T0108247

AS A DRIVEN LEAF

By Milton Steinberg

WITH FOREWORDS BY

RABBI DAVID WOLPE
&
CHAIM POTOK

BEHRMAN HOUSE, INC.

www.behrmanhouse.com

Also by Milton Steinberg
THE PROPHET'S WIFE

To Edith
in tribute to her love,
in gratitude for her collaboration

Library of Congress Cataloging-in-Publication Data
Steinberg, Milton, 1903–1950, author.
As a driven leaf / by Milton Steinberg ; with a foreword by Chaim Potok.
pages cm
Includes bibliographical references and index.
Summary: "A magnificent work of fiction brings the age of the Talmud
to life and explores the times of Elisha ben Abuya, whose struggle to
live in two worlds destroyed his chances to live in either. Now with a
new forward by Rabbi David J. Wolpe"— Provided by publisher.
ISBN 978-0-87441-950-4 (alk. paper)
1. Elisha ben Avuyah, approximately 70–approximately 135— Fiction.
2. Jews—History—168 B.C.–135 A.D.—Fiction. I. Title.
PS3537.T32343A9 2015
813'.54—dc23
2014047090

Copyright © 1939 Milton Steinberg
Foreword copyright © 2015 Rabbi David Wolpe
1996 Foreword copyright © 1996 Chaim Potok
Published by Behrman House, Inc.
Millburn, New Jersey
www.behrmanhouse.com
ISBN 978-0-87441-950-4

Printed in the United States of America
Cover design by Marc J. Cohen
Cover photographs: OlegSam/Shutterstock (leaf),
Eddie Gerald/Alamy (wall), kavram/Shutterstock (sky)

Library of Congress Catalog Card Number: 75-32237

Excerpt from The Prophet's Wife copyright © 2010 by Behrman House, Inc.
Original Milton Steinberg text copyright © 2010
by David J. Steinberg and Jonathan Steinberg

Wherefore hidest Thou Thy face...
Wilt Thou harass a driven leaf?

JOB XIII: 24-25

FOREWORD
ஃ

BY RABBI DAVID WOLPE

AS HE LAY DYING, ELISHA BEN ABUYAH's father expressed a wish for his child: "I am concerned only over one thing. I hope you will be wholehearted, not torn in two...."

Why has this book captured generations of readers? Partly it is the pageantry: before us is the magnificence of Roman civilization and the quaint but compelling world of the Talmud. Each is vividly realized and transports us to a strange, yet familiar, place.

The deeper power of this book, however, lies in a father's wish for his son that did not come true, just as it has not come true for us. Along with the main character, Elisha ben Abuyah, we are torn in two. We are divided between the twin pulls of assimilation in the modern world and faithfulness to the tradition of the old. We yearn to be citizens of the world while craving the rootedness and comfort of our grandparents. We are split citizens of modernity, with one foot in pluralism and the other in particularism.

The reader understands that the author's heart is also torn. Rabbi Milton Steinberg was a lover of Western thought who nonetheless, above all, cherished his Jewish heritage; he was as representative of his age as the Talmudic rabbis he writes of were of theirs. Born in 1903, he died in 1950, at only forty-six years old. Not blessed with a robust constitution, this gifted thinker and writer worked tirelessly on behalf of the establishment of the Jewish state even after a near-fatal heart attack. As the rabbi of Park Avenue Synagogue on Manhattan's Upper East Side, Steinberg stood at the very center of the first post-immigrant generation and was a much-loved figure in American Jewish life. In addition to his synagogue duties, speech-writing, and fund-raising, he wrote several popular books on Jewish thought and polemics. My father once told me that as a rabbinical student, he and his friends would walk to Park Avenue on Saturday mornings to hear the country's preeminent sermonizer recast traditional teachings in modern eloquence. I used to envy my father that he got to see Babe Ruth play and Milton Steinberg preach. Giants once walked the earth.

Steinberg taught Latin and Greek—and the world of the Greeks, so vividly portrayed in the novel, lived in its author. The conflict of Athens and Jerusalem, reason and faith, stirred Steinberg; it propels the narrative of *As a Driven Leaf* and has captured generations of readers. In reading this work we become students of the preeminent pulpit rabbi of the twentieth century. The magic of Steinberg's novel is the uncanny way it shows our own conflicts enacted in the world of the Talmud. This is a book about a very specific time and place, with insights that apply to all times and all places.

As a Driven Leaf tells a gripping story of Elisha ben Abuyah, the only Talmudic sage to be denounced and cast out as a heretic. It explores the two forces acting on us today—assimilation and tradition—as Steinberg divides the novel between two worlds and two women. We first see Elisha in the world of tradition, among the Rabbis and enchanted by Beruriah, the wise wife of his student. The second half tells of Elisha in the city of Antioch, bedazzled by the great, powerful, and wealthy empire that was secular Rome and a worldly woman, the courtesan Manto.

For the rabbis of the Talmud, living under Roman rule, Greek civilization was the great cultural challenge. We even know of cases where Jewish men, intent on hiding their identity, underwent painful operations to reverse their circumcision in order to compete in the Olympic Games, where Jews were barred and the athletes were nude. Through Elisha's quest, Steinberg shows us the seductions of Greco-Roman culture. As these two worlds powerfully clash, Elisha is unable to fully repudiate his origins or embrace his newfound destiny, and we the readers, heir to the same forces, feel our role as inheritors of his dilemma and ambivalence.

As a Driven Leaf is largely a story of "faith versus reason." Steinberg uses it to remind us that the rabbinic tradition was based on reason, but a reason directed at seeking the deeper meanings of tradition and transcendence. One of the most parsed and enigmatic passages in rabbinic literature, central to the story Steinberg tells, is the tale of the four rabbis—Akiba, ben Zoma, ben Azzai, and Elisha ben Abuyah—who enter 'pardes' (seemingly some version of paradise—a mystical state here on earth). We are told that one died; one became mad; one became a heretic; and that only one, Rabbi Akiba, emerged intact. Steinberg uses the tradition to posit a secret Torah-study fellowship, gathered to help Elisha reconcile himself to a life of Torah. Like the four sons of the Haggadah, we can each find ourselves in the fate of these rabbis who try to find a path through the thickets of competing cultures.

The novel shows us the Rabbis debating whether Greek learning can have a place in rabbinic practice or a traditional life. Devastatingly, Rabbi Joshua, Elisha's teacher and mentor, decides that Greek culture is too destructive; he concludes that outside wisdom will destroy commitment to a life of Torah. But is walling oneself off from the larger world the only way to preserve Jewish tradition? Steinberg shows us simultaneously how old and how current is this question.

Through a powerful story and vivid characters, *As a Driven Leaf* moves us to consider the essential dynamics of spiritual life. Elisha's primary emotional attachment to the world of the Rabbis is represented by Beruriah, the wife of Rabbi Meir.

Beruriah is the only woman designated by name in rabbinic literature as a teacher of Torah.

Beruriah represents the loveliness and allure of wise piety. Rabbi Meir was Elisha Ben Abuyah's premier student. That they spent a great deal of time in each other's company is to be expected. For Steinberg to invent a romantic interest in Beruriah seems both reasonable and novelistically compelling. It also reminds us, as we might expect from a rabbi who was confronted daily with the vagaries of the human heart, that a philosophic quest is as often impelled by frustrated love as by unanswered questions.

With Beruriah as with Rabbi Joshua, Rabbi Akiba, and others, Steinberg creates fully rounded modern characters out of Talmudic adages, stories, and intimations. Rabbi Akiba, probably the greatest of the rabbinic sages, is lovable, wise, and faithful, a portrait true to the Talmudic image of this martyred hero. Akiba and his students suffered the consequences of revolt against the Roman Empire. Steinberg, again developing Talmudic hints, suggests that Elisha helped the Romans in their struggle against the Jews using the knowledge he had gained from the Sages to aid in their destruction.

Romans destroyed the Second Temple and murdered many of Israel's greatest sages. Yet *As a Driven Leaf*'s portrait of Rome, despite its catastrophic role in Jewish history, is honestly appreciative. The cruelty of Rome does not cancel its grandeur, just as the passionate piety of Israel does not negate its narrowness. Elisha studies with scholars such as Antiphanes, and the novel does not condescend to their scholarship, as though learning existed only among the rabbis. Moreover, the cruelty of Roman villain Rufus is paralleled in Israel as well; the reader can only imagine that given the power of the Roman potentate, Shraga, the Jewish zealot, would act with just as little regard for the life of his antagonists.

Beruriah's Roman counterpart is the courtesan Manto. Intrigued by Elisha's virtue, as Elisha is by her worldliness,

Manto has the freedom that Beruriah lacks. Although she may not match Beruriah's modesty and learning, Manto wields a power that would be denied to her, and presides over a court of suitors and admirers who are themselves distinguished intellectuals. In the full-blooded and appreciative portraits of both Beruriah and Manto, we might be hearing the echo of the brilliant Edith Steinberg, the author's wife, who encouraged him to expand and enrich the novel's portrayal of women.

Sexuality is both a divide between the societies and a driver of Elisha's actions. Unsurprisingly, it is never made fully explicit in a book written by a rabbi in the 1930s. Some of Elisha's intellectual passion is sublimated or redirected after a cold marriage and frustrated infatuations. Alongside his own yearning, there is a distrust of libertinism, a fear that a life of passion without restraint is less worthy than one devoted to God's law. Caught between these conflicting and powerful impulses, we recall the heartbreaking words Elisha speaks to Beruriah: "We all want more than life permits."

Intimacy and intellectuality are woven together, and philosophy both ancient and modern echoes throughout the book. When Akiba tells Elisha "Doctrines themselves are not important to me, but their consequences are," we hear the philosophy of John Dewey, so popular in Steinberg's youth. Elisha's infatuation with the violent Roman amphitheater, and his own disgust with his enchantment, is a recasting of a crucial episode in Augustine's Confessions. Steinberg is subtle, his erudition tucked unobtrusively into a story about the limits of learning and the infinities of desire.

Intellectual conflict and a more primal frustrated desire are both central to Steinberg's portrait of a yearning sage. Almost ten years after the publication of his novel and just a year before he died, Steinberg had occasion to eulogize a wealthy industrialist, Bernard Armour. Armour had given his life to work, never building a family or developing close friendships. Steinberg said the following:

"There is a lesson in this for all of us, an admonition as to priorities in living, a reminder that the solicitudes of love and comradeship openly expressed and unashamed stand before wealth or fame or power. It is these, the treasures of the heart, not the treasures of the marketplace, which in the end are indispensable to human happiness."

Elisha ben Abuyah was on an intellectual quest to be sure, but he was also on a search to fulfill his affections. This is a novel of both head and heart. Elisha finds that without a bedrock faith, something that cannot be doubted, his life is unmoored. Yet his tragedy is not only the lack of certainty, but a lack of society. Not fully at home in the synagogue or the pagan court, this ancient sage reminds us that competing values of pluralism and particularity will always thread through our lives. We cannot erase the world, nor can we negate our past.

Steinberg was a rabbi in a congregation. He married couples and eulogized and counseled those in despair, and so he knew that while faith waxes and wanes, the treasures of the heart are in the end indispensable to human happiness. Elisha ben Abuyah will not give us the answer, but like the rabbi who brings him to life, he will journey with us, and help us feel a little less alone.

1996 EDITION FOREWORD

By Chaim Potok

ONE DAY IN MARCH 1950, while hurrying through a crowded hallway during a break between college classes, I overheard two students talking in Yiddish.

One said: "Did you hear the news? Milton Steinberg died last night."

The other said: "Really? He was young."

To which the first responded: "Now they're punishing him for his books."

That was all I caught of the conversation. It startled me to hear it said of a person so recently deceased that he was being punished for what he had written. I wondered who Milton Steinberg was and what had spurred the student's belief in the rush to judgment by the Heavenly Tribunal.

Later that day, I searched for Milton Steinberg's name in the catalogue of the college library, and discovered that he was not listed. My query to the librarian elicited the terse response: "We do not keep his books here." And to my further question as to why not, came the answer, laden with scorn: "He is from that other school, and a heretic."

In my school, the locution "that other school" meant the Jewish Theological Seminary, located some sixty blocks to the south in Manhattan. So, Milton Steinberg was a Conservative rabbi. What could he have written to earn him such reproval from the guardians of my faith?

A cousin by marriage was then a rabbinical student at the

Jewish Theological Seminary. In his personal library I found two books by Milton Steinberg, a work of non-fiction and a novel.

From my cousin came a brief account of Steinberg's life. Rochester, New York, had been his place of birth, in 1903. His family moved to the Harlem section of New York City when he was fifteen and a half. At City College of New York, he studied with the philosopher and iconoclast Morris Raphael Cohen, and at the Seminary he came under the influence of Mordecai Kaplan, the founder of Reconstructionist Judaism. He read Plato and Aristotle in Greek, knew Latin, was entirely at home in English literature, and possessed a thorough knowledge of modern philosophy and theology. In 1928, he received his rabbinic ordination at the Jewish Theological Seminary. He then served as rabbi in Indianapolis, Indiana, where he once came out publicly on the side of the workers during a strike at a hosiery factory whose owners were noted members of his congregation. In 1933, the Park Avenue Synagogue in New York invited him to become its rabbi, and he accepted. He had a wife and children, and was forty-six when he died.

How strange that his books had eluded me, especially his novel. I was then reading my way through many literatures like a person possessed, and thought that someone in my school—a fellow student or an English professor—might have brought his work to my attention. In retrospect, I think quite probably they would have—were he not allied with Mordecai Kaplan's Reconstructionism, whose ideology, though it emphasized Jewish observance, denied the chosenness of the people Israel, the existence of a personal God, and the divine authorship of the Torah.

I turned to the two books by Milton Steinberg. One, *The Making of the Modern Jew,* published in the early 1930s, was a work of history. The second was the novel, *As a Driven Leaf* published in 1939. I decided to read the history first.

There was a pure, stately caliber to the writing, a clarity

and reasonableness, as he navigated through the rocky quest he had set for himself: answers to the mystery of Jewish survival, and an understanding of the nature of modern Jewry. I was awed by the author's wisdom and lucidity as he conveyed me through the often glorious and too-often tragic centuries of Jewish history, sparing neither the Jews for their foibles nor the Christians for their cruelties. I had never before read that kind of candid Jewish history.

Finishing it, I turned with some apprehension to the novel. I was fine-tuned to fiction and knew that it was one thing to write a good history and something else entirely to write a good story. Moreover, who had ever heard of a rabbi taking on serious fiction!

It did not take me long to realize that there was a story in the novel, a gripping story. But as I read it that first time, I found myself becoming slowly convinced that the novel was far more than a mere story, that its central drama—a conflict between religious and pagan ideas, between faith and reason, between postulates of creed and science, as experienced by the early Talmudic sage Elisha ben Abuyah—was emblematic not only of all Jewish history but probably of Milton Steinberg himself. The novel seemed to me to be an extension of the same quest he had set for himself in *The Making of the Modern Jew*: an exploration of Judaism in conflict with a vigorous and powerful surrounding culture, in this instance the pagan world of Greece and Rome. Steinberg had traveled back in time to arrive at the cradle of Rabbinic Judaism—and his hero was a heretic.

Little is known about the historical Elisha ben Abuyah—the central character of the novel. His father appears to have been a wealthy Jerusalemite; we are told nothing of the son's early education. His character seems mysterious, enigmatic. There is considerable debate about his role in Jewish history and his relationship to the sages: he is accused of being an apostate, a dualist, a Sadducee, a lover of harlots, a betrayer of the Jews to the Romans after the debacle of the Bar Kochba rebellion in 132-135 C.E. He was a student of Greek, loved Greek poetry, and apparently had more than a surface knowledge of horses, architecture, and wine. He read forbidden books, which he kept concealed in his clothes. Here and there in classical Rabbinic texts are found some of his utterances. He dabbled in mysticism or Gnosticism and is believed to have had some sort of ecstatic experience. His lasting fame—or infamy!—rests on his having been one of a minute number of rabbis excommunicated during the entire eight hundred years of the Rabbinic period. The reason for the excommunication has come down to us in a tale. It appears that one day Elisha ben Abuyah stood watching as a man climbed up a ladder to send away a mother bird before taking down its nest of fledglings, in conformity with the law in Deuteronomy, for the observance of which the Bible promises a long life (22:6,7). Instead, the man fell to his death. Enraged and appalled by what he had witnessed, Elisha ben Abuyah denied divine providence with the words: "There is no justice, and there is no Judge." And was excommunicated.

From these sources, Milton Steinberg fashioned a singular tale. He gave Elisha ben Abuyah a mother who died while giving birth to him, a father assimilated to Greek and Roman wisdom and way of life, a devout uncle, friends, tutors—and a rich Jewish education and upbringing during the time in Judea after the destruction of the Second Temple by Roman legions. With his knowledge of classical sources, Steinberg sculpted in realistic detail the intimate lives of ordinary Jewish men and women, the hills and valleys of the Judean countryside, the rabbis in lively and quarrelsome debate; and left us gritty images of cruel and sybaritic Roman rulers, and Jews fighting Jews, and the horrors of the Bar Kochba rebellion.

The novel is in essence a *Bildungsroman* in which we witness the forming of the mind and heart of a Rabbinic sage and find ourselves in the world of the men who created the extraordinary culture known as Rabbinic Judaism. It is a novel of ideas and passions, the story of the man Elisha ben Abuyah caught up in an often fiery confrontation of cultures—in a struggle of contradictory Jewish and pagan core concepts about the world and the human experience. How poignant the resolution of that conflict in the heart of that sage—and no doubt in the heart of Milton Steinberg himself, who believed that philosophical reflection was the beginning of piety, and that without a worldview one could never stand firmly on the ground of faith. Separated in time by two thousand years, sage and rabbi were joined in the pages of this novel on a quest for a theology and a way of life that would bring together Jewish tradition and prevailing speculative thought.

I had been studying Talmud from the age of eight, lived deep in its winding argumentations and dialectics. But nothing I ever heard or read before was able to bring the world of the rabbis so vividly to life for me as Milton Steinberg's novel. Perhaps more important—at that point in my life, I too was caught up in a conflict of ideas, much of it inchoate, and *As a Driven Leaf* began to give it form. Conjure that, if you will: a renegade Talmudic sage and a contemporary Conservative rabbi reaching into the heart of a very Orthodox yeshiva boy through the power of the imagination resonating in the pages of a novel!

The uniqueness of this novel lies in the unceasing nature of the struggles it depicts, in its dramatic power, and in the quality of the writing. It thus renders its world as forever contemporary, and continues to have life in times quite unlike the decade when it first appeared. It retains its ability to enter the heart of pious and seeking Jew alike.

People who knew Milton Steinberg personally have told me that he was an intense man, somewhat tall, with an angular sharp-nosed face, shining brown eyes, an intimate voice. He spoke in a flawless and at times polysyllabic English, which revealed now and then the twang of the upstate New York region of his birth. His speech was as measured and impeccable as his writing. Students at the Seminary would walk to his synagogue on Shabbat to listen to him preach; one of them, a rabbi now in his eighties, once said to me that Steinberg's sermons were "brilliant and blinding."

What a tragedy, his early death. I have always deeply regretted that we never met. It is no small consolation to be linked with him now in the pages of this memorable novel. As for that distant day in March 1950 and the student's offhand reference to Milton Steinberg in the hallway of my school—I thank him for bringing that exceptional man into my life. And regarding the remark about the worth of his books—I feel certain that the Heavenly Tribunal indeed judged Milton Steinberg for his writings. And quickly passed him through, with praise and applause, to his deserved eternal reward.

AS A
DRIVEN
LEAF

PROLOGUE

THE SAGES OF THE SANHEDRIN sat in a sweeping half-circle, motionless like some conclave of graven images. Round about them stretched gray-green vineyards. To the east, the jumbled buildings of the town of Jamnia stood in sharp-lined whiteness against the deep purple of the distant mountains of Judea. To the west toward which they looked, tawny sand dunes rolled down to the sea. A cloudless sky arched high above, spanning the horizons. And in all that vastness, only the unsteady droning voice of an old man was heard, broken intermittently by the tinkling of a camel bell afar off, the dull murmur of the sea or the whisper of dusty leaves as the wind played through them.

Seventy members composed this High Court, civil and ecclesiastical, of the House of Israel. Most of them, their faces pale, their beards white with extreme age, were elders in more than title. A few were in the prime of vigorous manhood. Long robes, gray and brown, interspersed with bold crimsons and glowing blues, flowed in loose folds from their shoulders to the ground. From each hem dangled the fringes ordained by Moses, the greatest of the sages. On each forehead a phylactery gleamed. About the fingers of each left hand a black leather thong wa s twined in an ancient mystic symbolism.

For many hours they had sat in this place. Daylight had streamed over their shoulders from behind when the Patriarch Gamliel, a mountain of a man with the flowing black beard of an Assyrian king, had put before them the question: "Shall it be forbidden to a faithful Jew to study the tongue of the Greeks, to read their books and to think their thoughts after them?" On that issue, bitter with memories of old controversies, they had divided passionately. Angry debate had whipped back and forth across the arc. The western sun shone now into their eyes and still they were not agreed. Yet ever since the old man had risen to his feet, slowly and painfully as if his many years weighed him down, they had put aside argument and recrimination to listen unmoving as though some spell had fixed them in their seats.

The faltering voice of Rabbi Johanan, the son of Zaccai, was so faint that it was sometimes lost in the rustling of vine leaves when a breeze blew in from the sea. The skin of his face behind the white wisp of his beard was wrinkled parchment. His hands shook incessantly. No one knew the sum of his days. He had been well past the prime of life when he had fled the doomed Jerusalem and coaxed from Vespasian permission to found an Academy in this place. For this alone he would have merited the reverence which they accorded him. But now he remained one of the last of those who had once sat in the Court of Hewn Stone in the Temple—these ten years a ruin, naked except for the bramble and briar through which jackals wailed of desolation to the moon.

The minutes crept by as the old man spoke of unity and brotherly harmony, of the danger of dissension to the welfare of a people sore oppressed, a danger before which they should stand as one.

"It is apparent, Masters," he concluded, "that we cannot agree. I should suggest that we do not put the question to a vote. It would be wiser to leave it where it rests now, where it has always rested. Let us neither commend nor prohibit the study of Greek wisdom."

Johanan remained standing uncertainly as though there were more which he must say. His face in repose was weary with years and their tribulations. For a long, painful interval he groped for words.

At that moment the line of the horizon cut the sun in half. A path of fire flowed across waters toward land and sent long shadows into flight before it. The hills turned mauve and purple, presaging the quick twilight. A stronger breeze blew in from the sea coaxing the vine leaves into a bolder whisper. The air danced with angry dust. Garments snapped in the wind, wisps of hair were blown about. The sages shivered in the sudden cold and drew their fringed robes more closely about them. The silence broken so feebly by one thin voice now became clamorous with other sounds: the hiss of the wind, the rustling of fabrics, the call of some bird, the bleating of sheep in a distant fold.

The old man breathed deeply and spoke.

"Think not," he said in a voice raised against the rising wind, "that because I am old, I do not understand the heart of those who defend the learning of the heathens. There was a time, long, long ago, when I too adventured among the pagans. They possessed, I had heard, sciences derived from reason alone, something which, it seemed to me then, might perchance be stronger than the doctrine of our fathers, rooted in faith. But their wisdom failed me altogether as it will fail you and all others who look to it hopefully. For there is a strange paradox which men are wont to forget."

For a moment his voice and words were strong as though the energy of all his spent years was in them.

"There is no Truth without Faith. There is no Truth unless first there be a Faith on which it may be based."

They looked at him, not quite comprehending, as though a revelation were coming to them, but in an alien tongue. As in a dream they watched him grope backward toward his seat.

The Patriarch Gamliel glanced toward the sun. Its upper rim curved over the sea.

"The time has come," he announced, "for evening worship. Our assembly is adjourned until tomorrow. Let us withdraw to the synagogue for prayer."

The sages rose; a babble of voices broke forth. In a long straggling line they walked through an avenue of twisting vines toward the town at the crest of the hill. By the time they had reached the first houses of Jamnia the world was entirely dark and the dust-laden wind played about in senseless confusion.

PART I

CHAPTER I

TOWARD THE END OF THE first century, in the spring of the last year of the reign of the Emperor Vespasian, two entries were made in the Roman archives of the district of Galilee. The first registered the fact that a male heir had been born to one Abuyah, Jewish patrician, and master of an estate on the outskirts of Migdal. The second, inscribed five days later, recorded the death of Elisheba, wife of Abuyah and mother of the still-unnamed child.

Thus, only kinsfolk in the first degree and the most intimate of friends gathered at the sorrow-shrouded villa on the eighth day after the birth of the baby to witness the rite of circumcision.

At the appointed hour Sapphirah, the wet nurse, stood in one of the corridors of the house, holding the sleeping infant close to her full bosom.

"Poor little mite," she crooned to the blanket-enveloped face. "Soon they will call us in and hurt you. And you will cry. And well you may—what with her buried these two days."

For a time she wept silently out of pity for the child and his ill-fated mother.

Her grief giving way to curiosity, she freed one hand and lifted aside the curtain which hung in the doorway. In the chamber beyond, the guests conversed quietly. Over a table littered with instruments and bandages, Jacob, the surgeon, a man noted for his skill and piety, whetted his knife. Tobias, the steward, his fat short person exuding an air of importance, fluttered protectingly over the sideboard. In the center of the room Amram, the child's uncle, talked to two men. As she recognized them, Sapphirah gasped with pleased surprise. "Ah, ah, baby," she crowed, shaking her head in awe, "they came after all, the great rabbis. For your uncle's sake no doubt. No matter why—they are here. And someday, little one, you will be proud. You will tell your children that sages were your godfathers."

She held the sleeping infant upright. "They say that what a little boy sees on the day of his circumcision, that he will become. That graybeard, he is the Rabbi Eliezer, learned, rich, famous. Regard his haughty face; so an aristocrat bears himself. And now the other one, the ugly one (God forgive my words) that is Rabbi Joshua, the wisest and kindliest of all the sages. Look well, my dove, then you too will be rich, famous, wise and good. Beautiful you are already, as the day at dusk."

While she held the baby so, the surgeon finished his preparations.

"The child?" he asked.

Conversation ceased instantly. Tobias scurried forward.

"In a moment, Masters, in a moment."

"Well, well," he whispered toward the curtain. "What are you waiting for, the Messiah?"

Sapphirah crossed the threshold.

"If you must know, wise one," she responded fiercely, "I was waiting to be called."

"Blessed be he who cometh," the surgeon intoned, taking the baby from her arms.

"This is the Throne of Elijah," the assembly responded, as Jacob laid the child on the table.

"The father," he asked, "where is he?"

The guests looked about, observing in bewilderment that Abuyah was missing. Amram stepped forward, a frown on his thin dark face, his close-set eyes burning with anger.

"Tobias," he snapped, "go find your master."

"Immediately, Master Amram, immediately."

After several minutes the awkward silence was broken by the return of the steward. "He is coming," Tobias explained as he entered the room.

Amram's bearded jaws were set tight.

"Do not be angry, Amram." Joshua's voice was soft and gentle. "He is distracted by sorrow."

"If that were the reason," Amram answered slowly, "would

I not understand? Was she not my sister?..."

His mouth quivered an instant, then grew firm and stern again.

"Nay, it is not grief alone which accounts for this discourtesy."

He was silent, lost in bitter thoughts of his brother-in-law, of the pagan philosophers who were his intimate friends, of the heretical books he was forever reading. This was not the first time that Abuyah had deliberately flouted everything that Amram held sacred. And now, this child, all that remained of his sister, was left in the hands of an infidel and scoffer. Hatred welled up within him.

Steps were heard at last in the courtyard, slow and heavy.

"Gentlemen, my apologies for delaying these rites. I was preoccupied." Abuyah stood silhouetted against the day, tall, slender, in a robe cut after the fashion of the Greeks. His face, dark with shadow, was inscrutable. But it was apparent that no earlocks hung over his cheeks, no fringes dangled from his mantle. Nor was his robe rent in the symbol of mourning prescribed by ancient tradition. Only as he came into the room where his features could be read more clearly could it be seen that his handsome arrogant face was ravaged with pain, that his brilliant blue eyes were dull with grief.

He looked down at the baby lying on the table, a wry smile twisting his lips.

"A bad purchase," he mused aloud, "bought at too high a price. Such are the bargains God forces on man."

A chill swept the room, freezing the men in it into immobility. They waited apprehensively lest another word translate the muttered hint of reproach into full-voiced blasphemous recrimination. But Abuyah said no more.

Hesitantly the surgeon lifted the child.

"Who are to be the godfathers?" he asked Abuyah.

It was as though he had not spoken.

"The godfathers," Amram ordered in Abuyah's stead, "will

be the two rabbis here."

Jacob looked at the child's father for confirmation.

Abuyah responded indifferently with a shrug of the shoulders.

Rabbi Eliezer's pale, haughty face burned with indignation.

"This child," he prayed stiffly over the bundle he had taken into his arms, "may God bless him with a believing heart."

He transferred his burden to his colleague, missing as he did so the glance of aversion with which Abuyah responded to the unmistakable implications of the prayer. Joshua nestled the child against his ungainly body. His gnarled fingers cupped gently about the swaddling clothes. Softly, as though imparting some secret to the uncomprehending baby, he blessed him.

"God make you great, little one. As we initiate you into the covenant of Abraham our father, so may we be privileged to lead you into the study of our holy Law, into the marital canopy, into a life of good deeds.

"A sweet boy," he added as he surrendered him to Jacob the surgeon.

An instant later a sharp wail of pain pierced the silent room.

Abuyah shuddered and turned aside.

"A merciful custom," he muttered resentfully, "the ordinance of a God of mercy."

Through the crying of the child the guests heard him with horror. Jacob's hands faltered momentarily among his instruments.

"How shall the child be called?" he inquired, recovering. Again Abuyah was silent. Once more Amram spoke for him.

"Name him Elisha, after his mother Elisheba. So also will he be called after the great prophet. Elisha the son—" he paused as though his throat were choked "—of Abuyah."

With fingers deft from long experience, Jacob dressed the baby and put him into Abuyah's arms.

"You will now say the father's blessing," he instructed.

Abuyah shook his head.

"But you must..."

"Not I," Abuyah answered bitterly. "I have never believed nor observed. Shall I begin now by thanking a God in whom I have no faith for the death of my wife and the mutilation of my child? If I had not felt that his mother would have wanted this, I..."

"Enough, enough," Amram interrupted hoarsely. "I will say it."

He reached out to take the baby from his father.

Abuyah stared coldly into his eyes.

"He is my child, not yours. You may recite any prayers you choose. But I hold him."

They glared at each other. Amram's hands dropped, his glance turned away. He pronounced the prescribed blessing, each word hard and bitter as though it were a curse directed at his brother-in-law.

"Here, take him," Abuyah ordered Sapphirah. She took the baby into her arms, put a knot of honey-sweetened cloth into his mouth. The infant sucked greedily, his sobs mumbling into silence.

For a few minutes Abuyah watched.

"Such are life's compensations," he said at last. "And now, gentlemen, you will excuse me. There are urgent affairs to which I must attend. Refreshments will be found on the sideboard yonder. I leave you in the care of my brother-in-law."

So still was the room after he left that those in it could hear the rustling of the curtain which swayed behind him. Jacob, the surgeon, looked about in perplexity. He had officiated at more rites of circumcision than he could count, but never one like this.

Then he remembered that the ritual was not yet completed. He raised a wine cup full to overflowing above Sapphirah and the baby, intoning the prayers of benediction.

"...and may his name be known in Israel," he concluded, "as Elisha the son of Abuyah."

As though in defiance of the irreverence he had witnessed, his voice was loud, his words distinct. He hoped that that base infidel of a father would hear them wherever he had taken himself.

The chanting over at last, a drop from the cup of blessing was put on the infant's lips. Sapphirah carried him from the room as the guests watched, bewildered and ill at ease. This was the moment for much eating, drinking and lighthearted banter. The service was complete; the House of Israel had been enlarged by one more accession.

But the memory of a woman who had died to bring this new life into being restrained their tongues. Even more were they oppressed by the manner and sacrilegious words of Abuyah. That he was not a believer was a common scandal, but never before in all the annals of their people had a father so manifestly despised a ritual sacred to all. They had not dreamed that, even in his bitterness, he would be so bold.

Tobias moved about, pressing dainties upon them. Amram strove valiantly to evoke something of a festive spirit. It was of no avail. They could not bring themselves to taste Abuyah's food. Within a few minutes the banquet hall was deserted of guests. The steward, his plump body sagging with disappointment, contemplated the sideboard ruefully. Amram stalked to and fro in the empty chamber, his heavy jaws fixed in determination, his eyes flashing hatred.

Outside, the visitors rode in a body down the sandy road from Abuyah's house to the main highway, skirting the sea of Galilee. Excitedly they discussed the events to which they had been witness. A babble of voices hovered over them like the dust cloud that rose in their wake. But, in a sudden silence, all heard an exchange of comment between the two rabbis.

"An evil sign," Rabbi Eliezer confided to his colleague. "An unfortunate beginning for the child."

"Let us not say so," Joshua replied. "Each soul molds its own destiny."

CHAPTER II

THE SUMMER DAY WAS DROWSY with heat. In the fierce light
of the sun the world was drained of its colors. The olive trees
and grapevines were gray. The sea of Galilee was a sheet of
silver. The great house shimmered in whiteness. To the east
the humped hills of Gilead marched like beasts of burden,
heavy laden, against the sky.

In an arbor on the hillside, Elisha sat with Nicholaus, his
tutor; the young man on a stone bench, the ten-year old boy
on a stool at his feet. About them was stillness except for the
shrilling of insects and the call of voices far off. Splintered
shafts of sunlight, alive with motes, broke from between the
leaves into the shadows and striped with yellow the grass
underfoot. A ray fell onto a scroll which lay unfurled on the
boy's lap, illuminating the writhing Greek characters over
which he pored intently.

Nicholaus, the son of Zenothemis, looked like a scarecrow,
so awkward and loose-jointed were his long limbs beneath his
threadbare robe. Like a bird's, his head projected before him,
too heavy for the thin stringy neck that supported it. His nose
was pointed and always red as though from intense cold. When
the servants had first seen him they had smiled. At the sound
of his high-pitched nasal voice they had snickered. It was five
years since Abuyah had introduced him to the household. In
that time they had all come to like him, which in itself was a
tribute for he was the only pagan among them. Now he sat,
his head resting on his large hands, his reedlike arms propped
on his spindly shanks, staring sleepily at the bowed head of his
pupil, kindliness in his eyes, affection on his lips.

"Well," he asked at last, rousing himself with an effort,
"have you read it through?"

The boy looked up and Nicholaus caught his breath. It was
strange, he reflected fleetingly, that he was still startled by the
flash of those deep blue eyes ringed with dark lashes.

"Yes, I have."

"Now do you understand why you were not reading it correctly, what I meant when I said that the passage must be recited tenderly?"

Elisha nodded.

"Then begin again with the words, 'So she met him now...'"

Nicholaus stifled a yawn and added with assumed energy, "And please be careful not to confuse the accents with the rhythm. Homer is not read properly unless the rhythm is clearly..." He groped for a word, failed to find it. His voice trailed off into an inarticulate mumble.

In a sweet, childish voice, Elisha recited the lines from the Sixth Book of the Iliad wherein Hector parts from his wife, Andromache, and his child, Astyanax. As he read on, Nicholaus's lids closed and opened slowly. Wearily he stretched himself out on the bench. The boy paused an instant to watch, his eyes alight with amusement.

"Go on," the tutor prodded, "I am listening."

For all his assurances, he would soon have dozed off as Elisha continued to read had not a mispronunciation jarred him. He sat bolt upright, his legs stiff along the bench before him.

"The word is *thalpore,* not *talpore.* I have still to meet a Jew aside from your father who knows the difference between a *theta* and a *tau.*"

"And I," the boy retorted quickly, "a Greek who can pronounce the Hebrew letter *shin.*"

"No impudence, my lad," Nicholaus replied, sinking back. "It happens that I am teaching you Greek, not being taught Hebrew by you."

His last words were addressed to the branches above him, which he saw hazily through sleep-blurred eyes. Elisha racked his brains for an appropriate retort. "Go on," Nicholaus urged, with drowsy impatience.

The boy resumed his reading. The story rolled on through

Andromache's plea to her husband to its climax wherein Hector tosses his frightened child in the air.

The rhythm of heavy breathing broke the regularity of dactylic hexameters. Shaken from his concentration Elisha looked up at the relaxed form of his tutor. A knowing smile came over his face. For a few moments he sat quietly, then coughed softly several times to test the depth of Nicholaus's slumber. Convinced that the man was sound asleep, the boy put the scroll aside quietly and tiptoed out of the arbor.

From the opposite hillside a shrill whistle sounded as soon as he appeared. Elisha looked across the valley. Again the whistle sounded. This time he spied a figure in white brandishing its arms to catch his attention. It was his playmate Pappas, who lived on the estate to the north of Abuyah's. Elisha waved in return and plunged down the steep slope. They met at their old rendezvous, the boundary stone.

"I have been waiting for hours," Pappas began as soon as they were together, "in the hope that you could come." Although two years older than Elisha, Pappas was almost a head shorter. His face was round like a full moon, his nose bulbous with large circular nostrils. His cheeks were shaded by a dark down of which he was inordinately proud. He would have seemed insensitive were it not for his mirthful little eyes and a crooked smile that pulled one corner of his mouth higher than the other.

"How did you get away this afternoon?" Elisha asked.

"My teacher has a headache—the heat, he says. Thank God for it. I was sick of repeating 'and the Lord spoke to Moses saying.' But tell me how did you get away?"

"Nicholaus fell asleep right in the middle of a lesson. He is good for the rest of the afternoon."

"Then let's go swimming."

Elisha shook his head. "I have a better idea. I heard Tobias say that one of our cows may calve today."

Pappas nodded approvingly.

"But remember, no noise. We may wake Nicholaus. Besides Tobias or Sapphirah may see us."

They climbed the hill to the villa, avoiding the arbor where Nicholaus slept, and struck off on a path to the barns which lay beyond. They walked quietly, on the alert to pass unseen.

But they did not escape notice. As they rounded the corner of the house, a voice came from a window in the second story.

"Elisa, Elisa…"

Elisha looked up at the little girl who leaned over the sill. "Hush up, Theo," he replied fiercely. "Do you want to wake everybody?"

"But I want to go with you."

"No, you stay where you are."

"Please," she coaxed.

"No, I tell you!"

"But I have nothing to do."

"Then play with your nurse."

"But I want to go with you," she whined.

"Where we are going is no place for a girl."

"All right then. I'll scream and say that you and that other boy are running away from your lessons. That's what you are doing. I know."

The two boys gaped.

"Who is she?" Pappas whispered.

"She is Theopompa. Her father and mine are cousins. They are visiting us."

"But why does she talk so funny?"

"They come from Alexandria. They talk Greek to one another, not Hebrew or Aramaic."

Pappas stared at the little girl.

"She is pretty," he observed. "Let her come along."

"No."

Then Pappas's dark eyes gleamed with cunning.

"What did you say her name is—Theopompa? I'll get rid of her…Theopompa," he called.

shall not be betrothed to the daughter of a half-pagan. I tell you, I will not have it!"

Abuyah's reply was calm and cold.

"Are you not forgetting yourself, Amram? It is not at all necessary for you 'to have it,' as you put it. I am his father. I shall determine whom he will marry. Your advice is welcome, but you must not give it as though it were a command." There was a deep silence in the room. Elisha knew that his uncle was struggling to control himself.

"Then let me make one simple request."

"By all means."

"Have the boy taught something about his faith. Don't make him an alien to his own people like yourself."

There was a pause after which Amram continued pleadingly. "I do not say that you should not give him his Greek lessons. But teach him at least to read and understand Scripture. Why should you not? By what right do you deny him a knowledge of God's word?"

"That is just the point," Abuyah answered. "I do not like to shock you, but you know full well that I do not believe it to be God's word."

"Everyone believes it," Amram commented bitterly, "except you."

"I am sorry. I cannot hold myself responsible for the opinions of others. Neither will I teach my son incredible myths."

"And that accursed Homer of yours, or those dramas to which you are so addicted, what are they but myths, and immoral ones, too?"

"Aye, but we do not accept them as facts. We recognize them for what they are, lovely tales of impossible events. You see," Abuyah continued, "if I did teach Scripture to Elisha I would have to present it to him as legend. And even from your point of view that would be worse than not teaching it at all."

"And why," Amram persisted, "can you not accept Scripture as fact?"

"I dislike to go into the question again. But"—Abuyah's voice was weary—"you know full well that I cannot believe in miracles, the crossing of the Red Sea, Joshua stopping the sun, and all that."

"And why not?"

"Because, as every sensible man knows, the Stoics are right when they say that nothing ever happens contrary to nature."

A shadow fell across the pavement before Elisha. Glancing up quickly he discovered Nicholaus towering over him.

"So, you rogue, here you are—eavesdropping where you have no business, loitering when you should be studying. I turn my back, and what do you do? Instead of memorizing the passage as I ordered, you play the truant."

He led the boy off by the arm.

"But, Nicholaus, you did not tell me to memorize those lines. In fact, you fell asleep."

"No stories, if you please. I will not have excuses."

Elisha gazed up at his tutor. Before the accusing stare Nicholaus smiled sheepishly.

"Perhaps I am mistaken. But can't you permit a fellow to save his face?"

They grinned at each other.

A few minutes later, this time in a room at the front of the house, the two were busy again with a lesson in grammar. Elisha was reciting aloud the conjugation of irregular Greek verbs when the clatter of hoofs broke in upon them. The boy looked through the window to see his uncle riding furiously down the roadway.

"Nicholaus," he began abruptly, "I should like to ask you a question."

"Well?"

"Do you believe that the Torah, that book Pappas studies all the time instead of Homer, is the word of God?"

At once Nicholaus was wary.

"A great many people do," he parried.

"And you?"

"No, I do not."

"But do all Jewish boys learn Hebrew books?"

"Most of them."

"Then why don't I?"

"Because your father is an unusual person and prefers to have you know Greek."

"And one more thing," the boy went on: "Do you believe in miracles?"

"For myself I cannot regard them as possible."

"But why?"

"Why what?"

"Why do you think that miracles cannot happen?"

"By all the gods," Nicholaus protested, "I never saw such a child before. Why, why, why—that is all one hears from him. Must you know the reason for everything?"

"Why not?" the boy asked roguishly.

Nicholaus groaned with mock despair.

"But father says that it is not right to believe things without thinking them out."

"On with your lesson," Nicholaus threatened.

Still unsatisfied, Elisha resumed his recitation. But he was pleased that his tutor agreed with his father rather than with his uncle.

CHAPTER III

IT WAS LATE AT NIGHT. Elisha lay abed, trembling in the dark, afraid to fall asleep. He felt that as long as he could stay awake and will it, his father would live.

Only a fortnight before Abuyah had been completely well. Elisha remembered clearly how vigorous had been his voice as he argued with Amram. Two days later he had complained of feeling ill. Then had begun the nightmare of a mysterious malady that baffled the physicians, of a fever that mounted day by day, of a growing apprehension that congealed finally into a fearful certainty. That very morning Amram had come to the villa, summoned in haste from his home. He had gone directly into the sickroom. When he emerged a few minutes later, his face was paler than ever and twisted by emotion. Elisha, his eyes large with fright, had looked up at his uncle.

"We must not despair of God's mercies," Amram had replied to the unspoken question, and the child knew that Abuyah must die.

Nevertheless, now, heart heavy with dread, he concentrated on keeping his father alive, trying very hard not to hear the scurry of feet through the corridor, the muffled weeping of maidservants, the quick pounding of hoofs when the physician from Tiberias rode up the stony roadway.

A light glowed through the draperies of his door. The curtain was pulled aside. Amram, holding high a flaming torch, stood over him. Elisha blinked and began to whimper.

"Get up," his uncle whispered. "Your father wishes to see you."

Elisha's fingers shook as he clothed himself. Wordless sounds broke from his lips.

The man laid his hand reassuringly on the boy's shoulder. "Do not cry, if you can help it," he counseled compassionately. "It will sadden your father. You are a big boy now. Strive to control yourself."

Silently they crossed the courtyard into which a white moon

threw a patch of pale unreal light. The air was cool with dew.

Outside Abuyah's chamber stood Nicholaus. Elisha had barely the time to observe the look of dumb misery on his tutor's face before a servant came out carrying aloft a lamp to light the way for the surgeon who followed.

"It is almost over," the surgeon whispered to Amram, wiping his hands on a stained towel. "I have just let blood, but it will be of no avail."

Amram plunged his torch into a bucket of sand and, holding Elisha by the hand, led him soundlessly through the doorway. A three-wicked lamp burned brightly on a high stand, lighting the beamed ceiling and upper reaches of the room, but leaving the lower recesses in half-shadow.

Abuyah lay on his bed, his disheveled black hair spread like a splotch of ink over the white pillow.

"Go to him," Amram whispered.

In terror, Elisha climbed onto a stool and, reaching across the high bedstead, timidly touched his father's hand. Abuyah opened his eyes wonderingly, turned his head slowly, and saw the boy standing beside him. He smiled, but only with his lips.

"Eh, my son," he said, "your father is drinking from the cup of wrath tonight. That old Greek who said that philosophy teaches one to die gracefully, he was a fool."

Abuyah's voice, exhausted by weakness, trickled away. Then he breathed deeply with a great effort, and continued, "Come...time is short. Your uncle insists that, as your father, I bless you. Abraham blessed Isaac. Isaac blessed Jacob—though the morality of that particular act has always seemed to me open to question—Jacob blessed his sons, and my father blessed me. Therefore, I must bless you."

Amram placed Abuyah's hands on Elisha's head. The boy's sensitive face was intent with fear. He remained standing where he was, at a loss as to what to do while the traditional blessing came to him in broken Hebrew phrases:

"The Lord make thee...like Ephraim and Menasseh...the

Lord bless thee and keep thee...

The hands dropped from the top of Elisha's head, rested lingeringly on his shoulders, and slid reluctantly down his sides.

"I wonder," Abuyah whispered painfully, "have I made a mistake with you, my child? You are a Jew, after all. I have been of two inclinations, one by birth, the other by preference....Now you will have to make your own choice, without me. The issue is out of my hands. Perhaps it is just as well....Amram will know what to do....I would never have been certain...."

For slow minutes Elisha's father gasped heavily. When he spoke again it was for the last time.

"I am concerned only over one thing. I hope you will be wholehearted, not torn in two...."

His labored breathing was heard no more. The room was quiet with a great stillness.

The morning of Abuyah's burial was bright with sunlight, for although it was well past the Feast of Tabernacles the winter rains had not yet broken. Slowly the procession moved along the highway to Migdal, the coffin borne before, elevated on the shoulders of servants; the mourners, their figures stooped, plodding behind it in silence.

But by the time Abuyah's body had been lowered into the thirsty earth the heavens were black with clouds. Tradition demanded that those who had attended the funeral return from the cemetery to the bereaved household, there to break bread with the mourners. But it was apparent that a storm was impending. So, one by one, friends and relatives dropped off at sideroads or hurried on ahead. In the end only Elisha, Amram, Nicholaus and the little band of servants climbed the hill toward the villa that stood white against the lowering sky.

In the courtyard they found uninvited guests awaiting them. On a bench against one wall two men were seated, pagans by their dress. They rose at the sight of the returning housefolk and came forward to meet them.

"I am an assessor from the district tax office," one began without a word of greeting, addressing himself to Amram. "We have come to take your books to Tiberias—the death duties, you know."

Amram's eyes flared, his jaws tightened so that his voice was strained.

"You didn't lose any time getting here, did you? You might have had the decency to wait until after the funeral."

The assessor shrugged his shoulders.

"Don't blame me. I'm merely doing my duty. They sent me and here I am. The Empire must be maintained."

"Empire!" Amram snorted. "Publicans and tax collectors, you mean. A precious lot of it will ever get to Rome."

"That's not my business. We're here to get the ledgers, the accountant and I. If you will…"

"No," Amram barked. "I will not have business done here until the week of mourning is over."

"But you will," the man insisted. "We want the books right now. We've had too much experience with altered accounts to take a chance. We should like to get started at once before the storm breaks. But if you insist, I can get an order from…"

"Give them the scrolls," Amram rasped to Tobias, "and let them go. And remember to get receipts."

Muttering angrily under his breath, the steward turned toward the record room. The other servants dispersed each to his own tasks, leaving Amram and Elisha with the two Romans. "So this is the young heir," the officer, uncomfortable before Amram's fixed stare, said in an attempt at affability.

Amram's hand rested protectingly on Elisha's shoulder.

"He'll be the heir if you vultures leave him anything to inherit."

The assessor laughed with forced heartiness.

"I wouldn't worry on that score if I were you. Judging from what I've been able to see, he'll never want for anything. You Jews have no reason for complaint."

"You will excuse us, please," Amram interrupted stiffly, turning away.

Silently the boy and he entered the banquet hall where stools had been set for them as symbols of their grief. A meal had been prepared by friends in token of their sympathy. The memory of their bereavement, obscured briefly by the incident in the courtyard, returned in full force. They ate but little and spoke but once.

"Uncle," Elisha asked, voicing a question that had worried him for two days, "what did my father mean when he said I must be wholehearted, not torn?"

"Someday you will understand," Amram said hesitantly. Thereupon, he rose, left the room and entered Abuyah's private apartment. At first his footsteps beat with slow regularity. Then they ceased. The boy was mustering his courage to get up and investigate when the click of Amram's sandals sounded again, briskly this time, as though he were acting upon a vital decision. A door opened, admitting a blast of cold air. The villa was still except for the whine of the wind outside and the occasional murmur of voices from the servants' quarters.

Afraid to be left alone, Elisha got up and went flying across the room which had been his father's, through its outer door into the open. The sky was an expanse of tumbling, shifting clouds, dark with threat. At the sight of it, he hesitated. But he was more afraid of the emptiness behind him. In a mounting panic he ran around the house, seeking his uncle. The first time he passed by the fallow field behind the villa he missed him. But as he came by it again, stumbling a little now, his breath coming in half-sobs, he noticed smoke rising in a slender column amid the weeds. Just as he stopped to observe, Amram, who had been stooping over the fire, stood erect. With a surge of relief the boy plunged into the underbrush.

As he came up to Amram, he was startled to see a pile of scrolls burning at his feet, and to observe the wax name-tag of some volume, boldly inscribed in Greek characters, melt into illegibility.

The boy's hysteria ebbed quickly, leaving curiosity in its stead.

"What are you doing, Uncle?"

"Burning Greek books."

As though to confirm the words, a roll of papyrus unfurled. The writing was exposed briefly and then obliterated by the eager flame.

"Don't, Uncle!" Elisha cried. "They were my father's and he loved them."

Elisha waited for a reply. None was forthcoming. Tears filled his eyes and he was lonely again. He started to turn away but Amram took hold of his arm and walked with him, talking gently.

"Let us not speak about your father, may he rest in peace." But there were other things Amram had to say. He had waited too long for this moment. And now that it was upon him his religious zeal, fierce even among the men of his own generation, burst forth. His grasp on Elisha tightened. He knelt, swinging him about so that their faces were close.

"Listen, my child," he broke out hoarsely, "you are a Jew. Do you know what that means? You think only that you belong to a nation like the Egyptians, or Syrians, or Greeks. Ah no, being a Jew signifies more, much more.

"Ages ago God selected our ancestors to be His Servants. To them He gave the Law and the Tradition. In these He promised that if we would obey Him we should attain to righteousness here and to eternal bliss in the world to come. And His prophets foretold that the day would come when all the peoples of the world would accept His way and thus find blessedness for themselves as well. Do you understand?"

Half-hypnotized, the boy nodded.

"Now," Amram went on, "if one is born a Jew ought he not give every moment of his life to God's will? That is why

it is wrong to waste even a minute on the study of those..."
Amram jerked his head contemptuously toward the smoldering ashes behind them.

"But, Uncle," the boy protested, freeing himself momentarily from the man's domination, "Father said that many Greek books are beautiful and true. You shouldn't have burned them."

Amram scowled.

"Aye, so your father believed, but he was mistaken. There is only one book that is true—the Scripture—and all truth is in it. The others are vanity and error." Amram's face closed in upon Elisha. He held the boy's eyes with his own and swept his resistance along with the rush of his words. "And you, my nephew, my child, do you not wish to know this truth?"

"Yes," Elisha replied uncertainly.

Hope flared in Amram.

At that moment the first cold rain congealed out of the moist air. Great drops pattered on the withered stalks about them and splashed in Elisha's face.

"Come, my son," said Amram, rising, "the storm is breaking.

Together they walked toward the house, Amram's arm about Elisha's shoulders, clasping the boy possessively.

"We shall begin soon," Amram continued. "Tomorrow Nicholaus leaves and I shall become your teacher." Elisha started. "Hush, child," Amram soothed. "I know you are fond of him, but the Lord is a jealous God who must be served with a whole heart. Someday, if He wills, I shall take you to a great rabbi for instruction—to Eliezer perhaps, or to Joshua...Aye, Joshua...And then you will become a learned and pious man, a great light in Israel..."

As they entered the house, the wind broke loose in full fury. All night it raged, working its wild will on the earth, bending tall trees to the ground, driving the rain, shaking the house as though resolved to sweep all things along with it.

It was as though a whirlwind took hold of Elisha, too. Before he was aware of what had happened Nicholaus was gone, and with him his world.

Amram took up residence at the villa. Each day thereafter he sat long hours with Elisha, teaching him and explaining a strange and bewildering book in a tongue that Elisha spoke but in which he had never read. The child followed, learned mechanically, dazed and overwhelmed by the restrained fury of a zealot's determination.

Subtly, imperceptibly, Amram remade him. Fringes appeared on his garments, his earlocks grew long. Into his mind filtered those beliefs concerning God, Israel and the Law of which his uncle spoke with so passionate an adoration. He got into the habit of praying regularly and observing rites meticulously until, though there was no flaming enthusiasm in him for the faith and practices of his people, there was, on the other hand, nothing of dissent.

Of Abuyah Amram never spoke, and the boy, sensing that references to his father were unwelcome, refrained from voicing the many questions that stirred in him. With time memory blurred and recollection awoke less frequently.

One day, during the third year after Abuyah's death, Elisha stood at a window looking at the field behind the house. It had been put under cultivation again. The weeds had been plowed under and the ground was striped with long furrows. But the charred patch where Abuyah's books had been burned was quite distinct. Elisha saw it and remembered.

CHAPTER IV

"ARE WE ALMOST THERE, UNCLE?" the boy asked wearily. He was tired, his throat was parched and his eyes smarted from the dust of the roadway.

"Soon, Elisha."

Then they were silent, busy once more with guiding their donkeys up the difficult, rock-strewn path.

When they reached the crest of the hill, Elisha was struck with awe at the desolation of the barren mountains of Judea, rolling away like brown waves toward the horizon. He pressed closer to his companion for comfort, but Amram, peering intently down into the sun-baked landscape, did not heed him.

"There it is," he pointed.

In the valley before them, a plume of black smoke hovered above a domed structure and a little house set in a sparse clump of trees.

"But, Uncle, it is a peasant's hut."

"It is the residence of your godfather, one of the most scholarly and saintly men of our time."

Then the boy blurted out the question that had been on his tongue throughout the journey.

"Why must I come here to live? Why could I not have stayed at home?"

"Because, as I explained to you long ago," Amram answered over his shoulder, for he had already prodded his animal into motion, "it is the custom for young students to attend sages. And I am eager that you in particular have the advantage of study under a great master."

Elisha's voice rose toward the treble singsong of a child's weeping. "Then why cannot a rabbi live at our house? Why must I come to this lonely place, away from everybody…?"

Abruptly, Amram pulled on the reins, waited for Elisha to come abreast of him and looked into his face.

"You are old enough for me to speak frankly. My boy, you

do not love me. No, no, do not interrupt. I will not say that you hate me. That is not the case either. But God's word must be loved. Therefore I am taking you to a teacher loved by all men, so that through him you may come to love the Law. It is no easier for me than for you. I shall miss..."

For a moment Amram's dark eyes glittered. He dug his heels into the donkey's flank and hurried on.

Elisha trailed behind him, acutely uncomfortable because he could not deny his uncle's charge.

"Does he live here all alone?" he asked when his embarrassment had abated.

"Aye, his wife is dead. His children are grown."

"But why in such a place?"

"In part, because he is very poor and can manage here on the little he earns at his forge. You see, it is forbidden by the Law to accept compensation for instruction or for service in the Sanhedrin. But most of all because, in this solitude, he can study and meditate without distraction."

The path they followed ended midway between the hut and the smoking dome which they had seen from afar off. They dismounted, hitched their beasts to a bush and set about shaking the dust from their garments.

From behind the workshop a figure appeared, Rabbi Joshua the son of Hananiah.

"Welcome, Amram, and you, my godson."

Elisha blinked. He had never seen an uglier man. The Rabbi's cheeks were puffy, pock-marked and wrinkled. His beard was straggly. Bulging under a begrimed robe, his belly shook as he walked. Nor was his appearance improved by the soot of the forge that streaked his hair, smudged his face, and made of his large nostrils two black holes.

Elisha's first reaction was dismay. Then perplexity. He recalled what he had heard about Joshua—that he spoke Latin and Greek as fluently as Hebrew and Aramaic, and that he was learned not only in Jewish lore but also in pagan sciences and philosophy. It was hard to reconcile his expectations with the man.

Their exchange of greetings over, Joshua indicated a trough in which they might bathe. From a barrel he filled two bowls with drinking water. Then he withdrew into his house to change his clothes. Refreshed by their washing, Amram and Elisha turned eagerly to drink. But thirsty as he was, the boy was unable to drain his bowl. The cistern water, warm and brackish with grains of dust floating in it, was so unlike the clear, cold well water to which he was accustomed that he was repelled and frightened at the same time. Terrifying contrasts assailed him—this hut and his own home, barren hills and green fields sloping to a blue lake, that hideous old man and faces sweet from familiarity. He would not stay in this place, he decided fiercely, clenching his fists.

"Uncle..." he began.

But Joshua had already come out of the hut and Elisha lacked the courage to speak in his presence. The sage had exchanged his working attire for a simple, dun-colored tunic, girdled with a rope. His straggling hair had been combed, his face scoured as though with pumice. He extended his hands, one to the man and the other to the boy, and led them around the house to a crude bench at the foot of an overshadowing tree.

"This is my pavilion of Solomon. Pray, be seated."

"Now, let me look at you," he addressed Elisha. "When last we met I could scarcely see you for the blankets." His heart warmed at once to the sensitive youngster, struggling bravely to conceal his fears. "Well," he said affectionately, "there is certainly more of you at thirteen than there was then, and what there is makes up a very presentable boy. If one may judge by appearances," this time he spoke to Amram "he ought to be a good student."

"So he is," Amram replied, amending quickly: "Of course, he began to learn only recently. As a result he is anything but advanced. If you will examine him now, you will see for yourself."

"All in good time, after we have become better acquainted. I hope you will be happy with me," he encouraged the boy.

"It is an honor," Elisha responded, stammering the phrases in which Amram had schooled him. "I trust that you will always find me a dutiful disciple."

The man's eyes studied him reflectively.

"You want to go home, do you not?"

Elisha did not answer.

"Of course you do. So would I if I were you. I can still remember the first time I left home to study under Rabbi Johanan. Well, you may leave whenever you wish."

Elisha's face lighted up. "You mean today if I want to?"

"But, Rabbi…" Amram's voice cut in harshly.

"Please, Amram, this is a matter between Elisha and me."

"Yes," he said to the boy, "today if you really think it wise."

"What do you mean," asked Elisha suspiciously, "if I think it wise?"

"You and your uncle have traveled two days to come here. Would it not be foolish for you to go back immediately without giving me a chance? Ought we not try it for a short time, let's say, two or three months?"

"Two or three months," Elisha echoed in despair.

"Dear, dear," Joshua complained. "You came here expecting to remain for years. I ask you to stay a few months and you are not satisfied. Twelve weeks is not forever and we are not going to read books all the time. You would be surprised at what interesting animals, insects and plants we will discover on those hills. To observe them is also the study of the Law. For God's will is written not only in words, but also in nature. Up there"—he pointed to the tree above Elisha—"there is a bird's nest on the second branch. Can you see it? The fledglings are just learning to fly. You and I will watch them every morning. So, each day we will learn afresh why David said, 'His mercies are over all His creatures.' And then you will help me in the forge....They will pass, those twelve weeks, never fear. This then is my proposal: If you agree to stay here for two or three months, your uncle and I will consent to whatever you decide afterward. Is that fair?"

The boy nodded.

"Good! Now let us see how much you have learned."

The next hour was given over to an examination in Scripture and the Tradition. Both men were pleased with the showing Elisha made. There were some questions he could not answer. But unlike Amram, Joshua was gentle, patient and quite willing to allow the boy to speak his mind. Very soon Elisha was sufficiently at ease to argue a point animatedly, much to the delight of the sage and the distress of Amram, who had always disapproved of his nephew's stubbornness.

All through the examination Joshua studied the boy, tracing the traits he exhibited to the persons who had influenced his character. Like his father, he was alert, inquisitive, tenacious in his demand for reasonableness. But Amram's repressive imprint was on him too. It had turned him in upon himself and had made him shy and uncommunicative. But with it all there was an appealing sweetness in the youngster. And Joshua could barely resist the temptation to slip an arm around him.

By the time the exchange of question and answer was over, Elisha's apprehension had disappeared. And when the man extended both his hands in congratulation, Elisha, smiling timidly, put his forth in response.

Even the moment of Amram's departure left the boy less lonely than he had expected. He embraced his uncle, bade him farewell calmly, and watched him as he rode up the hill. Only when the mounted figure disappeared did his eyes fill with tears.

Immediately Joshua led him into the forge to explain its equipment. From then on they were busy—working the bellows and the anvil, bathing in preparation for evening prayers and the simple supper which they ate in the open. Over their food they engaged in study. For, as the Rabbi said, their first day together ought not pass without a period of learning.

So, while the sky and the hills turned saffron, they interpreted the verse from Leviticus, "Thou shalt not curse the deaf nor put a stumbling block before the blind." They discovered that people might be sightless though possessed of eyes, that not all stumbling blocks were of wood or stone, and concluded that it was as sinful to take advantage of the weaknesses of a person's soul as of his body.

Hours later Elisha awoke with a start, oppressed by a great heaviness. For a moment, as he felt the straw matting beneath him, he could not remember where he was. Then he saw Joshua on the other side of the room, reading intently by the light of a dim lamp. It came back to him in a rush—the desolate mountains outside, the strange old man with whom he was to live, the water in which grains of dust danced. He thought of his own bed, of Sapphirah and of Tobias. Although he tried to cry quietly one sob escaped.

Joshua came to his side and rested a warm hand on his shoulder. Saying nothing, he remained there motionless until the child was comforted and fell asleep again.

On the very next day Joshua introduced his disciple to the routines of his new life—to periods of prayer, meditation and observance which the sage, by his explanations, invested with poetic significance; to careful instruction in Scripture and the Tradition, that vast body of lore, religious, scientific and historical, descended from the past; to their labors in the forge and garden patch; to excursions into the hills where they observed the wonders of earth and sky. Slowly the lonely unhappiness of the boy was transmuted into love for the man, his initial indifference into a keen interest in their studies.

Absorbed in his work, he ceased to count the days, forgetting eventually that his sojourn with Joshua was by way of experiment. Nor would he have noted the completion of the stipulated period had not the sage called it to his attention. Unhesitatingly he rejected the opportunity to return to Galilee. Thereafter it was assumed that their association was to be continued indefinitely

So they lived isolated, except for each other. But there were times when they left their valley. For the Sabbaths and holy days they traveled leagues across country so that they might worship with a congregation in the nearest hamlet. And intermittently Joshua's duties called him into the larger cities, to lecture at academies, to preside over district courts, to confer with his colleagues. On such occasions Elisha accompanied him. He listened to the addresses, met other disciples and saw, awestruck from afar, the great scholars and leaders of his land.

Once his trust in his master was established, Elisha gave voice to the questions he had never ventured to put to his uncle. Searchingly and without reserve, he inquired about his father and his devotion to an alien wisdom. Always Joshua replied with careful sympathy, describing both the virtues of the Greeks which had fascinated Abuyah, and their deficiencies which he had failed to perceive. Scrupulously fair in his evaluations, patiently considerate of the lad's sensitivities, he neither criticized Abuyah nor spoke deprecatingly of heathendom. But the perplexities, the divisions of loyalty which had disturbed Elisha, were dissipated. In the end, he emerged with an untroubled understanding of his father. At the same time he grew strong in his loyalty to the ways of his people as against those of the pagans.

CHAPTER V

ELISHA PAUSED INSIDE THE GATEWAY of the Sanhedrin enclosure and looked eagerly about him. It was as he had always imagined it. An open space amid vineyards was hemmed in on three sides by a low stone fence and on the fourth by rambling buildings where sessions were held in inclement weather. In this courtyard a half-circle of chairs reserved for the sages curved about the table at which secretaries sorted documents. Before them stretched rows of benches set up for spectators. As he stared, he discovered to his dismay that every available seat was taken and that those who had come late, as he had, were perching themselves on the rear wall.

"But, Rabbi," he asked anxiously of the man at his side, "where shall I sit?"

Joshua smiled up at his disciple. In four years the frail child had become a young man, tall, slender, bronzed by the sun, his body wiry with hard labor. A silken down was beginning to shade his cheeks.

"Well, now," the master replied, eyes glowing with mischief, "let us see. Yonder perhaps?" He indicated the thronelike chairs of the elders.

"Someday," Elisha retorted.

"All in good time, my boy, but right now I'd look elsewhere if I were you, and quickly, too, or you will have to stand."

The sage moved toward his colleagues. Elisha hurried along the wall. Spying a vacant space, he squirmed upward into it and then breathless with relief and excitement looked out over the scene.

Below and immediately before him sat a motley crowd. Some were litigants—merchants, artisans or peasants interested in cases on appeal; others, dressed in formal robes of state, legates from various communities, and the rest students like himself. In the first three rows advanced disciples were busy preparing styli and wax tablets for the taking of notes.

The sages, Joshua among them, stood before their places chatting idly.

Elisha had long since grown oblivious of his master's appearance. But now when Joshua was with his imposing fellows, the boy saw him again as he had for the first time, and ached for him. Pity welled up and an inchoate indignation against the unjust dispensations of fate through which one so sweet and kind in spirit should be so ungainly in body. Yet, a moment later, sympathy and protest were erased by a flush of pride. For when the sages seated themselves, Joshua took a position of distinction immediately between the Patriarch and the old Rabbi Johanan. And when the moment came for the proceedings to open it was on him that Gamliel called to invoke God's blessing.

Joshua's prayer, brief, simple and impressive, was no sooner over than, at a signal from Gamliel, the secretaries began to read in turn from the pile of correspondence on the table before them. Letter followed letter in an unbroken succession, each posing some question, theological or legal.

Might the evil of the world be imputed to minor angelic beings without impugning the sovereignty of God? Was the Book of Ecclesiastes to be regarded as Sacred Writ, despite its skeptical, cynical sentiments? Was it heresy to deny the resurrection of the body if one believed in the immortality of the soul? Was the recitation of the vesper service to be treated as obligatory or as a voluntary religious expression? Was it an indirect violation of the law against usury for a debtor to give his creditor special allowances on the prices of merchandise one sold the other? Might the restriction on labor on the Sabbath be waived in tending a sick person? Did the obligation to love one's fellows extend to all men, even persecutors?

In each instance the Patriarch suggested a response. Where the sages concurred unanimously, he authorized the secretaries to draft a communication embodying their opinion. Whenever signs of controversy appeared he curtailed discussion and referred the query to a committee of elders for further study.

At first Elisha listened closely, trying in each matter to foretell the decision. Once or twice he thrilled when his knowledge proved adequate. But most of the problems were far too technical for him. And the letters were monotonously uniform, one beginning very much like the other:

"From the congregation of Jews in the Exile, in the province of Cappadocia in the city of Pergamum (or Rome, or Syracuse, or Alexandria, or other towns so distant that their names rang romantic), to the Patriarch Gamliel the son of Simeon, to his colleagues the members of the Sanhedrin, the scholars of the land of Israel, may their light increase. Greetings of Peace and the Blessing of God."

Elisha's attention wandering, he shifted his position and jostled his neighbor on one side. At once he turned to excuse himself.

"Do not apologize," a friendly voice whispered. "In these cramped quarters one expects collisions." The man next to him was bald and large featured. A thick brown beard framed his face. His powerful body was garbed in the coarse tan homespun of a peasant.

"It is crowded," Elisha agreed in an undertone. "Are you a litigant?" he went on to inquire, making conversation.

"No, a student."

Elisha's eyes opened wide in astonishment.

"Rather old to be a student?" The other read his thoughts and was amused. "Or is it that I look more like a peasant?"

Elisha flushed. A hand reached up awkwardly in the narrow space between them and patted his forearm.

"Do not fret," the low voice went on. "You are right. I am a wood chopper by trade and my schooling began only five years ago when I was thirty. Until that time I could not even read."

"It must have been very hard," Elisha murmured.

"It was. I was not accustomed to studying. It took me

almost three years to learn how to learn. I can think of more flattering situations than being the one grown man in a class of children at the school I attended."

"To sit with children!" Elisha echoed in fascination.

"It would have been humiliating if both my wife and I had not desired it so much. But enough of me. Tell me who you are. Or, better still, let me guess. You are..." he hesitated, "nineteen years old. Judging by your accent you are a Galilean. Your father is, let us say, a prosperous merchant, or perhaps a landowner, and you are a student, too. Now, how have I done as a diviner?"

"Moderately well." Elisha grinned. "You were right in some respects. I am a student and a Galilean. But I am only seventeen, and my father—my father is dead."

"Oh, I am sorry..."

"But he was a landowner. Our estate is near Migdal. Right now I am living with Rabbi Joshua. There, that is the whole story."

"A paradox, as I live," the older man jested, turning the conversation quickly. "You, the patrician, reside with the chief spokesman of the plebeians, whereas I, a day laborer, study under the haughtiest aristocrat of all, Rabbi Eliezer. But then neither master would approve of what we are doing now, chattering here like sparrows instead of paying attention."

"But it's all over," Elisha cried in astonishment as he looked toward the sages.

"So it is," the man agreed, sharing his surprise. "They don't usually adjourn so early."

The rabbis were already on their feet. The disciples and spectators had risen too in a hubbub of talk and motion.

"You must excuse me." Elisha explained hurriedly, sliding from the wall. "I must attend Joshua."

"But come, now!" The older man detained him, descending after him. "We do not even know each other's names."

"I am Elisha, the son of Abuyah of Migdal."

"And I Akiba, the son of Joseph of Bnai Brak."

"I hope we meet again," Elisha said.

"I hope so, too," was the response.

Elisha elbowed his way through the thinning crowd. Akiba stood looking after him, an affectionate smile lingering in his eyes like the afterglow of sunset.

Joshua was plodding patiently at the side of Johanan as they walked together toward the town of Jamnia. Behind them younger men shuffled along, not presuming to push ahead of the great rabbis. Skirting the edge of the road, pushing aside the tendrils of overhanging vines, Elisha came up to his master. The two sages were not speaking. The only sounds they made were those of dragging feet and the uneven breathing of an old man toiling on his way.

"Peace," Elisha greeted Joshua and reached out to take the wallet which his teacher carried awkwardly under one elbow.

"Peace, my son, and thank you."

Johanan bent his gray head forward and peered at the figure which had taken its place at the other side of Joshua. "Who is the boy?" he asked.

"Elisha, the son of Abuyah. You knew his father."

Joshua's gnarled hand pressed a warning. "A promising disciple, but, alas, troublesome. He can think of more difficult questions than a whole Sanhedrin can answer. All in all, a half-broken colt, almost ready to have the Yoke of the Law put upon him."

But Johanan was not listening. He was trying to pierce the vague, drifting mists that obscured memory. "Abuyah, Abuyah . . . ." He recalled the name, but somehow not its association. And then the clouds broke. Across the abyss of thirty years he recaptured a picture.

He was again in a large chamber in Jerusalem, rich in magnificent appointments, one of several rabbis engaged in a heated argument with Greek philosophers. Between the two groups a handsome, dark, urbane man reclined indolently on a couch, interspersing amused comments to direct and revive the controversy when it lagged. Abuyah... that was the name... a Jewish Hellenizer and skeptic. And this was his son, a disciple.... The mist closed in again. Johanan sighed and shook his head. Children, he told himself, must not be punished for the sins of their fathers.

"God prosper your way, my son, and may you grow to be a light in Israel."

"Thank you, Master," Elisha murmured humbly, tingling with excitement over the blessing of the great old man.

The Sanhedrin met again the next day. But on this occasion neither students nor laymen were admitted to its deliberations. In consequence, Elisha, like others in attendance on the sages, was left to his own devices. Somewhat lost and bewildered, he whiled away the dull hours, drifting from place to place. Everywhere he found the disciples debating the political tactic of the Jewish people in its relationship to Rome. This was the issue with which, it was universally assumed, the elders were concerned. Much younger than most of his fellows, less informed and experienced than they, Elisha stood unheeded on the fringe of one group or another. He ventured no opinions but listened to whatever he could overhear. The discomforting sense that he was an outsider depressed him increasingly as the day dragged on.

Once he caught a glimpse of Akiba. In the midst of a band of vociferous, gesticulating disputants, some of whom were calling for open defiance of Rome, the man was defending the Sanhedrin's policy of peace. Hard-pressed, he nodded absently to Elisha, waved him a casual greeting and turned away to repel an attack. Feeling more friendless than ever, Elisha wandered disconsolately down the pathway to the Sanhedrin enclosure, there to await his master.

It was late in the afternoon when the warders threw open

"What do you mean?" he challenged, a surge of color suffusing his cheeks.

"He was a Hellenizer, wasn't he, always running after the pagans? And a traitor too, perhaps? Why else did the Romans spare his estate?"

"How dare you speak that way about my father?" Elisha cried furiously, attempting to rise, only to be trapped between the bench and the table. The room had fallen silent, all eyes centering on the man and the boy.

Then a warm, steadying hand rested on Elisha's shoulder.

"Come, sit with me," someone said soothingly. "I have friends I want you to meet."

Through his blurred vision Elisha recognized Akiba.

"How dare he?" Elisha flared. "I'm going to..."

"You're coming with me," Akiba calmed him, drawing him firmly from the bench.

As they made a circuit of the room Akiba murmured in his ear:

"Do not mind that fellow Shraga. No one takes him seriously. He isn't really responsible for what he says. Otherwise I would have put him in his place. That scar on his face accounts for everything. He was eight years old when the Romans sacked Jerusalem. He watched them torture his father, violate and murder his mother. And when he tried to intervene some soldier struck him with the blade of his sword and left him for dead. You can see now why he hates everything pagan."

"You mean," Elisha breathed, unaware of the fact that he was being guided into a seat, "that he is insane?"

"No," Akiba replied slowly. "He is sane enough—except on this one issue. And he studies hard. But his great dream is revenge against the Romans and Greeks. I know for a fact that he is one of the younger leaders of the rebel party. They're a strange pack, these fire-eaters. They're militarists in policy and rigorists in the Tradition, not out of love of God or man, but for the solidarity of our people. Fortunately, there aren't many of them among the disciples. But you planted yourself, innocently enough, of course, squarely in their midst. That was why no one near you came to your aid."

"But I still don't understand," Elisha broke out fiercely, his ebbing resentment in flood tide again. "Why should he insult my father?"

"More than he hates pagans," Akiba explained, "he hates Jews who have traffic with paganism. And as for the rich Jew who talks Latin or reads Greek"—Akiba shook his head —"that's another snarl in his soul. You see, he has always been fearfully poor himself.

"But come, let's talk of more pleasant matters than Shraga the Levite. I said that I have friends to present. And it was no pretext. Across the table sit my two companions, fellow disciples of Rabbi Eliezer—to the left, Simeon ben Azzai, to the right, Simeon ben Zoma. Gentlemen, this is Elisha ben Abuyah of Migdal."

Elisha saw the two men, both younger than Akiba, though not by many years. Simeon ben Azzai was tall, loose-jointed, gaunt. His head was weighted with a tangle of hair, graying prematurely. In contrast with him, the other Simeon seemed a mere wisp of a man, slight, swarthy, with gleaming dark eyes and mobile features.

Both smiled at the youngster encouragingly, sympathet- ically, as he acknowledged Akiba's introduction. At once the three men began to talk with gay animation. Elisha was fully conscious of the fact that they were attempting to divert him. But through their banter they were sometimes serious and it was soon apparent to Elisha that he was in the company of no ordinary disciples.

By the time the dinner was over, Elisha was at ease with them. And though the nervous quivering in the pit of his stomach still persisted, and his legs were shaky when he rose from the table, he managed to leave the dining room without betraying himself.

He never spoke of the incident to anyone. Not even to Rabbi Joshua. At first he thought of it constantly. With time it ceased to haunt him. But years later when the memory of it returned, he would feel a cold chill course his veins, a tightness about his heart and a tremor somewhere deep inside him. Sometimes on such occasions he wondered how many of his associates felt as Shraga did about him and about Abuyah his father.

CHAPTER VI

ALL THROUGH THE MANY YEARS of Elisha's apprenticeship to Joshua he returned to Galilee only for the major festivals. In consequence, the day of his arrival was always a holiday to the servants at the villa. For weeks in advance they planned for it, arranging to serve the dishes he preferred, to replenish his wardrobe and to entertain him.

But except for the sacred days when labor and the discussion of all secular affairs were forbidden, Elisha had little freedom during his vacations.

"You are growing up, my boy," Amram would say sententiously. "In time this estate will be yours to administer. We are all but frail mortals. And I want to be certain that when I am gone you will know how to care for your patrimony."

With an unswerving determination, such as he had exhibited in directing Elisha's education, Amram now set about equipping his nephew for his future station as a man of affairs. He introduced him into the complexities of ledgers and account books. He sent him out into the fields to work with the bondsmen. He taught him the principles and practice of animal husbandry and horticulture. He had the boy by his side whenever he inspected the gardens and grain crops of the tenant farmers from whose produce the great house derived a percentage rental. He made it a point to include him at conferences with Tobias when decisions, large or small, had to be made. Should the olive crop be poured into the presses for oil or sold to merchants in Tiberias? Would wine prices be up or down a month hence? Was it cheaper to card, spin and weave one's own fleeces or to dispose of them at shearing time and buy cloth ready-made? Elisha was taught the importance of all these matters. And Amram had little cause to complain of his pupil's progress for Elisha was especially eager to become familiar with the workings of the household which was his home.

Meantime people, who had during his childhood been vague shadows barely perceived, took on definiteness. He came to know and to like as individuals the sturdy farm hands who tended the grounds and lived in the rows of little houses back of the villa. He was always welcome at their homes where he called often to inquire after their health and to talk of random matters. The men treated him with amused deference, and their wives fluttered solicitously over the orphaned lad who, before their eyes, was growing into a strong young man.

Of all this course of training Elisha enjoyed most the trips he was sometimes allowed to make with Tobias to Tiberias. It was exciting to ride into town leading a train of ox-drawn carts laden to capacity with grain, olives, flax, jugs of wine or oil, bolts of homespun, as the case might be. Their passage through the streets, especially as they approached the market places, was an adventure in itself. For the bazaars were a welter of sound, smell and color, swarming with people, many of foreign costume and dialect. Here, men unloaded a wagon creaking beneath its freight of timber. There, camels paraded swaying under bales of wares. And through the confusion stalked the marshals of the Patriarch keeping the peace of Jewish law, and the agoranomoi, deputies of the Roman Government, assigned to enforce the commercial regulations of the Empire and to collect the taxes and tariffs imposed by its treasury.

In Tiberias the steward followed an immutable routine. First he sold the produce he had brought to town, haggling with equal ease and expertness in the dusty cavernous vaults of flour mills, or in the cool, fragrant offices of dealers in wines and oils. Then, elated by triumphs largely imaginary, he led Elisha to his favorite tavern where he dined and drank as befitted one who had done his task well.

In the early afternoon he set forth to the bazaars to purchase supplies which the estate did not provide for itself— metal utensils, imported fabrics, pottery and spices.

And Elisha, as he accompanied Tobias, came to recognize not only the merchants but their bondsmen and apprentices as well. These sat in the dim interiors of the shops fashioning lumps of clay on their magical wheels into jars, tapping away on sheets of bronze and strips of iron, or stirring soggy masses of textiles in the great vats in which they were being dyed.

Almost invariably before they left Tiberias, Elisha and Tobias visited the House of Ariston of Rhodes, bankers to the estate, to deposit part of the moneys they had received. Then, weary with exertion and excitement, they rode homeward with their purchases, the steward alternately scanning the wax tablets on which his transactions were recorded and fingering the purse heavy with coins which hung from his girdle.

When in his twentieth year, a fortnight before the season of the New Year and Day of Atonement, Elisha left Joshua to pass the holy days in Galilee, he expected no more than the usual routine of duties. But on this homecoming he was hailed with especial enthusiasm. When he leaped from his horse and stooped to embrace Sapphirah, she held him longer than usual. Tobias' smile was warmer, his pat on the shoulder more caressing than ever. The other servants addressed him with an extraordinary shyness and later seemed to be talking about him. Even Amram unbent to smile at him affectionately, a soft light in his normally stern eyes.

It was not until the sacred days were past that Elisha discovered the cause of the happy tension in the household. On the afternoon after the Great White Fast he was summoned into Amram's study.

"Pray be seated, my son." After some minutes of purposeless talk the man said abruptly, "I have a piece of very good news for you." Elisha waited expectantly, wishing that he would get on with it.

Amram seemed to be mustering his courage. He cleared his throat and hesitated maddeningly before he continued.

"You are now at an age when we ought to begin to think of your future. After all, you are two years past the time which, the sages say, is proper for marriage."

Elisha flushed. So that was it. He should have guessed. "Yes, Uncle," he said dutifully.

"And so I have invited a young woman to visit us. She will be here with her father this afternoon."

"This afternoon?"

"I was saving this as a surprise," Amram said guardedly, then continued at once. "I might tell you that the family is of modest means but of good blood, learned and pious."

It took a moment for Elisha to comprehend what he heard. When he did he leaped to his feet.

"But, Uncle..."

Amram looked at him, surprised by Elisha's reaction and the protest in his voice. "What is it, my son?"

"Uncle, you cannot mean that. I have always thought of Theopompa."

"Theopompa?" Amram had been sure that there would be no difficulty on that score.

"My cousin from Alexandria. The girl I was supposed to marry. I thought it was all arranged long ago."

"Yes, that was the original plan. But it is impossible now."

"Must you do everything contrary to my father's wishes?" Elisha challenged indignantly.

"Let me see," Amram began obliquely. "It is ten years since you saw her last."

"What difference does that make?"

"None at all," Amram answered softly, "except that you surprise me by even remembering her."

"Well, I do."

The doubt beneath Elisha's vehemence did not escape Amram.

"Well enough," he pursued, "to be able to picture her to yourself?"

All that Elisha could evoke was the image of a pretty little girl who spoke Hebrew with a quaint Greek accent.

Amram looked an unspoken reproach. Discomfited, the young man countered:

"Then let her and her father visit us so that we can renew our acquaintance."

"That," Amram said quietly but directly, "is just what I do not want."

Elisha's eyes studied his uncle keenly.

"Perhaps you will explain why."

"Because she has been raised in a city notorious for its sinfulness and frivolity. Few women in a place like that are virtuous, not even the Jewesses. You do want your wife to be chaste, do you not?"

"Of course," Elisha agreed, only to object: "But it's absurd to make such an assertion."

"This much I am certain of," Amram insisted firmly, "she is not a pious Jewess."

"How can you say that?" Elisha protested. "You met her only once, and that years ago."

"True, but I know her parents. Like so many Alexandrian Jews they are one half pagan and the other half infidel. Their daughter cannot help taking after them. Do not imagine, my son, that I have not thought long and carefully about all this. There is a brilliant future ahead of you—that I have always believed, and Joshua agrees. For that reason, if for no other, you must have a wife who will be a helpmate. Not a light-headed, wasteful, impious wanton, but a woman trained to be godfearing and devout."

Elisha wavered.

"Ask yourself this," Amram suggested slyly: "What would Joshua advise?"

To that Elisha had no answer. And as Amram went on to describe Deborah the daughter of Phineas, he listened with a resignation that slowly turned to interest. Uriel, the hostler, scurried up the path, his short bowlegs pumping furiously.

"They are coming!" he shouted.

All day long he had lain in wait on a knoll that commanded a view of the road, hoping to be the first to sight the young woman who was to be the new mistress of the household. Now, in his excitement, he so forgot himself that he burst into the room where Elisha and Amram were closeted and blurted out his information.

Amram scowled in reproof, then his thin lips curved in a smile and his eyes lighted up with expectation.

"Back to your post," he scolded good-naturedly. "Such distinguished guests must be attended when they dismount."

In a confusion of curiosity and apprehension, Elisha started toward the courtyard to catch a glimpse of his future wife.

"No, no." Amram pulled him back. "It would not be seemly for you to loiter in the gateway. Besides, the young lady may not wish you to see her until she has had an opportunity to make herself presentable. Off to your chamber, my lad. I will call you at the right time. And you might put on a fresh garment."

Elisha bathed his hands and face, comb ed his hair and hurriedly put on his best robe. The window of his chamber gave no view of the entrance to the courtyard. Nonetheless, he planted himself by it in the hope of hearing the first exchange of greetings.

At last the sound of hoofs came to him, next the rumble of his uncle's words of welcome. Then he caught his breath. She was saying something, but her words were too distant to be distinct. Her voice, however, was lovely, soft yet resonant, with an upswinging lilt that thrilled him. She spoke only briefly and when she was through Elisha felt a lifting of his heart.

A few minutes later, he mustered his courage and stepped across the threshold of the reception room. At once they looked for each other.

Deborah saw a lithe young man who, except for his intense blue eyes, might well have been taken for a pure-blooded Arab.

An almost imperceptible widening of her eyes revealed her approval.

A twinge of disappointment shook Elisha. She was not beautiful. From the sound of her voice he had expected some- one frail, but she was tall, almost too tall for a woman, and angular. Then before he had time to observe more, Amram was presenting her father.

His curiosity unsatisfied by his first disquieting glimpse of Deborah, Elisha turned reluctantly to meet his prospective father-in-law.

Phineas was a timid, colorless little man, obviously uncomfortable.

"It is indeed a pleasure, my boy," he stammered in his eager- ness. "I might say a privilege."

"Thank you, sir," Elisha replied simply. "I am honored."

Phineas would have gone on, but Amram interposed whim- sically, "The young people may want to meet each other."

As Deborah rose to be presented, as they exchanged con- ventional greetings, Elisha had the opportunity, for which he had been waiting impatiently, to study her. His second impres- sion was much more favorable. Her dark eyes were large and bright, her color high. There was a sheen and a silken texture to her straight brown hair. And if her face was strong rather than sweet, it was not unattractive.

All through the desultory talk which followed, Elisha looked at her covertly. He observed that her dress was in good taste, her manner reserved yet gracious, and her voice as lovely as when he had heard it from his own room. But it was of no avail. He could not recapture the lifting of the heart he had experienced when he had first listened to her.

Meantime Amram was trying very hard to stimulate conversation. He talked lightly and casually in the attempt to put the others at ease. But their answers were stilted and restrained. Everyone was relieved when, giving up the effort, he suggested a tour of the estate.

It was early autumn. The grounds, sunlit and fragrant, were riotous with nature's last luxuriance. Elisha had always loved the great house and the broad fields that surrounded it. Now he viewed them through the eyes of others, and thrilled with the pride of possession.

Overwhelmed by what he saw, Phineas cried out time and again with childlike wonder. He asked numberless questions, about the cereal crop and where it was sold, about the orchards and the income they yielded, about the stables and the bondsmen. He even ventured a guess as to the annual profits of the establishment.

Stately, almost majestic in movement, Deborah walked with them. She uttered no comments, but there was a faint smile on her lips.

"I hope you will not mind if I make a suggestion," Deborah said quietly yet firmly to her father as soon as they were alone in the chamber which had once belonged to Elisha's mother.

"Indeed not, my dear."

"Then, please, don't go into raptures over everything we are shown. I admit that it is all magnificent. But must we behave like paupers? Remember, if our family has been fearfully poor of recent years, our lineage is as good as theirs."

"You're right," the man mumbled contritely. "I shall be careful, and now I had better go and allow you to dress."

He had scarcely left the room when Sapphirah raised the curtain over the doorway.

"I am—or rather was—Elisha's nurse." She waited for an invitation to enter. "I raised him since he was five days old. And now he is going to be married!" Her great bosom heaved with emotion, her eyes filled with tears. She half-lifted her arms for an embrace.

At the moment Deborah was passing her slip, a long sheet of fine white linen, under her right arm and then drawing its two corners over her left shoulder to tie it. Her hands busy, she did not move in response to Sapphirah's gesture. The nurse's hands fell slowly to her sides.

"It is kind of you to take the trouble to visit me," Deborah said, glancing up and then looking down again to the knot on her shoulder. "Please come in."

Sapphirah obeyed with alacrity and plunged into the story of Elisha's life, talking volubly and disconnectedly but with deep devotion. As she spoke, Deborah shook out the folds of her stola, a formal mantle of deep blue linen with a band of white, embroidered in gold thread, at the hem.

"Oh, do let me help you," Sapphirah volunteered eagerly.

"Of course, if you like," said Deborah. With the nurse's assistance she put on the robe, bound a narrow white girdle under her breasts, covered her hair with a veil that flowed from over her forehead onto her back, slipped several bracelets onto her bare arms, and picking up a mirror, considered her appearance.

"Thank you," she said at last, opening a vial of perfume. "You may go now."

And as she withdrew Sapphirah knew full well that she had been rebuffed and that intimacies between servants and their mistress would not be encouraged.

The betrothal contract was signed that spring, but only after Elisha and Amram had argued and even quarreled about it for days. The young man had yielded in the end largely because he could advance no good reason for refusing to marry Deborah. He did, however, succeed in exacting from his uncle consent that the marriage would be deferred for several years. The interval seemed reassuringly long.

CHAPTER VII

ELISHA AND DEBORAH WERE MARRIED in the fall of the third year following their engagement. The ceremony took place just after the Feast of Tabernacles when the countryside was still dotted with the leaf-bedecked huts in which the Jews lived for a full week to celebrate the harvest and to recall the desert dwellings of their ancient ancestors.

On the wedding day a large crowd foregathered at the villa to witness the rites. Joshua and Eliezer arrived escorted by Akiba, the two Simeons and other disciples who were Elisha's friends. Kinsfolk of the bride and groom assembled from all parts of the land. And from the huts on the estate and farmhouses in the vicinity groups of laborers and peasants, dressed in holiday clothes, strolled across the fields to the great house. Long before nightfall every private chamber had been assigned to some visitor or other, and the courtyard swarmed with a multitude of men, women and children.

At dusk Amram and Phineas formally opened the doors of the banquet hall and invited everyone to enter. As they came into the stately apartment, the guests looked about with pleasure. The bronze oil lamps that hung from the cedar-wood ceiling had been kindled so that the place glowed with light. Wreaths adorned the walls and festoons of flowers stretched from pillar to pillar. Fresh rushes had been strewn over the flagstones. In corners tables had been set which the servants would move forth as soon as the service had been read. The snowy cloths that covered them bulged with the shapes of invisible goblets, platters and beakers. And directly in the center of the room a canopy of brilliantly colored silks was suspended from the roof beams. Beneath this symbolic representation of their nuptial chamber Elisha would stand to take Deborah for his wife. While the guests waited for the bride and groom a musician led them in the chanting of hymns. In former times, pipes and lyres would have sounded. But since the destruction of the Temple, a generation before, the playing of instruments at weddings had ceased and their voices now were unaccompanied. In the intervals between songs a jester entertained, directing quips indiscriminately at sage and peasant alike or making sly insinuations about the institution of marriage. Some especially bold sally had just evoked a roar of mirth when the curtain over one of the doors was drawn. The laughter died away abruptly. All eyes fixed themselves on the entrance where Elisha stood, flanked on either side by Pappas and Akiba, his groomsmen.

On his forehead a golden diadem gleamed. A silken robe of deepest purple swirled about him. Those of his kinsfolk who, living at a distance, had not seen him for some years murmured with pleased surprise. The boy they remembered had grown into a distinguished man, his graceful height the more striking in contrast with the stockiness of Akiba, and the squat fleshiness of Pappas. His fine-featured face, framed now in a tapering beard, silken and jet black, was marked with breeding and maturity. His clear blue eyes were luminous with health, yet soft with grave thoughtfulness. At the sight of him some recalled his long dead parents, others, aged and infirm, their own youth. A wistful silence settled over the assembly.

But he stepped across the threshold and the brooding sadness was dispelled instantly. The spectators broke into a chant, intoning and clapping their hands in rhythm with his stride, speeding him so to the canopy.

Once he stood beneath the cloth bower they turned to the door again, raising their voices now in salutation to the bride.

"Virgin, chaste and fair," they sang.

To the accompaniment of their music, Deborah appeared, attended by her father and matrons. Her gown was golden. Her hair and face were veiled. With her crowned head held high, she moved majestically, disregarding the rice and hops, emblems of fertility, which the guests showered upon her.

Under the canopy, the women lifted back her veil and

allowed Elisha to see her. On her lips was that same cryptic smile that had played over them when she had been taken on her first tour of the estate. Now, as then, it disturbed Elisha with its intimation of triumph.

Nevertheless, his fingers firm, his voice steady, he handed her the marriage token. "Lo," he pronounced, "thou art consecrated unto me by this gift in accordance with the tradition of Moses and Israel...."

Hours later, while the guests were still engaged in the song and mirth of the banquet, the groomsmen, holding torches aloft, escorted Elisha from the hall to the bridal chamber into which soon her attendants were to lead Deborah.

For a full week, innumerable meals were served and countless kegs of wine broached in the banquet hall. From dawn to midnight each day the villa resounded with laughter and music. But with the eighth morning after the marriage the festivities came to an end and the guests prepared to return to their homes. Singly or in little groups, they called at Deborah's apartment to pay her their respects. Then, as they emerged from the courtyard, they stopped at the gateway where Elisha stood to bid them farewell.

Exhausted as he was by the week's excitement, Elisha assumed a gay, carefree manner. He acknowledged felicitations with a smile or phrase of gratitude, and parried witty thrusts lightly. To the earnest farewells of Akiba and the two Simeons he responded with jests. Not once did his face betray his feelings, not even when Joshua departed, and Elisha, looking after him, ached with the intuition that his youth was disappearing down the pathway with the old man. So one by one they passed before him until the last of them was gone. Then, his shoulders sagging with weariness, he entered the deserted courtyard and sank onto a bench in a recess to rest.

He was tired, unspeakably tired. And one farewell still awaited him, the most trying of all. For Amram too was leaving the villa to resume residence after a lapse of years in his native town of Meron. Bridal couples had best be by themselves, he had insisted. And not all Elisha's coaxing had moved him. But he would not be leaving until the following morning, and in the meantime it was pleasant for Elisha to be by himself.

Leaning back, he propped his head and shoulders against the wall and savored the refreshing solitude. But he experienced no lifting of the spirit.

For it was not fatigue alone that weighed on him. It was rather the aching disillusionment that had been with him from the beginning, throbbing all the more perceptibly at this moment when he was free from distraction. On his wedding night he had approached Deborah expecting to meet with an ardor equal to his own. Passivity, dutiful and tolerant, had been her response, and his own eagerness had faltered before it. So it had been since then. Always the ecstasy for which he hoped had eluded him. His successive disappointments depressed him increasingly. Their cumulative weight rested on him now with all the urgency of some keen physical pain.

"As I live," a familiar voice broke in on his brooding, "I have been searching the house for you for an hour. Of all places to find you—and so dejected and alone."

"By the sanctuary, Pappas," Elisha threw back at him. "Isn't a man entitled to a few minutes by himself?"

"What's troubling you?" Pappas asked in quick anxiety.

Elisha looked up at him. There were some things a man did not share with anyone, not even his closest friend.

"Nothing," he answered offhandedly, "except sheer weariness of people."

Pappas scrutinized him. They knew each other too well for dissemblance, but when Elisha volunteered nothing further he did not press him.

"Very well," he resumed jocularly, accepting Elisha's pretense, "I will not disturb your precious privacy. I am on my way now. But you may be interested to know that this time

I'm going pretty far—and for good. To Antioch, in fact."

"Antioch?" Elisha gasped, shocked out of his self-concern. "Why, it's in another world."

"Exactly, and that's why I'm going. Palestine may suit you well enough. You have a wife, and a career to follow. But there is nothing to keep me here. Everything is so dull and proper in these parts. I want excitement and variety in living. And incidentally, it will be a relief to do as I please without having to worry always about the scruples of my countrymen."

"You can't be serious," Elisha protested. "It's just a passing fancy."

"Oh no, it's not. I've been thinking of it for ever so long. I would have gone months ago if it had not been for your wedding. Now that that's over I shall be on my way within a week."

"But why didn't you tell me?"

"I thought you might be disturbed by the news. I may have been flattering myself but it occurred to me that you might regret my going."

Elisha looked up at him. His friend's face was round and fleshy almost to coarseness. Little wisps of hair sprouted from the circular nostrils of his bulbous nose. He had not been handsome as a boy. Manhood had made him no more beautiful. But his eyes still sparkled with love of gaiety, as in his childhood, and there was affection in his crooked smile. Altogether he was very dear to Elisha.

"I shall miss you," Elisha said.

"And I you," came the immediate response. Briefly their glances locked.

"But come now," Pappas broke the silence, averting his eyes self-consciously. "It is not forever. I shall be back someday. And we will certainly exchange letters in the meantime."

The lonesomeness that already burdened Elisha became at the prospect of Pappas's departure almost intolerably oppressive. Fleetingly he wrestled with the urge to detain Pappas by confessing his need for old companionships. But pride prevailed and a reluctance to impose his requirements on his friend. He rose and opened his arms for an embrace.

"With all my heart, I wish you happiness," he said.

Amram's last words to Elisha and Deborah as he rode off were a promise of a speedy return. But almost at once his health began to fail, much as though, his guardianship of his nephew at an end, he were relaxing his hold on life. It was midwinter before he came to the villa again and by that time his stern face had softened with weakness, his hair was as white as the frost that shimmered on the ground. Thereafter he was too feeble to leave his home and for some months Elisha and Deborah were kept busy traveling back and forth between Migdal and Meron.

Just before the early spring feast of Purim they visited with him for the last time. They had hoped to find him recovered sufficiently to return to the estate in their company. He was confined to his bed and obviously unequal to the trip. But when they offered to remain with him for the holiday he rejected their suggestion decisively. The occasion, he argued, was too important to their servants and tenants for them to absent themselves. With a flash of his old peremptoriness he reminded them, as they took their leave, of the Tradition which forbade marring religious festivals with personal concerns.

Despite his absence and general anxiety over his welfare the celebration at the villa began auspiciously. By dusk, every bondsman and farm hand was present in the Great Hall with his family to hear the reading of the Scroll of Esther, to rejoice in Mordecai's triumph and Haman's downfall. The last accents of Elisha's recital were scarcely over when the assembly rushed unceremoniously for the doors. There was much to be done before the carnival. Costumes and masks must be donned, a play rehearsed, the courtyard prepared for the festivities.

"I am so happy the weather favors us," Elisha said to Deborah when they were alone in their chambers. "It is so much pleasanter to hold the carnival in the open. Now this outfit," he exhibited a fantastically colored robe, "is the very stuff of miracles. Observe for a moment and you will see me transformed into the most glorious Ahasuerus on whom you have ever laid eyes."

She smiled in amusement.

"I hope," she commented, half-earnest, half-teasing, "that once you become the King of Persia you will not indulge in the liberties he allowed himself."

"Indeed I shall. I intend to behave outrageously. But aren't you dressing?" he asked as he observed in dismay for the first time that she was not engaged in doing so.

"No," she replied hesitantly.

"But why?"

"I don't know," she evaded, going on to confess in a rush: "The truth is that I cannot do this sort of thing gracefully."

"Try it once. After all we are among friends, and everyone will be so disappointed."

"I'd love to. But it's just not easy for me to unbend."

He was very busy with the buckle of a belt as he said ruefully, "I'm sorry. I had it all planned to crown you my queen in the play."

"Thank you for the compliment. To my sorrow I shall have to do without the honor. And now if you will excuse me, I must see to the banquet hall."

He lifted his head to stare at her in amused surprise. "Again? You certainly are a conscientious housewife. Isn't this your tenth inspection?"

"One must," she responded somewhat ruffled. "It is simply impossible to trust servants to obey instructions."

"Please don't be offended. I merely wanted to display myself privately before you in all my magnificence."

"I shall be back in a moment," she replied, moving toward

the door, "and then I will admire to your heart's content."

But when she returned she was too annoyed to pay him heed. Her cheeks were flushed, her lips compressed into a thin line.

"Just as I thought," she cried as she swept into the room. "I told Tobias explicitly how to lay out the tables. And he had the impudence to tell me that he had always done otherwise."

"What of it?" he responded casually, piqued that she had not commented on his appearance. "No one will notice the difference."

"To be sure no one will," she agreed complacently. "He is redoing the arrangements now."

The courtyard swam with light and color. Flaring torches set in metal brackets fixed to the walls illumined the enclosure. The peasants and servants, dressed in bizarre, gaily hued disguises, had danced and sung riotously for over an hour. Now, exhausted, yet still excited, they were seating themselves cross-legged on the stone flagging, eager for the spectacle to be enacted on a crude improvised stage.

From her chair in a corner where she could command a clear view of the scene, Deborah watched, her eyes aglow with delight. It had all been a bit wearing, but more pleasant than she had expected, to observe the antics of these happy people, to accept their simple festival gifts, diffidently presented, to distribute little handfuls of coppers in return and to acknowledge their expressions of gratitude.

For the first moments of the play her elation persisted. And once while Elisha was scrutinizing candidates for the position vacated by the deposed Queen Vashti, Deborah regretted fleetingly that she was not participating. But later in the performance, as her husband warmed to his role and began to display an abandon that evoked storms of laughter from the spectators, a look of uncertainty came over her face and by the time the presentation was over her lips were pursed, her brows knit.

"Well, how did you like it?" he asked as he joined her.

"It was lovely." she responded at once. "Only…"

"Yes?" he encouraged when she paused.

"I wonder," she groped, "was it altogether dignified for you to…"

"Oh come, Deborah," he cajoled, "where's your sense of humor?"

"You have told me before that I lack one," she threw at him, with a toss of the head. "At least I have some feeling for propriety."

A flurry at the entrance of the courtyard drew Elisha's attention from his wife. Through the shifting crowd a messenger elbowed his way.

"Master Elisha," the man began, "I bring you news of your uncle. Amram is very ill. He may not live through the night. He has asked you to come at once."

A hush settled over those who stood near enough to hear and spread from them until the enclosure was altogether silent.

"Uriel," Elisha commanded, "saddle a fast horse for me and get a fresh mount for this man."

"Shall I go with you?" Deborah volunteered.

"I think not. Night travel is too strenuous and I shall be riding hard. You had better follow with Tobias at dawn."

Tugging at the fastenings of his costume which was suddenly grotesque, he hastened to his room to change his clothes.

His arrival at Meron was none too soon. When he entered his uncle's bedchamber, Amram had just completed his death confessional.

"I am glad you came so promptly," the old man greeted him. "I did not want to die without bestowing my last blessing on you."

He raised his trembling hands. Elisha bowed his head.

"Twenty-four years it will be on your next birthday," Amram whispered to his nephew when the benediction had been conferred. "A fleeting dream…"

Then a wan smile hovered over his lips.

"I am content. I have set you firmly in the ways of our people. Now may He take my soul for I am not better than my fathers."

With that he turned his face to the wall and sank into a sleep from which he did not wake.

CHAPTER VIII

SINCE THE DAY THEY HAD protected him from Shraga the Levite, Akiba and the two Simeons had become Elisha's most steadfast friends. At sessions of the Sanhedrin or at the various academies they frequented, they sought one another out unfailingly, sat side by side during the lectures, dined together in the taverns, exchanged notes and opinions, and traveled in a body as far as their routes homeward coincided. Among the other disciples their association evoked at first some comment, so disparate were they in age and temperament. They themselves would have been hard put to account for their attachment. Nor did they attempt to analyze it. It sufficed them that the three older men felt toward Elisha as they might toward a younger brother, loved both for himself and for his unusual gifts, and that he responded with a devotion reverential yet intimate. So inseparable were they that in the end their fellows slipped into the habit of referring to them simply as "The Four."

With Elisha's marriage a rift appeared in their companionship. A bridegroom could scarcely be expected to be faithful in his attendance at scholarly assemblies, and for over a year or so his friends saw him only sporadically. But by the time the second anniversary of his wedding had rolled round the old routine had been restored. And subsequently he was with them more constantly than ever.

Neither ben Zoma who was a widower nor ben Azzai who had never married saw anything untoward in the unswerving regularity of his presence. But Akiba, as a family man, was puzzled over the ever increasing length and frequency of the periods during which his young colleague was away from his home. Whatever his apprehensions, they were dispelled by the joy with which Elisha informed him one day that Deborah was pregnant. An anxiety lifted from him when he heard the tidings. And there was relief under his enthusiasm as he cried. "Every good fortune!"

"If it's a boy," Elisha went on exuberantly, scarcely stopping to acknowledge his friend's congratulations, "I shall call him Abuyah."

Affected by his excitement, Akiba took refuge in banter, inquiring in all gravity, "And if twins?"

"After Amram, may he rest in peace," came the instant unreflecting reply.

Then Elisha caught the gleam of amusement in the other's eyes. He flushed slightly and retorted to it, "Why don't you ask how I will call a girl, or twin girls for that matter?"

"Why not? One ought to be prepared for any contingency."

But as it turned out Elisha was not to have the opportunity on which he counted to use the names he held in readiness. And one gray wintry morning, months later, after Deborah had suffered her second miscarriage, he heard from the lips of a midwife that such an occasion might never arise.

They were standing, the woman and he, in a corridor just outside Deborah's chamber, their faces white with sleeplessness. In the cold and the pale light little jets of mist spurted from their mouths as they spoke to each other.

"I may be mistaken," the midwife confessed, "but I doubt that she will ever conceive again. After all, two uncompleted pregnancies in a little over a year. And she was so sick this time." She shook her head dolefully.

Through his crushing disappointment hot concern flashed. "You did not tell her that?" he asked frantically.

Muffled weeping from within the room supplied the answer.

"But she asked me." The woman cringed before his look of reproach. "I could not lie. I am sorry if…"

"No matter," he cut off her protestations and moved toward the curtained doorway. "She would have had to know sooner or later. You may go now."

Deborah lay flat on the high bedstead, one arm flung across her eyes.

Uncertainly Elisha bent down and kissed her forehead.

At his touch, she bit her lower lip to steady its sudden trembling. But sobs broke through, shaking her violently. Pitying and bewildered, he stroked her tear-drenched cheeks until she quieted.

"Oh, Elisha," she murmured, "I wanted it so, our child, an heir for the estate after us, and now it will never be."

"Hush," he soothed, his fingers pressing her in gentle restraint. "We are not certain that it is so."

"But it is," she whispered. "I felt it even before she told me. It is so hard to realize. I am so large, so strong, and such a failure...."

The desire to comfort her dispelled all other feelings in him, even his own sorrow. Tenderly he gathered her into his arms, striving to still her renewed weeping.

"What have I left?" she moaned as she poured forth her grief against his body. "What is there to which I can look?"

"You must not speak so," he chided gently. "Despite this disappointment we have much for which to be thankful. It is not everyone who is privileged to enjoy friends like ours, the security and comfort of our home...."

After that, though sobs continued to rack her, she quieted.

Elisha met his friends again at Jamnia a fortnight before the Passover. Not an explicit word passed between them and yet he could feel and was warmed by their sympathy.

On the last day of the convocation, Akiba invited them to celebrate the impending festival at his home in Bnai Brak. Like the two Simeons, Elisha accepted the proffered hospitality unhesitatingly. Deborah was quite well again, though still depressed, and a change of scene might do much to dispel her moodiness. On his return home Elisha found Deborah awhirl with the annual house cleaning which was a tumultuous but unfailing prelude to the Passover. To the enthusiasm with which she had always gone at directing the affairs of the villa there was in this instance an additional incentive. For the purifying of Israel's dwelling places of forbidden leaven was more than a matter of routine administration. It was a religious obligation as well. And Deborah, though unconcerned with moral doctrines, was meticulous about ritual observances.

It took Elisha some time after their first greetings to capture her attention, so distracted was she by her innumerable duties. But when he did succeed in getting her to listen and suggested a trip for the festival her immediate response was an expression of delight.

"You're quite sure you're strong enough to travel?" he persisted.

"Yes, indeed. But where are we going?"

"To Akiba's in Bnai Brak."

The glow of anticipation faded from her eyes.

"But, Deborah, I thought you'd be pleased."

"Well, in a way I am and in a way I'm not," she responded. "If you must spend the holy day with him you should have insisted on his coming here. Certainly he and his family would all be more comfortable with us. And we could accommodate them under our own roof, while they, in all likelihood, will have to send us off, for lack of room, to some foul tavern to sleep."

"Frankly," he admitted, "it did not occur to me in time. And when it did, Akiba had already invited ben Azzai and ben Zoma, who have been at his home regularly for years."

Hearing their names Deborah flushed.

"I must say," she cried, "I do not understand your taste in friends. Here we are to travel two days and for what purpose? To enjoy the company of three men, all of them older than ourselves. Our host a woodcutter, our fellow guests a weaver and a petty merchant, each poorer than the other. You know, Elisha, among the sages and disciples there are men of your class with whom you might associate."

For an ominous interval Elisha was forced to remind himself of the ordeal through which she had passed, the effects of which were still perceptible in her irritability and will to dominate. Only when he was master of himself again did he speak, and then very softly.

"Simeon ben Azzai and Simeon ben Zoma may soon become members of the Sanhedrin. Akiba is to be ordained at the very next session. They are scholars, pious men, and leaders in Israel. They have been kinder to me than I can say. I am proud to regard them as my friends. And if they are poor, since when has a man's worth been measured by the weight of his purse?"

She started to protest.

"No," he said gently but stiffly, "I regret that you are not happy over the arrangement. I promise that I will bear your preferences in mind next year. But I will not discuss the matter any further now."

She glared at him for a moment and turned to leave, stopping at the door to add, "There's another letter from Pappas waiting for you in the book cabinet."

Eager for diversion after the unpleasant exchange, Elisha broke the seal on the wax tablets, ripped off the binding threads and, throwing himself on a couch, began to read.

"...after all this time," Pappas had written, "I still cannot accustom myself to the marvels of this place. I shall not make another attempt to describe them. No account could do them justice. The only suggestion I can offer is this: You know something of Caesarea. Well, Antioch is to Caesarea, as Caesarea might be to Migdal. Almost a half million souls in one city, Greeks, Romans, Syrians, Egyptians and Jews all milling through the endless streets both by day and night, so that one might imagine no one ever sleeps. And as for amusements—theaters, arenas, gymnasia and bathhouses beyond number.

"But what is most exciting is the associations I have established. For a long time most of my acquaintances were, I will admit it, more than a little nondescript. Fortune, however, has smiled on me. I have been using my spare funds for an occasional speculation—shipping, contracting companies and the like. As a result I have had dealings with one Pompeianus, the shrewdest lawyer in the Empire. He took a liking to me and since then I have dined in the best households. I have won the friendship of distinguished philosophers, men of letters and governmental officials.

"One commandment of Scripture at least I am fulfilling here, the precept of Solomon: 'Rejoice, young man, in thy youth and walk after the impulses of thy heart and the sight of thine eyes.' Incidentally, as one learned in the sacred writ, you might explain to me some time how such a Greek idea ever got into the head of a Palestinian Jew...."

As he read on a glow thawed the chill in Elisha. Even when he had come to the end he did not put the letter aside immediately. A smile—half-amusement, half-affection—on his face, he sat for a time turning the tablets idly in his hands. The door of the book cabinet which he had closed insecurely swung open. The sight of the scrolls stacked within it recalled him to his duties. With a faint sigh he rose, slipped Pappas's letter into the cabinet, drew out a roll of notes and set himself to study.

Trailed by a cavalcade, Elisha and Deborah rode up to the tavern at Bnai Brak. Idlers in the courtyard gaped at the ostentatious retinue, and Elisha cringed inwardly before their scrutiny. He had wanted to travel with one or two servants at most. But he had been so relieved when Deborah consented to accompany him that he had not interfered with the arrangements, elaborate though he thought them.

Entering the public room of the inn, they came upon Rabbi Elazar ben Azariah and his wife. The man, a scion of one of the wealthiest, most aristocratic families of Palestine, was a frail person, with delicate features and prematurely gray hair. Gentle, soft-spoken, unfailingly courteous, he was one of the few members of the Sanhedrin popular both among the patricians, to whom he belonged by birth and position, and among the plebeians with whom he was identified in his sympathies. His wife, Miriam, of equally distinguished descent, was simple and unpretentious, a somewhat faded beauty. It was with wry amusement that Elisha observed Deborah's sudden affability during the exchange of introductions and greetings, and her transparent relief when she learned that they were to be fellow guests.

They did not tarry long in talk, for it was mid-afternoon, only a few hours before the setting sun would inaugurate the holy day. Having arranged with their wives to meet at Akiba's home, the men set out first for the baths, and from there, refreshed and robed, for vesper services.

The last "Amen" resounded through the crowded synagogue. The congregation streamed through its doors into the town square. Night had fallen. Riding high in the heavens a full moon dimmed the stars. Breezes scented with spring blew unsteadily past houses gaily illuminated in honor of the festival.

Briefly the worshipers loitered in the mingled light and shadow, extending the season's greetings to one another, and in particular to Akiba and his distinguished guests. Then they dispersed in little knots and hurried off to the banquets at which they were to celebrate Israel's exodus from Egyptian bondage.

Akiba, Elisha, the two Simeons and Elazar ben Azariah walked together; Joshua, Akiba's seventeen-year-old son, brought up the rear. Time had left no trace on Akiba. He was solid and firm, granitelike in body and mind as when Elisha had first met him. Simeon ben Azzai, however, had aged beyond his years so that his hair was altogether white. It was rumored that he had become a rigorous ascetic, and the fleshlessness of his body, the loose, wrinkled folds in which the skin of his face hung beneath his beard, gave confirmation to the report. His voice was hollow, his manner had become preoccupied as though with things beyond the vision of others.

The restlessness that had always characterized the other Simeon had grown more marked. His colleagues, disturbed by his increasing eccentricity and nervousness, sometimes said of him that he was the least bit mad. But of all the disciples he was the most highly reputed for the learning and ingenuity of his interpretations of Scripture.

Akiba's house, at the outskirts of the village, was scarcely more than a brick hut. Its one chamber, unpartitioned except for two portable screens, served normally as kitchen, parlor, study and bedroom. Tonight it had been turned into a banquet hall. It was brilliantly illuminated and a long table set for the feast ran its length. The scanty furnishings had been arranged to lend a festive air. If the tablecloth was threadbare, it was spotlessly clean. The dishes of cheap earthenware were distributed among bowls of meadow flowers and many lamps. And over the improvised couches bright-colored covers had been spread.

Rachel, Akiba's wife, her careworn face relaxed with serenity, stood just inside the doorway to greet her guests. Elisha marveled at her composure. Disinherited by her father, she had left a luxurious home to marry Akiba, then but an ignorant peasant. Now despite years of toil and privation, she preserved a simple dignity of manner. But the affection between her husband and herself was perceptible even to the most casual observer.

In a very few minutes, the men reclining, the women seated upright, they began the sacred service. Over cakes of unleavened bread, reminiscent of the Exodus, sprigs of bitter herbs symbolic of the slavery of their ancestors, and cups of wine to gladden the heart as with freedom, they told the old story of Egyptian bondage and the miraculous deliverance from it. From time to time they chanted hymns or interrupted the ritual to discuss some one of its aspects. Then, with the evening far advanced, they dined. After the meal they continued tirelessly with song and prayer, intoning their grace and reciting psalms of praise. It was late when the last prescribed syllable had been uttered. Even so, they were loath to leave the table. They remained as they were, about the littered board, talking at random of the past of their people and the lessons to be drawn from it.

Their conversation drifted into a discussion of a subtle point in theology, absorbing to the men but too technical for their wives. Rachel listened intently and tried to follow the involvements of the argument. Miriam sat quietly withdrawn into her own thoughts. Deborah, openly bored, stared about the room, studying its furnishings critically. Her roving glance did not escape her hostess. Following it for a moment as it fixed itself on a chipped bowl, a bunch of wilted flowers and a battered lamp, Rachel frowned and turned her attention to the discussion again. Some minutes later her frail calloused hand moved a dish to expose a neat patch in the tablecloth. Then she raised her eyes to meet her guest's and as their glances held a flush swept Deborah's cheeks.

Elisha had been watching his wife, observing the elaborateness of her gown in contrast to those of the others, noticing that, unresponsive to ideas as always, she was making no effort to interest herself in the conversation. Now witnessing the byplay between the two women, his eyes blazed. Only with an effort did he refrain from giving voice to the flaring of his indignation.

But before the evening was over, Deborah volunteered comments so injudicious that the memory of them rankled in Elisha for days. Their talk had wandered from abstractions into gossip of the courts and academies. Someone referred to the Patriarch, complaining that he had become so intolerant of difference of opinion that no one dared disagree with him, that he had been high-handed even with Rabbi Joshua, and had virtually driven Eliezer, his own brother-in-law, out of the Sanhedrin. Their resentment against Gamliel grew greater as they talked, and they set about debating whether it might not be necessary to take steps to limit his authority. Here Deborah intruded herself.

"I must say," she broke out indignantly, "I do not see how you dare talk that way about him."

They were all mildly amused by her unexpected defense of their presiding officer.

"And what makes you think that we are being presumptuous?" Simeon ben Zoma asked, his eyes dancing.

"Because," she threw at him, "the position is his by birth. His father was Patriarch before him, and his grandfather all the way back to Hillel. Why, the office has been hereditary in his family for five generations."

"But," Akiba interposed gently, "what if there is no living with him, if his actions are disrupting the Sanhedrin?"

"That does not matter," she answered with astonishing assurance. "It is his privilege to behave as he chooses. Certainly it ill befits artisans and hucksters to tell an aristocrat such as he is how to conduct himself."

A painful hush settled over the table. Elisha stared at her, aghast at her affront to his friends. She paled as she realized how unfortunate her remark had been. But she did not apologize. Instead she held her head higher in defiance. Almost at once Akiba attempted to turn the conversation. But the constraint persisted and they all rose to depart very soon thereafter.

CHAPTER IX

WITHIN THE YEAR THE SANHEDRIN indicated formally its recognition of Elisha's growing mastery of the Tradition. On the last day of the autumn convocation the Patriarch announced that the sages had voted unanimously to accept Elisha ben Abuyah of Migdal as a candidate for ordination, that they had assigned him a seat on the first of the disciples' benches in token of their readiness to elevate him to their number. The signal honor accorded him despite his youth surprised Elisha but no one else, and cries of felicitation greeted him from all sides as he rose to make his way to the place to which Gamliel beckoned. Neither Shraga nor his friends, scattered in the obscurity of the rear rows, joined in the applause. But the rumble of their dissent was drowned in the outburst of spontaneous acclaim. Elisha was altogether indifferent to it in the whirl of congratulations with which elders and disciples hailed him as soon as the session was adjourned.

Two days later, Elisha and his attendant riding along the paved Roman highway which skirted the sea of Galilee between Tiberias and Migdal, caught their first glimpse, over dull green waves of foliage, of the red tiled roof of the villa standing against the cold autumnal sky.

"Please, Master," the servant renewed his coaxing, "allow me to go on ahead to inform them of the good news."

Elisha had denied the request at least a dozen times that day. Amused by the lad's persistence, he now gave his consent. In a clatter of hoofs and a scurry of motion, the self-appointed messenger bolted forward and disappeared with astonishing rapidity from sight.

By the time Elisha approached the gate of the courtyard, some of the servants were already gathered before it.

"Blessed art thou who comest," Tobias called toward him. Soon they surrounded him, chattering enthusiastically while Uriel helped him dismount, pulled the saddlebag from before the pummel and, slinging it over his shoulder, grinned at him affectionately.

"Well, Master, was it a good trip?"

"Master?" a lyric voice corrected. "Rabbi from now on." Deborah stood in the doorway, her tall form stately in a formal gown, her face flushed with pride.

A sudden hush of reverence came over them.

But Elisha shook his head. "Not so fast," he disavowed; "that is a long way off."

Their babble broke forth again.

"Yes, Rabbi to all of you," Deborah said again, savoring the syllables, "if not now, then very soon."

Again they were silenced, but this time as though they had been reproved. After an awkward interval Uriel pulled impatiently at the reins of the tired horse. The other servants turned away self-consciously.

"See me this evening, Tobias," Elisha called to the retreating back of the steward. "We shall go over the accounts."

"Yes, Master...pardon, Rabbi." Tobias answered, pausing in his waddling retreat.

"You must not call me that," Elisha insisted. "I have no right to the title."

But he was gone, and Deborah and Elisha were alone. "Welcome, Elisha, and my congratulations."

He smiled and slipped his arm through hers as he led her into the house. In his study the saddlebags had been unpacked, the soiled linens were being removed. The tablets of notes he had taken during the ten-day session just ended had been piled neatly onto a little table. The servants retired as soon as Elisha and Deborah entered.

"Will you have your bath now," she asked, "or do you want first to tell me all about what happened?"

"The bath can wait." Comfortably settled on a couch by her side, he described the convocation of the Sanhedrin from its very opening.

Deborah listened intently until he was recounting how his name had been proposed for advancement. Then she rose and restlessly paced the room, her eyes aglow.

"Tell me," she demanded as soon as he was through, "how soon will it be."

"What?" he asked blankly.

"The ordination, of course."

"Oh," he paused. "Three, five, ten years."

"As long as that?"

"They are under no obligation to elect a man to the court simply because they have allowed him to become a candidate. Besides, I can think of people who would not be happy to see me ordained. Shraga the Levite, for example."

"Shraga the Levite?" she queried. "Is that the man with the horrible scar on his face?"

Elisha nodded.

"But what can he have against you?"

"I've never been able to discover. He is identified with the rebel party to which I'm opposed. But it runs much deeper than that. He disliked me the first time he laid eyes on me, years ago. Since then, to make matters worse, the sages have promoted disciple after disciple over his head. They don't trust him and his eccentricity, and they have little sympathy for his frantic hatred of everything that is not Jewish. Now they have passed him by again and for the person he resents most."

"Does he exert any influence?"

"Among the sages and disciples? Very little. But he has become one of the leaders of the secret army. In fact, he is almost its unofficial spokesman in the academies."

"Could he prevent...?" Her face was pale, her voice strained with anxiety.

"Who knows? Generally the Sanhedrin is immune to pressure. But a determined opposition might sway its decision."

She stood in the center of the room, calculating so intently that her arms were stiff at her sides. Then releasing her pent-up breath, she relaxed.

"Elisha," she insinuated softly, "why should you have opponents when you could so easily convert them into allies? A gracious word, a pleasant smile, perhaps an invitation to Shraga and some of his associates to visit us..."

"There's something you don't understand, Deborah," Elisha interrupted coldly. "Someday I may be a member of the Sanhedrin. Certainly I am working hard, in part, I suppose, out of ambition but also because I enjoy it and think I can be useful in office. But it is not a matter of life and death. And even if it were, I would still not curry favor with people who hate me and for whom I have no respect. Nor will I flirt with subversive movements so that I may advance myself. In brief, I will not scheme my way into ordination."

For a moment she was too stunned by his firmness to reply. Then she rallied and turned on him with a great show of indignation.

"Why must you always misinterpret me? Do you imagine that I would suggest cheap trickery? All that concerns me is that you be on good terms with everyone. And what, pray, is so shameful about that? Why even our Tradition teaches that he who converts an enemy into a friend..."

Her pretense of principle was more than he could stand.

"Please, Deborah," he broke in, "let's talk of something else...."

Irritated by his dismissal of her advice, furious that she had exposed herself to him so unfavorably, she was too unnerved to speak.

Then he went on to suggest, "What's been happening here while I was away?"

All her repressed rage exploded and vented itself on the first available target.

"Elisha, the situation has become simply intolerable."

"What's wrong?"

"Wrong?" she echoed. "Can anything be right in a household where servants grow more insolent day by day?"

"Oh," he murmured wearily, "so it's that again."

"I wish," she snapped, "that you would not act so bored and resigned whenever I try to tell you something about your precious staff."

"But I have talked to them every time you have suggested it."

"Precious little good it's done. Look at Uriel..."

"And what has he done now?"

"It isn't what he does, but what he says."

"He always had a short temper and a long sharp tongue," Elisha explained, smiling tolerantly. "Even my uncle Amram could not get him to be respectful. And if he failed, no one will succeed. Years ago, the other servants used to refer to him as 'the angel'—a brilliant instance of the inapposite. But they stopped soon enough after daring to call him that to his face."

"There you are again," she exclaimed, "justifying them. No matter what I say, it does not count just because they have been here such a long time! Sapphirah, for instance, always meddling with the cook and the chambermaids, as though she were mistress here."

"What do you suggest? Shall I send her away?"

"Why not? She is absolutely worthless."

"After all her years of service?"

"What has that to do with it? Servants should be retained only so long as they earn their keep." Deborah's voice was altogether devoid of its normal loveliness. "Let me tell you, idle servants can eat up an estate. My family was not always...we once had wealth, too. But my grandfather, like you, let them devour him. I refuse to allow this to happen to us."

"Please let them alone, Deborah," Elisha urged. "Everyone has faults, and theirs are not serious. You go at them the wrong way. Win their loyalty and affection and they will do all they can to please you."

But she was not appeased.

"Then you will not reprimand Uriel or Sapphirah?"

Elisha would have agreed to speak to them again, advising them to be more deferential, had she been less vindictive. But the hardness of her face and the rasp in her tone repelled him.

"No," he answered decisively.

Wordless with fury, she left the room.

It was all one, he thought despairingly, her condescension toward his friends, her suspicious surveillance of the servants, her criticism of him whenever he failed to conform to what she regarded as the proprieties of their station. These were scars left on her spirit by a girlhood nurtured on poverty and tales of the vanished glory of her family. He had hoped at first that time and a growing sense of security might efface them. But since her second pregnancy her haughtiness and ambition had become more aggressive than ever, as though reinforced by the thwarted energies of motherhood.

He understood her behavior well enough; he could even excuse it. But that made it none the more lovable.

Late that night he and Tobias sat by the light of a lamp examining the account scrolls. At one time the oil burned low and Tobias was compelled to replenish it. Deborah walked about in the next room, preparing to retire, the sounds of her movements unnecessarily loud. Elisha heard. But he remembered their quarrel and did not stir.

The steward looked at him. His mind wandering from the papyrus scrolls, he pinched the tip of his beard between his thumb and forefinger, carried it to his mouth and caught the strands between his lips. So he held it for a long time—an infallible sign to anyone who knew him that Tobias was thinking unhappily.

Gray swirling clouds moved sullenly across the sky, filling the air with shooting lines of water. Fog blanketed the lake and rested uneasily over the valleys and hills. The parched earth had drunk greedily at first like a camel fresh from the desert. But now, after two weeks of continuous downpour, it was surfeited so that the fields oozed moisture like Gideon's fleece, and little ponds gleamed where the ground was low and flat. Streams of muddy water ran noisily down the hillside, rippling about wet rocks.

Elisha stood at the doorway of the room that had once been his father's and watched the winter rains through the lattice. Myriads of little sounds, the gurgling of water on the tile roof overhead, the tapping of raindrops on the shutters, the hum of the wind and the low murmur of the rain, blended into a pulsing monotone. Fascinated by the dull pageant, he lost track of time until, chilled by the raw air, he drew his woolen cloak closer about him, and returned to the scrolls and wax tablets he had put aside some time before.

In the center of the chamber a charcoal fire burned on a bronze brazier. Along one wall beneath the shuttered window stood a low couch. A cabinet of exotic wood gleamed with moist redness near the inner door. Two stools, a bench and a high-backed formal chair completed the furnishings.

Stretching himself out on the couch, Elisha resumed his review of old lecture notes.

An hour or so later, the rain ceased abruptly. The gloom of the chamber burst suddenly into brightness. Distracted by the flood of unwonted light Elisha got up and threw open the lattice.

Tumbled masses of cloud still rested on the mountains of Gilead in the distant east. In the foreground the mists broke and withdrew like squadrons of cavalry in slow retreat. The sea of Galilee, flooded with sunshine, became a sheet of metal. Far off to either side the roofs of Tiberias and of Migdal shone in glistening whiteness. A great rainbow spanned the sky.

Devoutly, Elisha recited the benediction prescribed for one who sees the band of colors vaulting the heavens: "Blessed art Thou, Lord our God, King of the Universe, Who remembers

Thy covenant with Noah." The call of a familiar voice startled him. Pappas emerged from the olive orchard, the rain clogs on his feet sticking in the mud, retarding his steps as he struggled up toward the house.

Surprised and delighted at seeing his friend whom he had supposed to be still in Syria, Elisha hailed him excitedly and stepped out to meet him. They embraced affectionately, thumping each other on the back, exchanging greetings. Once inside the door Pappas stooped to unstrap his footgear, straightened again to throw off his raincoat, a great Cilician cloak, woven of goat's hair, and stood frankly inviting Elisha's reaction to his appearance.

"Well," Elisha cried, "your stay abroad has certainly turned you into a Greek!"

"It's just that we have exchanged roles," Pappas grinned, looking down at his clothes in satisfaction. "They are quite the vogue. Look at this paenula." He indicated his garment. "I am glad the rain did not get at it. It cost me a small fortune. And the tunic under it." Undoing a jeweled clasp on his left shoulder, Pappas opened his robe to exhibit a stretch of linen undergarment.

"And these boots." They were laced with colored leather thongs that twined about the calf to the knee.

"And this haircut." His broad, curving brimmed hat came off to uncover his black hair cut at the nape of the neck in a blunt semicircle and in front so that a curling wisp descended onto the forehead.

"And now, what do you say of the total effect?"

He held out his hands and turned slowly, like some tailor's mannikin.

"Elegant! Altogether fit for the agora of Athens," Elisha teased, "even to the sweet little love curl on your brow so that Iris can drag your soul to the Elysian fields when you die."

"Never mind," retorted Pappas quickly. "The rabbis may not approve of it and it is certainly not recommended by the

Law of Moses, but it is better-looking than your earlocks. Listen, my boy, Syria is not Galilee. In Antioch, one dresses like a Greek."

"Well, each man to his taste," Elisha goaded. "Only some of us have more important matters on our minds."

"I beg your pardon," Pappas said with an obeisance. "You men of affairs…"

"And speaking of men of affairs," he broke out seriously, "here you are—a candidate to the Sanhedrin, with all Galilee buzzing with excitement—and I have not had even the courtesy to congratulate you!" He threw his arms around Elisha and embraced him again. "I am *really* pleased. You do deserve it all, and more." Then he lapsed again into mockery. "Shades of your father and Nicholaus. You have come a long way."

Smiling broadly, Elisha called through the curtained door and Uriel appeared. "Some wine," he ordered, "and please tell your mistress that we have a guest."

Pappas strolled over to the couch and picked up a wax tablet.

"A list of the points of disagreement," he declaimed aloud, "between the School of Hillel and that of Shammai…" He looked at Elisha in inquiry.

"Notes of a lecture I heard at Usha some time ago."

"Well," Pappas replied, shrugging, "as you put it so well, 'Every man to his taste.'"

Uriel returned with a tray bearing a flagon of wine and two goblets. Elisha filled the cups, handed one to Pappas and began the traditional blessing.

Pappas blushed. "A moment more and I would have toasted some lady or poured a libation to the gods." He dropped onto a stool. "Typical Palestinian wine," he commented, making a wry face at the first sip. "Thin and dry, like life here. I suppose I have been spoiled. Those pagans know how to drink, as they know how to live. What a place Antioch is, Elisha!" he exploded. "You must visit it some time."

"Well, if you like it so much, what could possibly have torn you away?"

"The estate. Two of my bondsmen are finishing their sixth year. They demand their quitclaims. You know, 'And when thou sendest him away, thou shalt not send him away emptyhanded. Thou shalt surely endow him....' Well, my latest steward is a Gentile. He has refused to pay. They are suing him in the court at Tiberias and I have had to come home for a week or so. Now the Greeks—they handle their slaves intelligently. No six-year terms, no release years, no jubilee. A slave is a slave and serves for life, unless his master wishes to free him. No quitclaims either. The slave pays the master for his freedom, not the reverse as with us. I had half a mind to write to my steward and tell him to refuse to go into the Jewish courts. Let those ingrates try Roman justice and see how far they get."

Elisha lowered his cup.

"You wouldn't dare...."

"No, I guess not. The whole House of Israel would come down on my head. Just the same, Jewish law ties us owners hand and foot. First, we have to pay special taxes to the government. Then, our servants are so protected by Moses and your colleagues that they become a liability instead of an asset. No wonder we cannot produce for the same markets as the Gentiles."

"Well, your bondsman is a human being, too!"

"Maybe, but not according to the Greeks. Aristotle says that some people are slaves by nature. And that seems reasonable to me. If they were not slaves in character, they would be freemen."

"Nonsense."

"Perhaps it is," Pappas admitted grudgingly. "But it was God who made them bondsmen, was it not? Let Him provide for them. Why should I?"

"Oh, Lord," groaned Elisha, interrupting him, "we're off on theology. Quick, lets talk about something cheerful."

"All right.... How is Deborah?"

A shadow passed across Elisha's face.

"Quite well."

"And you?

"As you see."

"Tell me, Elisha," Pappas looked searchingly at his friend, "you can be honest with me—after all we have known each other since childhood—do you really believe all that you profess? I mean, all this about a God in Heaven who gave us the Torah and the Oral Tradition, who ordained quitclaims to bondsmen, and forbade shaving the corners of one's head?"

Elisha flushed angrily, then grinned.

"What is one to do with you?" he asked helplessly.

"I am sorry," Pappas apologized contritely. "It was like asking a man whether he is honest. Only you know me. My Jewish education was wasted on me. My father tried hard enough, I suppose. I simply could not understand it, and, for that matter, don't now. It is difficult for me to believe in God. The world looks too crazy and unreasonable. And as for the Law, why shouldn't a man eat swine's meat if he wants to? Or why must he leave just the corners of his field uncut for the poor? Charity would be just as welcome out of the center of the crop. I cannot imagine that God, if there is one, really cares. And then that story of how the world came into being. The Greek scientists say that the world has existed forever— though that scarcely makes sense either. And as for the Jews being God's chosen people, it hardly looks that way. If I had to select God's favorite nation, I should say it is the Romans. Not that I really care. I have always felt that a man is a fool to waste his time on questions he cannot answer."

Elisha listened tolerantly, serene amusement on his face.

"Here I pour out my heart to you," pouted Pappas, "in one of the longest speeches I ever made, and you're not even impressed."

"I am sorry, really, and I suppose I ought to be concerned

over your soul. But I have the feeling that nothing will ever change you."

Neither Elisha nor Pappas noticed the sunlight fading as they talked. They started at the first patter of returning rain upon the roof above them.

"Raining again," Pappas groaned, "and me with my best clothes on. What a climate this is! Six months of furnace heat when only the dew keeps the ground from catching fire, then six months of rain."

He rose from the couch, put his empty wine cup on the table and went to the door, Elisha following him. He slipped his hat over his head, stooped to fasten the rain clogs on his booted feet, and to pick up the Cilician cloak, which he had dropped carelessly to the floor. As he shook its long stiff folds a parchment cylinder slipped out.

"By Mercury, I almost forgot.... Like a good Greek I have brought to my host, who neither invited me to come nor urged me to stay, a genuine Greek Xenia, a guest gift." He retrieved it from the floor. "I doubt whether you will approve of it. But whether you do or not, it will be superior to your wine. Guess what it is?"

"A book, I hope," Elisha said eagerly. "I enjoyed the others you sent me thoroughly."

"Right, but you will never guess which one this time! Evil reading for a rabbi-to-be."

"Who thanks you nonetheless," Elisha completed.

"Well," Pappas added, "it is worth what it cost me if it prevents Nicholaus's instruction from having been wasted on you." He thrust his present into Elisha's hands. "Here, read it. I loved it. I am sure you will, too. Now I am running for home before this Noah's flood drowns me. I'll see you tomorrow."

Elisha attempted to thank him, but Pappas did not wait to listen.

Someone stirred just behind Elisha. He whirled about to discover Deborah looking after Pappas over his shoulder. "I am sorry," he said, "that you did not get here in time. Pappas inquired after you."

"Very kind of him. But I did not wish to see him. You know what he is—a profligate and an infidel."

"Oh, come now, I am not so easy to corrupt."

"Perhaps not, but his reputation... What do you suppose people will say when they learn that you and he are still friends?"

"So it is that again," Elisha thought, but said aloud, "No one who is fair-minded will misunderstand."

"And those Greek books..." Deborah was not to be denied. "I see he brought you another. What is he trying to do to you?"

"They are poetry. There is nothing wrong—"

"Do you think it proper for a future rabbi to waste his time on such frivolities?"

They would have quarreled again but the memory of their last disagreement was still too painfully fresh. With an effort he talked of other matters. But his courtesy was conscious, a thin, cold covering of resentment.

When his wife left the room Elisha picked up Pappas's gift. *"An Anthology of Poets"* the name-tag read, "selected by Meleager of Gadara."

Tempted, Elisha pulled the papyrus roll from its sheath and sampled one or two short passages. But the failing light recalled him to his duties. Laying the book on the couch, he began the vesper worship, his lips moving rapidly in familiar recitation. Unnoticed by him, the tight-rolled Greek scroll unfurled, spreading over the list of debates between the schools of Hillel and Shammai.

CHAPTER X

GAMLIEL'S HANDS RESTED HEAVILY ON Elisha's bowed head. His great voice boomed over him in the ancient formula of ordination: "Moses received the Law at Sinai from the Holy One, Blessed be He. He transmitted it to Joshua; Joshua to the Judges; the Judges unto the Prophets; the Prophets unto the men of the Great Synagogue...."

His own hands clasped before him, Elisha looked down at the strip of sandy ground visible between the fringed hems of their robes. But, as though his mind were disembodied, he pictured the entire scene. Himself, overshadowed by the towering massiveness and the arms of the Patriarch; the members of the Sanhedrin standing in a line at their seats, watching in reverent attention; and the respectful crowd of disciples and visitors, arrayed at their benches behind him. He knew that picture to its last detail—every face among the sages, every vine that hung from gnarled olive branches and straggled over the stone wall, that very wall on which he had sat for the first time thirteen years before.

Much had happened since then. There was scarcely an important teacher under whom he had not studied, not an academy from the southland of Judea to Usha in Galilee where he had not attended classes, rarely a session of the Sanhedrin which he had not visited. And of late, since he had been accepted as an advanced disciple, he had done his share of lecturing and of sitting as adjutant judge in district courts.

It seemed incredible that he was the same person as the boy perched on the ledge. His heart pounded with the thrill of achievement.

The voice of Gamliel went on, intoning the formula to its end: "In accordance with the will of God and with the authority vested in me by the Sanhedrin, I endow Elisha, the son of Abuyah, with the title of Elder and with membership in this body. I declare him a Rabbi in Israel. I name him

Companion to all the Scholars and Sages. From this moment forth he is authorized and declared competent to adjudge matters of ritual law. He may try cases, civil and criminal. He may determine issues regulating the sanctuary and its perquisites. What he declares ritually impure is impure. What he declares ritually clean is clean. What he declares forbidden is forbidden. What he declares permitted is permitted. He may teach the Scripture and interpret it. He may preach; he may reprove. He may exhort to the Glory of God and to the enhancement of His Word. Henceforth he shall be called by the title Rabbi, by the title Companion, by the title Sage, by the title Elder. These shall be the terms of reverence by which he shall be addressed in Israel, and may God prosper him in all his ways. Even as it is written in the words of David, 'And may the pleasantness of the Lord his God be upon him, and mayest Thou establish the work of his hands, yea the work of his hands, establish Thou it.' "

Gamliel reached forward quickly and enfolded the new sage in an embrace of welcome. Elazar ben Azariah, the associate Patriarch, and Tarfon, the vice-president of the Sanhedrin, took positions at either side of their newly ordained colleague. With the measured tread of a ritual act they escorted him to the seat which awaited him at the very end of the curving line. Joshua, his teacher, looked at him proudly as he passed before him. Rabbi Ishmael whispered a phrase of blessing. The two Simeons smiled at him broadly. Akiba was stationed on the other wing of the half-circle, but Elisha knew without seeing him that his eyes were aglow with happiness. He stood before his assigned chair while his escorts returned to their own positions. At the Patriarch's order they seated themselves and sat together quietly for a moment as a symbol of their new bond of enlarged union. And then Elisha arose to deliver his ordination lecture.

He had worked over his address long and carefully. Its theme was eminently appropriate—an analysis of the Scriptural sources for the authority of the Sanhedrin. He knew that he had developed it with impressive learning and ingenuity. It had been approved without reservation by Akiba and the two Simeons, when he had discussed it with them to get their criticisms. Nonetheless nervousness assailed him. But when he heard his own voice, surprisingly calm, he took on confidence. He was pleased to observe as he continued that the attention of his colleagues was more than polite, and gratified when at his last words a chorus of approving comments broke forth.

The Patriarch rose, thanked him graciously for his message and declared the session adjourned. In an instant Elisha was surrounded by an excited crowd, all congratulating him enthusiastically both for his ordination and his address. They patted him on the back and wrung his hand. Those who knew him well embraced him. Akiba came across the enclosure, working his way through the milling group.

"Thou hast expounded well," he said as he came up to him, using the conventional phrase of felicitation. But as he threw his arms around Elisha's shoulders, he whispered into his ear, "Beautifully done. I am so happy."

Insistent hands and voices came between them. A rush of bodies tore them apart. Someone plucked at Elisha's robe to catch his attention. Eager newcomers flocked around him, pressing his hand until it ached. His head whirled with excited talk. In a daze he acknowledged their congratulations. Then they melted away slowly, leaving him face to face and alone with Joshua, whose eyes were bright with tears. Elisha's mind cleared.

"I owe it to you, Master."

Joshua's voice was soft and gentle as he responded. "It has been a pleasure, my son—my colleague," he corrected.

"I do not know how to thank you. You have been a second father to me."

"Do not try. It was my duty and my privilege. Only serve God and treasure His Law, and I shall be repaid abundantly."

They turned and walked together across the deserted assembly floor, up the road toward Jamnia. Elisha escorted his master to his lodgings and came back to the tavern where Deborah and he were staying.

Eagerly he stepped into the public room only to hear a voice sounding from the ladies' parlor to one side, unmistakable in the richness of its timbre and tunefulness of its inflection. He stopped to listen.

"I have always felt," Deborah was saying, "that the sages ought to be not only men of learning, but of wealth and breeding as well. The common people cannot be expected…"

A frown knit his brow. He hesitated and then went directly to his own chamber.

His first task after his ordination took him to the town of Usha, sprawled over the side of a Galilean hill like a pile of toy blocks dropped by some careless child. Houses, standing on different levels so that the windows of one overlooked the cornices of another, jostled each other along the narrow streets and winding alleys. One building loomed above the confusion of roof tops—the synagogue—which was also the seat of a district court, and an academy of great repute. The little city was a sleepy place except during those seasons when college and courts were in simultaneous session. Then the taverns were crowded. In the bazaars purchasers haggled with merchants, shouting to make themselves heard above the din of voices. The stream of life stormed through the twisting streets like flood waters along the bed of some rivulet.

It was on a morning appointed for the opening of the courts that Elisha rode into the town. Uriel followed him, his short legs sticking out stiffly from his mount. From time to time they were hailed by passersby as they forced themselves through the shifting crowd.

"It is like the locust plague of Joel," Uriel called forward to him. "The inn will be a madhouse."

"Prophet of ill omen," Elisha retorted.

But Uriel had foretold well, as Elisha was compelled to admit when they rode into the courtyard of the tavern and looked upon the swarm of men and animals that filled it.

"We shall be fortunate if we have a bedchamber to ourselves," Elisha said, dismounting. "Even so, it will probably be impossible to sleep in this tumult."

"Just what I was thinking, Master," a voice spoke from behind him.

Elisha turned to find himself confronted by a young disciple, Meir by name.

"Master," he began after they had greeted each other, "the inn is dreadfully crowded. Will you be our guest? Modest as our home is, it will be more comfortable than this place."

Elisha smiled appreciatively. Ever since he had been accepted as a candidate for ordination, he had from time to time acted as a lecturer in one or the other of the academies. So he had come to meet some of the students. From their first random encounter he had been attracted by Meir's Grecian features, glowing light hair and beard and blue eyes, all lending credence to the romantic story that he was descended from a noble pagan family that had been converted to Judaism. He was a likable young man and Elisha was fond of him. But, tempted though he was to accept the invitation, he hesitated.

Meir, he had heard, was a scribe and like most of his fellow craftsmen fearfully poor. To accept his hospitality might work a hardship on him. And there was always the possibility that a prolonged stay at his home might prove a bore. "Let me visit you for the Sabbath," Elisha suggested by way of compromise.

"As you say, Master."

An hour later, Elisha stood at the doorway of the court. He was breathing quickly with excitement. He had sat as judge on some occasions in the past, but always in the capacity of an adjutant. This was his first experience as a fully ordained elder.

The hall, a lecture room with a raised platform at the end,

was crowded with litigants—a motley of Palestinian Jewish society, from the rich and the powerful to the poor and the helpless.

Approaching the dais, he found three of his colleagues talking before it. Two of them he had expected, Simeon ben Azzai and Simeon ben Zoma, who were to be his associates. But he was surprised to see Akiba among them. They turned as he came nearer, and smiled warmly.

"Peace, Elisha," Akiba began. "I have no business here. As you know, I am lecturing in the academy today. But I could not resist the temptation of being present to observe the opening moments, at least, of your career as a sage. I shall probably be late for my class, but it is worth it."

He patted the younger man's arm and Elisha immediately covered the hand with his own.

Ben Azzai, who was to serve as presiding elder, and ben Zoma, who completed the roster, were equally cordial.

They chatted for a few minutes, the older men reassuring Elisha by amused recollections of their own nervousness over their first assignments.

Meantime, the secretary of the court arranged his records on a table before the platform. The marshal, wand in hand, took his station behind the judges' chairs. With a concluding word of benediction Akiba left. A hush came over the room as the three men mounted the platform. The spectators rose for prayer.

"Our God and God of our fathers," ben Azzai intoned in his hollow voice, "we stand before Thee, prepared to judge Thy people Israel in accordance with the Law which Thou didst give to us through Thy servant Moses. Do Thou give us wisdom so that we may obey Thy precepts even as it is written, 'Righteousness and righteousness alone shalt thou pursue.' Strengthen us that we may fulfill Thy commandment: 'Thou shalt not respect the person of the poor nor regard that of the mighty, but in righteousness shalt thou judge.' Let us regard ourselves as though Thy sword were always over our heads, waiting to descend should we pervert justice. Then shall we administer Thy Law in fear and in trembling until a redeemer come unto Zion and to those of Jacob returning from transgression. Amen."

They seated themselves. The marshal tapped with his staff; the business of the court began. All through this day and the two that followed, it moved before them without cessation. There was little in it that was novel to Elisha or unprecedented. In the main it consisted of routine cases. A bondsman sued his master, exhibiting an eye which had been blinded in a beating and asking for release from his covenanted years of service. Husbands and wives haggled over dower rights, bills of divorcement, all the many details of domestic life. Debtors sought release from their obligations on the grounds that their indebtedness was tainted with usury forbidden by Moses. A group of porters were sued for damages in an action based upon their negligence toward merchandise entrusted to them. The laws of personal and property rights, leases, rentals, debts and pledges were applied in turn.

On the third day of Elisha's stay in Usha the court of which he was a member adjourned its sittings. Together with his colleagues he moved to the academy. Again he was apprehensive, this time at the prospect of addressing advanced disciples and maintaining his thesis against their criticism. Yet he delivered his inaugural lecture fluently and well. Once that was over, he was entirely at ease. By the morning of the second day, his audience had grown in size and come to include some of the most promising students. It was with deep satisfaction that he began his final discourse on the afternoon before the Sabbath. His theme, the Law of Bailments, was not an easy one. He enjoyed the challenge implicit in it and the burst of spontaneous applause which marked the end of his address. Flushed with pleasure, he stepped down from the dais. Young men crowded round to congratulate him.

"Master, thou hast expounded well."

"May thy strength increase."

CHAPTER XI

THE SUN HUNG LOW OVER the hills when Meir and Elisha joined the crowd of masters and disciples who hurried from the lecture halls. Laborers bustled about the narrow streets hoping to complete their weekday tasks before dusk. Shopkeepers busily cleared their counters of wares or hung shutters before their booths. Children, enjoying a half-holiday, ran about shouting to one another excitedly. From open windows the fragrance of Sabbath delicacies scented the air with a homely, sweet savor. Buffeted on all sides, Elisha and Meir made their way to the bathhouse. Men stood in line before the door awaiting their turn. They parted respectfully to allow the master to enter at once. Some time later the two men emerged, cleansed and refreshed, into the cool air of late afternoon. The Sabbath lamps were being kindled in the houses they passed. They shone forth one after the other as stars light up at nightfall. Within a few minutes the entire town was aglow. Usha was quiet and serene, as befitted a Jewish community over which the Sabbath angels hovered.

As they walked on Elisha felt curiosity stirring within him at the thought of meeting Meir's wife for the first time. The sages never talked about women, except in the abstract. They might in their preaching and lawmaking discuss the morality of the home, the jurisprudence of marriage, divorce and dower. But gossip and frivolous talk concerning any specific woman were unbecoming the piety and dignity of a scholar. It was taken for granted that every daughter of Israel was chaste and God-fearing, as it was assumed that her husband was kind to her and faithful. When that had been said, there was no room left for idle comment.

To this rule of reticence Meir's wife was an exception. She was the daughter of the distinguished Rabbi Hanina ben Teradion. From her father she had learned to quote Scripture and the Tradition as readily as the most advanced student. It was reported of her, too, that her humor was fresh and sometimes delightfully irreverent. Some of the primmer elders did not altogether approve of her. A learned woman, especially a beautiful one, was to them a contradiction in terms, a phenomenon vaguely suggestive of impropriety. But the younger men, masters and disciples alike, were universally frank in their admiration.

They passed through the courtyard of a large building perched on a hillside, climbed the flight of stone steps which led into various apartments and entered a tiny chamber, furnished with several chairs, a table on which lamps burned, a chest for books and a couch. Elisha's saddlebags, transferred from the tavern by Uriel, stood in a corner. Two doors led to the chambers beyond.

"Beruriah!" Meir sang out.

A curtain parted and Meir's wife stood before them. For all his expectations, Elisha was unprepared for so lovely a young woman, slight, dark-haired and vibrant.

Meir stepped to her, slipped one arm about her and presented her to Elisha. "This, Master, is my wife."

Beruriah bowed. "Welcome, Master Elisha, to our home, and my congratulations on your ordination."

"Thank you on both scores," Elisha replied. "And may I add that I have finally discovered the meaning of the verse, 'The beauty of Japheth in the tents of Shem.'"

"You disappoint me, Master," she teased, her eyes flashing up at him. "From your fame I had been led to expect better. It is Meir here with his blond hair who is a descendant of Japheth."

"Then let me correct the quotation. Let it read, 'The beauty of Shem in the tent of Japheth.' You see, on the presence of the beautiful I insist."

Beruriah flushed slightly.

"One quality at least masters and disciples have in common, the flatterer's art against which they preach so steadfastly. But please be seated. And will you excuse me—I left the children only half-dressed. I shall be with you in a moment. Make yourself comfortable," she added at the doorway, "and if you can think up any more compliments, please do. Frankly, I love them."

She reappeared a few minutes later, her two boys entering the room before her. At the sight of Meir, they swooped forward. He stooped and gathered them in his arms. An excited babble arose. Beruriah watched for a moment, smiling. Then gently disentangling the children from their father, she took them by the hand and led them before Elisha.

"These," she explained, "are our twins, Saul and Samuel. And they get along with each other about as well as their namesakes. And this," she said to the boys, "is a friend of your father. His name is Rabbi Elisha. Now say that he is welcome."

Shyly the children lisped the word "Peace."

"I hate to do this to you, Master," Beruriah excused herself. "But you will have to entertain the twins while Meir and I set out our supper. I hope you find your learning helpful."

With that she turned to the table.

What did one say to little children, Elisha asked himself. Desperately he attempted to make conversation. In response to his questions they told him which was Saul and which Samuel, that they were both almost four years old, that Samuel was an hour the older of the two, that they did not yet attend school though they would begin the next year.

"But we are learning to read already," one of them volunteered.

"Yes, Mother is teaching us," the other added.

Then he was altogether at a loss. Noticing the silence, Beruriah paused midway from the kitchen, a dish in her hand.

"What, Master, are your resources already at an end? Come, come, you will have to do better than that or I shall have them under my feet and we will never get to dine."

He looked at her hopelessly, pleading for help. She smiled and continued setting the table.

"Do you know any games?" said one.

"Or any stories?" the second suggested.

Stung by her amusement, Elisha extended himself. He showed the boys tricks with his fingers which he had played as a child. In the end, the youngsters were on his lap listening intently to a story which he improvised as he went along. The pressure of their little bodies warmed him. As he looked down into their eager faces, he felt in himself a sadness such as he had never experienced before. Unconsciously his arms tightened about them. And when Beruriah stood over him, smiling appreciatively, to announce that dinner was ready, he released them reluctantly. For a moment after he had put them down, he was overcome by a sharp emptiness.

But it was gone once they were at the table. First the children stood alongside their father who, with his hands on their heads, blessed them. Next, at Meir's request, Elisha arose, took up a wine cup and chanted the benediction that sanctified the Sabbath day. In the midst of it he looked down to discover that Meir and Beruriah were smiling happily across the table at each other. He sang the rest of the ancient melody with fervor and sweetness that evoked exclamations of pleasure when he was through. They bathed their hands, blessed the loaf of bread, broke it and settled back to eat.

The food before them was simple but satisfying. Elisha found himself eager to hear Beruriah talk. But she was busy with serving and helping the children. Only after the dessert, a bowl of fruit, had been put before them did she give him some sustained attention.

"Have you had a pleasant week?" she asked. Stimulated by her interest, Elisha described his reactions with a frankness and humor of which he had never dreamed himself capable.

"The poor dears," she interrupted, noticing that the children's eyes were heavy with sleep, "it is very late for them. I am sorry," she apologized to Elisha; "I did not mean to interrupt you. But we had better say grace so that I can put them to bed.

Then we can have the rest of the account."

The last hymn sung, the children rose, kissed their father and, after some coaxing on Elisha's part, him as well. Beruriah led them from the room. In her absence the two men felt no impulse to continue the conversation. They sat and listened to the voices in the next chamber and the murmur of bedtime prayers. But when she had returned first to clear the dishes and finally to take her place with them again, Elisha picked up the thread of his tale. Under her encouragement he talked easily and well. His elbows were propped on the table, his hands clasped. His blue eyes sparkled.

"But you are not listening to me," he protested on one occasion as he saw Beruriah purse her lips soundlessly into a kiss in Meir's direction to which Meir responded in kind. Both of them were embarrassed.

"But we are," Beruriah reassured him. "You must not mind us. It is a silly habit. It does not even mean affection. Meir and I resort to it generally to disconcert each other. When Meir is preaching or lecturing and I am in the audience, I wait till I catch his eye and then this is what he gets. I love to watch him stumble over words and look about for fear someone has observed."

"That woman has a demon in her," Meir complained.

"Don't you like it?" she challenged. "Or would you rather have me solemn and grave?"

"As though I had any choice."

"Answer my question."

"No, I would not."

"Such a falsehood." she threw her hands up in horror. Her laughter tinkled through the room. She rose, stepped behind Meir, bent down and kissed him lightly on the top of his head.

"One would think," she said to Elisha over Meir's shoulder, "that after a time he would learn how to handle my teasing. I am afraid your pupil may be learned but he will never be adroit."

She ran her hand through the blond hair and returned to her seat.

And Elisha watched with delight.

"We return to you, Master," she prodded. "For Meir that is a safer subject, and welcome, too. You have no idea how devoted he has become to you. But as a woman, I am interested in your wife. I should very much like to meet her. To be honest with you, I have made inquiries about her. But no one seems to know her. She must be a secret treasure that you keep jealously to yourself."

"She is rather reserved," he explained awkwardly, "and doesn't like to travel."

Beruriah noticed the change in his manner. She began to talk of other things, trivial, amusing incidents. He listened with but half his attention until at last she broke deliberately into his brooding.

"Master, melancholy is forbidden on the Sabbath."

He forced a smile to his lips and gave her his interest. In a few minutes he was chuckling over tidbits of gossip or shrewd, penetrating observations of character. He found himself staring at her, watching each expression of her face, each gesture. Once she looked up and their eyes met. She diverted her glance but a slight flush came into her cheeks. Thereafter she was even more animated in manner.

It was late in the night when Meir and Beruriah retired to their own room, leaving Elisha exhilarated and much too awake for sleep. He rummaged in his bag for something to read and took out an anthology of love poems which Pappas had sent him recently. Love after all had been the motif of the evening.

Aglow with his discovery of such delightful people, Elisha persuaded his wife to accompany him when official business next took him to Usha. But the meeting proved an unhappy experience for everyone. Suffering by contrast with the wit, vivacity and colorfulness of her hostess, Deborah accented her normal hauteur. Her aloofness chilled even the irrepressible Beruriah. As a result, they were all so self-conscious and constrained that

Elisha found himself waiting impatiently for the hour when it would be proper to leave. Once thereafter he dutifully suggested a second visit but Deborah begged off, pleading that the journey was fatiguing, that she saw in Meir and Beruriah none of the extraordinary qualities which she had been led to expect. Relieved, he neither coaxed her then nor invited her again. And though he visited Usha with increasing frequency, it was always alone.

But if Deborah never accompanied him, she did not fail to observe that to her husband Meir's apartment was becoming virtually a second home.

"I must say," she protested on one occasion, after Elisha had traveled to Usha recurrently and at close intervals, "it cannot be judicial assignments that take you to that place so often. And if it is those friends of yours, I cannot see what you find so attractive in them."

"What indeed?" he echoed silently, evoking in response a multitude of disjointed pictures. Impressions and recollections of the bare, neat little apartment flashed through his mind: Meir's face at once alert in concentration over some discussion and soft with the devotion of a disciple for an adored master; the bittersweet feeling of the children's hands searching his robe for hidden gifts; the high, animated talk; the delightful unpredictability of Beruriah, now incapable seemingly of seriousness or of reverence for any sanctity whatsoever, now revealing in some chance remark depths below depths of still, sensitive thoughtfulness; and her profound if unostentatious piety, concerned with beliefs and aspirations, which was so much more congenial to him than Deborah's scruples over details of observance. But it was none of these, nor yet the sum of them, that drew Elisha to the young people. It was rather the spirit that breathed through the whole, the binding circle of a mutual love which had been opened to include him, the unity of purpose between husband and wife in which he had been permitted to share, and, most of all, the filling, even if only partially and vicariously, of the voids left in him by his own marriage.

He smiled ruefully and, thinking that Deborah's question had been more challenging than she had intended, made some belated, inconsequential reply.

CHAPTER XII

THE INCIDENT AT TIBERIAS BEGAN innocuously enough with Elisha's receipt of a communication from Gamliel.

Rabbi Tarfon, the messenger informed him, was ill and could not fulfill his engagement to attend the forthcoming district assizes. Since the court was to be under lay auspices, the bench consisting of two unordained scholars and one presiding rabbi, the presence of some sage was imperative. Would Rabbi Elisha be so kind as to give his services in his colleague's place?

Without the least hesitation Elisha accepted the call. The year since his ordination had been an unbroken round of assignments, judicial and academic. This special request was so much of a piece with a familiar routine that it never occurred to him to inquire the identity of the lay judges nor the nature of the business with which they were to deal.

Only when he rode into Tiberias the next morning did Elisha receive the first intimation that inadvertently he had involved himself in a tangled situation. The streets seethed with people, Roman soldiers patrolled the marketplace and a restless assembly stood before the courthouse.

As he entered the building, Elisha came upon one of his disciples loitering in the doorway.

"Why all the excitement?" he asked curiously.

"Master," the young man replied, amazed, "haven't you heard? Two days ago the laborers of Benjamin, the linen-weaver, asked for higher wages and, when he refused, quit their work. Now he wants the court to compel them to return. What's more, he is suing them for damages. It seems that they left flax in the vats. He is inside waiting for the judges. And he has been swearing great oaths that if he cannot get justice here, he will go to the Roman courts for it."

"But why are the soldiers on the streets?"

"That's his work too. He claims that he has been threatened

with violence, that his workshop may be attacked. A lie, Master, I'm sure. You know those men. Do you believe…"

"Hush," Elisha shut him off. "The case is still to be tried."

At the dais Elisha found one of his colleagues, Jonah the merchant, a venerable old man greatly respected by the townspeople for his piety and learning. They were exchanging greetings when he sensed that a third person had joined them. Turning about, he discovered Shraga the Levite. Both men were taken aback. For a moment they stared at each other.

"I thought when I accepted the assignment," Shraga began tentatively, "that Rabbi Tarfon was to preside…."

As he spoke, he drew from his wallet a parchment sheet splotched with a great official seal.

But Elisha, who had recovered his composure, waved the credential aside.

"Welcome," he said politely.

After an awkward interval in which no one said anything, the three men took their places.

The preliminary rituals were performed, the first unimportant cases on the docket heard and decided with every appearance of deliberateness. But the judges like the spectators were eager for the airing of the dispute that had disturbed the entire community. And if there was no untoward haste, the court proceeded with dispatch. Meantime, Elisha and Shraga addressed each other only when necessary and then with meticulous courtesy. Of the latent tension between them neither gave overt sign.

It was shortly before noon that the marshal announced the case of Benjamin the linen-weaver against his laborers. A stir of suppressed excitement passed through the spectators. The plaintiff, a portly, ruddy-faced man, came forward, exuding an air of prosperity and self-importance. The half-dozen defendants, shabbily dressed, pale from their habitual confinement indoors but determined in manner, collected themselves at the other end of the dais.

Without waiting for an invitation, Benjamin stated his

complaint, relating with blustering impatience the story which Elisha had already heard.

"But we had to quit, Masters," one of the defendants said resolutely when the weaver was done. "You know what corn prices have been of late. That man must work to live was God's ordinance to Adam. But where is it enjoined that one must labor to go hungry?"

"Am I responsible for the fact that the grain crop failed last year?" Benjamin retorted angrily. "Is it my fault that bread has become so expensive? Or do I control the linen market? The pagan weavers use slave labor. If I am to pay the wages these fools demand, I shall have no work for them at all. And then they will starve altogether."

The laborers looked at him contemptuously.

"That's not so, Masters," one of them denied. "He makes a great profit. He could well afford—"

"That," Elisha interrupted, "is totally irrelevant. What is more, if you were determined to quit work, why did you wait until your stoppage was certain to ruin an expensive consignment of flax?"

"But, Master," the workers protested in chorus, "that was our only course."

"Whenever we broached the question he refused to talk to us."

"We thought we could compel him to deal with us."

"Is my workshop an academy," Benjamin roared, "that I should engage in conferences? I hire men to work. If they do not like the wages I pay, let them go elsewhere."

"Exactly," one of the laborers crowed. "Then why have you hailed us to court?"

A tumult broke out at the dais and spread through the courtroom. Only after administering a sharp reproof to litigants and spectators alike did Elisha restore order.

By then it was well past noon and, since the case for both sides had been set forth, Elisha declared a recess.

Over a simple luncheon, served by the marshal in a chamber back of the courtroom, the judges considered the case.

On one point they agreed instantly: Benjamin's weavers had acted within their rights. "Unto Me are the children of Israel servants," Scripture said. From this statement, the Tradition had drawn the deductions: "No Israelite may be coerced into working for another" and, as a further inference, "The laborer shall be free to quit even at high noon."

With authoritative, unequivocal principles to guide them, the three men voted unanimously and unhesitatingly to deny Benjamin's petition that his men be ordered back to his factory. But when they had finished polling one another on the second issue, whether the weaver was entitled to compensation, Elisha smiled quizzically. For he, the patrician employer, had balloted for the laborers, as had Jonah, the prosperous merchant, while Shraga, the penniless plebeian, notoriously resentful of men of wealth, had sided with Benjamin.

"The influence of your teachers on you, gentlemen," Jonah chuckled, alluding to Joshua's liberalism and Eliezer's conservatism.

Perplexed by the paradoxical turn of events, Elisha turned to Shraga for an explanation.

"Perhaps," he suggested affably, "you will interpret your position. Here we are all agreed that the right of a laborer to quit work is unrestricted. Now every stoppage involves some injury to the employer. If then, employees can be held liable for restitution, their liberty of action is limited in effect. In fact, under certain circumstances it is annulled altogether."

For a long time Shraga did not reply. He sat arranging the earthenware dishes on the table into a symmetrical design. But his hands were unsteady and his lowered face very pale.

"And the public welfare?" he muttered at last, without raising his head.

"Public welfare?" Elisha echoed wonderingly. "What Jonah and I are doing is in the best interests of our people. Is it not the central motif of all our law—yes, and its unique virtue in contrast with that of the heathen—that we put the rights of persons above that of property."

"Words, high-sounding, empty words," Shraga rasped, shoving the dishes into disarray with an impatient gesture. "Do you know that a war is coming—a war with Rome . . . ?"

The old obsession, Elisha thought wearily. Aloud he said, "I know nothing of the kind. But even if you are right, what conceivable relevance can that have to this case?"

Shraga looked up and fixed his eyes on Elisha. The scar on his face was livid.

"I am no rabbi," he said in a soft trembling voice. "I am not regarded as worthy to be a rabbi. And I hold no brief for rich Jewish employers. But we shall need their wealth when the next clash with Rome comes. They are having enough difficulty competing with Gentiles and their slaves. If our law penalizes them further and gives our laborers too much latitude, do you know what will happen? We will force them out of business, impoverish them and through them our whole country. I tell you," he rose slowly, his voice mounting meantime, "this land is being bled white. It is our duty to husband our resources, or we shall have none to conserve. And then where shall we derive our power? To perdition then with sophistries over human and property rights, and with logical deductions. Only one policy is right, that which trains our hands for battle and strengthens our sinews for war.

"What is more, we have no right to force upon Jews defiance of our authority, to foment breaches in our national unity. Do you imagine that Benjamin will abide by our decision? Have you not heard what he has been saying? He will walk out of this building straight into the basilica where pagan judges can be relied on to be sensible."

"He will not dare," Elisha countered confidently. "And if he should, since when are questions of Jewish law determined by threats?"

"Go ahead," Shraga threw at him furiously. "Hasten the debilitation that is spreading through our land like a creeping paralysis. Undermine our discipline by driving Jews into the Roman courts. What can one expect from the son of—"

"Silence," Jonah thundered, his open hand slapping the table resoundingly.

Shraga stopped short. For a moment he was discomfited by the old man's angry face and Elisha's cold stare. Then he shrugged to demonstrate his unconcern. Elisha breathed deeply once, while he regained his self-control, then spoke with a steady voice.

"No purpose will be served by further discussion. I had hoped to obtain a unanimous verdict as would be desirable. But failing it we shall perforce be content with a decision by majority vote. Shall the laborers be ordered to return to work?"

Three nays sounded together.

"Shall they be held liable for the damages?"

Two nays and one aye, that of Shraga, were spoken simultaneously.

The persons standing in the aisles or before the benches scurried to their seats as soon as the judges appeared in the courtroom. The plaintiff and the defendants resumed their places at the dais. The hall was altogether quiet even before the marshal tapped the floor with his wand and proclaimed, "The suit of Benjamin the weaver against his laborers."

"The court rejects," Elisha announced through the tense silence, "the petition of Benjamin that his employees be ordered to return to work.

"The court holds further that the laborers are free of responsibility for any damages..."

Whatever his last words were, they were lost in the uproar that rose in the room. Men climbed onto benches and called excitedly to one another and to the defendants who were embracing one another enthusiastically.

Benjamin the weaver had paled with anger on hearing the

verdict. He stood struggling to control himself.

"No," he bellowed above the din, "I will not comply."

A gasp of incredulity swept the chamber. The clamor of voices died away.

"I beg your pardon?" Elisha inquired softly.

"I said," Benjamin shouted defiantly, "that I refuse to accept the verdict."

"I still do not understand," Elisha persisted, a forbidding frown knitting his brow. "Exactly what do you propose to do?"

Men held their breath for fear of missing the least word.

Benjamin's lips opened for speech. But he looked into the narrowed blue eyes of Rabbi Elisha and his courage failed him. His mouth closed slowly. A flush mounted his cheeks, deepening in hue until his face was aflame with embarrassment.

"I shall appeal to the Sanhedrin," he mumbled lamely.

"That," Elisha commented coldly, "is your privilege."

Then, as Benjamin and his opponents joined the spectators streaming toward the door, Shraga's voice, thin and tense with passion, sounded in Elisha's ears.

"You have despised my counsel. I shall remember that fact. You have handed down a dangerous verdict, one that may do harm to our people. I shall hold you responsible for it."

The arrogance of the remark was so egregious that Elisha was first stunned, then amused. Deliberately he smiled into the blazing eyes before him, and turned away.

Thanks to Benjamin, who complained bitterly of the trial to every merchant he met, and to Shraga, who hastened to spread a report of it among his acquaintances, the proceedings at Tiberias became a matter of comment and debate throughout the land.

When then, as good as his word, the weaver appeared at the next session of the Sanhedrin to ask for a reversal of judgment, the sages, with few exceptions, were thoroughly familiar with the issues involved. They listened to the plaintiff and to the defendants, interrogated the three judges, and after a brief discussion, voted by a substantial majority to sustain Elisha's verdict.

To Elisha, the action of his colleagues was a source of relief. His judgment was vindicated and he was rid at last of a distasteful controversy. But he was not yet done with the quarrel between the weaver and his employees. For Benjamin, although he uttered no protest to the Sanhedrin at the time of its verdict, proceeded promptly to appeal from Jewish justice to Roman. He entered his suit in the civil court at Tiberias and out of malice named the scholars who had presided over the first hearing of the case as material witnesses. In consequence, Elisha had scarcely returned from Jamnia to his own home when he was summoned to appear in the basilica at Tiberias.

Once again, Elisha met with Shraga and Jonah at the airing of a dispute of which they were by now thoroughly weary. But this time they sat abjectly among the spectators, waiting to be heard. In accordance with Roman legal practice, both the plaintiff and the defendants were represented by professional counsel. And when at long last the Jewish judges were called to testify, Benjamin, hiding behind his Gentile attorney, exacted a safe, subtle revenge through the humiliating examination to which they were subjected.

After three days of proceedings the ordeal came to its end. The Roman judge, a wizened, nearsighted man, read his findings in a thin dry voice from a papyrus roll. It was a learned document, replete with references. It alluded to a stoppage by free workers in Egypt under Ptolemy Euergetes II, to a strike in a factory at Pergamum during the reign of Attalus Philadelphus, to a rebellion of slaves at the Athenian mines at Laurium, and to other precedents in Greek, Hellenistic and Roman law. But through the confusion of citations the purport of the decision was clear after its first words. The entire verdict of the Jewish courts was being reversed. Approaching the end of the document the judge paused, looked up from the scroll and peered at the spectators. His manner suggested clearly that he was about to make a statement of grave import. The silence in the room was suddenly tense with expectation.

"The plaintiff," he resumed, "has appealed to this court for protection against an edict of excommunication with which he is threatened by the authorities of his people. To penalize recourse to the justice of the Empire is to deny a free man his rights. Wherefore, I enjoin the rabbis and the Sanhedrin against attempting to punish Benjamin of Tiberias by any ban or restriction whatsoever."

Instantly Elisha was on his feet protesting furiously against the decision as an infringement of Jewish autonomy. But the judge was adamant.

"The case is closed," he snapped decisively and, refusing to listen further, withdrew from the chamber.

Stunned by shock and dismay, Elisha was scarcely aware of the angry talk which shook the chamber. But he did hear with painful clarity two gibes hurled at him.

"I congratulate you, Rabbi," Shraga cried wildly in his ears. "You have made a great contribution to the welfare of our people."

"Master," Benjamin chimed in sneeringly, "may I give you your own advice. You may appeal for a reversal—to Caesarea."

But as they turned to leave, the smirk of satisfaction faded quickly from the weaver's face. For, confronting him with clenched fists, stood his fellow Jews, glaring with a hatred so palpable that in panic Benjamin looked about for aid. The sight of the Roman soldiers stationed in the hall reassured him somewhat. Yet he was pale and trembling as he made his way through the crowd that parted sullenly before him.

That night a group of stalwart young Jews slipped through the cordon of guards stationed to protect Benjamin's home. What they told the weaver in the privacy of his own bedchamber the townspeople of Tiberias never learned. But when, the next day, his employees failed to appear at his workshop he made no complaint to the Roman authorities. Nor did he ever attempt to collect the damages which had been awarded him.

In subsequent months he was given additional occasion to rue his wiliness and insubordination. For though he had succeeded in heading off an edict of excommunication, he was benefited but little. Spontaneously, the Jews of Tiberias, indeed of all Palestine, leagued themselves against him as in obedience to a formal ban. No one conversed or traded with him. Eventually, his business ruined, his will broken by universal hostility, he traveled to Jamnia to apologize to the Sanhedrin for his disobedience. On the eve of the next Day of Atonement, he did public penance in the great synagogue of Tiberias. Only then was his ostracism mitigated. Thus, quietly, unobtrusively but effectively the verdict of the Roman court was nullified.

Yet, it had its damaging consequences. For the Sanhedrin could not accept passively even in principle any restraint on its right to impose penalties. It appealed first to Caesarea, then to the proconsul at Antioch. In the first instance its request was evaded, in the second denied. Finally, a legation sailed for Rome. When it, too, returned empty-handed, a wave of exasperation swept Palestine. Many who had hitherto remained aloof from the illegal army now joined it as recruits. Everywhere throughout the land people talked with increased gravity of the inevitability of conflict with Rome.

Nor was Elisha left altogether unscathed by the general indignation. Among sober responsible persons, it was understood that he had acted in the light of reason and conscience. But the popular mind tended to regard him as responsible in some vague fashion for the trial and all its unfortunate consequences. Blinded by animosity and fanaticism, Shraga in particular made much of the incident, charging that like his father the young rabbi had been motivated by sympathy for the heathen world and gross disloyalty to the interests of his own nation. Few people took Shraga's grotesque accusation seriously. But into the members of his group with whom his influence was considerable, he succeeded for the first time in inculcating something of his resentment of Elisha.

CHAPTER XIII

THE LAST ECHOES OF THE unresolved conflict in authority between the Sanhedrin and the Roman Government were just fading into inaudibility when a new, graver danger arose to threaten the Jews of Palestine. The plague visited the land. Hearing the report of it, people paled and trembled, each for himself and his own. And when it became apparent that the dread malady was not to be confined to the seaports where it had first appeared, men turned indifferent to their habitual pursuits and ambitions. Bound together in a fellowship of fear, they spoke only of the terror that froze their blood, exchanging with morbid fascination reports of the stricken and rumors of eerie deaths or miraculous cures.

All that spring no one drew a free breath, so weighted with anxiety was each heart. Then with the coming of summer the incubus lifted slightly. For, though scarcely a town was spared, the disease was obviously not becoming epidemic. Cautiously old interests began to reassert themselves. Life slipped toward normality, without however attaining it altogether. For death still lingered. And as long as it tarried, no one could feel himself secure.

On a blazing Sabbath afternoon during this season of calamity, Elisha and Meir sat side by side in one of the synagogues of Usha. The auditorium baked like the interior of an oven. All that week the sun had glared with a fury extraordinary even for a Palestinian summer at its height. Outside now not a breath of wind stirred, not a wisp of cloud flecked the dimming sky. But the two men did not feel the heat nor were they attending to the speech of a preacher who droned interminably from the pulpit. They were thinking with unbearable apprehension of Meir's two sons who even then tossed and moaned in their little bedchamber. For the fire within them burned ever higher, parching their skin and glazing their eyes. Physicians, blood lettings and potions had proved unavailing, and Beruriah, ministering to her children with a hypnotic calm, revealed her desperation only in the pallor of her face and the tonelessness of her speech.

From a corner of the room the sobs of some bereaved woman broke forth, shrill and uncontrolled. Meir shuddered at the sound, and Elisha reached out and pressed his hand. But his gesture of confidence was only a pretense. Too vividly did he remember the deaths of a young disciple, of a burly laborer on the estate, of an old sage, of a Syrian peddler who dropped in his tracks on the highway before the villa.

"God is just and merciful," he murmured, reassuring himself as well as Meir.

The droning of the preacher came to an end. One of the elders of Usha descended the three steps to a depression before the Ark so constructed that he who prayed for the congregation might literally fulfill the words, "Out of the depths have I called upon Thee, O Lord." In a prescribed chant of great antiquity he called forth the invitation to prayer.

When the brief service was over, the congregants greeted one another hastily and exchanged wishes for a happy week. Then they dispersed, each man to his own home, his own weekday tasks and concerns, or, if so unfortunate, to the sick-bed of a kinsman. As Elisha and Meir stepped into the open street, the air, still hot with day, rose from the cobblestones to smite them with an angry hand. A white moon illumined the world with an unreal light.

Meir walked so rapidly that Elisha was barely able to keep abreast of him. He led his teacher into the courtyard of his home and climbed the steps with precipitate haste. The room, when they entered, was silent and dark save for such fragments of the universal whiteness of the moon as poured through its windows.

Beruriah rose from the shadows to greet them. "A happy week to you, my master and husband, and to you, my master and teacher." Her face was a shimmering white mask, its expression inscrutable.

"A happy week," the two men responded.

Then Meir burst forth, "How are the children?"

"Better," Beruriah replied and turned to a cupboard to fetch a lamp, a spice box and a cup of wine.

"It is still the Sabbath here," she said monotonously. "When we have discharged our duty to God we shall talk of our own affairs."

Reassured by her calm, Meir kindled the first light of the new week, pronounced a blessing over the wine cup of division between days, sacred and profane, shook the spice box so that the Sabbath angels might depart in a cloud of fragrance, and uttered the words whereby the week which was about to begin was marked apart from the Sabbath.

The echoes of Meir's last words of prayer had not yet died away when Beruriah began spinning out a parable.

"A man came to see me some years ago," she said in a voice quiet and half-hypnotic. "He left in my care for safekeeping two precious stones. Today, just before you returned, he appeared again. I am loathe to part with them. Tell me, must I give them back to him?"

"Of course," Meir responded guardedly. "They never really were your property, no matter how long you have held them. But why is it so still here? Are the children asleep? Why do you talk of such strange matters?" His voice faded to a whisper, word by word. "Why do you say nothing about the boys?"

Without waiting for answer, Meir turned toward the children's chamber, moved as if to enter and then stopped, struck with sudden comprehension. Like one in a trance, he came back until his face was close to Beruriah's. He stood staring into her eyes, waiting for the interpretation of the parable he dreaded to hear.

Beruriah raised both hands to her quivering lips. "The jewels," she said, through her fingers, "are in that room."

In the feeble light of the lone flame the face of Meir was transfixed. He pushed abruptly into the children's chamber.

For a moment there was only silence behind the swaying curtains. Then through it there cut the horrible rasp of rending cloth. Elisha covered his face. He knew that sound. It was the tearing of a garment in the presence of death.

He did not see Meir when he came out of the room. But he heard with intolerable clarity his stumbling steps and uneven breath. When he opened his eyes again Meir was sinking onto a chair before the table. "The Lord hath given," he droned, "the Lord hath taken away. Blessed be the righteous Judge." He bowed his head upon his forearms and wept.

As though the words of ultimate resignation were a command, Beruriah's hands went to her dress, her fingers tugging at it. The cloth tore under her insistent pulling. With the stiff gait of a sleepwalker, she moved silently into the room where life had been born to her and where, together with her heart, it had died.

And Elisha, to whom these children had become as his own might have been, dug his fists into his chest to keep his tortured heart from breaking.

In the shadows of Meir's home the stillness was broken only by the sobbing of a grown man. A hot wind blew through the open door and extinguished the solitary lamp. For a moment all was darkness. Then the unperturbed moon sent in its spectral light, and the room was peopled with creeping shadows.

CHAPTER XIV

FOR DAYS THEREAFTER, THROUGH THE funeral service and
the week of mourning during which he never left Meir's home,
Elisha's eyes looked out as always to the ordered world of men
and things. His speech and actions were addressed to it, but
his thoughts were turned inward on the seething chaos of his
anguish.

On his long journey to Jamnia, at the sessions of the
Sanhedrin, pain continued to flow through him like a deep
unfailing river, pain for two little boys who would never laugh
or weep again, pain for Meir and Beruriah, who behind the
drawn veils of pallid, impassive countenances, restrained
gestures and considered speech, were wrestling each with a
private horror too monstrous for him to conceive.

The last day of the convocation was one of fitful sunlight
and erratic wind. Great fleecy clouds alternately stood fixed
in the sky and raced rapidly across it. From far out to sea a
galley beat its way toward land, its sail a white patch on the
blue waters. But of all the panorama of earth and heaven,
Elisha responded to only one detail. The breeze redolent with
odors of autumn blew across his face. As he inhaled it, he was
reminded of the heavy fragrance of a spice box, and he knew
then that always the scented dusks of Sabbaths would be
associated with tragic memories. Again he relived the aching
turmoil of those unforgettable hours. Whence, he marveled
anew, came the imperturbable faith that sustained that mother
and father in their bereavement, that restrained them even in
their extremity from cursing God and dying? Aye, and where
were the justice and mercy of that God?

This last desperate question, born within Elisha at the very
moment when he had heard the rasp of rending cloth from
the children's bedchamber, had been in the beginning but a
fleeting ripple of protest over the first upsurge of his sorrow.
But with time it had interpenetrated the depths of his being,

much as a sullen sky might project its colorations into a river exposed to its baleful light. Now it obsessed his entire consciousness. Deaf to the voice of his colleagues about him, blind to their movements, he watched like some spectator held motionless in fascinated horror the advance and retreat of his belief before assaults of doubt.

"The soul that sinneth, it shall die," Ezekiel had asserted. Where was the offense of those two innocents? "Of things too wonderful for me, things which I knew not, have I spoken. Wherefore I abhor my words and recant." So Job had reconciled himself to the enigma of his fate. But had not the man of Uz yielded too easily? Had not the Almighty dealt deviously with him? Had He not tricked him into submissiveness, exploiting his ignorance of the workings of nature to obscure the relevant issue, the equity of His way? Might the answer be found in the next world? It could not be. No future bliss would render less wanton a present cruelty. There remained only the dictum of the sages: "It is not in our power to explain either the happiness of the wicked nor the sufferings of the righteous." But how could he make a truce with mystery when his soul cried out for understanding? Was there then in all the realms of the Tradition no light equal to the menacing darkness? Were its doctrines so weak against reality, so impotent to save when the challenge of evil crowded close and would not be denied? A vast, inchoate misgiving welled up in him.

"I tell you," a harsh voice dinned in his ears, "there is too little of faith among us."

On hearing the words, hurled seemingly in accusation of his secret thoughts, Elisha started violently.

Rabbi Eliezer was standing before his chair, his aged face white, his arms, outflung in a gesture of protest, trembling with passion. With relief, Elisha observed that the old sage was addressing the entire assembly. Jolted out of his introspection, he listened as Eliezer went on:

"Aye, ours is a generation puny in its trust. Wherefore, I

will not hold my peace. It does not concern me that the session has already been prolonged, that you are all eager for its adjournment so that you may return to your homes. Nor will I defer even to the Patriarch when he requests that I withdraw my resolution. His contention that the issue has been debated before and in vain does not impress me. The time has come to act on the Lord's behalf. I insist that here and now we impose an interdict upon the study of the Greek tongue and upon the cultivation of pagan wisdom.

"How long shall we be like those false prophets in Scripture who cried, 'Peace, peace,' when there was no peace? How can there be peace in Israel so long as we contaminate ourselves with the abominations of the pagans? So long, I say, as there are those in our midst, here among us, entrusted to preserve the sacred faith of our fathers, who sanction and defend this fornication of the spirit.

"What do they seek to gain, those to whom God's word is not sufficient so that they must take Greeks and Romans as their tutors? I can tell you what we will achieve, unless once and for all time we prohibit this intercourse with Greek learning. Our young men will read their books. They will become godless as the pagans are godless. They will associate with them and learn their corrupt ways, exercising in gymnasiums, sitting in circuses, lounging all night in drunken symposiums and running in pursuit of harlots. And our sacred traditions, the expression of God's will, will be abandoned. Whence came these Christian and Gnostic heresies into which so many have fallen away, if not from our failure to do fifty years ago what we still hesitate to do now? Or consider our brethren in Alexandria, their flouting of the Law, their disregard of its explicit commandments. What, pray, could one expect from them, living with and among pagans? The Holy Books were not good enough for them in the Hebrew tongue. They must have it in Greek. I say to you that the day when Scripture was done into Greek was as grievous a day for Israel as that on which our ancestors erected the Golden Calf.

"And now mark my words. We are a small people in the vastness of the pagan world. Our faith is a pinprick of light in the night of their darkness. They have stripped from us everything which gave us strength. Our commonwealth is gone. Our Temple is gone. This very land," Eliezer stamped the ground, "is being sold from under our feet. Only if we keep ourselves apart can we hope to live at all. Otherwise—the extinction of the people and its Tradition. 'Make a fence about the Law,' said the men of the Great Synagogue in generations gone by. 'Make a fence about the Law,' I repeat to you.

"Some among you may object to our withdrawal from contact with the pagan world. They may plead that it is immoral for us to keep our truth to ourselves. 'Throw open the windows,' they will argue; 'let the light go forth to the Gentiles.' A noble argument, doubtless—if only one could be certain that the great darkness would not engulf the little light.

"I say to you, this is not the time. Ours is an evil hour. A plague is abroad in the world—a plague of godlessness and immorality. Bar the doors, I tell you, bolt the windows that you and your seed may live."

While Eliezer was uttering the last words, the sun hanging low over the western horizon slipped from behind a cloud. The galley, now close to land, was silhouetted against it. Passingly it was outlined with light, rimmed in fire that danced along its sails and spars, and flickered over its oars as they rose and fell in a rhythm like deep breathing. The beat of a drum on board ship throbbed through the air.

"Masters, if you please—" Joshua's voice was gentle but strong as he rose.

"I recognize the son of Hananiah," Gamliel replied immediately.

"It was said long ago," Joshua began calmly, "by the sages who went before us, that truth is the seal of God. We have been taught and we teach others that truth must be the beginning, the middle and the end of all things, even as the first, the middle and the last letters of the alphabet spell its name—*Emeth*. We have recounted from every pulpit the ancient legend concerning the scrip which fell from Heaven on which was found inscribed the single word *Truth*.

"I do not quote to weary you with maxims. But if the essence of the Law be the service of truth, then this resolution of Eliezer's is a betrayal of that Law and a profanation of God's name. I know the shortcomings of the Greeks—better than most of you for I have had extensive associations with them. But I know that in certain realms where we have not looked they have sought the truth and found it. They have plotted the movements of the stars; they have diagrammed the earth, its seas and its lands. The very geometry which we use is theirs. Even from their artisans we can learn. Can a bridge be erected without a knowledge of some truth to hold its arch suspended in space? Can a statue be carved, even if it be in the detestable image of a heathen god, if there be not valid principles in the mind of the sculptor?

"See," Joshua pointed to the galley, "there moves a ship built by their hands. Each plank lies fitted alongside its fellow. The sail has so been ordered as to catch the lightest wind. Have not the shipbuilders of Alexandria, Piraeus and Rhodes a truth concerning the building of ships? Is not the discovery of this truth and its communication also a service of the Holy One, Blessed be He, Whose glory is made manifest in the marble, the sailcloth and the principles of geometry? Remember, my brethren, that truth is many-faceted like a well-cut gem, that their wisdoms are merely different facets from those at which we look, that in all of them alike the light of God shines.

"It is written in Scripture: 'In all thy ways know Him.' In *all* thy ways, in looking at the heavens above us, in measuring the earth beneath our feet, in considering the ship at sea. And I say to you, that to adopt this resolution is to refuse to see the fullness of God. It is to fail to know God in all our ways. In brief, it is sacrilege."

Joshua's last word hung before them, pulsating in space like some awesome tangibility.

From the very beginning Elisha had known that he would vote against the proposal. Like his master, he had never been sympathetic to the program of Jewish isolation. Yet in this instance Joshua had spoken too persuasively. For he had opened the floodgates of memory in his disciple. Recollections that had not visited him in years came now to Elisha as from another, half-forgotten life. He saw his father poring over some Greek tome in a room drenched with shadow; he heard Nicholaus intoning lines from the Iliad on a hot summer's day. Even as he brooded over the sadness of vanished things, an old issue that had never been altogether resolved revived in him. Abuyah and Nicholaus had been wise with that wisdom to which Joshua had alluded. They, too, by the sage's testimony, had revered the truth, and sought after it. And yet neither to them, nor to multitudes like them, had the doctrines of the Tradition appeared valid. To the death of Meir's children they would not have responded with an assertion of faith in divine rectitude. Elisha's misgivings returned with fearful urgency, reinforced by his awareness of the dissent of all the world except his own people.

But there was no time to think of that now. Eliezer had risen again in an outpouring of angry words.

"Masters," he was shouting, "what nonsense is being spoken here? All this talk about our truth—their truth—all facets for God's light." He snorted in scorn. "Greek truth, forsooth. Does Joshua forget that scene in the Forum at Rome which we both witnessed—a beggar shivering in cold, without a rag to cover his nakedness, while the marble statues were carefully protected with mats lest they crack in the winter's air? Does Joshua consider this a wisdom, this disregard for human beings and this concern over unfeeling stone? He has referred to yonder galley as a demonstration of those supposedly divine truths which they possess. Listen for a moment, I beg you, listen." He stopped and waited significantly. In the sudden silence all heard the ship's drum, throbbing in an inhuman rhythm.

"Do you hear that drum? Have you forgotten what it means? Beneath those scientifically fitted planks, under the sails woven with so much skill, below the feet of the captain who has found God's truth in the movement of the stars, a ship's officer beats upon it and with every blow the slaves bend to the oars. Woe betide the one who does not pull his weight, for the arm of the taskmaster is long! For all their truths, the Greeks have not learned that slaves, too, are made in the image of God. Joshua pointed to the galley. I point to it, too. Here is Greek truth in one crushing example. I say to you, let us have sailors who know less about the stars, and shipbuilders who do not build so well as the Greeks. But let them know more about God and the sanctity of men. For this is the whole Law."

At once men sprang to their feet, calling for the right to speak.

"Silence," Gamliel thundered through the clamor. "Silence, I say. Who dares turn the debates of the Sanhedrin into a tavern brawl? Is this a theater or circus that all decency is forgotten?"

Voices died away. Men sank back, ashamed.

"We have debated enough," the Patriarch said decisively when order was restored. "There is no purpose to be served by prolonging our discussion. Unless I hear an objection, I shall proceed to the ballot."

He stood there threateningly and no one dared to utter a word. "The issue before us," he continued, "is this: Shall we forbid the study of Greek culture among us? Let the roll be called."

Instantly the elders turned their eyes to Elisha who, as the most recently elected among them, must vote first. Such was their practice that the younger members might make their decisions freely, uninfluenced by the example of their seniors.

"Elisha ben Abuyah," the secretary intoned.

"Nay," Elisha responded firmly.

Then from somewhere near at hand, he heard a voice mutter, "So votes the infidel's son."

Flushing, Elisha veered about to discover the source of the comment. But he failed to spot the person though he was certain instantly that it was one of Shraga's intimates. By the time he had returned his attention to the progress of the voting, it was already apparent that Eliezer's proposal was destined to rejection.

The journey homeward from Jamnia lead Elisha along a road that mounted steadily into the hills of Samaria. Everywhere the countryside bore testimony to the fury with which Jews, Samaritans and Romans had fought out the great rebellion forty years before. Of the forests and groves which had once clothed the mountains all that remained was blackened stumps. Terraces still climbed the slopes, but so broken that the soil had long been washed from behind them. In the valleys the ruins of flour mills stood desolately alongside dried-up watercourses. Here and there, deserted villages, half-hidden by weeds, melted slowly away into the tawny ground.

It was just past noon when he reached a decaying village a bit beyond Antipatris. The town was little more than a straggling collection of houses built of sun-dried brick. Its forum was unpaved. Its only public buildings were two dilapidated temples dedicated to obscure local gods. Its inhabitants, pagans and Samaritans, were poverty-stricken and disease-infested. Normally the traveler saw of them at most a face appearing for a moment in a doorway, some beggar stirring sleepily on the temple steps or a group of ragged children who trailed after the stranger pleading for alms.

But on this day the forum was crowded with townspeople

and peasants. A troupe of actors had put up their booths and crude stage in the square, and the whole countryside had come out for the spectacle. At the moment of Elisha's arrival a shabby little fellow with cunning beady eyes stood on the platform beside a large vat filled with water. His flowing robe, adorned with crudely sewn signs of the Zodiac, was soiled. But he spoke fluently and persuasively in a facile mixture of common Greek and Aramaic. He was telling his audience that, to him, a reader of horoscopes and Chaldean numbers, the future was as clear as the present to others. He could relate to them things about their lives which they themselves had forgotten. He could guide them to lost possessions. He had with him philters for health and potions to win love. He could predict what the years would bring. But they must not take him at his word. Most magicians, he admitted regretfully, were frauds. But he could prove his competence. He would perform a sign and wonder to convince them. Then those who chose could consult with him privately for a trivial fee.

Amused by his glibness and the gaping awe of his spectators, Elisha drew in the reins of his horse and without dismounting, watched idly.

The magician stooped quickly. When he straightened up he held a bronze bar in his hand. He struck it against the hoops of the vat. The unmistakable clash of metal on metal resounded through the forum. Then, bending forward, he asked the spectators closest to the platform to feel and lift it. It was, they agreed, bronze, not wood.

"This bar," he challenged, "can it float?"

No one answered. "Well, I shall make it float, here, before your eyes in the water in this vat."

"Is it water?" an incredulous voice called out from the crowd.

"It looks like water, does it not?"

"Aye, but we cannot see it very well."

"Then come closer."

A burly countryman jostled his way forward.

"Closer than that," the magician urged.

Standing on tiptoe the peasant put his face on a level with the rim of the vat. Unexpectedly the performer dropped the bronze object into the water. The peasant was drenched by the spray. Shamefaced, he slunk away while the crowd hooted and roared with laughter.

"Metal in water," the magician cried over the uproar, "and I shall make it float."

But some of the townspeople were not satisfied. Despite the splash, they insisted on looking into the vat to see whether the object was really there. Shrewdly the magician objected and the altercation across the front of the stage grew heated. Then, when the moment was ripe, and with a pretense of reluctance, he yielded. The local skeptics mounted the platform, saw the bar resting on the bottom of the vat and climbed down abashed.

Through the deep quiet the performer intoned a charm, his hands alternately dipping into the water and hovering over it. A gasp broke from the peasants when glistening metal appeared on the surface.

Applause swept the forum. A few voices called, "Fraud," "Deceit." But they were drowned in the tumult of cries, "A miracle, a miracle."

"Aye," the performer shouted exultantly, "a miracle— absolutely contrary to the laws of nature."

Elisha smiled condescendingly, dug his heels into his horse's flank and started onward. For cleverly as the trick had been executed, he had been able to see from his mount what had been invisible to anyone else, the momentary gleam of a thin thread reaching from the vat to the magician's hand.

As he continued homeward, the whole incident struck him as strangely reminiscent of a tale told in Scripture about his namesake, the prophet:

"As one was felling a beam, the axhead fell into the water.

"And the man of God said, 'Where fell it?' And he showed him that place. And he cut down a stick and cast it in, and the iron did swim..."

Centuries ago, had it also been a fraud? Had other peasants in their credulity taken it for a miracle?

The boast of the magician still ringing in his ears, Elisha remembered the words of his father, "The Stoics are right when they insist that nothing ever happens contrary to the laws of nature."

But if that were so, what became of all the miracles of Scripture—the burning of a bush that was not consumed, a sea dividing to allow one host to pass through and closing to engulf another, fire descending from heaven to kindle a sacrifice, the revival of a dead child with a breath of a prophet's lips—were these too deceit or naive legend?

But if miracles were rejected, where was the veracity of a Scripture that recorded them as fact? And if the authority of Scripture were shaken, then there was no firm basis for the Tradition which rested upon it.

Yet it was from Scripture and the Tradition that Elisha's world derived its system of living, its jurisprudence and ceremonial rites, its faith in the immortality of the soul and reward and punishment after death, even its belief in God. Every doctrine was so interwoven with every other that the denial of one meant the renunciation of the whole.

It was all like an avalanche. A pebble is disturbed. The soil behind it slides. A rock rolls. A bush strains at its roots and gives way, and the whole mountainside is in roaring destructive motion....

CHAPTER XV

THE EMPEROR TRAJAN SAT SLUMPED in his seat over-
looking the long auditorium of the basilica of Caesarea. His
heavily pouched eyes were half-closed. His broad flat face was
lined with fatigue and sagged with boredom. The tour of the
Eastern Provinces and his brief visit to the capital of Palestine,
an annoying incident, had left him exhausted. And he was
frightened too. The dull pain which came so frequently of late
reached now through his chest from shoulder to shoulder.

It had all been a mistake, this war with the Parthians.
What was worse, it could have been avoided. The Armenians
had offered satisfactory terms. But he had been drunk with
intoxicating visions of new triumphs. It had all seemed so
easy on the maps. How could he have foretold that the Syrian
legions would be corrupted, disorganized and undisciplined?
His generals had lied to him about their readiness for war.
After a year of strenuous efforts the Eastern Army was still
badly trained. It was so long since he had served in Syria that
he had forgotten what it was like. He thought with distaste of
the rawness of the rainy season which chilled him now, and of
long marches through the fearful heat of the Arabian desert
that awaited him the next summer.

No, the campaign would not be easy. The Parthians were
not united but they were resourceful and cunning foes. They
would not stand in pitched battle. They would withdraw into
the somber, sun-baked hills of Iran. He would follow and lay
open his lines of communication, exhausting his soldiers. And
then they would attack, suddenly in clouds of arrows and
swarms of cavalry, to disappear as quickly as they came. There
would be no conquest of Parthia, that he admitted now, despite
all the elaborate preparations. He would be fortunate to be
victorious at all. And even if he pushed the frontiers forward,
adding new provinces to the East, who could say whether they
would be tenable? And what would the Empire gain by a land

that burned by day and froze by night, a frontier that must be garrisoned so heavily that it would drain the already strained treasury? It would be little enough that he would bring back with him for so much effort, even if the gods smiled on him and he won.

Ruefully he thought of Alexander and Caesar, wondering how they did so much with smaller armies. He had had his successes, too. The victory over the Dacians had been worthy of the triumph accorded him. But that had been a conquest of greater strength, of engineers rather than of soldiers, of bridges and roads rather than strategy. There must be, he told himself, a real military genius that transcended efficiency as truly as the natural grace of some untutored dancer surpassed mere studied elegance.

It would have been pleasant to be back in the Sabine Hills again, amid fountains and quiet walks, where secretaries could annoy him only during prescribed hours. There were so many things there that demanded his attention. The new forum was still unfinished, his triumphal column not yet completed. What a stroke of genius that was—to inscribe the full record of the Dacian war on a shaft of stone so that one read the story of his achievements in an ascending spiral of sculptured pictures. There would be a triumph for him again when he returned no matter how the campaign went. The Senate would see to that. His gorge rose at the thought of the conscript fathers. He handled them with respect—it was good policy. But he knew them for what they were—a band of slimy sycophants and verminous, cheap politicians eager to vote a triumph in the hope that the Emperor might learn who first proposed it. And the worst of the lot were the few authentic aristocrats who had survived the proscriptions of his predecessors. He knew that they despised and hated him as an upstart Spaniard. Only his control of the army kept them loyal, and the recognition that he was better than another Nero or Domitian who might succeed him.

It was not good to be Emperor. When he had been simply

Marcus Lepius Trajanus, he had wanted it desperately. He had worked hard in the army for that day when old Nerva had adopted him as his successor. He had thirsted to be famous, to have his name on everyone's tongue, to be ruler of the world. Now there was no way of letting go. One relaxation of vigilance and a knife would be at his throat. He spat in disgust.

The head of the Nabatean delegation was so startled at this exhibition of vulgarity that he lost his place in the petition he was reading on behalf of the tribe. Trajan dismissed him wearily.

"Your plea," he commented, "will be referred to the proper departments.... What is next, Lucius?" he asked his secretary. "Are we almost through?"

"I am sorry, Caesar, but it will be several hours before the audiences are completed."

Trajan shifted in his seat and looked down the long hallway. In the half-light that came in through the upper line of windows, the crowd of generals, petitioners and attendants wavered before his sight. Someone else now stood before him bowing low. Distantly he heard comments about a statue erected in his honor in the city of Philadelphia Ammon. From force of habit he expressed his appreciation in a partial remission of taxes. Next an artist submitted the model of a triumphal coin. The inscription amused Trajan: "The East Having Been Pacified."

"A bit premature and overly optimistic," he grunted. "But let it be approved. Win or lose, that will be our story."

Secretaries bustled about, leading forth a group of men. One, a giant with a full graying beard, held a bulky scroll in his hand. From it he read what seemed to be a long list of complaints—about a temple, taxes and unfair land laws. On and on it went. A fly buzzed about Trajan's head. He brushed it off angrily. An attendant hurried forward with a fan.

"Who is he, Lucius?" the Emperor asked irritably.

"A member of a committee from the Jewish Court of Elders," the secretary explained.

"Well, let him talk. When he goes back to his village,

wherever it is, he will brag about how bold he was before the Emperor. But I do wish he were through."

"Please, Caesar, this whole area is very restless. It is better that you listen. It will save you trouble. You do not have to do anything about any of these petitions. Just tell them that you will take them under advisement."

Trajan settled into his seat. In his boredom, his glance wandered across the faces of the members of the Jewish legation. One of them looked vaguely familiar and set him groping at recollection.

"By Hercules, that ugly fellow over there. I remember him from somewhere. I say there, come nearer."

Gamliel continued reading.

"Hush, you," he silenced the Patriarch.

"Now tell me," he said to the sage whom he beckoned forward: "What is your name?"

"Rabbi Joshua."

"Now I know," Trajan cried, remembering. "You are the Jew who gave that quick answer about how it came to pass that so much good sense could be deposited in so ugly a person. All Rome laughed over it for a week. Come a little nearer."

As Joshua approached self-consciously, Lucius whispered in the Emperor's ear.

"Blast dignity!" Trajan interrupted impatiently. "This is the first amusing face I have seen since that clown in Antioch. Come on, tell me, what do you men want?"

There were vast possibilities in the Emperor's mood and Joshua's eyes narrowed.

"O Caesar," he said, "our national shrine was destroyed, as you know, by the Emperor Titus. We want your permission to have it rebuilt." He made no reference to taxes and land laws.

"Is that all you want—a building?"

"That is all."

"Then you shall have it. It is so ordered."

Lucius bent forward, whispering nervously into the

Emperor's ear. "If it please you, Trajan, the request is much more complicated than appears. These Jews have been a rebellious people. To allow them to have their Temple again would encourage disturbances in Palestine. Please, do not make quick, rash promises which are inadvisable."

Trajan hesitated, visibly perplexed.

"Imperial Caesar," the alert Joshua broke in hastily, "there is no better way of guaranteeing the obedience of the Jewish nation than by allowing them to rebuild their shrine. If we have that, we who are your faithful servants at all times will serve you even more devotedly."

"You are right," Trajan agreed. "We must have order here, behind our backs, while we are in Parthia. What's more, there are tens of thousands of Jews in Babylonia. I'd rather have them friendly than hostile." He turned to Lucius, and commanded, "Have a secretary draw up the edict. I shall sign it immediately. And hasten it on to Rome with my request that the Senate confirm it."

"But, sire," Lucius protested, "it is contrary to the policy of years."

Trajan flushed with anger. "I will hear no more from you," he shouted in the voice of a.drillmaster. "There are countless temples in the Roman Empire. There surely is room for one more. This man—whatever his name is—shall have what he asks, do you understand? And as for the peace of the Roman Empire, I will attend to that."

The secretary bowed and stepped back in humiliation. The rabbis, incredulous with joy, pressed up to thank the Emperor. But the excitement had brought back the pain in Trajan's chest and he was suddenly impatient.

"That is all," he waved them away. "You have what you want."

In their exultation the sages could not let the matter rest at that point. They felt they must give more fitting expression to their gratitude and Gamliel began to speak again.

But Trajan was now irritable.

"You are dismissed, I say," he snapped. "And if you want that Temple you had better leave before I change my mind. Now go home," he concluded more affably.

Chastened, the elders bowed and withdrew, keeping their dignity until they were in the open. Then they turned and threw their arms about one another's neck.

"It has come," they cried; "it has come! Blessed be God who is good and doeth beneficently. He has answered our prayers."

Outwardly Elisha, too, was elated. Yet he had been shocked to see his older colleagues treated with good-natured contempt. It was humiliating to realize how lightly the Romans regarded them, to watch Gamliel and the others accept a discourteous dismissal so humbly. They had obtained what they asked for entirely as a matter of chance. And caprice was a double-edged sword. Now it had worked in favor of the Jews. It might just as well in the future operate against them. Trajan had been pleased to allow the Temple to be rebuilt. He might just as well have seen fit to close the synagogues. In either case, the Jews were powerless, dependent on the arbitrary will of pagans. The recognition of the impotence of his people disturbed Elisha. What hope could there be for a nation whose very existence was determined not by its own will but by the casual and careless decisions of others?

Joining ostensibly in the jubilation, he was nevertheless depressed by a newborn awareness of the overwhelming might of the pagan world.

From Caesarea Gamliel dispatched Elisha on a pastoral tour of Galilee. The Patriarch was quite apologetic about the especially arduous assignment. He went to great lengths to point out that as a young sage of independent means Elisha must assume burdens heavier than those laid on his older fellows who in the main earned their own livelihood.

Eager for new scenes and faces, Elisha required little persuasion. Since the death of Meir's children and the performance in the Samaritan village he had been engaged in a constant, frantic struggle either to suppress his doubts, to will himself into his original unreflecting acceptance, or to dispel them by an appeal to reason. In the course of several months he had met with not the faintest glimmering of success. Indeed, his very preoccupation with the questions that haunted him had served only to heighten and intensify his disquiet. A round of strenuous activity was then a welcome prospect. It might well prove the very distraction of which he was so desperately in need.

Wherever he went, he found the populace almost delirious with joy over the news of Trajan's edict. But the normal routines of life persisted. Bazaars and workshops were busy as before. Congregations assembled as always for worship and instruction, students gathered for lectures, district courts convened for the adjudication of disputes.

In Haifa, on the first Sabbath of his trip, he preached at the great synagogue. The theme of his sermon, the Scriptural sources of the doctrine of the immortality of the soul and of the resurrection of the body, was not of his choosing. It had been forced on him by the elders of the community eager to offset the influence of a group of Sadducees who denied these articles of the faith. By sheer will, Elisha completed his address, but once or twice in the midst of it his words stuck in his throat.

Many another incident added to his unrest. In Acco where a court met under his presidency his fellow justices argued him into punishing a poor peasant for a violation of the Sabbath. He had little heart now to enforce ritual practices by coercion. The precedents on the matter were quite clear, giving him no loophole for evasion, but he hated himself for performing these prescribed duties.

In the Academy of Pekiin where he taught for several days, he lectured once on the approaching festival of Hanukkah, which celebrated the rebellion of the Maccabees against the Greeks. He had always loved that holy day with its kindling of lamps, increasing in number on each of eight nights to a final triumph of light. Now he wondered about the effects of the war against Antiochus. There was no way in which the Jews could have averted it. Their entire faith and culture had been at stake. Yet, as he spoke, Elisha wished that events had worked themselves out differently, so that Judaism might have been free to absorb more of the wisdom of the Greeks.

Increasingly aware of the discrepancy between his conduct and thought, he made his way from town to town, arriving finally at Meron. He was scarcely settled in his lodgings at the tavern when a distracted woman sought him out in the public room. A young man, seventeen or eighteen years of age, accompanied her with obvious reluctance.

"Master," she began, approaching Elisha and addressing him nervously. "This is my son Zebulun. He was always a good boy. You can ask any of the people here. But he went off last summer to Gadara, to deliver my husband's wool to the market there. He fell in with evil heathen. Since his return, I cannot do a thing with him. He will not pray. He will not learn. He says he does not believe any more...."

Loiterers in the room interrupted their conversations to listen.

"Hush," Elisha silenced her. "Let us go to my chamber where we can discuss this quietly."

"Now," he said to the boy in the privacy of his own room, "tell me exactly what troubles you."

Zebulun, suspicious of the kindliness in Elisha's voice, shook his head sullenly.

"Come," Elisha urged, "you can talk openly to me."

After much coaxing, the story came out, an incoherent tale of confused thought.

Elisha reasoned with him for hours, answering questions, arguing, persuading. Won over by the patience and interest of the rabbi, the boy yielded grudgingly point by point.

"Yes, Master," he acquiesced at last.

"And you will behave as a Jew should?"

"Yes, Master."

"Thank God," the woman exclaimed. "Master, I cannot begin to thank you. You have saved my child."

She stooped quickly to kiss the hem of Elisha's robe.

"Please," he begged awkwardly, drawing back. "I have done only what any rabbi would have done for you."

Alone again, Elisha sank despondently onto a stool and buried his face in his hands.

His tour completed, he returned home, but his unhappy preoccupation continued.

"Elisha...Elisha," Deborah repeated late one night as they were preparing to retire, "you haven't heard a word I've said. What's the matter with you?" She had been talking about some unimportant matter only to discover that, as was so often the case of late, he was not listening.

"I am sorry," he apologized. "I was thinking of something else."

"Something is bothering you," she persisted. "All you do is brood."

"But it's not so," he protested. "I'm quite all right."

"I do not believe it. Are you sure you're well?"

"Of course," he replied at once.

"Is it anything I've done? Sometimes, in temper, one forgets...."

"Oh, no," he reassured her, "it's not that at all."

"Then there is something. Why should you keep it from me? After all, I'm your wife. Your problems are mine...."

The impulse to unburden himself, to ease his inner strain by confiding in someone, had long been strong in him. Now under her sympathetic concern it was overpowering.

Pacing the room, he told her what had befallen him. He spoke slowly at first, then in spurts of words, describing how he had begun to doubt, how he was in a constant turmoil out of which he was unable to think his way.

"Do you mean," she whispered aghast, "that you don't believe in the Torah, the Tradition, our whole religion any more?"

"That's not quite it. I don't actively disbelieve. I'm just horribly uncertain, so that every time I pray or perform some ceremonial, I begin to wonder whether it's true or right. Worse, much worse, is having to preach to others when I'm not sure myself. I feel so hypocritical...."

"But it's mad," she exclaimed. "You mustn't even say such things. They are sinful."

"But I think them."

"Then stop it."

"I try, but it's impossible. No one can control his thoughts."

"Very well, then, think as you choose," she warned, "but not a breath of this to anyone. It will ruin you."

A look of concern came over her as she heard her own words and realized their full purport.

"You can't afford," she went on with mounting intensity, "to take chances with your position. You can get over this. You must! Stop reading those Greek books. Above all, stop talking about it, even to me."

He should have known, he told himself, that it would be a mistake to confide in her. A woman like Beruriah would have understood or at the least shown sympathy....

"I am sure of it," Deborah added confidently. "The more we discuss this, the more confused you will be." His discouragement deeper than ever, he lapsed into silence.

A few days later while sorting notes, Elisha came upon a tablet he had drawn up when first attempting to reason his way out of his difficulties. In the hope of fixing his doubts so that he could deal with them, he had listed questions to be resolved.

Now, after the passage of weeks, he reread them.

"Are miracles possible?" he had written.

"Is Scripture the Word of God?"

"If not, what basis can there be for the Tradition, its law, its rituals and beliefs?"

One item was not on the list. He had not inquired, "Is there a God?"

That was still the one article that had escaped the catastrophe which had overtaken every other in his system of belief.

His position, he realized instantly, had become intolerable. He could not remain in it, yet he could not extricate himself from it unaided. In some quarter he must seek help, the assistance of someone stronger and more confident than he.

The thought of Joshua occurred to him at once, and his pulse quickened with hope. Such a one possessed of serene faith and worldly sagacity might deliver him from the snare in which his soul was entangled. But even as he stayed himself with the idea, he had already renounced it. For he had spent a night in Joshua's company in Caesarea after the still incredible audience with Trajan. And the man was old and feeble; the strain of the day's events had exhausted him. His strength was not equal to the imposition of additional burdens. There was another deterrent too. Joshua was manifestly proud of his disciple and his career. He had not merited that his reward be disillusionment and a fresh anxiety. Love and gratitude commanded silence as well as communion.

But if not Joshua, then who? Who, that would willingly assume the weight of another's faltering?

A moment later, he was writing feverishly to three of his colleagues urging them to meet him in the tavern at Usha. He did not state his purpose.

"Uriel," he called, tying the tablets and sealing them.

The house stirred at his voice.

"Uriel," he repeated impatiently, "where are you?"

The little man appeared in the doorway.

"What is it, Master?"

"Deliver these letters at once. Two go to Rabbi Akiba and Rabbi Simeon ben Zoma at the academy in Usha, the other to ben Azzai in Tiberias. Give them only to the rabbis in person. Now hurry—no tarrying on the way."

"They are already delivered, Master."

Now that it was done Elisha's excitement diminished. The prospect of confession became embarrassing.

Back and forth he paced, weighing how to present his problem. Deborah entered the room. In his absorption he paid her no heed.

She waited for some time. When she spoke it was sharply. "Uriel tells me you are going away tomorrow."

He nodded absently.

"But why? You have no assignments for some days."

"That is true, but something of extreme importance has arisen. I hope you do not mind."

"But I do. You are never at home."

"I am sorry, but this is extremely urgent. And I shall be back soon."

Just then an idea occurred to him, a cryptic statement of his case that would invite their assistance without self-exposure.

"...ashamed before the neighbors and servants," he heard her say, "a husband who is always fleeing his home as though his wife were a leper. It would not be so bad if it were only when you were compelled to go. But you must find excuses to take you away. And even when you are at home, you sit by yourself in this room all day and all night."

The promising thought was eluding him.

"I have already made my arrangements." he said curtly.

"Of course, and without the least consideration of my feelings." Remorse touched him. She was left a great deal to herself.

"Deborah..." he began.

"You may spare yourself your apologies," she said, leaving the room; "I will get along without them."

"Deborah, Deborah..." he called after her, prepared to explain. But she was gone. He would have followed to console her, were it not for the fact that he must record his idea before it evaded him again. Hastily he fumbled in a cabinet for a fresh wax tablet.

CHAPTER XVI

THE ATTIC INTO WHICH THE innkeeper ushered Elisha was low-ceilinged, dreary and unfurnished except for a tumbled bed in a corner and several rickety stools scattered over the unswept floor. A smoking oil lamp hung from a roof beam throwing a patch of murky light onto the center of the room but leaving its outer darkness intact. Through a window lattice, a breeze blew moist with the drizzling rain that fell on the darkened, silent streets of Usha. At its hesitant touch, the tongue of flame overhead wavered so that the lurking shadows now darted forward boldly, now retreated to cower against the walls.

"I am sorry," the man apologized, "but every other chamber is taken. Now if the Rabbi will reconsider and agree to use one of the public rooms…"

"No, we shall require privacy. This will have to do."

"As you say. But may I fetch some refreshments for the master and his guests?"

"I think not."

"Then there is nothing else?"

"Except to direct the other rabbis here."

Bowing deferentially, the tavern owner withdrew.

The palms of Elisha's hands were moist, his stomach was slightly nauseous with apprehension. To dispel his nervousness, he busied himself with selecting the firmest chairs and arranging them where the illumination was strongest. But his movements were sporadic and intermittently he lapsed into reflective immobility. Ought he discard the artful presentation he had prepared so deliberately and reveal himself without protective deceits? But that might cost him their friendship, for how could they continue to associate with one who tottered on the brink of apostasy. And if they deserted him he would be altogether alone. Perhaps he ought to abandon the entire enterprise, keep his own counsel and find his own deliverance. But he could not return to the wretchedness that plagued him without exploring his only hope of liberation from it. There was then no course except that on which he had already determined.

Quick steps sounded on the staircase. Elisha's tongue flicked out to moisten his parched lips. He cleared his throat.

"What is the deep mystery?" ben Zoma hailed from the doorway.

"Shall we wait for the others?" Elisha evaded, postponing the dreaded moment. "And if I am not mistaken, here they come."

Almost immediately ben Azzai and Akiba entered the room, and the four men greeted one another in a flurry of conversation. Questions flew back and forth, bits of scholarship and morsels of gossip were exchanged, brilliant with learning, aglow with mutual affection and confidence. And Elisha, though he assumed a smiling composure and forced himself to participate in their sparkling talk, felt, for the first time since he had come to know them, that he was not of their company. Aching, he perceived that, having lost their securities, he had become in part an alien to their fellowship. What evil compulsion, he brooded resentfully, was driving him from the familiar comforting communion of his people and friends?

"Shall we get on with our business?" he interjected abruptly, eager to confront the crisis as soon as possible.

His voice was so strained and peremptory that the others were startled. Interrupting their conversation, they glanced at him in some perplexity. But when he said nothing more, they seated themselves on the chairs he had set.

"I feel," he began, employing the exact phrases he had been rehearsing all day, "that I owe you an apology for summoning you so hastily. I hope the letters you received did not alarm you. As a matter of fact, the issue I wish to put before you might just as well have awaited a more convenient occasion. But once I conceived my project, I was so afire with it that I allowed myself to be carried away."

Accustomed to easy spontaneity, they were perplexed by the stilted formality of his speech. They smiled uncertainly to indicate their interest, to conceal their bewilderment.

The wavering encouragement on their faces unnerved him. Again he was assailed by the temptation to frankness, only to repel it. It was not safe, he cautioned himself, to discard a carefully conceived policy for impulse.

"This is the project that occurred to me," he went on mechanically, as though reciting by rote. "We are all students of a Sacred Book, recipients and interpreters of a tradition which has grown up about it. Now most people are willing to accept our doctrine on authority. But many, not content with faith alone, demand demonstrations of the articles we expect them to believe. For that reason I would have this group undertake to work out a system of argument to support our faith. If you agree, we might draw not only upon our own resources but from the Greek philosophers as well. I might have attempted this alone, but several of us working together can complete it more quickly and effectively. This is my plan. I shall be pleased to hear your comments."

An awkward stillness followed. The two Simeons who had been altogether misled by Elisha's obliqueness were manifestly baffled. Only Akiba, traces of an unhappy surmise on his face, studied his friend searchingly through the unsteady light.

It was ben Azzai who first broke the silence.

"The suggestion we have just heard," he said gropingly, his colorless eyes fixed on the shadow-haunted wall, "is interesting. In fact, it has often occurred to me that we might utilize our meetings for some co-operative enterprise. But my notion was always of an altogether different character. There is, I think, but one goal to all human aspiration, the knowledge of God. But the experience of Him cannot be attained through the mind, not even fully through Scripture. Like color, it is a matter of direct apperception. It is as though one wishes to see a great king and holds in his hand a map of the palace and keys to its doors. That map is Scripture, those keys the reason of man. But the king is perceived only when one looks upon Him as Moses did, face to face. And I have sometimes thought that we might together evolve techniques...."

With a start he remembered the others.

"You will pardon me, I was rambling. But to be honest with you, Elisha, I see no special point to your suggestion. There is no widespread skepticism among our people to justify it. And if there were, I would not be too confident of the powers of systematic argumentation to allay it."

"Nor am I," ben Zoma broke in. "I hope you will not be offended, Elisha, but why this sudden interest in logical systems and Greek philosophy when we possess in Scripture all the truth we need? If there is anything lacking in us, it is that we concern ourselves too little with the deeper significances of the Writ. Now that would be a project in which I could join wholeheartedly—to study the hidden meanings of Scripture. But as for your idea..." He squirmed in his seat and was quiet.

"I am afraid that both of you have missed my point," Elisha countered, driven to greater openness. "Doubt is a natural phenomenon. No one, and I include myself, is spared by it. Now what other function can there be for reason except to corroborate the truths of revelation? As custodians of the Tradition, we shall have failed in our duty to our people and our own souls unless we exploit every device to render faith secure."

His words rang with a despairing appeal. He could say no more without engaging in full confession. But that his friends were beginning to understand he could sense in the tautness of their bodies, in the intentness of their staring, and in Akiba's utterance when he spoke, hastily as though to head off a final disclosure.

"Elisha is altogether right. Against the evil of skepticism there is but one defense, a bold, logically developed assertion of faith. To be frank with you, I myself would profit from a procedure such as Elisha suggests."

Elisha was not deceived. He knew instantly that Akiba was protecting him by exposing himself. His eyes met Akiba's in a momentary communication of unspoken gratitude, and turned away. Neither of the Simeons uttered a word, but Akiba must have read agreement in their faces for he went on after a slight pause to put the discussion safely on the plane of the impersonal.

"There are additional reasons for Elisha's proposal. We ought to know Greek philosophy so that we can defend ourselves against it. What is more, the number of proselytes who come to us has dwindled of late—an unmistakable consequence of our stubborn refusal to speak to the Gentile in the idiom of his own life. Out of all these considerations I urge that we act on the recommendation. Ben Azzai, what do you say? Are you willing to join us?"

"Gladly, in the light of your explanation."

"And you, ben Zoma?"

"Of course, of course."

"Good then," Akiba concluded with a reassuring nod toward Elisha. "We are agreed."

From that moment forth, Elisha's friends were all solicitude and co-operation. With dispatch they arranged to assemble regularly after each session of the Sanhedrin when they would be together in any case. Readily each undertook some special assignment, ben Azzai to lead discussions in mystical methods, ben Zoma to clarify troublesome passages in Scripture, Akiba and Elisha together to survey important texts of pagan philosophy. They even quarreled good-naturedly over who was to travel to Caesarea to purchase the Greek books they would require. and it was only because he was insistent that they allowed Elisha to assume that responsibility.

Elisha longed to voice his appreciation of their willingness to assist him. But by unspoken consent they all pretended that they had entered into the enterprise for its own sake, and any expression of personal gratitude would have nullified their face-saving fiction. It was only when, their business done, they had descended to the public room of the tavern for refreshment that Elisha was afforded an occasion to give vent to his feelings.

"To faith," Akiba cried, raising a brimming goblet, "abundant, clear and strong as this wine, for us and for all Israel."

"And to friendship," Elisha added, his voice soft, "that like this bread stays man's heart."

On the next morning Elisha awoke to find that his elation of the night was sadly diminished. In the light of day he saw all too clearly that what he had won was a preliminary skirmish, not a decisive battle. The co-operation of his friends was a first, indispensable step. It was not of and by itself a guarantee of the solution of his problems.

Disturbed by depressing misgivings, in contrast with the lightheartedness of the previous evening, he prepared for his trip to Caesarea. Before he set forth he paid his customary visit to Meir's home. Since the death of their children he had called there more frequently than ever for the sole purpose, he believed, of diverting and cheering them. But the attraction which drew him to their household was stronger than friendship. There was in it a yearning toward them which their presence both allayed and heightened at the same time.

They were, as always, genuinely pleased to welcome him. But the whiteness of Beruriah's face and the tenseness of her manner tortured him. Torn by concern for her, restless with his own problem, he sat at a table, his fingers drumming on it. During a lapse in the conversation their beating sounded inordinately loud.

"Master," Beruriah said gently, "something is troubling you."

"Yes," he replied, caught off guard and touched by her insight and the warmth of her solicitude.

"I thought so. We women know how to read trivial signs. Is it anything you can discuss with us?"

He opened his lips to speak but, reconsidering, shook his head.

"Perhaps not."

"Is it important?" Meir persisted.

They watched him intently.

"Very."

"Well, whatever it is," Beruriah encouraged, "I am sure that it is not so serious as you imagine. Few things ever are, except..."

That was all. But when he left he knew that their devotion and anxiety on his behalf, asserted in the midst of their own sorrow, had strengthened him.

At a fork in the highway where a battered roadside Hermes stood amid the mound of stones thrown in his honor by pious travelers, Elisha drew in the reins of his horse, hesitated for a moment, and then rode through the North Gate of Caesarea into its pagan quarters. Although he had his colleagues and friends in this populous city, the metropolis of Palestine, he did not wish to see them now. This was no time for formal welcomes, for invitations to preach in the synagogue, for all the courtesies which would be extended to him as a rabbi and member of the Sanhedrin. There was urgent business at hand, the seeking out of a dealer in Greek books.

Once inside the walls, he stared about with open curiosity. He had visited Caesarea often but, except for that one audience with Trajan, never outside its Jewish district. The great avenue that stretched before him swarmed with freemen and slaves, with litters, chariots, caravans and drays about which the stream of pedestrians eddied. Everywhere, from the sidewalks, the colonnaded arcades and the countless shops, he heard a babble of voices speaking in the *koine,* the debased Greek dialect which was the universal tongue of the Orient.

Wondering where among these unfamiliar buildings he could find a bookstore, he paused beside a group of boys who played in the center of the street, sliding discs over a diagram scratched on the stone pavement.

"Can you tell me, please?" he called in Greek, "where I can find a bookshop?"

Dirty faces looked up at him.

"The next side street, to the left," one of the urchins volunteered.

Rounding the corner of a narrow alleyway, he caught sight of a terra-cotta plaque affixed to the wall over the stall to which he had been directed. On it were portrayed representations of books, papyrus, parchment, wax tablets, ink, pumice, quills and styli. Beneath it, fronting the street, stretched a counter strewn with scrolls. Dismounting, he fingered title-tags and found himself in the main familiar with neither the books nor their authors. A sense of depression came over him as though he were in a strange land where men of alien tongue conversed in his presence incomprehensibly.

"Is there anything I can sell you?" a nasal voice queried. The sound of the words stirred Elisha vaguely. From the shadowy recesses of the mart a man approached him, tall and loose-jointed. Elisha stared incredulously, his heart lifting with pleasurable recollection as the full light of day fell on a well-remembered face.

"Nicholaus?" he cried excitedly.

The bookdealer glanced at Elisha inquiringly.

"Then you do not recognize me?"

"No, I cannot say that I do. If I should, I apologize."

"But I am Elisha."

"Elisha?" Nicholaus stared at him. "It cannot be," he stammered, unbelieving. "Elisha was a little boy and you...Of course, of course..." He stepped forward quickly and opened his arms. They embraced joyously. As they drew apart Nicholaus held him at arm's length, looking at him eagerly. "To be sure. The same features, the same eyes. It was your height and the beard that deceived me. But I should have recognized your Greek. And you remembered me at once."

"Naturally. How could I forget you? Besides you have not changed very much. A little older perhaps, your hair somewhat gray, but that is all." He looked down at the hands on his arms. "Why, I should have known your fingers," he smiled whimsically. "I remember them so well, beating the rhythm of Homer."

Nicholaus grinned. "Can you still recite the poetry I made you memorize?"

"Not much of it, I am afraid, although I still read verse."

"I feared it would be so when Abuyah died. But come inside. I want to hear all about you." He slipped an arm around Elisha's shoulder and led him into the shop, past tables loaded with writers' supplies, into a back room. The walls were stacked with circular cases, crowded with scrolls. "Sit here," Nicholaus invited, drawing up a stool, "and tell me everything that has happened since I left your home."

"But I want to hear about you," Elisha countered.

"No," Nicholaus insisted. "You first."

They wrangled good-naturedly over precedence. In the end Elisha yielded, giving a brief account of the major events in his life but avoiding carefully all references to his recent confusion.

"And now you are a rabbi," Nicholaus mused, "an elder, a great man among your people. I congratulate you. Yet I cannot help thinking that it would have been otherwise had your father lived. You would have been a free citizen of a great world and with your wealth and intelligence...But then," he went on with a quick change of mood, "who can say that you would have been happier? There was a time when I was quite certain about everything. Now, as I grow older, I am not so sure. In any event, it is done beyond our power of remaking."

The possibility that life might have been different, perhaps happier and freer, had its accidents fallen otherwise, stung Elisha.

"And so," he picked up the thread of conversation, twisting it deliberately, "I have become a rabbi, and you...what have you done all these years?"

"Nothing exciting. I had little heart for tutoring at any time, and less after I had to surrender you. Fortunately, your father paid me well. I bought this shop and have been here ever since. It is hard to believe that it is a matter of over twenty-five years. But, to be more cheerful, what are you doing in these parts? It is not often that Jewish scholars visit Greek bookshops. Unless matters have changed, they approve as little of our philosophers, scientists and poets as of our sculptors."

Elisha chilled at the reminder of his enterprise.

"There is," he said a little stiffly, "some difference of opinion among our sages concerning the merits of Greek literature."

"Perhaps," Nicholaus agreed, noting a look of discomfort on Elisha's face. "Now what can I do for you?"

"Strange as it may seem," Elisha replied, "you may sell me Greek books. Some of my friends and I plan to study philosophy—which makes my finding you all the more fortunate."

"Philosophy?" Nicholaus queried. "Have you any specific works in mind?"

"No. We are quite at a loss where to begin."

"Then let me see what I have on hand."

Elisha followed him to a wall cabinet and watched while he read title-tags.

"Here is something you will certainly want," Nicholaus pulled cylinder after cylinder from a case. "A full Plato. A Ptolemy?" he muttered, turning to the next cabinet. "No, astronomy is a little too remote. The Geography of Posidonius? Good, but not relevant...Strabo...Polybius...Cicero. Do you read Latin?"

"Not a word."

"That rules out the essays and Lucretius the Epicurean. Just as well. You most assuredly would not want that. The

Analytics of Aristotle. The *Ethics*. The *Metaphysics* especially. All these, of course. Hold on. Here is something quite rare...a copy of Euhemerus, the most blasphemous book ever written, but brilliant."

Moving from cabinet to cabinet they selected and rejected until a sizable heap of scrolls was piled onto a table. At the last cabinet Nicholaus paused.

"Here is something," he said, "which is only a school text —the *Elements of Geometry* by Euclid. It is not really important except that it represents the best example of clear thinking that has ever yet been penned. It might be useful to you not so much for its contents—I know that some of your people are fine mathematicians—as for its method. Had I remained with you, you would have spent years over it. You really should have it. If you do not want to buy it, accept it as my gift." He tossed the bulky cylinder onto the others. "There," he concluded, "that's all."

Nicholaus shook his head sadly over the disordered pile of manuscripts. "Alas, it is a motley lot. I am worried about pre-scribing so badly planned a diet. It may make you sick." Taking a large mesh bag from under one of the tables, he slipped the volumes into it, tied the binding cord firmly and pushed the bundle across the table.

"Here they are."

"Can you arrange to get additional books for us as we will need them?" Elisha asked, counting coins out of his purse and forcing them on Nicholaus. "You have a general idea of what I want. I can leave the selection to you."

"Of course, but only if you promise to call for them in person. I have thought of you often during all these years. And now that we have met, I do not want to lose you again."

"I wish I could stay with you longer today," Elisha replied. "Unfortunately, I must return to Usha at once for my classes."

"Then it is good-bye for the present."

"Yes, I am afraid it is."

The two men stood facing each other, one of Nicholaus's hands closed about the coins, the other resting upon the bag of books. As though it were against his will he broke forth abruptly:

"Please pardon what I am going to say. After all, I am more than a merchant. I am your friend. Do not take these books. Why should you concern yourself with them? Go back to your own people and its traditions and be happy. These philosophers of ours will give you nothing. They have never given me anything. They will merely confuse you. They are liars, glib with promises which they never fulfill. Why should you open a Pandora's box in your heart or sow your mind with dragons' teeth?"

Through the shadows Elisha looked toward the well-known, well-beloved face.

"The box is already opened," he whispered. "The teeth have been planted."

Nicholaus's heart sank, his face was lined with solicitude. "Then there is nothing left to be said except this: if ever you need my help, you can count on me. Meantime the Agathos Daimon go with these books, and the God of your people. May you find whatever it is you seek."

"Thank you," Elisha said simply. "We shall meet again."

"Often, I hope."

"Yes."

"Then peace."

"Farewell."

Elisha slung the packet over his shoulder. Nicholaus followed him to the doorway, dropping the coins absent-mindedly from hand to hand. He watched Elisha mount his horse. They waved to each other. Elisha turned and rode away.

"So we have prevailed after all, Abuyah and I," Nicholaus brooded unhappily as he looked after the retreating figure. He made a wry face as though a bitter taste were in his mouth. "Eh," he spat forth resentfully, "victory is not always sweet."

The morning sunlight streamed through the open windows of the tavern at Usha, falling directly onto Elisha's face. He stirred in his sleep and opened his eyes. It was still early. The streets outside were quiet and cool with dawn. The long trip from Caesarea had tired him, but he had slept well and now, as he lay abed, he felt thoroughly refreshed, almost lighthearted.

Throwing the covers from him, he rose to his feet, bathed his hands and face in a washbasin and dressed rapidly, reciting mechanically with each act the blessing of thanksgiving prescribed by the Law. His phylacteries bound onto his arm and forehead, he murmured his morning worship in a rush of well-remembered, unnoticed words. Then he turned eagerly to the table on which the mesh bag rested. As he untied the binding strings the cylindrical scrolls rolled out in confusion. Pleasurably perplexed he seated himself on a stool, picked one of the volumes at random and scanned the crimson name-tag which dangled from the open end of its parchment sheath. It was entitled *Concerning the Creation of the World*, by Philo the Jew of Alexandria. He slipped it from its container and skimmed the first few columns of text. Its interpretations of Scripture interested him. Reluctantly he put it aside to continue his examination. Out of its sheath he extracted a slender roll done in a careful hand on the finest papyrus. When he read the title-tag, *Concerning the Gods*, by Euhemerus, he recalled that this was the work to which Nicholaus had called his special attention.

Without turning his eyes from the book before him he drew a wax tablet and a stylus into position and from force of habit began outlining the decisive points in its argumentation. The gods, he noted, have no real existence but are merely human heroes who have been deified. But he had no sooner jotted a few lines than he lost confidence in the thesis. It was bold but entirely unsupported and seemed, on more sober consideration, unreasonable. He shoved the scroll away and picked up Euclid's *Elements of Geometry*.

That, too, disappointed him on his first survey. It seemed a mere statement of mathematical principles with which he had long been familiar. The rabbis and their disciples were well-trained mathematicians who used convenient and simple rules of thumb. But this, he realized in a flash of insight, was a mathematics different not in content but in method from that which he had known. This was no business of additions without an abacus or of the calculation of weights and distances. It was rather logic in motion. Pure abstract reason proceeded relentlessly from definition through close-knit argumentation to final unchallengeable conclusions.

Carefully he went back, sampling postulates, examining the inferences from them. It seemed to hold wherever he tested it. But whether or not every detail was proved completely—and only an exhaustive study could determine that—the whole embodied a magnificent conception. For it was transparently an attempt to order the processes of thought into a series of rigid demonstrations.

Yet it was less the intellectual boldness of the design that fired Elisha than the implications which he glimpsed. Assuming that this system of mathematics had attained to the certainty it professed, enterprises in other realms might be equally successful. What was more, it was something akin to this for which he had been groping in his religious thinking. After a fashion, he too had been trying to find axioms and a succession of propositions on which the doctrines of the Tradition might rest.

The mounting noises of the street broke in on him and reminded him of the day's duties. Stepping to the window he observed that he was already late for his class at the academy. From among the litter of books he collected the tablets on which he had outlined his lecture and left the tavern, not stopping long enough to take breakfast in the public room. He arranged his memoranda as he strode along the street and found, included among them by accident, the notes he had made of Euhemerus' book. Impatiently he slipped it into his robe to get rid of it and hastened on.

The auditorium was crowded with students. Without preliminary, he plunged into his theme, a discussion of the Day of Atonement, its ritual and its moral significance. He was in high spirits. The attendance pleased him, the glow of discovering Euclid had not yet disappeared, and the close attention with which he was followed stimulated him further. Rising from his chair, he walked back and forth along the edge of the platform, the scratching of styli on wax sounding a shrill overtone to his enthusiastic words.

Then it happened. His movement dislodged the tablet in his bosom. Through his girdle, down his leg it slipped. Before he could catch it his swinging foot had kicked it and sent it sliding off the platform onto the floor. Several students stooped to pick it up. As the one who retrieved it brought it forward, his eyes dropped onto the large Hebrew characters scrawled over it. "God has no real existence," he read aloud and gasped.

A deathlike hush settled over the room.

"Master," the student stammered, thrusting the tablet toward Elisha. "You dropped this."

Accepting it, thanking the student casually, Elisha reflected quickly. Ought he account for the unfortunate sentence and explain that the sentiment was not his own but that of a pagan philosopher, that the word read as God should really be read the gods, for in Hebrew the singular and plural were identical? It was wiser, he decided, to let the incident pass as something innocent, which indeed it was. Calmly he tossed the tablet onto the table and continued his lecture at the point at which it had been interrupted.

But he was disconcerted when he looked up again, to read suspicion, cold, almost hostile, on the faces before him.

CHAPTER XVII

FROM PALESTINE THE REPORT OF Trajan's edict spread to all the Jewries of the world. It moved ahead of the Roman army along the trade routes eastward into Babylonia and Persia. It was carried by merchants and special couriers southward into Egypt. Fleet galleys and lumbering freighters brought it to Ostia whence it traveled with the speedy flight of a bird across the Alps and down the Rhine. Word of it reached the colonnaded synagogue of Alexandria built like a basilica and so vast that the sexton waved a flag so that worshipers in the rear might know when to respond with the prescribed Amen. To a tiny chapel in Cologne, to a shrine built of sun-dried brick far to the south of Carthage where the caravan trails from the Sahara debouched onto the plains of North Africa, to Sura and to Nehardea, standing across the silt-choked canals of Babylonia, came the good tidings. Throughout the dispersion of the House of Israel the great Hallel, the paean of thanksgiving from the Book of Psalms, was chanted. "I will give thanks unto Thee that Thou hast answered me. I love the Lord, He hath heard the voice of my supplication."

The Patriarch made no official request for moneys to rebuild the Temple. But almost immediately the pious were sending contributions. A trickle at first, coming from Palestine alone, the flow of gold and silver turned speedily into a torrent of coins as the news spread to more distant and richer lands. Within six months there were funds at hand sufficient to begin operations. But when a full year had passed without the Senate's confirmation of the edict the sages and people alike grew anxious. Representatives of the Sanhedrin were constantly at the governor's palace in Caesarea. Urgent messages were sent to the Jewry of Rome asking that its influence be exerted on individual senators to effect speedy action. A legation was dispatched to follow Trajan to the East to inform him of the delay in implementing his order.

In the meantime, the Patriarch, yielding to the universal impatience, appointed commissions. A committee sat for long hours examining the genealogical records of priestly families. Hundreds of Levites came before it, requesting their hereditary privilege of serving in the secondary rites of ministration.

Another group, designated especially for that purpose, studied the traditions, written and oral, concerning the structure of the sanctuary. It interviewed old men who, as children, had seen the Temple. Apartments in Jamnia were assigned to architects, many of whom had been summoned hastily from Alexandria. Each day they listened to the descriptions of the building as it had once been. Each night they drew on great tanned hides the lines which indicated how it was to be reconstructed.

The house of Autemaus which for centuries had compounded the sacred incense announced that it still preserved the esoteric formulae of its ancestors. The family which had baked the show-bread of old now asked that that task be assigned to it again. The Jews of Palestine lived in a joyous half-trance, as though to each individual there had come a rare good fortune, something so beautiful that it could scarcely be believed.

Elisha too was caught up by the contagious excitement. All his life he had prayed for the rebuilding of the Temple and on the seventeenth of Tammuz and on the ninth of Ab, days associated with its destruction, he had participated each year in the dramatic rites of mourning. What surprised him most was the discovery that even Pappas was pleased with the prospect of a Temple rebuilt.

"Needless to say," his friend wrote from Antioch, "our brethren here are wild with delight. As one who is neither a pagan nor a Jew, I worship at no shrine. But the symbol of our disgrace is gone. Like me, my Gentile friends here in Antioch take little stock in any religion or any nationality. Nevertheless, I have been able to discern in them an added respect for our people. We have ceased to be different from every other nation in the Empire. We too have our sanctuary."

At last the day came when the decree of the Senate was delivered into the hands of the Patriarch at Jamnia. Within an hour thereafter horsemen rode at breakneck speed through Palestine informing the populace and calling the Sanhedrin into special session. That very night the tidings strode from hilltop to hilltop in flaming beacons to the dispersions in Syria, Babylonia and Egypt.

Two days later the sages assembled at Jamnia to hear the Patriarch read the official text of the decree. So long as he held in his trembling hands the parchment scroll with its great seals, so long as his voice pronounced the sonorous Latin words, they were silent as though they would never breathe again. But when it was finished, a clamor broke iorth. Men wept, shouted and embraced one another. Then a stentorian voice roared over them, "Come, let us go up to the mountain of the Lord." Without a formal motion, without debate, without a ballot, every sage knew that on the next day the Sanhedrin would as a body travel in pilgrimage to the place where The House had stood aforetime and where it would stand again.

By the end of the first watch that night, the large public room of the tavern of Jamnia was almost empty. Tables and benches stood irregularly as they had been left when the diners had risen some hours before. The air was heavy with the stale smell of food and the acrid scent of the oil lamps that hung from the ceiling. Propped on a chair in one corner, an itinerant merchant slept, his chin resting on his chest, his beard splayed over it. Most of the sages who frequented the place had retired early, leaving Akiba, the two Simeons and Elisha to hold their conference undisturbed.

For a time they had argued animatedly. But eventually they had fallen silent, not with agreement, but out of despair over the power of words to persuade. Now their stillness was alive with a resentment that was in part fear and in part hostility.

Seven times in a period of two years they had met. On each occasion ben Azzai had talked of his mystical speculations, ben Zoma of his interpretations of Scripture, and Akiba of his reasoned theology. And still Elisha was not convinced. It was not that he ever denied openly or rejected their arguments outright. At each meeting he listened attentively. But just when they would grow hopeful, he would inject one of his detestable questions and explode their eloquence. By indirection he challenged the basic assumptions on which supposedly they were all agreed. Then, unable to answer him, they would be left gaping.

Their inability to silence him troubled them increasingly. It was not easy to face denial regularly and remain unshaken. The two Simeons especially had been much disturbed by the series of discussions. After each, they restored their own confidence only by plunging themselves further into their habitual modes of thinking. They had come to dread these gatherings. If they could, they would have stopped them. But they refused to admit even to themselves that the faiths by which they lived were too weak to overpower dissent. They continued to meet with reluctance, apprehension and, above all, with increasing bitterness against the doubter in their midst.

Such were the thoughts that occupied them now. And as for Elisha, he knew full well how they had come to feel toward him. It was impossible to misread the significance of their gestures of annoyance, their exclamations of impatience, their occasional spurts of temper. He told himself that he ought not dispute with them, that there was no point in shaking their faith. But he could not abide their half-reason and their shoddy logic. He had learned from Euclid what the proof of a proposition should be like. And although he recognized that he was alienating his closest friends, he was unable to keep his objections to himself.

Of late, like them, he would gladly have dissolved their futile association. But there was no way of doing so with any semblance of graciousness. And all the time he was sinking deeper into the morass and dragging them down with himself.

He sighed unhappily.

The faint sound broke the spell. They stirred.

"It is late," Akiba commented heavily, "and it has been an exhausting day."

"Aye," ben Zoma responded, "and it will be a hard trip tomorrow."

They rose and with careful courtesy bade one another good night.

A heavy mist hung over the low hills of the seacoast as they marched, several hundred masters and disciples, upward toward the Judean mountains. Moisture dropped from trees and shrubs, condensed on the halters and hair of their animals and seeped through thatched rain hats and woolen outer garments. The early spring weather was cold, raw and unpleasant. But as they traveled, they chanted together, "I rejoiced when they said unto me, 'Let us go up to the house of the Lord.'"

All day long from the moment when the sun rose in a blur of mist until late afternoon they chanted on their way. The countryside, faintly seen through the drifting fog, grew wilder and more desolate. Bleak hillsides, denuded by the Romans in their campaign to take Jerusalem, ran with water. It seeped through broken terraces, washing away the soil where once gardens and olive groves had flourished. These mountains had become indeed a land which the Lord had cursed, which had vomited forth its inhabitants.

And that night when the sages were encamped near Emmaus where once Judah the Maccabee had won a great victory, they intoned together an ancient Song of Ascents. "When the Lord turned the captivity of Zion, we were as those who dreamed. Then were our mouths filled with laughter and our tongues with joy.... Aye, the Lord hath done great things for us. Wherefore we were glad. Turn Thou, O Lord, our captivity like the rivulets in the southland...."

The night was chill and dark vapors shifted spectrally about their feeble campfires. The thought of those who had perished in blood and fire wove itself into a melancholy spell. Out of the dark desolation and out of the broodings of their hearts a minor note crept into the joyous chant as it continued, "He who goeth on his way weeping, bearing his measure of seed..." With sunrise the mist turned into a spanking spring rain. In the sodden discomfort the exhilaration of the night before, even its yearning, poignant sadness, was dissipated. Sages and disciples bathed, bound on their phylacteries, recited the abbreviated morning service allowed for those engaged in travel, ate a hasty meal and pressed onward.

No longer did they sing, not even while climbing the slope of the Mount of Watchmen from the crest of which they would see where Jerusalem once stood.

At the very moment when they reached the hilltop, the wind shifted and tore the veil of rain asunder. A moan broke from them at the sight of the utter waste before them. Below and at their feet curved the Valley of Jehoshaphat, for centuries the burial ground of Jerusalem. Weeds crowded about the great tombs of ancient nobles and blanketed the untended graves of the humble. Across the valley and beyond the Sacred Mountain towered the Akra, fortified as in the days of Jewish glory but garrisoned now by a cohort of the Tenth Legion Fretensis. On one of its crenellated battlements a Roman sentry, his armor hidden by a gray hooded raincloak, stood huddled against the wind and rain, like some bedraggled bird of ill omen brooding over the valley below. Everywhere, as far as the eye could see, the hillsides bristled with skeletal thorns and thistles, burned out by the fiery heat of the preceding summer. The Temple Mount itself was a desolation naked even of bramble and briar, so thoroughly had the Romans sown it with salt.

A graybeard in the party lifted a quavering thin voice,

chanting the doleful lines of the Book of Lamentations: "How doth she sit desolate, the City great in people, the Princess among kingdoms…!"

The shrill elegy was broken by Gamliel's booming voice. "Enough, enough," he interrupted. "Weeping hath endured for the night. Joy hath come with the morning. Come, let us thank Him."

Together, with one accord, the pilgrims recited a benediction: "Blessed art Thou, O Lord our God, King of the Universe, who is good and who doeth beneficently." Their voices rose steadily with each word climbing in a crescendo of exultation as they went on to pronounce, "Blessed art Thou, O Lord our God, King of the Universe, who buildeth Jerusalem anew. Amen."

Moving wordlessly, they descended the steep hillside through tall, wet weeds that snapped at them as though the flowers of desolation resented the disturbance of their malignant peace. Stumbling over rubble, slipping through mud compounded of pulverized rock, they enter the Tyropean Valley where a fragment of the western retaining wall of the Temple still stood. This alone the Romans had spared as a symbol of the might of the city which had fallen before the fury of sword and firebrand.

Rain fell once more as the sages climbed a rough path strewn with shattered hewn stone upward toward the Temple plateau. At its crest they stopped, recalling the injunction which forebade Jews to walk upon the site of the ruined shrine lest in their ignorance they tread upon the Holy of Holies where only the High Priest was permitted. Panting from their exertions, the weary men stood, the wind lashing at them and beating into their faces so that none could tell whether his fellows' cheeks were wet with rain or tears.

With palsied hands the oldest among them pointed out the location of the Court of the Gentiles and the Court of the Women. Yonder had stood the golden screen built like a vine, hanging with clusters of golden grapes. Here had been one altar, there another. The younger sages followed the various descriptions fitting their book knowledge of the Temple to its actual site. But their eyes returned again and again to the Stone of Foundation, that great natural outcropping of rock where Abraham had willingly bound Isaac and where once a year the High Priest had offered the sacrifice of atonement. In the uncertain light it gleamed darkly, the channel for sacrificial blood barely perceptible. The area about it was littered with cut stone left by Roman artisans who had begun the erection of a shrine to the Capitoline Jupiter. This project had been abandoned quickly when Vespasian discovered that the Jewish people, although exhausted by one defeat, might attempt a second rebellion to protect the ruins of their sanctuary.

Drenched to the skin, Elisha stared at a great block of battered blue marble which lay at his feet. At one side an inscription was discernible. Splashed over it was a blotch of fused gold, melted doubtless in the last conflagration and, through some chance, escaped from the rapacious eye of the plunderer.

A sense of the impossibility of the project depressed him.

"Master," he said to Joshua at his side, "it will never be done."

Joshua put a restraining hand on his arm.

"Can anything be too wonderful for God?" he quoted.

But Elisha shook his head unconvinced.

A group of their colleagues stood near enough to overhear.

"Is that all that you can say at a time like this?" one of them barked at Elisha.

"An encouraging attitude," another chimed in resentfully.

"Hush," Joshua quieted them. "He has merely expressed what we all fear."

They turned in unison and descended slowly into the valley.

CHAPTER XVIII

FOUR MEN RETURNED FROM THE pilgrimage to Jerusalem, each to his own home.

In his hut in Bnai Brak, Akiba the son of Joseph read from a long Greek scroll unfurled across the rude table before him. A group of children played noisily in the street. Their shrill excited cries beat upon him through the open door. His wife, busy with numerous tasks, moved quickly about the chamber. From the brick oven built into one wall heat radiated, and the fragrance of baking bread. Over the fire below it a pot simmered, scenting the room with the pungent smell of cooking vegetables. Assailed on all sides by sounds, odors and movements, Akiba sat, interrupting his reading from time to time to give absent-minded responses to his wife's comments. His large eyes were fixed unswervingly on the writing before him. His fingers, restless with the strain of mental effort, stroked his full coarse beard. He looked up once, half-awakened from deep thought by a sudden outburst of voices. Smiling vaguely, he rose, asked the children to continue their games more quietly, and returned to his text. They went on with their play as though he had not spoken.

It was a great work, this *Analytics* of Aristotle, he reflected, clear, profound and helpful. He wondered whether this system of logic was to be preferred to that employed by the rabbis. The problems to which they addressed themselves were dissimilar, of course. The pagan philosopher was interested in reasoned demonstrations of propositions whereas he and his colleagues sought to expound a sacred text. Argumentation and exegesis were radically different activities.

It would be an interesting theme for discussion with the other three at their next conference. He frowned. The sessions were becoming increasingly difficult. They were obviously disturbing both ben Azzai and ben Zoma, driving them further from reality into worlds of their own. And as for Elisha—concern wrinkled Akiba's brow.

At the foot of a blossoming apple tree, Simeon the son of Azzai stood, the fragrance of the flowers scenting his thoughts, his eyes bewitched by the tracery of leaves, branches and petals. His heart pounded within him at the thought that he might be at long last on the verge of a great discovery. In his hands he still held the scroll in which he had been reading when, his own room growing too small for him, he had fled into the open.

His resentment against Elisha was gone. Instead, he felt indebted to him. For if they had not studied together, one denying and the other fearing, he would never have entered upon his researches into Gnostic doctrines. They had not been easy, these two years of questing. More than once he had hated Elisha in his heart for destroying his peace, for forcing him to read strange books and think alien thoughts.

But this very day as he puzzled over the scroll, he had caught a glimpse of the key to the Great Mystery. Unexpectedly he had comprehended, as one who has long struggled with a puzzle may suddenly see the solution and, having seen it, marvel that he had not perceived it before.

Perhaps it was true, he speculated, his great colorless eyes dilating with wonder, that the realm of sense was the work not of the True God, but of some lesser spirit. Certainly the physical world, weighted by death and sin, swayed by rigid merciless law, gave little testimony to a Deity who was perfection and infinite love. It might well be that there were two Gods, one, the lower being, the creator of the material universe, the other pure light and compassion, removed far above transiency and decay.

But if there be a God beyond God, He could not be grasped through the senses, for these and the things on which they fastened were stamped with the blurred seal of the lesser divinity. Nor could reason help, since all law, even that of human thought, was a confinement, a delimitation, and hence incapable of perceiving the infinite.

Here, then, lay the secret of the failure of his mystical exercises in the past, of his confusion and uncertainties before Elisha. He had mistaken the inferior God for the Highest. Now, with confidence he would begin to fast once more, to pray, to lay his soul open through meditation. And he would wait until that light of salvation which was invisible to sight, inconceivable to thought, dawned over him.

A wan smile touched his pallid face, illuminating it with hope. He put his shaggy head back slowly, rested it on the gnarled tree trunk and looked upward into the tangle of weaving branches toward the glimpses of the sky visible through them....

The foot of ben Zoma pressed nervously on the treadle of the loom, sending the shuttle back and forth in jerking flight. Like a harp player's, his fingers flowed over the threads. The weaver's frame stood against the doorway of his workshop, the web of warp and woof cutting the light with thin lines and drawing fine black tracings over the houses and men beyond. But his eyes saw no further than the intertwining strands and their pattern, so tightly did his thoughts hold him.

It was sinful to hate Elisha. But how could one cherish love for a blasphemer to whom Scripture itself was no sanctity? And his denials, unspoken as they were, were insidious. There were times when even he, Simeon the son of Zoma, was seduced into wondering....

A spasm shook his body, his hands faltered in their automatic movement. For a moment he contemplated the vista which opened before him. Its bleakness chilled him. Deliberately he submerged himself in the comforting warmth of old researches.

"And the spirit of God hovered"—what mystery lay hidden here in that word suggestive of the circling motion of a bird, as though the Presence were in some way akin to a winged thing?

"Over the face of the waters"—but the world, its rivers and its seas had not yet been called into being. Might it be, as some Greeks believed, that water was a primeval substance as old as God, that the creative word had given to material things not existence, but only form?

"Let us make man in our image...."

Wild surmises gleamed in his eyes as he dwelt on the baffling plural pronoun. The shuttle darted more quickly, ben Zoma's body twisted, his lips writhed suddenly. Who, he asked himself, was with Him in that awesome moment when man was conceived in the womb of Eternity?

Snapped by his uneven touch, a filament sagged across the web in lifeless spirals. Disturbed in its rhythm, his thinking leaped from one cryptic passage of Scripture to another...from the mystery of creation to that of revelation, to the vision of the chariot which Ezekiel saw when he was among the exiles by the River Chebar.

"The four creatures...and each had four faces...wheels within wheels...and their rims were full of eyes...." He tried to visualize it, but it was too complex to be conceived, too intricate to be interpreted.

"...a firmament like the color of a terrible ice...the likeness of a throne, as the appearance of a sapphire stone...the likeness as the appearance of a man...colored like the bow that is in the cloud in the day of rain..."

His foot pressed with increasing ferocity on the treadle. The strip of woven cloth mounted apace, until it blotted out the world, leaving him only the dizzy intertwining of myriad threads that lost themselves in convolutions about one another....

Elisha stood at the door of his chamber staring out toward the blue black waters of the Galilean Sea. A wind blowing in from the lake flowed gently but steadily across his drawn face. Overhead, stars looked down upon him as they had upon Amorite and Hittite and the Nephilim, the great giants of old.

Steady and sure they gleamed undisturbed by the rise and fall of empires and by the troubled hearts of men.

Wistfully Elisha whispered a passage uttered by one of the sages who had gone before, "Consider ye the heavens which I created above you. Have they ever modified their habit? Has the sun ever risen in the west to set in the east? Have the stars in their constellations ever departed from their path? Consider the earth which I have created to sustain you. Has it ever varied its character? Hast thou ever planted wheat and harvested barley, or planted barley and harvested wheat? Now consider yourselves whom I have created to serve Me. In all the wide world it is only you who know not your law, even as it is written, 'The ox knoweth his master and the ass his owner's crib. Israel doth not know, my people doth not understand.' "

If only man, Elisha brooded, could know his law as the stars knew theirs. If only he could move unswervingly along a course charted for him as they followed their destiny so that all things might be at peace in God.

But where was that orbit for man which was also harmony with the universe? And knowing it, how was one to be certain that one had charted it aright out of all the infinite lines that might be drawn through space?

This much only he knew: he was not finding it. After two years of travail he was no nearer to serenity. At their very next meeting he was determined he would release his friends from a futile task they had come to hate.

But then what? Somewhere in Israel there must be a surer truth. Might it be in the possession of one of those heretical sects, the Gnostics or Christians perhaps, of whom the rabbis spoke so slightingly. He must learn for himself. No stone must be left unturned lest it conceal the mouth of the fountain of life.

With but little hope, he resolved to explore the possibility.

Once again he looked up at the stars. Their calm clarity reproached his bewilderment. Sadly he sighed and returned to his couch.

CHAPTER XIX

THE TEMPLE MOUNT AND ITS environs swarmed with men. On the plateau builders were at work leveling the ground preparatory to the laying of foundations. Imperiling their lives to clear the cliffs of weeds, laborers crawled cautiously from hold to hold over sheer precipices. In the valleys below, masons and carpenters toiled busily, piling high the mounds of hewn stone and massive beams which porters were soon to haul up the temporary road, gouged out of the rock.

The silence of the site, so long unbroken, throbbed now with sounds—the drone of saws, the shriek of planes, the thudding of axes and the voices of men.

Aquilas, the proselyte, surveyed the scene from the crest of the hill and was satisfied with what he saw. It had been almost midsummer when at the request of the Sanhedrin he had laid aside his still unfinished translation of Scripture into Greek to become overseer of building operations. The progress he had made justified the sacrifice.

He frowned as the gleam of armor on the fortified crest of a neighboring hill caught his eye. If only the Roman garrison would be withdrawn!

Aquilas was zealous for the faith he had adopted. It offended his piety that heathen should be free to look irreverently on the sacred enclosure. What was worse, their presence was dangerous. They were forever inciting his men, sneering at them whenever they came within earshot. Someday they would overstep the bounds. Something too provoking would be said. As he told his men time and again, the Temple must be built in peace. Even David, for all his virtues, had not been allowed to erect the first sanctuary because, as a warrior, he had spilled blood.

Withdrawing his gaze from distant Akra, he watched a band of cavalry ride over the hillcrest from the northwest and enter the gates of the Roman fortification.

An hour or so later, his duties completed for the day, Aquilas descended into the valley to find unwelcome guests awaiting him; Milo, commander of the Roman garrison, and an adjutant. There was a parchment scroll in the officer's hands, and pleasurable malice in his eyes.

"Call off your men," he ordered abruptly; "tell them to stop work."

"What do you mean?" Aquilas stammered.

"I mean what I say. Call them off. There is to be no more work."

"What right have you to give such an order? You have no control over us."

"Maybe not," Milo sneered. "But the Emperor has, and this"—he brandished the scroll—"is an order from Antioch. The Emperor has issued a decree. There is to be no more work done on this spot. And no more Jews allowed either. The old rules are in force again."

"But it is impossible.... We began on the basis of an imperial decree!"

"It has been canceled. The Emperor has changed his mind. You will have to call in your men. Here is the order—read it yourself!" He thrust the parchment into Aquilas' hands.

Laborers attracted by the dispute began to cluster about. "Move on," Milo ordered. "I am talking to your overseer, not to you."

The men did not budge. The report of what was happening now spread over the hillside. Other laborers came on the run, carrying their axes, mattocks and spades, until a sizable crowd hemmed in the officer and his men. The workers rumbled with anger.

"It is a lie!"

"A Roman fraud!"

"We will not quit...."

"Let us go back to work!"

Milo heard the last remark.

"I will arrest the first man who raises a finger."

"You will, eh?" a voice called. "Try and do it!"

A roar of rage ascended from the Jews. Picks, axes and shovels were raised. Milo looked apprehensively at the angry mob.

"These aren't my orders," he called appeasingly. "They are the Emperor's."

With a show of confidence they did not feel, the Romans turned into the wall of men that opened sullenly before them.

They walked casually, so casually that one of the Jews they passed saw the pallor of their faces, the cold sweat on their brows.

"They're scared," he jeered.

Others picked up the cry. Hoots and insults pursued the Romans until they were out of sight. Then the laborers, deprived of a butt for their rage, began to mill about, arguing, cursing, gesticulating savagely.

Recovering his authority, Aquilas called, "Back to your huts. Put away your tools."

No one moved.

"Do as I say," Aquilas insisted. "Do you think it is easy for me to give this order? You are not in charge here and I am not either. The Sanhedrin is. It now rests with them."

A burly stonecutter from Galilee protested from the midst of the crowd.

"Why must we obey the decree?" he asked. "There are five hundred of us here. They are a handful up there. They will not dare to interfere. I say that we continue!"

"Aye, aye!" voices called on all sides.

"And if they try," the laborer went on, emboldened, "we will know what to do."

"You will stop work until further orders," Aquilas thundered. "The Sanhedrin may still get this decree recalled."

"No," the stonecutter shouted. "We are tired of waiting for the rabbis. We have started, and by the God of Hosts this time we will finish the job, rabbis or no rabbis."

"So, it is you Naphthali"—the overseer's words dripped with guileful sarcasm—"blaspheming the name of the Lord in vain oaths, swearing by God's name. Who appointed you ruler and judge in Israel? Speak once more and you will have an excommunication to deal with. Is there to be no discipline among us? I have said that you will cease work until the sages can be informed."

Naphthali grumbled inarticulately. The crowd shifted sullenly but no one dared defy the authority of the Sanhedrin. With bowed heads the laborers made their way back to their barracks.

A few minutes later riders rode at breakneck speed, one toward Jamnia, the others in various directions to carry the evil tidings to the populace of Palestine.

All through the night the Roman soldiers on the Akra drank, diced and laughed uproariously, glorying in their triumph. Their voices carried through the clear air to the huts where the laborers sat listening. With each outburst the Jews stiffened, and talked the more resolutely of the hour having come.

The Sabbath was drawing toward its close. Meir's apartment was cool and shadowy with approaching twilight. It had been a slow, heavy afternoon with but little talk, and that dull and desultory. Both Meir and Beruriah had given up trying to hide their feelings. They had turned quiet, speaking gently to each other, but rarely and with no trace of the banter that once sparkled in their conversation. And Elisha, who was visiting with them, had come to Usha to suggest to his colleagues that they discontinue their group meetings. The prospect was not pleasant. Fretting over it, he had not been able to pretend lightheartedness.

Just before dusk, Meir set out to call on some friend who was ill, leaving Elisha and Beruriah alone. Meir's footsteps died away. The room was very quiet. Elisha looked up from the scroll in which he was reading. Beruriah was seated by an open window, the waning light illuminating her pale delicate face. Her frail hands drooped listlessly on her lap.

Pity surged up in him and his desire to comfort her was so strong that he could barely refrain from rising and putting his arm around her. With an effort he forced his eyes back to the manuscript. But he did not see the words. He was trying desperately to rise above the pulsing awareness of her presence.

Wild surmises checked the tumult of his feelings abruptly. Why was excitement thrilling through him now that they were alone? Why had her memory haunted him so constantly of late? Why had he returned so steadfastly to this place? Was it, as he had always imagined, so that he might enjoy the company of both of them, or, actually, so that he might be with her? He brushed his hand across his forehead. Had he fallen in love with Beruriah?

He must think clearly. From the very beginning he had been aware of the fact that he was idealizing this lovely woman. But now he was treading on dangerous ground. She was another man's wife, and that man his disciple and personal friend. And there was too short an interval between adoration and desire. Restless and hungry as he was, he might have to admit an urge of the flesh to her. It must never happen. He must never...

Hope and happiness died within him.

The letters on the scroll danced before his tortured eyes. The silence of the room pressed on him suffocatingly as he rallied himself for an inevitable renunciation. Sick with the effort of it, he lifted his face, strained and drawn, to gaze at her, hoping to provide himself for the future with memory.

Troubled by the intentness of his stare, Beruriah began to speak.

"You are leaving Usha after the Sabbath?" she inquired.

"Yes. I am on my way to ben Azzai's home in Tiberias." Elisha's voice was low and his manner quiet.

"How soon will you be back?"

"I am assigned to the court a fortnight hence."

"You will stay with us?"

"I am afraid not."

"Why?"

"I have accepted another invitation," he lied.

"Oh, I am sorry. Then the next time."

He did not answer.

"You will stay with us on your next visit, of course?" she repeated.

"I am afraid I impose on you too often...."

"Tell me honestly, Master"—she looked at him searchingly—"is it anything we have said or done? Have I offended or hurt you? Has Meir?"

"Oh, no," he reassured her, "it's not that."

She seized on his inadvertent admission. "Then there is something wrong!"

"No," he groped, "nothing specific. I do not think I ought to come here so often."

"Why so?"

"The expense to you..."

There was such indignation in her eyes that he was ashamed of his stupid excuse.

"Please don't urge me," he pleaded, his control almost gone.

Thoroughly concerned Beruriah insisted. "Pray tell me the real reason."

"Very well," he yielded. "I ... I ... Seeing you has come to be too important to me. I cannot come here again." He ended in a rush of words.

Her eyes widened, then she glanced down at her hands now clasped so tightly that even in the half-light he could detect the whiteness of their knuckles.

"I see," she whispered. "And I am sorry. It will be very hard. You have become so dear to us—to both of us. But it would be better to do as you say."

Elisha's heart was pounding so loudly against his ribs that

it took him several minutes to realize he was hearing also the pounding of a hard-driven horse in the streets. Amazed even in his distraction by the unprecedented violation of the Sabbath, he rushed to the window in time to catch a glimpse of a rider, coated with dust, tearing past the courtyard gate.

A moment later people returning from the street wailed the news that the Romans had stopped the building of the Temple.

"Master," Beruriah gasped, turning to Elisha, "is that possible?"

He nodded slowly, painfully.

"I knew all along it would end this way. We never had a chance against the Romans. They are too strong for us."

"But what will we do?"

"Nothing," he said heavily. "There's nothing any of us can do. We all want more than life permits."

CHAPTER XX

In the hall of ben Azzai's home in Tiberias, Akiba, ben Zoma and Elisha waited for their host. He had not been at the door to greet them when they entered. He was, the porter informed them, meditating in his study. Indeed, he had locked himself in two days before and had not come out since. Servants had entered his room to bring their master food and once to inform him of the disaster at Jerusalem. Except for those brief moments no one had seen him.

Seated on divans the three discussed the depressing news of the day before. They considered it from every conceivable angle, debated as to what should be done, and speculated anxiously over whether it would be possible to restrain the outraged populace. On one fact only they agreed immediately—their impotence against the Romans.

Elisha had to drive himself to attend the conversation with even half-hearted interest. He could not talk or care about an issue so remote as the rebuilding of the Temple. A more intimate sorrow, the parting from Beruriah, possessed him. The subject of discontinuing the meetings of the four would also have to wait for a time when, ceasing to feel, he could think again.

The rasp of curtain rings called their eyes to the door. There ben Azzai stood, framed in the lintel and posts, his hands groping feebly before him.

There was in his eyes a glittering vacancy, an intent absence of sight such as they had never seen before. Without a word of greeting he walked to the center of the room and stood trembling as with the ague. Akiba half-rose to help him. But ben Azzai began to speak, so softly that they could scarcely hear. Yet had he shrieked he could not have captured their attention more completely. Akiba sat down on the edge of his chair.

"For years." he intoned, "I have sought Him in vain. His footsteps, the imprint of His hand, the signature of His wisdom are all about me. On every leaf, in each mote, in the industry of the ant, the rage of the lion, the cunning of the spider, I detected traces of His presence. In Scripture I held His letter of love. Most of all, I felt closest to Him within my own mind and heart. But when I looked inward, lo, He was gone as though He had just passed from sight. And I stood like one who knows that his beloved is in the chamber with him, who senses her presence, recognizes the fragrance of her perfumes, who yearns to touch her but cannot. And I said to myself with Job:

> "'Behold, I go forward, but He is not there;
> And backward, but I cannot perceive Him:
> On the left hand, where He worketh, but I cannot
> behold Him;
> He hideth Himself on the right, that I cannot see Him.'"

"Long ago, I concluded that my body was a wall between us. Wherefore I fasted and denied myself the desire for woman in order to break it through. And when they asked me why I would not fulfill the first commandment of Scripture, 'Be fruitful and multiply,' I told them that mankind and its future generations could be maintained by others.

"It was a long, dark, weary way I traveled. But never did I doubt that I would arrive at my destination to drink there from the fountains of salvation. Then Elisha almost persuaded me that there was nothing beyond the veil—that my painful quest was a pilgrimage to nowhere.

"I hated him for murdering my dreams. Hush, Elisha, hear me out. Now I thank you because through your denial I was driven to the truth. For I had mistaken the demiurgic world-soul for God. Was it to be marveled at, if, having aimed at an illusory target I could not hear my arrow strike? Now since my discovery, my progress has been rapid. I am almost at the end of the road. Stay here, my friends, and watch while I walk through the last curtains and enter into His Presence. With you I would share the glory of the moment that is coming."

The three men sat transfixed, their skin crawling with terror. Even ben Zoma was frozen into quiet, as ben Azzai circled waveringly to face the wall. Standing before the blank expanse of plaster, he raised his hands and beat weakly, rhythmically against it, chanting a strange perversion of the Song of Songs:

"The winter is going, the rains are passing, the blossoms appear in the fields, the voice of the dove is heard at last. Open unto me, my beloved, my perfect one!"

Then his hands were still and there came as though across long leagues of distance a voice hushed with awe and wonder: "The veil is lifting. The wall is breaking through. Light flows over me and an intoxication as of wine. There is sweetness, too, sweetness within and everywhere. 'And God saw all which He had made and behold, it was good.' It is good, all good, aglow with light. The whole world is aglow with light…brighter and brighter…too bright to see, too dazzling, for no man may see Thee and live. I have asked after Thee, sought Thee in the night watches, and called out of the depths. Now do I, Simeon the son of Azzai—see—I see…"

He stiffened in a spasm, then his shoulders drooped forward onto the wall. Slowly he slid to the floor until he sat cross-legged; his great shaggy head scraped down along the plaster and came to rest between his knees.

Akiba, the first to reach him, groped for his wrist.

"He is dead," he cried out incredulously. "Blessed be the Righteous Judge."

Elisha and ben Zoma repeated the ancient formula after him. For a full moment the three stood so. Then they carried ben Azzai to a couch. His large form was surprisingly light, like a shell from which all inner substance has been burned.

CHAPTER XXI

RAIN fell steadily on the sodden streets of Caesarea, quiet with night except for the continuous patter of water or the resounding footsteps of some late passer-by.

Within the shuttered shop a flickering lamp threw a patch of light on the unmoving form of Nicholaus and the table on which his forearms rested. Its rays struggled through the shadows to touch here a sheet of parchment and there the gleaming name-tag of some scroll. In the darkness of a corner, the face of Elisha was a white mask shining forth from obscurity as though disembodied. He was talking easily, almost casually, his voice perfectly controlled. But his words, for all their restraint and understatement, were freighted with desolation.

"...My position, I am afraid, is scarcely enviable. It is taken for granted pretty generally that in some devious way I who loved him dearly, who owed him so much, am responsible for what befell Simeon. And the worst of it is that in a sense the suspicion is justified. He was always a strange, withdrawn person, forever delving in mysteries. And he had worn himself out with fasting and self-mortification. Yet I cannot help feeling that had he not tried to help me, he might never have met so sudden, so tragic an end. At his funeral everyone avoided me studiously. And when I arrived at the Sanhedrin the day before yesterday, my colleagues were, it seemed to me, quite reserved, though I may have mistaken their concern over the Roman edict for personal coolness. But what I could not understand at all was the absence of Shraga...."

"Who?" Nicholaus queried.

"One of the disciples, a fellow who for some reason or other has always schemed against me. I had confidently expected to be treated to the spectacle of him and his friends scurrying about triumphantly, trying to create a public scandal out of Simeon's death. Then the news came that the populace had taken matters into its own hands and that an army was gathering at Beth Rimmon. The riddle was solved. Shraga and his associates had other more important business on hand than stirring up trouble for me. In any case, the session adjourned at once so that a committee of rabbis might set out to avert a rebellion.

"But my escape from the open inquisition with which I was threatened does not blind me to the fact that suspicion of me is spreading rapidly, that I am dangerously near the edge of a precipice."

Indignation flared in Nicholaus, the anger one feels with a brother who hurts himself wantonly.

"In the name of all the gods," he exploded, "what are you doing to yourself? What are you looking for? Wealth? Prestige? Position? You have all these right now. You should be altogether happy. And yet you are miserable—I can feel it for all your brave speech. Can you not be satisfied? And this way of living that fills you with restlessness and discontent—I am not a Jew but even I have sensed something lovely in Judaism, in its faith and in its morality with its emphasis on pity. Even its rituals are not without poetic grace. See how many Gentiles have been converted to your religion. Does that not prove that it possesses virtues which the Greek world lacks? These are at your disposal now. What more do you want?"

"You know, Nicholaus," Elisha replied obliquely, "I have of late made an interesting discovery about the processes of living. In our Tradition there are a number of epigrams about the prerequisites of human happiness. One of the sages generations ago enumerated truth, justice and peace as essentials; another, God's law, His service and acts of mercy. Actually, the stuff of spiritual peace is of a much less heroic character. A man has happiness if he possesses three things—those whom he loves and who love him in turn, confidence in the worth and continued existence of the group of which he is a part, and last of all, a truth by which he may order his being."

"But what has all this to do with you?" Nicholaus challenged.

"These are just the qualities that are passing from my life. My friends are slipping away from me. I have little hope for the Jewish people. Sooner or later it must be engulfed by the Roman Empire. And as for beliefs—of all the doctrines I once accepted none seems sure to me any longer. There is one article I still hold. I am convinced of the existence of God. But for the others, I vacillate between doubt and outright denial. Prop after prop has been withdrawn from inside the structure of my life until the whole edifice is virtually suspended in space."

"But who is withdrawing those props?" Nicholaus protested in exasperation. "You yourself. You can rewin your friends and their respect if you want to. You can restore your confidence in your people. Your colleagues seem to experience no difficulties in that regard. But these are not the crux of the matter. It is obvious that your unhappiness springs from your religious perplexities. That, too, you can mend, if you will it. Force yourself to believe and the problem is solved."

"Do you suppose I have not tried self-suppression?" Elisha sighed. "It's no use. I cannot prevent myself from thinking. Come what may I must reason my way out. If the old truth has failed me I must find another."

"Phrases, empty phrases," Nicholaus snapped, all the more sharply for his concern. "Truth—certainty—both pretty words. Do you really know what you mean by them?"

"Yes, indeed," Elisha replied calmly, simply. "I am seeking a theology, a morality, a ritual, confirmed by logic in the fashion of geometry so that one need not forever wonder whether what he believes is true."

"An obsession," Nicholaus breathed in despair, "a veritable obsession. Do you think man capable of attaining certainty in these matters? Do you imagine that life is as simple as lines, points and planes to be reduced to a series of propositions?"

"It has been done in mathematics," Elisha replied stubbornly. "Why not elsewhere as well?"

"Granted that it can be achieved, must you sacrifice your

peace and comfort for it? Are you so blind as not to reckon the cost?"

"Of course, the price is high. But that makes no difference. According to our sacred literature there once was a man called Job who stood before the inscrutable universe and demanded an answer to its mystery. It did not reply. Therefore he repeated his question, hurling it again and again into its unresponsive face. And when his friends protested that he was destroying himself by his obduracy, he turned and challenged the Presence behind things—

" 'Wherefore,' he demanded, 'hidest Thou Thyself from me? Wilt Thou harass a driven leaf?'

"I know how he felt. The great curiosity is like that. It is not a matter of volition. It is stark inner compulsion, dire necessity. And he against whom it moves has no more choice than a leaf driven in a gale. No, there is no retreat. Forward is the only way."

"But how?" Nicholaus asked, his misgivings submerged momentarily by the surging passion of Elisha's determination.

"Two courses are before me. I wish first of all to make contact with the Christians and Gnostics here in Caesarea."

"What good will that do you?" Nicholaus inquired, wary now.

"It is not impossible that they can teach me some principle to give me direction."

"And what will your colleagues say of your association with heretics?"

"There is no reason why they should learn of it."

"But suppose they do?"

"Then what have I to lose? I cannot remain as I am."

"And the other course," Nicholaus suggested hopefully, "to which you referred a moment ago?"

"The last resort," Elisha replied laconically. "To begin at the beginning. You see, Nicholaus, it is just that which I have never attempted. I have always started at the end. My procedure has been ever to try to demonstrate predetermined conclusions, the doctrines of Tradition. I have spoken glibly of the method of Euclid without ever applying it seriously. If I am driven to it, I shall do exactly as does the geometry book. I shall lay away all beliefs, principles and affirmations, and set out afresh accepting only what is as thoroughly self-evident as the axioms and postulates of mathematics. . . . "

"But," Nicholaus interrupted, shaken, "that means abandoning everything."

"Only tentatively, of course, until I arrive at my conclusions."

"In the meantime continuing to conform to the rites and practices of your people?"

"Yes, if I can without compromising my conscience."

"But look here," Nicholaus cried, discerning a possibility he had not envisaged before. "Suppose the results of your experiment are not consistent with the Jewish religion?"

Elisha's voice was strained, as though his throat had tightened, but he did not falter.

"I have considered that possibility, too. I hope it may never become an actuality. Yet, should that be my destiny, I am prepared to assume it."

"The Nazarenes, or Jewish Christians," Nicholaus sighed heavily, choosing the lesser evil, "conduct services daily in a synagogue off the Via Herodiana. As for the Gentile Christians, one is an old customer of mine. His name is Justin. I can easily arrange a meeting for you. Regarding the Gnostics, I shall find out, if you like, when and where the next public lecture will be held."

"I want to thank you," Elisha said when later they stood in the doorway.

"Please," Nicholaus silenced him, "do not thank me. I've loved you since you were a boy. No matter what other doubts we may entertain, we cannot question the reality of friendship. And in a world where so little is certain that is a great deal."

CHAPTER XXII

FROM CREST TO CREST THE amphitheater-like valley of Beth Rimmon swarmed with a motley assembly of artisans, merchants, students and peasants turned into soldiers. The call to rebellion had gone forth and they had come from all over Palestine in numbers so large that they blanketed the earth solidly among the pomegranate trees after which the place was named.

Before the rostrum, a heap of stones piled on the top of a mound, a stalwart farmer from the Southland exhibited a crude weapon to admiring acquaintances.

"I beat my ploughshare into a sword," he commented dryly. A roar of excited laughter followed the sally, ominous with auguries of war.

Stunned and bewildered, a little group of sages sat near the platform, observing the turbulent scene. They had come uninvited. For this meeting had been convoked not by them but by a secret government, by those little groups of zealots who in caves and cellars forged arms in preparation for the inevitable struggle with Rome. Only at the last moment had the Patriarch learned of the meeting. Instantly he had adjourned the Sanhedrin then in session and set out with a group of selected colleagues. When they had arrived in the valley they had been greeted with cold respect. Now they sat together knowing that they would be listened to but not obeyed, that other hands had taken the reins from theirs.

Two weeks had passed since the laborers on the Temple Mount had reluctantly laid down their tools. The first frenzy of the people had been supplanted by cold anger and a growing determination that a long-cherished hope would not be frustrated again. A commission of rabbis was to sail for Rome. The men of Palestine received the news with indifference. They were done with negotiations. If the Emperor would not give them what they wanted they would take it—even if the price were war.

A man mounted the rostrum, raised his hand for attention. The terraced hills stirred momentarily with increased motion as men settled themselves to listen, and then were quiet. Among the sages only Gamliel knew his name.

"It is Julianus of Tarsus, their leader," he whispered to his colleagues. The rabbis regarded him intently. They had heard of the chief of the insurgent party though none of them had met him, so hidden had been his movements.

His right arm upraised, he stood commanding silence, slender, graceful, almost effeminate in his elegant robe made in the Greek style. It was apparent even at a distance that his forelock, ear curls and beard were but of recent growth. No more than a month ago, the hair over his forehead had been clipped after the fashion of the pagans.

Patiently he waited until the silence was complete. Then he lowered his arm slowly and left the silence unbroken for a long minute. Into the stillness he hurled a challenging question, "What are we waiting for?" The hills alive with men roared in answer. He smiled at the full-voiced din, turned to the Patriarch and invited him respectfully to speak. Gamliel mounted the rostrum. Quiet had not yet been restored when he began so that his opening words were lost to all except those near by. He spoke earnestly, insisting on Israel's ideal of peace. But the crowd, even when it heard, was in no mood to respond to sermons. It applauded his remarks feebly. When he was among his colleagues again he shook his head in discouragement and self-reproach, whispering, "It was of no avail. I did badly."

"Do not fear, Gamliel," Joshua said resolutely. "Somehow we shall stop them yet."

The sun stood directly overhead as Julianus rose again, his shadow a little black patch about his feet.

"My brethren," he began in Aramaic, faulty from unfamiliarity, but skillful in devices, "enough of talk. The time has come to put words away and to lay hold on deeds. Are you agreed?"

A thunder of approval rolled back from the terraces.

"But you will do the fighting," he went on. "Therefore you must vote, group by group, so that there be no mistake as to who is launching this rebellion, whether it be our masters here"—he bowed with mocking politeness to the members of the Sanhedrin—"or you men of Israel. You shall ballot in a moment, but before you do let me give you point by point the arguments of war."

He held up before them a delicately manicured hand clenched into a fist.

"One," he counted, his index finger snapping erect: "The Emperor Trajan is now dangerously ill. Whether he live or die, and you know my preference, the whole Empire will be beset with convulsions. Already Roman generals are trying to buy the Pretorian Guard. On the Rhine, on the Danube, on the Euphrates, in Mauretania, in Alexandria and in Antioch, every military commander has his soldiers prepared to seize the crown for him.

"Two," he enumerated, liberating a slender second finger: "The Empire is exhausted by the Parthian campaign. The treasury is empty. Do not let yourselves be fooled by reports of Trajan's victories. He has won none. Rome cannot stand another war.

"Three," he continued, projecting his thumb: "We have been in communication with foreign powers. The Parthians have promised their assistance. There are provinces in Asia Minor with whom we have established secret relations. I do not wish to mention their names for we doubtless have our share of spies and informers here. But now is the time to strike."

Another finger unfolded as he shouted explosively, "Four: We are ready for war. Every one of you is armed. Our secret committees have vast armories. Even our strategy has been worked out and our commanders chosen. Never fear, we will not make the mistakes that were made fifty years ago. This time we will not shut ourselves up in fortified cities and allow the Romans to besiege us at their leisure. We will fight as we did under the Maccabees, in the hill country with sorties and surprise attacks. We know this land and the Romans do not. In this kind of warfare, we can hold out for fifty years."

The full hand was unclenched as he shouted, "Five, last and most important: It is not the Jews of Palestine alone who strike. If we go into war, one hundred and fifty thousand of our brethren are ready in Egypt and Cyrenaica, fifty thousand in Cyprus alone, another hundred thousand in Asia Minor and Syria. This can be told, and let any Roman spy or Jewish informer carry the news back to his master for his harlot's hire: our armies in Africa and Asia and the islands move on the first of the month of Kislev whether we do or not. A few weeks hence they raise the standard of rebellion. If we do not support them, they will be fighting on behalf of a pack of sniveling curs who lack the courage to fight for themselves. Will you leave them in the lurch? You will not."

The hand fully unclenched hung in the air over his head, its fingers moving slightly, like the legs of a spider, as he went on, "Now is the time. As for the reasons, who does not know them? Freedom for our people, release from oppression and, greatest of all, the rebuilding of our Temple. They have toyed with us, these Romans, make no mistake about it, as one teases a dog or a child, offering it what it desires and then withdrawing it. But we are neither dogs nor children. We are the descendants of the Maccabees. If they will not give us what we have a right to, we will take it. By force of arms we shall win our freedom, our land, our Temple, and our self-respect. Now is the time to strike and this must be our answer to their perfidy!"

He ceased to speak and looked up in silence at his hand poised above him. Thousands of eyes followed it, watching it drop slowly to shoulder height, and then close quickly into the bold, clenched fist of violence.

"This is our answer, I say. What say you?"

Swords and spears waved over the valley like branches tossing in a tempest. They beat with mad clamor against shields, or thumped against rocks and soil. Through the din, wild cries rang like the breaking of the whirlwind.

"The answer," Julianus screamed over the tumult, "is apparent. It is unnecessary to vote."

The sages sat in stunned silence, overawed by this strident passion. Gamliel leaned over to Joshua. "The demon is in that man. In Heaven's name, get up. Say something before it is too late."

Joshua shook his head. "I will try," he said.

He waited until Julianus had restored order and was prepared to continue. As the rebel's mouth opened, Joshua called out suddenly in a voice that resounded like a thunderclap: "Hold on a moment, Julianus, our Strategos!"

Men craned their necks to see who had interrupted. Fascinated by the promise of drama they watched the old sage climb the side of the rock pile. When he stood on the rostrum so that his ugly face was visible in the clear light, a whisper swept through the crowd, "It is Rabbi Joshua."

Julianus hesitated and stepped back on the mound.

"Hold on, Strategos," Joshua repeated to him over his shoulder.

The multitude snickered at the satirical title with which Joshua had hailed Julianus. For whether by design or accident he had addressed him with the Greek word for general.

Joshua's powerful voice rolled out over the tiers of men. Calmly and slowly he enumerated the advantages of peace and detailed the risks of war.

"Two freedoms there are," he argued, "which we desire: a freedom of our souls and a freedom for our bodies. The first we have. We teach our Torah and live our own life. The Roman government ventures not to interfere. In great measure we possess freedom of the body, also. Bit by bit, the old restrictions are being lifted. The Jew tax is no more. To be sure, there are galling restraints imposed on us. But then, the whole world is in thralldom, the mighty lands of Egypt and Gaul as well as little Palestine. It is not given in our present world order for men to be absolutely free."

Then, when he knew he had their full attention, his tone changed subtly until his voice was sharp with satire.

"You have heard much from Julianus here and from his advisers. They have spoken of their carefully laid plans. 'We have prepared this, we have decided that, we are ready for such and such a circumstance.' What puzzles me is, who are they that they shall act as our rulers? Who has appointed them princes and judges in Israel?"

Joshua turned toward Julianus, pointing a gnarled finger at him.

"This is the first time," he shouted in acid words, "in the history of our people that one who would lead us offers as his qualifications the fact that he dresses like a pagan, wears his hair like a heathen, and speaks our tongue with a Greek accent. Whence, O Julianus, comes that noble passion of yours for Jews and Judaism, seeing that it finds voice in the mouth of one who is by every sign a half-Jew? What personal grudge, what selfish ambition, do you serve under this guise?

"The provocation Julianus tells us is there," he went on without waiting for an answer. "The Romans have denied us the Temple they offered us. Aye, we grieve over that fact, Gamliel, the sages, you and I. But pray, why should Julianus be so concerned? What would he do with the Temple if it were built? Would he visit it and pray in its courts? Would he let his earlocks grow longer and turn from half a pagan into a full Jew?

"I am a Jew. I have been a Jew, not for one month or year, but all my life. My earlocks are not a growth of this season. And I say to you, yearning for our Sacred House as I do, that we must keep the peace."

Joshua paused, smiled, and went on in a voice so soft that men leaned forward to catch each word: "Once the lion fell ill of a bone that had lodged in his throat. He promised vast rewards to anyone who could cure him. Along came the crane and offered its services. The great jaws were opened, the bird stuck its bill down the beast's throat and took out the bone. The lion coughed with relief, rolled over on his side and promptly fell asleep. The crane squawked demanding its compensation. The lion did not answer. The crane shrieked, the lion did not hear. The crane opened its puny beak and prepared to tweak the lion, to peck at him, or to twist his fur. Then the lion decided that matters had gone far enough. 'You want your reward? You have your life. Go brag to the birds of your feather that you put your head in my mouth and that it is still on your neck.' "

The audience gasped at the appositeness of the fable, then broke into self-ridiculing laughter.

"I am a rabbi," Joshua continued, "a preacher, and you are perhaps at this moment impatient of sermons. But let me tell you just one more parable. There is an old tradition, handed down from our fathers, that generations before Moses the tribe of Ephraim, wearied of Egyptian slavery and determined to liberate itself, rose in rebellion against the Pharaohs. After a long war it fought its way out of the land of bondage. But its victory was unavailing for the time was not yet ripe, God was not yet ready. Into the wilderness they moved, only to die, because they sought to anticipate the end. So with all evils in the world. There comes a time when the poisonous fruit, full-ripened, falls from the tree by itself. He who plucks it too soon must perish in agony as its venom courses through his veins. Do not, my brethren, anticipate the end. Do not force God's hand. His sword of judgment lies in its scabbard. Some day it will come forth, flashing with lightning—but only when He is ready. The Master of the Orchard knows when to shake the Tree of Evil. Until then, to your tents, O Israel, you have no share in the house of Julianus." No one obeyed. But dissension swept the valley like the rippling of wheat in the wind. The voice of the old sage became that of a commanding king: "In the name of the Sanhedrin, the rabbis and teachers of Israel, who are its only properly constituted leaders, I command you. To your tents!"

Men stirred uneasily, unable to arrive at a decision. Then, at the fringe of the crowd, someone unhitched his horse and slung his saddlebag over it.

Julianus scrambled forward across the mound. A stone rolled under his weight. He stumbled and fell to his knees. Frantically he attempted to recover his footing. But his ankle was caught between two boulders. He cursed madly as he jerked his leg and though his lieutenants helped to tug and push he was trapped.

From the writhing knot, one figure detached itself. It was Shraga the Levite. His eyes glowed with an insane anxiety. His scar a white stripe across his writhing face, flecks of foam on his lips, he rushed toward the rostrum. But with a darting movement Joshua planted himself in his path.

"Not another step," he commanded.

"Out of my way, Master," Shraga shrieked. And when the sage did not move he twisted to one side to pass.

Joshua's gnarled hands seized an arm.

"Let me go, Rabbi. Or by the Lord of Hosts, I shall strike you down."

"Hold your tongue," the old man snapped.

For a moment the two men strained against each other. Then Shraga looked into the blazing eyes before him and quailed.

By this time Julianus had torn himself free. Skirting the two men, he reached the crest of the mound and shouted for attention. Not even thunder could have been heard in the tumult that had arisen. For the whole valley had come alive as though a dam had burst, releasing the impounded humanity. His associates clustered about him, gesticulating, offering frenzied suggestions. But no device could check the long lines of men who plodded through the passes homeward bound.

So an insurrection was averted in Palestine. But in Egypt,

Cyrenaica and Cyprus, it burst forth and raged for bloody months. Despite initial victories, the defeat of the rebels in those lands was complete. They were slain by the thousands, enslaved by the tens of thousands. When the war was over, the Romans were stronger than ever, the Jews weaker. In their convocations the sages of the Sanhedrin worked indefatigably to minimize the losses. But in their secret meeting places the zealots of Palestine still forged arms in preparation for their next opportunity.

CHAPTER XXIII

ON THE DAY WHEN JOSHUA addressed the Assembly at Beth Rimmon, Elisha walked along the Via Herodiana looking for the Nazarene conventicle to which Nicholaus had directed him.

The morning was bright and clear, an interlude of fair weather before the rainy season settled into a continuous downpour. The early sun threw long shadows across the deserted streets. The neighborhood through which Elisha passed was the most poverty-stricken of Caesarea. Dilapidated houses, the dwellings of poor artisans and starving freedmen, fronted the main thoroughfare. Between them, at intervals, narrow alleys opened leading to a maze of passageways, slimy and foul-smelling. In one of these he found the shabby building which was his destination. The droning chant of worship informed him that despite the earliness of the hour the service had already begun.

The little room into which he slipped was furnished with crude wooden benches and lighted only by dim windows and a flickering oil lamp over the Ark of the Law. The congregation of some thirty or forty people seemed, as far as Elisha could discern from a seat in an obscure corner, to be entirely Jewish. Every worshiper wore the conventional phylacteries and fringed garment. The prayers were those with which he was familiar except that at one point the reader omitted the passage recently inserted by the Sanhedrin against dissenters and their heresies, and that at another, he declaimed the Ten Commandments, a practice which the synagogue had abandoned largely because some Christians insisted that of all the Tradition only this need be observed.

Just before the close of the service a scroll was taken from the Ark. When the reading began Elisha expected to hear a selection from the Law of Moses. The passage however turned out to be an extract in Aramaic from the sayings of Jesus. The moral epigrams and parables he heard were lovely. He was stirred by their ring of authoritativeness strangely combined with bold kindliness. But aside from the phrasing and one report of a miracle, there was nothing in the citation which was new to him. Indeed in some instances the aphorisms were quoted literally as they had long been current in the academies.

It was during this reading that someone recognized him as a member of the Sanhedrin. A wave of whispering went through the congregation. People looked at him quickly and averted their eyes. Several persons seated near him edged away. He could well understand their unfriendliness, for the official leaders of Judaism had of late been hostile to these sectaries.

The service concluded with the singing of a hymn. Phylacteries were stripped off. Several men picked up bags of tools and rushed off to their day's labor. The congregation disbanded quickly. Then the reader who had conducted the service approached Elisha. He was a kindly Jew, soft-spoken and respectful for all that he was unmistakably suspicious.

"To what, Master," he asked cautiously, "may we ascribe the honor of the attendance of so distinguished a guest?"

Elisha, always uncomfortable before deference, smiled shyly. "I am not present," he assured him, "as a member of the Sanhedrin. I merely wish information concerning the beliefs and practices of your group."

Warily at first but with mounting enthusiasm as he was convinced of the friendliness of the stranger the Nazarene described his sect, its doctrines, its morality, and above all its Saviour. And it was not out of policy that at the end he stressed the fact that he and his fellows were fully and completely loyal to the Tradition.

"The great rabbis and the members of the Sanhedrin are not fair to us," he protested. "We are good Jews, devout Jews, observant Jews. The only difference between us and other Jews is that we know that the time of which the prophets spoke has been fulfilled, that the Messiah has already come in the person of Jesus of Nazareth. Otherwise we follow the law to its last jot and tittle for so He enjoined upon us. Nevertheless, the sages insist on confusing us with the followers of Paul who are mainly Gentiles and who contemn not only God's revelation but the Master's injunction as well, in disregarding the ordinances prescribed by the Law of Moses."

"You will come to our service again, will you not?" he added, emboldened by Elisha's affability. "You see, we are all very simple folk without a single advocate in the Sanhedrin. At one time Eliezer the son of Hyrcanus was very friendly to us. But that was years ago. A few rabbis like Joshua have been kind enough to recommend letting us alone. But it would be gratifying if a great man like you would take an active interest in us and intercede occasionally on our behalf."

His sweet humility and unfeigned piety reminded Elisha of dozens of simple Jews whom he knew and loved.

"Of course," he promised. "I shall do what I can."

The man smiled, gratefully.

"Perhaps," he went on, "the Rabbi is interested in studying our faith for his own sake. He may have heard of our Savior and, like so many others, felt himself attracted to Him."

"Not exactly," Elisha corrected. "Right now I am merely seeking information. Most of all, I want to know on what your belief rests."

Without hesitation the Nazarene replied, "On Scripture, of course, which we revere as you do."

"On anything else as well?"

"Why yes, on the life and teachings of the Messiah also."

"And that is all?" Elisha asked eagerly, reckless of the implications of his question.

"What more," the Nazarene replied, startled, "would the Rabbi want than the fulfillment of the words of the prophets?"

"It's quite enough," Elisha conceded without conviction.

From beyond the door someone waiting for the Nazarene called impatiently, "Levi, you will be late."

"You will excuse me, Rabbi," the man said reluctantly. "I am a tanner by trade. Much as I should like to stay, I cannot. Will you visit us again?"

"Thank you," Elisha replied equivocally.

"But I have had no chance to answer your questions."

"Quite the contrary," Elisha assured him; "you have."

Somewhat perplexed, the man considered his answer.

"In any case," he said at last, "if you can put in a good word for us at the Sanhedrin, please do so."

"Of course."

"Thank you. And now I bid you farewell."

"Peace be to you," Elisha responded.

With that he was gone.

Elisha stood at the doorway of the deserted chapel and looked after the man until he was lost from sight on the Via Herodiana, now bustling with activity. He had come to the conventicle in the hope of finding some clue. He had met a lovable human being. He had been touched by an example of piety and untroubled faith. But he had not been helped.

Upon returning to his tavern, Elisha found a note informing him that Nicholaus had arranged an interview for him with Justin, the leader of the Gentile Christians.

At the hour appointed for the meeting Elisha knocked at a gateway in a wall fronting on a sunlit suburban street.

A porter appeared.

"My name is Elisha. Your master is expecting me."

"Pray come this way," the porter said.

Leading Elisha across a little garden into the house he showed him into a room. A man dressed in the negligee of a Greek gentleman greeted him.

"You are Rabbi Elisha?"

"Yes."

"I am Justin. I am delighted to meet you. Please be seated," he said, cordially indicating a chair. "And let me give you something to drink. The day is quite warm, you must be tired from your walk. Then we can have that talk for which I have been waiting."

Justin rose to fetch a flagon and cups. He was a frail person of middle years. His face, pale, lined and tired, was that of a student, an impression confirmed by the bookcases along the walls and the scrolls and tablets that littered a table.

"This may be tepid," Justin apologized holding out a cup, "but it should be refreshing."

Elisha withdrew the hand he had extended, saying, "Is this wine?"

"Why yes. And good wine, too, imported from Greece."

"I am sorry, but I may not drink it...." As he spoke, Elisha winced over the contrast between his external conformity and internal rebellion.

"A thousand apologies," Justin burst out contritely. "I had forgotten the prohibition of your law against the wine of the Gentiles. But you will take a cup of water?"

"Yes, of course, thank you."

Justin summoned a servant to bring it.

"Then," Elisha surmised, accepting the cup, "you do not heed the injunctions about foods?"

"No," Justin replied. "We do not believe that one is infected with idolatry merely by drinking of a brew, some of which may have been poured as a libation to some pagan god. As we see it, it is not what goes into the mouth but what comes out of it that defiles the spirit."

"So you have renounced the Law of Moses?"

"Not quite," Justin corrected. "To be sure, we no longer observe the rituals prescribed in it. But that is because we insist that they have been superseded by a new dispensation of our Savior. In their time they represented the divine will. In our age we have a fuller, simpler revelation of it."

"Again revelation," Elisha sighed inaudibly.

Justin proceeded to outline the doctrines of his group:

how Adam, created for innocence, had corrupted himself and tainted his seed with sin; how the law of Moses, given for salvation, had served only to multiply the occasions for transgression; and how, for the redemption of mankind, God had taken on human form and suffered death so that through belief in Him men might be saved.

Of all this Elisha had some knowledge. The Jewish academies were not uninformed of what was happening on the fringe of their religion. But what surprised him was the number of differences between the two Christian sects, Jewish and Gentile, and the bitterness with which they disagreed on the crucial point: had the Law of Moses been annulled or was it still binding?

From the description of the internal life of the new church the conversation drifted into a discussion of the interpretations to be put on certain passages in the Old Testament. Justin insisted that the divinity of Jesus and his co-existence with the Godhead had been foretold in Scripture. Elisha denied the assertion. For a time they argued in a friendly fashion over the fact that one of the Hebrew words for God was plural in form. They discussed the line, "Let *us* make man in *our* image" and whether the verse in Isaiah should be read "behold a virgin" or "behold a young woman shall conceive and give birth to a son."

The afternoon was far advanced when they were done with the theme.

"I give it up," Justin cried with a despair not altogether pretended. "I once argued these matters with Rabbi Tarfon, and with no more success. Well have you Jews been called a stiff-necked people."

"Perhaps," Elisha teased, "our stubbornness is the result of the fact that we are right."

"Now, now," Justin chided, "do not bait me. We will be quarreling in a moment. Besides I have a feeling that it is not for this that you sought me out. You must have had some question which I, ungracious host, have submerged in a flood of words."

"Frankly," Elisha replied, "that is so. I came less to learn of the details of your belief than what it is on which you base it."

"On Scripture, of course," came the instantaneous answer, "on the prophecies of the Old Testament. On the evidences of the life of the Christ."

"Then you do not rest your belief on logical reasoning as well, on philosophy, on scientific proof?"

"Of course we do. We assume, naturally enough, that anything attested by the Word of God must be reasonable and demonstrable."

"I am afraid that you do not understand me. What I mean is this: Do you accept your basic presuppositions on faith and then use reason to confirm them, or do you first demonstrate them and then set them up as doctrine?"

"Ah," Justin murmured, "so that is it."

His face, which all through the conversation had been animated by interest, now sagged again into lines of fatigue. For a while he reflected without speaking. "Let me tell you something about myself," he said, as though he had arrived at some difficult resolve. "You will find my answer in what I shall have to say."

With that, he proceeded to recount the story of his life, the tale of a young Samaritan who set out to study philosophy, who went through system after system only to find none altogether convincing and who finally stumbled onto Christianity.

"You see," he concluded, "these were the alternatives: either faith or nothing. How I chose you can judge for yourself. Does that answer you?"

Elisha nodded.

Later, on his way back to his lodgings, Elisha felt, underneath his pleasure at meeting Justin and the stimulation of talking to him, a sad disappointment. He had not had high expectations of being helped by the Christians. But he was depressed nonetheless that he had found no more than he had anticipated, two versions of the old, faith-anchored Judaism, differing from it only in their elaborations.

In his little room in the tavern Elisha prepared the next night for the third of his adventures among the sectaries, a Gnostic lecture to which Nicholaus was to escort him. This was to be his introduction to a group predominantly Gentile and Nicholaus had cautioned him not to be too conspicuously Jewish in dress. He pushed his earlocks behind his ears. The fringes on the corners of his garment he tied into little knots until they were almost unnoticeable. Holding a mirror before himself, he considered his black beard and decided it would pass. The wearing of beards was as much a Greek as a Hebrew mode, although of recent years under the influence of the Roman fashion the smooth-shaven face had become popular among younger pagans. Elisha had long ceased to regard matters of hairdress as important. Nevertheless, compunctions troubled him as he concealed the most conspicuous marks of his identity.

There was a tap at the door. Expecting to welcome Nicholaus, Elisha threw it open. To his surprise three men stood in the hallway. At first he did not recognize them. Then with dismay he identified them as the syndics of the Jewish community of Caesarea.

The tall man was Musaeus, a local merchant-prince and banker who, it was rumored, was the owner of twenty galleys. In the half-light Elisha observed his peculiar garb which, like his name, might be either Greek or Jewish, representing a nice compromise between the demands of the Tradition and the exigencies of Greek commercial life.

In the center stood a trembling graybeard, Reuben the son of Asher, lay head of the great synagogue of Caesarea, and first officer of the Jewish civic council. The man on whose arm he leaned was his son-in-law, Abba, the principal of the local academy, but a scholar of insufficient attainments to be a member of the Sanhedrin.

Elisha was shaken. He had thought that his presence in Caesarea was unknown to his fellow Jews. The three men, too, seemed taken aback as though they had not believed when they knocked that they would find him. Forcing a show of composure, Elisha greeted his uninvited guests and ushered them into the room. He remembered his costume but it was too late to do anything about it. The three men seated themselves, their staffs of office across their knees, their faces inscrutable.

When he had recovered his poise Elisha opened the conversation.

"To what," he asked politely, "do I owe this honor?"

"We had heard," Reuben replied, speaking for his companions, "that you were a visitor in our city. It pained us that you paid us no official visit. After several days went by we resolved that if the man of learning would not come to us we would go to him, no matter where he might be found."

The oblique reference to the obscurity of his lodgings did not escape Elisha.

"Gentlemen," he said with elaborate formality, "I owe you an apology for the seeming discourtesy of which you complain. But, as it happens, I am in Caesarea on urgent personal business. I had hoped to slip in and out of town, thus avoiding social obligations which, pleasurable to be sure, would nevertheless constitute a drain on the time of which I have so little."

Reuben nodded his head as though he understood. His two companions followed his lead. No one commented on Elisha's dress. There was an awkward silence in which Elisha offered no information and they dared not ask questions.

"But pray," Elisha inquired at last, as much to make conversation as to satisfy his curiosity, "how did you learn that I was in Caesarea?"

Both Musaeus and Abba looked to Reuben. The old man hesitated. When he spoke it was with a half-apologetic smile. "The rumor spread yesterday that a sage had visited a conventicle of the Christian sectaries. Indeed, some of the heretics boasted that they were going to make a convert of him. Naturally we were interested. We made inquiries, learned that it was you, discovered where you were staying, and here we are."

Reuben said all this without the least suggestion of criticism in tone or word, as though it were most normal for a distinguished scholar to slip furtively into Caesarea and to associate with heretical groups. Honeyed with blandness though his words were, there could be no mistaking their reproach. Beneath his courtesy he was expressing the censure of the Jewish community.

"It was very kind of you to make these inquiries," Elisha murmured.

"Not at all," the three protested.

"And how long will the Master be in town?" Reuben continued.

"I expect to leave for my home tomorrow morning."

The three men considered his answer. The regret in the old man's voice rang ungenuine.

"Alas, I had hoped you would remain over the Sabbath so we might have the privilege of hearing you preach."

"Ah, yes," Abba added, "and I had planned to invite you to lecture at the academy."

But the scholar was by no means as skillful a dissembler as his father-in-law. He was transparently relieved that he was being spared inviting Elisha to deliver an academic address. The satisfaction of the two was so painfully obvious that Musaeus, the merchant, hastened to put a better face on the whole matter.

"Master," he urged with the wiliness of a trader, "will you not reconsider your decision to leave?"

"No, I am sorry. My business was completed today. I must leave tomorrow."

"Your business, Master?" Reuben asked. "Perhaps an assignment to investigate the activities of heretics or something related to the unfortunate gathering at Beth Rimmon?"

The question was put with timid hopefulness. All his life the old man had revered rabbis. Now he was reluctant to accept the situation on its sorry appearance. Obviously he wanted to hear that Elisha was in Caesarea on behalf of the Sanhedrin, engaged in some unimpeachable mission which required anonymity and disguise. But Elisha could not bring himself to lie.

"No," he reiterated, his head erect, "my business is entirely personal."

At that very instant Nicholaus put his head through the doorway, calling breezily, "Well, Elisha, are you ready? Oh, I beg your pardon!"

Ruin was complete. With the bravado of one who knows that all is lost Elisha invited Nicholaus into the room. There his heathenism was glaringly revealed in his gray philosopher's mantle. In dour amusement Elisha presented him to the three men. The Jews rose, acknowledged the introduction stiffly, murmured to Elisha that they would take no more of his time, and withdrew.

Nicholaus dropped into the chair vacated by Abba, a look of concern on his face. "I am afraid I walked in at the wrong moment. Who were those fellows?"

"Three leaders of the Jewish council here. Somehow they found out that I have been visiting the Nazarenes and the Christians."

Nicholaus whistled softly.

"I hope my breaking in did not do any harm."

Elisha smiled wanly.

"No, the damage was done in any event."

"Perhaps we had better not attend the lecture tonight," Nicholaus said after a moment. "If it was so grave an offense to visit the Nazarenes who, after all, are Jews, this will be worse."

As Nicholaus spoke, Elisha began to perceive the full import of the incident. The elders of Caesarea could scarcely be expected to make a secret of their discovery. Ultimately the story must become common knowledge. To the suspicion of him, already widespread, there would be added this first overt, unmistakable indication of apostasy. What was more, even if his colleagues should prefer to ignore the entire episode, Shraga and the war party would be certain to exploit it to the full. Their influence—and it had increased of late—might be sufficient to precipitate an official investigation. He might be asked for an accounting of himself. Questions would be addressed to him, questions which he would be unable to answer....

Nicholaus saw his thin face turn pale, his jaws tighten.

"Can they do anything serious to you?" he asked anxiously. "After all, you're a Roman citizen."

"It's not violence I'm worried about. But they may indict me. If they should, there would be no escaping excommunication."

"Look here, Elisha," Nicholaus counseled. "It was I who was eager to protect your position, who wanted you to turn back. But you've gone too far. Don't wait for them to ruin you. You are still young. A man not yet forty has the best of life before him. Cut loose now. Go to Italy or Syria, where you can work out your problem in quiet."

The prospect of the peace and freedom to be found outside Palestine held Elisha in breathless contemplation for a moment. Then his sobriety reasserted itself.

"No," he rejected the suggestion resolutely. "I am no criminal that I should run away. Mine is a dignified enterprise, a quest for conviction. I owe it to my self-respect to take its consequences. Besides it may well be that I may find here among my own people what I seek. To doubt as I do is not yet final denial. It would be stupid to reject the Tradition altogether until I have exhausted its last resources.

"Most of all," he paused and went on more softly, "this is the only world I have ever known. In it are all the persons I love, all the scenes that are dear to me, all the habits of living that are as natural to me as breathing. Leaving it for some strange, alien land would be half-death. And," he added with a wry smile, "I am not yet ready for suicide, even in part."

CHAPTER XXIV

ONE MORNING SOME MONTHS LATER Simeon ben Zoma failed to appear at a lecture at which he was expected. At first no one took the fact seriously, not even after casual inquiry disclosed that he had arrived in Usha the preceding day. Always erratic, he had become increasingly undependable. Joshua and Akiba took over his classes.

But when Simeon was not present at vesper worship in the synagogue that night, his colleagues grew concerned. A disciple, dispatched to the inn where he lodged, brought back the report that the luggage of the missing sage was in his room but that no one at the tavern had seen him since the evening before. A quiet search was instituted. By midnight every house in Usha had been visited without yielding a trace of him.

Thoroughly alarmed, the sages, disciples and townspeople procured fagots and lanterns, divided themselves into groups, allocated districts about the village to one another, and set out to hunt for him in the countryside.

Joshua, Akiba and Meir joined a party assigned to one of the main highways. Spread out on both sides of the road, where Joshua walked so that he might be spared the difficulty of traversing broken fields, they moved forward slowly, torches glaring in an irregular line, calls passing back and forth. By the time they came to a crossroad the lights had burned out. Only the blue glow of stars shone on a marble pillar of Hermes, God of Wayfarers, which marked the intersection of routes. There they gathered about Joshua for consultation.

Into the whispers of the group a faint weird chanting penetrated. Instantly they were quiet. Peering through the darkness in the direction of the sound, Meir was the first to see something white shimmering eerily at a distance. The superstitious among them, already unnerved, trembled with fear. Shrinking, they made their way forward in a body. Leaves rustled, dead branches snapped underfoot, the wind hummed an accompaniment to the incessant intoning.

At the foot of a plane tree his friends found Simeon. He gave them no heed when they encircled him. Crouched, he crooned without pause:

"From the earth to the firmament is a distance of five hundred years' journey. And from the topmost firmament to God's throne is an equal distance. And the upper firmament is so close to the lower that a bird flying between them would brush both with each stroke of his fluttering wings. Even as it is written, 'The spirit of God hovered.' So short is the interval between things celestial and earthly. And yet so far that man cannot span it. It is written in Scripture, *V'noshantem ba-aretz.* 'Ye shall grow old in the land.' Now the numerical value of the phrase 'Ye shall grow old' is eight hundred and fifty-two. So long was the duration of the first Commonwealth to have been before the Exile. And yet it endured only eight hundred and fifty years. What secret shall this discrepancy conceal?"

Joshua spoke to him. He continued to babble Scriptural quotations.

Meir clutched Joshua's arm.

"Master," he asked, "what does it mean? Has Simeon…?"

"God pity him," the old sage replied, "he is mad."

Sick at heart two disciples lifted Simeon by his arms, raised him to his feet and half-carried him back to Usha. With each step he quoted Biblical verses, interpreting them with an insane, fantastic ingenuity.

In the quiet streets of Usha, the townsfolk stood about in assemblies of stirring shadows. A murmur of horror swept through them when they heard Simeon's speech and the explanation of it whispered hastily to them by his companions. Then they fell silent, retiring uneasily to their homes or gathering before the doors of the tavern into which the stricken sage was borne.

In his chamber, Simeon lay abed raving without surcease. Physicians bustled over him, administering futile sleeping potions, consulting one another worriedly. Joshua, Akiba, Meir and other disciples sat wordless with apprehension and concern.

Just before dawn, without pause in his talk or change in his tone, Simeon veered abruptly from his garbled weaving of Scriptural verses.

"Elisha," he chanted, "does not believe.... Elisha denies everything.... Hush... I must not say so—not to anybody. He is my friend."

Those who stood about gasped. Joshua, Akiba, Meir looked anxiously from Simeon to one another. And when the report reached the men outside their faces became grim in the gray light.

As soon as Meir entered the dining hall Elisha knew that he bore bad news.

"Meir," he asked in a half-whisper, rising slowly from the table, "what brings you here so unexpectedly?"

Meir looked at Deborah and Tobias who were watching him intently and withheld what he was about to say.

"I have come," he extemporized, "to notify you of a special meeting of the Sanhedrin to be held at Caesarea next week."

"Why?" Elisha asked suspiciously.

"To intercede with the Roman governor for the rebels who have been arrested."

A hiss of pent-up breath sounded faintly through Elisha's teeth. For a moment he had envisaged a court of inquiry at which he was to be the defendant and the elders of Caesarea his prosecutors. Then it occurred to him that this could scarcely have been Meir's sole purpose.

"You will excuse us, please," he said to Deborah, who moved to invite Meir to be seated. "Come with me," he suggested to his disciple, leading him toward an adjoining room.

"Now," he asked tensely when they were alone, "what is it?"

Meir's composure dropped from him like a crumbling mask.

"Master, a terrible thing has happened. Joshua and Akiba sent me here."

"I know," Elisha said, almost relieved that the long awaited crisis was at hand, "they have heard about Caesarea."

"Oh, no, Master, that too, but there is something else, something fearful."

"In Heaven's name, what have I done now?"

"Master, the night before last ben Zoma went out of his mind."

Elisha looked blankly at his pupil.

"Yes, Master, insane."

"I don't believe it. He was always eccentric."

"No, this is different. He babbles all the time, and he mutters about you...."

Elisha reached out and took hold of Meir's hand, his fingers tightening until the younger man winced.

"Meir, listen to me," he demanded. "You have been trying to tell me something. What, I still do not understand. Now begin at the beginning...."

Most of what he heard seemed to Elisha at first to make no sense; the rest was too fantastic to be credible. But he understood at last. And from his tardy comprehension two threads of thought unraveled themselves simultaneously, each distinct, each tragic with a sadness peculiar to itself. One was a succession of pictures, the fleeting, disjointed recollections of a man of eager eyes and restless body who had once worked at a loom, loved his friends and gone adventuring after a truth. The other was the inquisition of his own conscience, its protest against his accursed touch which had destroyed his most devoted friends, first ben Azzai, now ben Zoma.

Slowly he released Meir's hand from the convulsive grasp in which he still held it, found his way onto a couch and sat looking blankly into space. His mind continued to dwell on the two sequences, elegy and self-reproach, that wove through each other like a pair of compelling voices intoning together.

"Master," Meir broke into the silent privacy into which Elisha had withdrawn.

"Master," he pleaded desperately, "you must listen to me. You must. You are being blamed for all this. And it is no longer a matter of Shraga and his group. Everybody is talking now—in the academies, in the bazaars, in the streets. There are rumors of a trial, of impeachment, of excommunication. You can have no notion of how general the sentiment against you has become, or how bitter. I know. I hear what people say. I have argued and defended. . . . "

"Poor wretch," Elisha murmured in response, "have you not suffered enough in your own life that you must involve yourself with me? You cannot approve of what I have become any more than the others."

"Oh," Meir exclaimed impetuously, "surely friendship is like the eating of a pomegranate! One savors the seeds and is sustained by them. Who gives a thought to the rind?"

"That," Elisha teased bravely to hide the sting of the bittersweet judgment of himself, "is a good epigram. But," he went on after a pause, grave again, "there are no seeds. It is all rind. I have nothing left to teach you. Your knowledge almost equals mine. Your faith exceeds mine. What sustenance is there in me?"

Meir's eyes were steady but bright with tears.

" 'That love,' " he quoted from the Tradition, " 'which is founded on earthly circumstance vanisheth with the circumstance; that love which is beyond circumstance abideth forever.' "

And Elisha was still with grateful wonder.

"You must go to Caesarea," Meir resumed eagerly, "with the legation. That is the message which both Joshua and Akiba asked me to convey. They say that your presence will tend to discourage discussion among the sages while your absence might be taken as an admission of guilt. You will go?" he asked hopefully.

Elisha nodded.

"Good," Meir cried. "But most of all, both of them, each separately, instructed me to warn you to be discreet. They believe that they may succeed this time in preventing the Sanhedrin from adopting official measures against you. But one more untoward incident and not even they will be able to avert an indictment. Please give them your word that you will be careful."

"I shall try," Elisha said tonelessly.

"A promise," Meir begged. "As you love them, as you love me. For our sake, if not for your own. I shall not be able to rest...."

But Elisha shook his head. How could he promise as long as the intractable confusion of his mind persisted, as long as he was ignorant of its ultimate issue?

"I shall try," he repeated.

"But you do not understand," Meir renewed his supplication. "You are no ordinary person. You are a member of the Sanhedrin. Your colleagues will be forced to put you on trial with the next semblance of dissent. They will have no choice except to indict you...."

"Then they will indict me," Elisha replied calmly.

"God of Mercy," Meir breathed, "do you want that? Is that why you are so little concerned?"

"No," Elisha disavowed, "I am not eager to be excommunicated, to be ostracized by my friends, to become an alien to my own people, perhaps to be driven from my native land. What sane man could invite such a fate?"

"Then forestall it," Meir argued passionately. "That at least is in your power."

"No, not even that. You see, Meir," he spoke cautiously, selecting words that would explain without revealing him altogether, "ideas and opinions are germinating within me. It is still too early to predict their full-grown character. That is why I can give no guarantees, not even that I will not invoke destruction on myself. For decision lies not in my will, but in my conscience, and over that I have no control. But it is sweet to know that, come what may, there are those who love me beyond themselves."

His own words reminded him of Simeon. A commingling of sorrow and guilt pervaded him again.

"What does it matter?" he whispered. "No indictment could incise a wound deeper and more painful than that which I have inflicted on myself."

When Tobias left the dining hall, Deborah tiptoed to the door between the two chambers and stood hidden behind the curtain where she could overhear every word of Meir's and Elisha's conversation.

As she listened, her initial fear became panic. By the time Elisha rose to escort Meir from the house, her entire world hung, precariously balanced, over an abyss. Fiercely she hated her husband for imperiling their welfare, for making their name a stench in the nostrils of decent people.

Her first impulse was to give free rein to the turmoil of resentment and accusation within her, to administer to Elisha such a tongue lashing as he had never in his life had before. Striding about she indulged her fury and hysterical fright by imagining the hard things she would say to him.

Then she sobered, remembering how often they had quarreled in the past. Her rage had never served to deter him. And this time he must be stopped before it was too late. She would win him over, control her temper, be soft and gentle, and so coax a promise by her sympathies.

Elisha came into the room and sank onto a chair. The courage he had exhibited before Meir was gone, leaving blank despondency in its stead. At the sight of him, real pity swept Deborah unexpectedly. The gentleness with which she bent down and put her arms about him was not assumed.

"Hush, Elisha," she whispered, pressing his head against her bosom, "do not fret. I will help you."

She felt his unyielding stiffness and held him more closely. To her own surprise it was suddenly important that he turn to her. But he was unresponsive. Her sympathy came too late. Then she recognized how estranged they were, how powerless she was to reach the core of his being. It was the hurt of this, as much as the failure of her scheme, that filled her with a sense of defeat.

CHAPTER XXV

M. Lusius Quietus, commander of the Roman armies in Palestine, moistened his thin lips with the tip of his tongue.

"Come, gentlemen," he said quietly to the delegation of rabbis as he settled back onto his cushioned chair, "you may speak frankly to me."

He was a Moor, slight of form, catlike in his movements. His face was thin, sharp-featured and bony. About his exquisite robe and carefully dressed hair hung the scent of rare ointments. His soft voice was more encouraging than the sages had dared expect. They had been shocked when they first entered his private apartments by the voluptuous furnishings, the perfumes and, above all, the sight of the rouged cheeks of the young male attendants. The intimations of cultivated vice had sickened them. Now they forgot their aversion in a surge of hope.

"You must not hesitate to say whatever is in your minds," he assured them. "I know the rumors concerning me which you have doubtless heard—that I am a monster devoid of mercy. But it is my duty to punish rebels against the Emperor—a painful duty, I assure you. Tomorrow, fortunately, my distressing task will be completed. I presume that it is on that score that you have come to me. If my assumption is correct, I am afraid..." He shook his head as over an impossibility. "I do not want to put those rebels to death—that fellow Julianus and the others. Unfortunately I have no choice. But," he went on, his face brightening, "if you can give me good grounds for commuting their sentences I shall really be grateful to you."

Gamliel stared, dazed by the sympathetic distress in Quietus's voice.

"But, sir," he began incredulously, "these men have not actually been rebels..."

Emboldened by the manner of the Roman, he spoke on earnestly, pointing out that, whatever might have happened in Egypt or Cyprus, Palestine had remained at peace, that the mere thought of insurrection was no crime.

Quietus listened intently. Time and again he asked leading questions. Only once did he interrupt to enter a reluctant contradiction to a chance statement.

"I wish it were true," he said sadly, "that you Jews really averted the war. I know that some of you tried. But really now, you must admit that the government maintained its own authority. Our spy system functioned well. An unfortunate necessity, this business of informers, to be sure—but a necessity nonetheless. We knew of the meeting in Beth Rimmon, who led it and when it was to be. As proof, let me adduce the facts. First, within a week after it was held, the Fourth Scythican Legion entered the country; second, we knew exactly whom to arrest though as yet we have not apprehended them all. It is not a large point," he admitted impartially, "but you really cannot urge that your people prevented hostilities. We had some share in it, too." He smiled in self-deprecation. "Go on, gentlemen, I am still open to conviction."

Encouraged by his reasonableness, they took turns in speaking. Always it seemed as though one more word, one more contention would win him. As they argued with increasing vehemence, until they were pleading and begging at once, his watery eyes glowed and the tip of his tongue flicked out rapidly.

His manner changed as though he had grown sated of some pleasure.

"I have heard enough," he interrupted, rising abruptly. "There will be no reprieves and no commutation of sentence. These men planned rebellion against Rome. They will die tomorrow. With most we shall be merciful. We have erected crosses at the army post. The twenty least prominent of them will hang on them." His voice rose a pitch as he continued, "Unfortunately, we have not enough crosses. I am afraid that several of the more important rebels will have to be burned. As for Julianus, he has been a stubborn dog. Not one bit of information could we get from him. I have not quite decided how he will die, but it will not be quickly or painlessly. Gentlemen, our interview is over."

Quietus picked his purple-bordered toga from the floor and started from the room. Halfway, he stopped and looked back at the horror-stricken faces of the members of the Sanhedrin. Relishing in anticipation the effect of his words, he added slowly, "I beg your pardon, Masters, I had almost forgotten the courtesies. May I, on the Emperor's behalf, the Senate's and my own, express to you our deepest gratitude for your part in preventing a rebellion in Palestine."

His hearers winced and from the lips of Joshua a grunt escaped as though he had been dealt a violent blow in the belly.

The sun beat down on the vast crowd that thronged the parade grounds on the outskirts of Caesarea. But though he stood directly in the glaring heat, Elisha trembled uncontrollably as with the ague. Crosses stood black against the sky, alive with the crawlings of the men nailed to them. From stakes in the center of the field the charred remains of human figures hung limp. Near by the executioners were attempting in vain to restore the bloody body of Julianus to consciousness so that they might resume their torture of him. In a throne-like chair set on a high dais, Quietus sat, his eyes aglow with feral pleasure, his lips drooling saliva.

Frantically, Elisha looked for relief to his colleagues who stood about him in a little knot. Like him, they had come to offer last ministrations to the condemned. Their harrowing task was completed, their presence now was unavailing. But they remained, powerless to move or to console one another. Seeing their pale, anguished faces, Elisha shut his eyes to blot out the diversity of horrors. As he extinguished sight, the scent of scorched flesh stank in his nostrils. He retched violently.

Akiba's arm supported him.

"Come, Elisha, we may as well go. There is nothing we can do here any more."

Elisha shook his head resolutely.

"But I must go," the other insisted.

Elisha opened his eyes, glimpsed the pallor of Akiba's stolid face, the whiteness of his lips.

Together they plunged furiously through the dense crowd, concerned only with escaping into fresh clean air, to scenes which a man might view without despising his senses.

Far outside Caesarea an abandoned estate stretched up a hillside from the Mediterranean. Once the residence of the Herodian family, it had been a garden of trimmed trees, smooth lawns and glistening white statues. Its cultivated beauty had long since disappeared. During the great rebellion, over forty years before, the palace on the hillcrest had been sacked and burned. The statues had one by one been consumed in lime kilns. Now the flower beds were overgrown with weeds, the untended trees arched over ponds green with scum. The place was sad with neglect and the memories of vanished glory.

It was here that Elisha and Akiba took refuge. They had fled blindly, caring not whither. And when they found themselves in the deserted park, by unspoken consent they entered it, climbing a long slope to a marble arcade where they might rest.

The rear wall of the colonnade was mottled with traces of pictures that had once adorned it. Wild vines held crumbling columns in their shaggy embrace. Lichens and moss spread patches of green across the uneven tessellated marble floor. They seated themselves on a yellow stone bench supported by two battered griffons and stared through the foliage toward the sea. The day was lazy with mid-afternoon heat. Birds called in the trees, insects hummed and shrilled in the twisted shrubbery. The leaves rustled faintly.

"God, it was fearful," Elisha exclaimed, addressing Akiba articulately for the first time.

At once, the agony of the morning pervaded them anew.

"Please." Akiba shuddered. "Let's not discuss it. What good will it do? Let's talk of something else."

But Elisha could not free himself from the evil spell. "And all so hopeless."

"Hopeless?" Akiba's great bald head came erect. "What do you mean?"

"Oh, the whole business," Elisha replied disconsolately. "Trying to keep a little people alive against the Roman Empire."

"And what would you have us do?" Akiba challenged. "Give up the effort?"

"Why not? The sooner we admit our defeat, the better. They will destroy us in the end in any case. The only issue is how costly the process will be."

"Elisha," Akiba cautioned, "you're distraught."

"Distraught, am I? Then suppose you look realistically at our position. The Temple gone, and the hope of rebuilding it, too. The land passing from under our control. Suffocating laws, crushing taxation. And our own ranks, especially in countries like Egypt, depleted by constant desertions to Christianity, Gnosticism or unadulterated paganism. We have run our course."

"Not by far," Akiba retorted confidently. "Do you imagine that any earthly power can crush a people that lives to communicate a God-given message of faith, justice and mercy to all men? All the empires of the world united in unholy league have not the might to exterminate us."

Elisha averted his face and did not reply.

"So," Akiba breathed unsteadily, understanding stirring in his luminous eyes. "Elisha, what strange things have you been thinking? I knew that you were disturbed but I never dreamed it had gone so far. Am I correct in believing..."

"Yes," came the toneless reply, "everything is gone, not steadily and all the time, but quite generally—everything except for faith in God."

"Impossible!"

"So I sometimes think. But it is so."

"Then you must make an effort to recapture what you have lost. I will help you gladly."

Elisha shook his head obdurately.

"Then what will you do?" Concern rang clear in Akiba's voice.

"I am going to start at the beginning, by laying aside all prejudices, all preconceived notions, all my beliefs and affirmations."

"I am afraid," Akiba faltered, "that I do not understand. What will be gained if you substitute blanket denial for a wavering faith?"

Elisha rose and began to walk up and down the length of the columned porch, as Greek philosophers and rhetoricians had done when, a century before, they had met with royalty in this place.

"Let me put it this way. We have both studied Euclid's *Elements of Geometry*. You must have been impressed by the lucidity of the reasoning and the sureness of its results. For some time, I have been conscious of the contrast between the method of the Greeks and ours. Their success, I am convinced, followed from the fact that they started from the foundations. We, on the contrary, have always tried to bolster a pre-established case."

He ceased pacing and stood over Akiba.

"Akiba, we have been friends for many years. You have been dearer to me than a blood brother. I would not hurt you or disturb your peace. But I know you. You are honest to the very core. Never have I seen you tolerate a lie or an evasion. Therefore, you must undertake this effort with me. Let us start at the beginning together."

The issue had been stated. In all the subsequent wrestling of their minds over it, they did not refer even once to the ordeal of that morning. But the memory of it persisted, coloring, flavoring their discussion, investing it with an urgency and import that transcended the decisions of individuals.

"But I still do not understand," Akiba had protested, "how you can expect me to discard beliefs even tentatively if I am really possessed by them. Your suggestion is like the procedure of those Greek philosophers who say, 'I do not trust my reason, but I will use it to prove that I have no right to use it.' A man may insist that he lays a doctrine aside, but if it is integral to him, he will carry it with him wherever he goes and will inevitably find it again since it has never left him."

"But certainly one can put an attitude away."

"You can only remove from yourself that which is not part of you. To be altogether honest, Elisha, I think that you might engage in such a project. I could not."

"You mean," Elisha struck, "that you are afraid to subject to honest examination any proposition which you like to accept?"

"Let us not abuse each other," Akiba demurred. "We owe each other no explanations. Certainly I have no right to ask for any. You who have few, if any, beliefs left are sufficiently detached from our traditional faith to be able to suspend it. I am not."

"Suppose then you tell me," Elisha asked in agitation, "how, knowing as much as I, you can still maintain a naive faith?"

"The purpose of life," said Akiba softly, "is to live well. Whatever contributes toward that end is right and true. My first and last criterion concerning my proposition is: Does it help man to live better? You may remember a lecture in which I asserted, 'All is foreseen by God, yet man possesses freedom of will.' "

"But Akiba…"

"Hear me out, Elisha, please. I am aware that, judged by the logic of Aristotle, my thesis is a contradiction in terms. But there is a higher logic, a rationality that springs from the necessities of human nature. Does not man face life with greater assurance if he believes that a benevolent providence foresees the future? And yet he must at the same time be confident that his will is free, otherwise moral effort is meaningless altogether. Doctrines in themselves are not important to me, but their consequences are. For example, I urge upon men that they regard themselves as embodiments of the divine essence. If I convince them, their days are endowed with a sense of abiding significance and unturning glory. Then not all the misfortunes and degradations to which they may be subjected can take from them their feeling of oneness with angels and stars. And as for our people, persecuted and dispersed, they live under the shadow of death, cherishing a dream that is recurrently shattered by the caprice of tyrants and then dreamed again half in despair. What can enable such a people to persist except a conviction of a special relationship to God?"

"And the objective truth of that conviction?" Elisha broke in impatiently.

"A large and terrible question, I grant. Nevertheless, the first and ultimate consideration, I insist, must be of effects. If any doctrine enlarges life, then it possesses truth in realms beyond Aristotle's logic."

"Surely now," Elisha retorted, unable to contain himself longer, "all wisdom will die with you. Why, every fool who cherishes some superstition, every rogue who seeks to persuade someone else of a lie, can justify himself by insisting that so he will live the better. The murderer can argue that his days will be enriched if the person he hates is put away. The thief can contend that his existence takes an added significance as he obtains possession of another's property. Every adulterer pleads that his life is not worth the living unless he wins the body of his paramour."

"You are deliberately making an absurdity of what I said," Akiba broke in resentfully.

"Indeed not. Yours is a good principle to be sure. Alas, it proves too much. It justifies everything and its opposite. What is more, you know as well as I that if there be no God, it is a lie to speak about Him no matter how well such a falsehood functions. And your readiness to believe, your willingness to accept doctrines on blind faith and then to defend them on grounds of expediency..."

"By what right," Akiba protested, "do you presume to call my attitude blind? Belief need not be unseeing. Is it a darkening of counsel to admit that truth is not a matter of the mind alone, but of the heart and experience also? Since it cannot be obtained by reason unaided, faith is indispensable both as a base on which thought may stand, and as a check-rein when logic goes astray.

"He who wishes to trace a circle must first select out of all space one point about which to draw it. The choice of the point makes possible the line which circumscribes it. The utility of the circle in practice will determine ultimately whether the point has been well placed. So with faith. It is the axis about which we move—an axis that must be posited as an act of will. The fate of man determines whether he has located it properly. That is all I am saying—that belief is the beginning, that it may be tested by experience, but that it must exist, or nothing can be."

"Arrant nonsense," Elisha interjected contemptuously.

"It was to be expected," Akiba went on heatedly, "that you would say so. To speak of faith to the man without faith is like communicating the experience of color to one who is blind."

His last words stung Elisha. Tears started in his eyes. Abruptly he turned his back on Akiba and looked through dimness into the distance. He could not believe simply because it was easier or more expedient. He could not have faith unless first his mind were satisfied. He had set himself to a task, the discovery of truth by reason, pure and unafraid.

Akiba was contrite. Rising quickly he laid a reassuring hand on Elisha's shoulder. "Please do not take what I have just said personally. I have no desire to hurt you. I recognize that you, in your own way, are seeking some light as I in my way believe that I have found it. We are all poor blind moles, trying without eyes to perceive more than our frail natures can apprehend. It ill befits one of us to charge the other with a deformity we all possess alike. But, Elisha, my friend, my brother," he urged, his fingers tightening their grasp, "it is a dangerous way you are traveling. Turn back and in time all things will be clear."

But Elisha was not listening. He stood erect, head high, his eyes fixed on a flock of birds ranging above the sea. As he watched, their formation broke. Most of them settled into a thicket of rushes at the water's edge. A few flew on for a time until one by one these, too, swerved back to their fellows. In the end, only one was left flashing whitely in the sunlight. Then it, too, was lost to sight.

CHAPTER XXVI

A FEW DAYS LATER, ELISHA lectured in the academy at Usha. He expected his audience to be small. Attendance at his classes had been dwindling. Yet when he came into the room assigned to him to find only Meir and a half-dozen other disciples present, he was, for all his indifference, deeply chagrined. It was with an effort that he composed himself, mounted the dais and plunged into the discussion of his theme—the legal and moral duties of parents to their children.

"A father," he cited from the Tradition, "is obligated to circumcise his son, to instruct him in God's Law, to teach him a trade from which he may honorably earn his livelihood...."

But his heart was not in it and when he was through there was not the slightest suggestion of applause. No one congratulated him. No one so much as asked a question. The handful of disciples rose at his gesture of dismissal, leaving Meir and him alone.

As they walked toward the tavern Meir did not refer to the lecture. Instead he coaxed Elisha to spend the evening at his home. Discouraged by persistent refusals, he had of late stopped extending invitations. But this time he was stubborn, eager in the hour of his master's humiliation to show his devotion.

Elisha yielded at last, sensing that he was at the parting of the ways, that very soon he might have no further opportunities to be with Meir and Beruriah. Before that befell, he longed to see Beruriah again.

Thus it happened that for the first time in more than a year he found himself in her presence. But the sight of her, far from bringing him joy, sharpened into new acuteness the compassion and yearning which separation had dulled. It rendered almost intolerable his intuition that this was the last time he would look upon her.

Once, while Meir dozed in his chair, the desire to speak

of his love for her almost overpowered him. He felt in that brief moment of indecision that if once he poured his soul out in speech, his pain would be forever lighter. But loyalty to his friend sealed his lips.

And so, all evening long, they talked of inconsequential matters. And of that which all but consumed him he uttered not a word.

Hours later, master and disciple sat opposite each other, each absorbed in the scroll before him. From afar, Elisha heard the town sentry calling the end of the first watch. He looked up across the table. The traces of the bitter years were written legibly on Meir's pale, weary face.

"Meir," Elisha prodded, "it is nearing midnight."

"I know, Master," he replied, "but I must finish my studying."

"It is too much," Elisha objected. "Diligence is a necessary and admirable quality in a student but to work as you do, day and night, is the excess of a virtue."

"One must forget somehow," Meir murmured.

Silenced, Elisha returned to his scroll, and to the Greek lines that marched over it. As he stared at them, unseeing, a new discontent filled him. It was still difficult for him to read these pagan philosophers. His knowledge of academic Greek was deficient. And the books at his disposal were at best a disorganized miscellany.

At first he had been relieved by his determination to begin at the beginning. But he was discovering now that his resolution had not brought him to a starting point. He must go back even further and set about mastering the language over which he stumbled, studying the natural sciences until references to them were a help rather than a hindrance. Then he must read the works of the great philosophers in logical succession. If only it were possible to start afresh like a Greek child in Athens—or Antioch....

"Antioch...Antioch," he repeated to himself, considering

the possibility. Then from his bosom he drew a letter which that very afternoon had been forwarded from his home.

"To Rabbi Elisha, the son of Abuyah, from Pappas, the son of Joseph, greetings of friendship and peace:

"I have heard the strangest reports from people who have visited Antioch. I do not know how much credence to put in them. If they are true, you must have changed considerably since I last saw you. Perhaps it is your father coming out in you after all.

"Be the cause what it may, I am writing to tell you that if for any reason you should find it necessary or wise to leave Palestine, my home is open to you. There is no Sanhedrin here to criticize one's conduct or beliefs. Antioch is a center of culture. I could introduce you to philosophers, scientists and rhetoricians. Needless to say, I would love to have you as my guest. Perhaps I should add that if you decide to come to Antioch for any length of time, you can arrange your credit through the House of Ariston of Rhodes which has a branch office here...."

The lamp burned lower, its light wavered, the shadows crept closer. He sat weighing his life and pondering a difficult choice. When the sentry called the end of the second watch he had reached no decision but a taste as of wormwood was in his mouth.

During the course of the following week Elisha attended a meeting of a committee appointed by the Patriarch to plan lecture cycles, preaching schedules and judicial assignments for the coming season. The dozen rabbis who assembled at the villa of Simeon, Gamliel's son, disposed of their routine duties by late afternoon. Then, on their host's invitation, they withdrew to a garden for refreshments. As they stepped from the house into the open they caught their breath in wonder at the prodigies visible in the heavens. Gray clouds, rimmed and plumed beneath in pinks and mauves, mottled the sky.

Fashioned after the creatures that inhabit nightmares they stood sharply outlined in the windless air.

Slowly, as they watched, the firmament turned solemnly black except that at its western rim a band of luminous scarlet glowed like an open bloodshot eye. In the last light of the setting sun every face, cloak and tree shimmered with redness.

The palpable quiet that weighed upon the world, the almost tangible awe that breathed over it silenced the sages. They made no attempt to break the deep hush through which no bird called, no insect hummed, no voice was heard. All was still as it had been at that moment before God, brooding over the infinite void, had spoken the first explosive word of creation.

It was at this moment of strange, ominous sunset, when the world weltered in gore, that the end came for Elisha.

At the edge of the garden, down a long slope of lawn, a peasant and a boy circled about the foot of a lone tall tree.

"Get all the eggs, my son," the man said in a voice that reached the rabbis but faintly. "Be careful to send the mother bird away."

Nodding, the boy set about climbing the tree.

One of the sages shook himself from his hypnotic trance.

"That boy will live long," he muttered whimsically. "For observe, in one act he is fulfilling two commandments, the reward of which is expressly stated as length of days. He is obeying his father, and it is written, 'Honor thy father and thy mother that thy days may be prolonged upon the earth.' He will send the mother bird away, thus conforming to the injunction. 'If a bird's nest chance before thee…thou shalt surely send the mother bird free that it may go well with thee and that thou mayest prolong thy days.'"

A few moments later wings fluttered about a treetop and a bare, slender arm waved toward it from among the branches.

Then a treble cry shattered the silence.

A sprawling body plummeted downward. Simultaneously a deeper voice sounded, inarticulate with panic.

Instantly the rabbis rushed headlong down the grassy slope.

The peasant was already on his knees gathering the boy into his arms.

"Tell me," he said, lifting a distorted face to them, "does he still live?"

One of the sages bent over the boy, then rose, shaking his head. "Blessed be the Righteous Judge."

"But, Masters," the father moaned, "he was a good boy, a good pupil—you can ask his teachers. Oh, his mother..."

Tears streaming into his tangled beard, he rose to his feet, warding off the hands that offered assistance.

"I picked him up the moment he was born; I will carry him now."

He walked away, bearing his burden with rough tenderness.

Against their will, the rabbis stared after him and saw with fearful clarity the limp hanging limbs and dangling head of the dead child.

Elisha trembled from head to foot. A cold perspiration covered him. Nausea writhed through his entrails.

The scene he had just witnessed brought with sudden vividness to his mind the tragedy that had befallen Meir's children. The two pictures merged into a unity, insane and incredible. A wild protest stormed up in him against the horror of it, its senseless waste of life, its wanton cruelty.

The sages turned and slowly mounted the slope together, talking meanwhile, trying to restore their confidence, to solidify a crumbling universe. At first, Elisha did not listen, so stunned was he, so dazed his senses. But as his mind recovered from its initial disorganization, he heard one of them say, "He will have his length of days. God is just. It is hard to understand but let us remember that there is a better world, in which it is all day, a day that stretches for eternity." At once Elisha knew the answer to the question he had never ventured to face before.

A great negation crystallized in him. The veil of deception

dissolved before his eyes. The only belief he still cherished disintegrated as had all the others. The last tenuous chord that bound him to his people was severed.

And when the sages droned on, their words buzzing like flies, revulsion swept Elisha. He could no longer tolerate their deliberate blindness. In cold desperation he silenced them.

"It is all a lie," he said with a terrible quiet in his voice. "There is no reward. There is no Judge. There is no Judgment. For there is no God."

The wind blew in from the sea across horror-stricken faces. The sun weltering so long in its own blood, died slowly.

CHAPTER XXVII

IT WAS DONE. HIS ARRANGEMENTS were complete. With relief, Elisha stepped out of the office of the House of Ariston of Rhodes. He turned and walked briskly down the main street of Tiberias. That very morning he had received the third in a series of letters from the Patriarch Gamliel. The first, coldly courteous, referred obliquely to a distressing incident and made vague reference to emotional stresses under which even sober men might be momentarily irresponsible. It had closed with the suggestion that Rabbi Elisha appear before the Sanhedrin to offer explanation. The second letter, ten days later, was curt and peremptory. The Patriarch and sages demanded an immediate accounting from Rabbi Elisha of blasphemous remarks made in the presence of witnesses. The Sanhedrin had patiently overlooked successive indications of heresy. It would be patient no more. Now Elisha carried in his wallet the last letter which informed him that one week after its receipt he would be tried by his colleagues as an infidel and rebellious elder.

Elisha had no intention of appearing before them. He had done nothing which called for justification. What was more, he hoped to spare those sages who were his friends the pain of a trial at which he could only confirm the charges made against him. All he wanted was to get out of Tiberias without encountering someone he knew.

But it was not to be. For as he was passing the synagogue he saw two of his colleagues walking in his direction. Even at a distance he recognized them easily, Rabbi Ishmael by the bold crimson robe he always affected, and Rabbi Tarfon by his corpulence. Quickly he looked about for cover. He could not enter the synagogue which might very well be their destination. Through the open windows of the schoolhouse across the street he heard voices reciting the text of Scripture. Turning, he stepped through the door into a classroom. As his eyes adjusted themselves to the sudden dark, he saw the long benches and the little forms bent over them. The teacher, a former pupil of Elisha, arose, obviously embarrassed and uncertain as to how to greet his uninvited visitor. Like everyone else he had heard rumors of the impending impeachment. But the habit of deference prevailed. He tapped on a desk with his pointer.

"Boys, we are honored. We have with us Rabbi Elisha, member of the Sanhedrin. Perhaps he would be so kind as to address us."

Elisha shook his head.

"Just a few words," the teacher coaxed, still impelled by politeness.

It was impossible for Elisha to refuse and yet what could he say to them?

"My dear children," he began tentatively only to pause.

The phrases he had once uttered so freely stuck in his throat. He could not tell these children to believe what he no longer believed. Then it came to him that little boys were being taught doctrines that were untrue, that among them there might be some who were being prepared for the anguish and disillusionment that had been his lot.

"My dear children," he said with soft urgency, "a long time ago a little boy about your age sat and learned what you are learning. They taught him stories and beliefs that they said were true. And he grew up and discovered that it was all legend and fable. I say to you, do not believe what they tell you here. Do not take it too seriously. Go out and be shoemakers, tanners, carpenters, farmers, merchants. Make things with your hands, real things that you can touch and taste. Then perhaps you will be happy, and make others happy, too."

He was saddened to see a fascinated horror in the children's eyes. The teacher and his assistant came toward him. How he got out of the room he could not remember afterward. He had a confused recollection of a scuffle, of a din of voices, calling at him "Infidel," "Atheist," "Apostate." When he came to himself he was on the street. Only then was he aware that his right cheek smarted. He raised an unsteady hand to it. It came away wet and sticky with blood. Holding a corner of his garment against the scratch, he left the town.

Several hours later, he mounted the pebbly path which led to his home. Avoiding the house, he made his way directly to the barns at the rear and called. Tobias came forth. Briefly and decisively Elisha told him that he was leaving on a journey, that the revenues of the estate were to be paid regularly to the House of Ariston of Rhodes, and that the account books were to be taken to Tiberias for periodic examination.

Whatever he thought, whatever he felt, Tobias nodded over each item of instruction and said nothing. Only when Elisha ordered him to arrange for a saddle horse, and a pack mule, did he reveal his emotions, and even then not by words but by twining his unsteady fingers in his beard.

Elisha was touched.

"You have been a faithful servant," he said. "I know that you will be as loyal to the mistress, should she remain here, as to me."

Then there were so many things to be said that they did not speak of any of them.

One more task remained, the most painful of all. He entered his wife's room.

Deborah rose. Her eyes fixed themselves on the scratch on his cheek but she remained silent. She had not spoken to him since the report of his final outbreak had reached the villa.

"Deborah," he began quietly, "I am afraid I have unpleasant news for you. I shall have to go away."

"That is no novelty," she gibed.

"It is this time. I shall never return."

Deborah remained motionless, uncomprehending, so that he was compelled to explain.

"A ban of excommunication is to be pronounced before the

week is out. I want to get out of the country while people are still permitted to talk to me."

The disdain she had affected of late crumbled away.

"I knew it," she burst out bitterly, clasping her hands. "I saw it coming long ago. And I tried to save you. But no, you were resolved to ruin yourself and me, too."

"Please, Deborah, there is no point in going into all that now. It is too late."

"But is it?" she seized on his remark, her voice instantly firm. "You can prevent it. Go to them. Make peace with them. They do not want a scandal either. If you turn penitent . . . " Her words trailed off at the sight of his calm and resolute face.

"Penitent?" he echoed. "For what?"

"Where will you go?" she asked hopelessly.

"To Antioch."

"Of course," she sneered, "to that wretch Pappas who started all our trouble. If it hadn't been for him—"

"Stop it, Deborah," Elisha interrupted, cutting off the threatened tirade. "There is a more important matter that must be settled right now. You must decide your future, too."

A look of fear came into her eyes.

"You mean," she breathed, "that I must go with you, leave our home, become an outcast, live among strangers? Besides, wouldn't the ban fall on me, too, for consorting with you?"

"You need not come with me," he informed her, "unless you want to."

"But how can I stay here," she protested, "married to you, and you far away? What sort of life is that?"

"There is a way out."

"What?"

"I hate to say this. You haven't had an easy time with me and I am sorry for a great many things. Neither of us has been particularly content with our marriage. But now that we have come so far, perhaps you would like to be free, to have another chance to live your life the way you want to. It's not easy for me to suggest this. But I feel that you might be happier if we were divorced."

His last words were barely audible. He stood still, watching the woman he had never loved. In spite of that, he hoped that she would want to come with him. Otherwise, their years together would be too intolerable a travesty.

"Divorce?" she cried incredulously. "So you can do that to me, too!" Tears of hurt sprang to her eyes. "And I'd have nothing," she went on an instant later as she realized the implication of his suggestion. "How long could I live on my dower money? Even while it lasted I'd be half a beggar...."

Disappointment and loneliness settled on Elisha.

"You do not understand," he interrupted. "I intend to support you no matter how you choose. Your dower money would be paid to you, and a regular allowance besides."

"And the house?"

"It shall be yours as long as you live."

"In my charge?"

"Yes, if you prefer it so, and I'll put it in writing—but subject to the contract I have just made with the banker, Ariston of Rhodes."

Deborah breathed more easily now that her future was secured. It was an attractive offer, that of the estate under her control. It would be virtually hers except for its legal title. For an exhilarating moment the prospect held her. Then she looked up at Elisha and the glow of anticipation faded. In its wake she experienced an agonizing twist of the heart. He stood before her, slender and erect, handsomer than ever in spite of his tortured eyes and the faint sprinkling of gray in his hair at the temples. It was like cutting off a limb to surrender him. She hesitated.

"What do you wish me to do?"

"It rests entirely with you."

Even had he given the answer for which she hoped, she would not have decided otherwise. But certainly the moment would have been less bitter had he even pretended to urge her.

"Then write out the documents," she instructed.

And he felt his heart sink over the blank nothingness which had been their marriage.

Elisha withdrew to his own room to find Tobias, Uriel and a maidservant packing his belongings. He strode back and forth, stopping once to point at an open bag.

"Take the Hebrew books out," he ordered glumly. "I shall not need them."

Then he sat down at his writing table, picked up his quill pen and tried to write a bill of divorcement. He knew the formula well but his fingers slipped and his mind played queer tricks on him. Only on the fifth attempt did he finally have it done and even then he was not certain that it was accurate. Next he drew up a writ of settlement.

"Tobias, Uriel," he called. "You will attest these documents."

The steward picked up the sheets, read them and turned pale.

"I do not like to do this," he began nervously.

"Please sign," Elisha insisted.

Reluctantly the servants affixed their names.

"And now come with me. You will serve as witnesses of their delivery."

He led the way into the next room. Deborah had remained standing. Elisha handed her the document attesting to the financial agreement. Then he held forth the bill of divorcement. But it was a moment before he could find the voice to say, "With this I send thee forth from being my wife. Thou art henceforth free to marry whomsoever thou choosest."

The sheet slipped from her nerveless fingers and fluttered to the floor. Yet it was enough. She had made no gesture of refusal. Therefore, in accordance with the law, they were no longer man and wife. But in the interval between the delivery of the two writs a turmoil had broken loose within her. For, once the guarantee of security was in her hand and her anxiety as to her future allayed, the other hurt made itself felt, filling her with bitterness. At the touch of the second document her seething resentment exploded into hysteria.

"I hate you," she spat at him. "I am glad they have found you out. You deserve to be excommunicated. If they ask me, I will stand up before the whole Sanhedrin and tell them how you, a rabbi, have treated me."

He attempted to calm her.

"Deborah," he reasoned, "it is better so. In time, when you are more composed . . . "

"Stop," she shrieked, "stop trying to make it easier."

"But we do not love each other. We never have...."

"You mean," she screamed, "you have never loved me."

At the memory of old humiliations she leaped forward and clawed at his face. He raised his arm to ward her off, but not quickly enough. For the second time that day his cheek was streaked with blood.

With one final glance around the room he turned and left the house. Deborah followed to the door, hurling curses after him. They pursued him into the open. He picked up the reins of the pack mule, got onto his horse and rode off. His last impression of the woman who was no longer his wife, as the first, was of her voice. But now it was shrill and unlovely. In his eagerness to escape its stridency he neither took leave of his servants nor looked back to the house that had been his home since birth.

PART II

CHAPTER I

LONG BEFORE HE CAME WITHIN sight of Antioch, Elisha knew that his journey was nearing its end. The road he traveled had, for some distance, been lined with great estates and congested with freight wagons, carriages, litters and pedestrians. Yet his first glimpse of his destination was almost accidental.

He had halted to gape at a giant aqueduct that spanned the highway before him. Its massive arches curved over the crest of a hill, vaulted the spot where he stood and continued their bold striding toward a valley below. It was while his eyes followed their descent that he saw, through a haze of smoke and dust, the mass of buildings that was Antioch, capital of Syria and third largest city in the world. It lay on both sides of the river Orontes, sprawling up the flanks of mountains that ringed it in.

Elisha breathed deep with wonder. He had heard many reports concerning it, but he had not expected it to be so vast. As he stared he became aware of a sound intermingled with the hiss of the rushing waters overhead—a dull, sustained hum, like the purring of some great contented cat. Overawed he rode on.

His passage for the first time through Antioch was terrifying and confusing. He was amazed beyond all else by the swarms of people. In contrast, the streets of Caesarea had been deserted. The author of the book of ben Sira, it occured to him, must have been thinking of scenes such as this when he wrote, "I am hidden among multitudes of men. What is my soul in their great numbers?"

And the farther Elisha went into the city, the denser the crowd, the greater the tumult, the higher the houses until, buffeted on all sides, he was riding between buildings of five and even six stories.

He stopped in front of a shop to watch a waiter ladle out bowls of broth to customers standing on the street before the counter. Again, he passed under an arcade into a world swimming with shadows where long shafts of light probed, touching indiscriminately the bronze vessels of a cooper, the fly-infested wares of a butcher, and the diversely colored garments of people moving out of darkness into darkness.

Of all his impressions the most vivid was that of a heroic marble statue, bearing on its circular pedestal the inscription, "THE TYCHE OF THE CITY OF ANTIOCH." It stood in the center of the Forum, the symbol of this mighty city—a crowned goddess with arrogant face, indifferent to all things, even to the sportive little god, half-boy, half-fish, representing the river Orontes that played at her feet. That image remained with him, catching as it did so fittingly the spirit of the place.

But for the rest, all was a chaos of sight, smell and sound. In the end, after much bewildered wandering and frequent requests for directions of people who, as often as not, shrugged their shoulders and hurried on without answering, he rode into the courtyard of an apartment house.

"Does Pappas live here?" he inquired of the porter who lounged in the arched entrance.

The man nodded.

"Which are his rooms?"

"On the second floor, that staircase in the corner."

"Please stable my horse and mule, and hold my saddlebags," Elisha instructed as he dismounted and started up.

"Pappas," he called tentatively through the open door at the head of the flight of steps. The room before him was empty but from a chamber beyond he heard his friend's voice in response.

"Who is it?"

"It's I—Elisha."

Instantly Pappas appeared, delight and surprise on his face. Arms extended, he rushed toward Elisha.

"Elisha," he cried and embraced him joyfully. "Welcome, welcome. I had no notion when I wrote to you that you would accept my invitation so promptly."

Still holding him by the arms he drew away and abruptly was silent.

"Elisha," he whispered, aghast. "What has happened to you to make you look so haggard?"

"I'm tired," Elisha winced. "All this travel…"

"Oh no, it can't be merely that…"

Remembrances, obscured during his journey by the excitements of the road, assailed Elisha anew.

"It's a long story," he evaded.

"Whatever it is," Pappas remarked, concern flickering in his eyes, "it can keep. But sit down here, on the couch where you can rest, and tell me about everybody—yourself, Deborah, Joshua, Meir…."

But to his inquiries, the answers were constrained and halting, as though wrested from Elisha.

"Something is troubling you—fearfully," Pappas said at last. "Let's have it."

Though Elisha drew a deep breath before he replied, his voice was unsteady when he spoke.

"I have been excommunicated."

Pappas shook as though under a violent blow.

"God, Elisha," he breathed, "how horrible! What you must have gone through! No wonder you look like a ghost. Do you want to tell me about it now or would you rather …"

His head bowed, his hands clasped before him, Elisha responded by beginning his story. Not once did he raise his voice, yet there was such anguish in his tonelessness, such desolation in the purport of his disjointed broken phrases that, after a time, Pappas rose silently from the stool he occupied and, seating himself by his friend, laid a comforting hand over the two locked so tightly.

"That," he said decisively when Elisha was done, "is all over now. You have come to Antioch to begin life afresh. And the first step in that direction is to forget the past altogether."

"As if I can," Elisha murmured disconsolately.

"You will. I'll see to that."

"Then the ban won't affect our relationship?"

"You precious idiot," Pappas cajoled. "You put that question to a renegade like me? Why, the only difference between us is that you have exhibited principle and courage while I have played cautious. But I insist, not another word from either of us about what was! Not even an expression of sympathy from me—at least not until the ache is out of it.

"Where are your bags?" he inquired briskly with a quick change of manner. "With the porter? I'll send my boy for them at once." He snapped his finger in recollection. "I completely forgot that I left my hairdresser waiting. All the better! We will use him on you after he is done with me."

"Come on." He tugged at Elisha's wrists. It was obvious that he was deliberate in his babbling. And Elisha, already somewhat easier in mood for having unburdened himself and strengthened by the spontaneity of Pappas's sympathy, was not at all loath to be diverted further. His shoulders straight, he got to his feet and allowed himself to be led onto a balcony where a man and a boy waited.

"Get my friend's luggage," Pappas ordered the lad. "And finish quickly with me, Cleon," he urged the barber. "I have another, more important, task for you.

"You could not have come at a more opportune moment," he managed to inform Elisha through the snipping of scissors and the fluttering movements of the hairdresser. "I am going to a fashionable dinner tonight, and you are coming with me. Hmm, let me see…" He considered him critically. "You will need clothes."

"But I have several changes, all of them quite good."

"For the Sanhedrin perhaps, but not where we are going. I will lend you something until we can get to a tailor."

"I am done, Master," Cleon said, pulling the apron off Pappas with a flourish.

"Good. Now what suggestion have you for this gentleman?"

The barber looked at Elisha thoughtfully. "He should be clean-shaven, of course. That beard ages him. And I should recommend a haircut in the Roman fashion. It generally suits that thin dark type best."

"Right," Pappas concluded after studying Elisha, "though I am not so optimistic about turning him into a younger Cato or Brutus. He is a little too dark, and not stern enough. But it will be becoming."

"Well," he cried as he rose from the stool and waved Elisha toward it, "do we cross the Rubicon?"

Elisha hesitated. Things were happening to him with bewildering rapidity.

"Quick, Cleon," Pappas ordered, "get a sidelock before he protests."

The shears snipped and a black curl slipped down to the floor. Elisha looked at it and resigned himself to the skill of Cleon. For almost an hour the barber was busy with scissors, razor and pleasant smelling oils and ointments.

At last Cleon appraised Elisha triumphantly.

"What did I tell you?"

Pappas smiled in agreement.

"You were right. You can always be trusted to be right. You know, Elisha," he went on, half in banter and half in earnest, "you are really a personable fellow, a bit Oriental, to be sure, but quite passable."

"I should like to see what I look like," Elisha broke in. "After all, I may as well know the worst right now."

"Hold on a moment, let us do this properly."

Pappas darted into the house and returned almost at once, carrying a large mirror in one hand and a gaily colored cloak in the other. "Slip this on and then look at yourself."

When the mirror was held up and Elisha saw himself reflected, he scarcely recognized his own face, so youthful did it appear without the beard and earlocks.

"You know," he commented impersonally, stroking his chin, "it is not bad."

"I am not certain," Pappas chuckled, "that you are as beautiful as you think. But you are quite presentable. And now we had better dress or we will be late to dinner."

"But I have not been invited…"

"You have a great deal to learn. It is no longer necessary to be invited. The newer mode allows guests to bring guests. 'Shadows' we call them."

"But who is our host?"

"Hostess," Pappas corrected. "Her name is Manto. I promise you the best food and talk in Antioch."

"That sounds exciting," Elisha said, his spirits more cheerful than in many a week. "But who is she?"

"What difference does it make?"

"None, but I am curious."

"You shall see for yourself."

"Why are you so mysterious?"

"Because I want you to make up your own mind about her."

"But are you sure she will not resent my coming?"

"Oh, not at all. I know her well enough to bring along a 'shadow.' In fact, I rather think she will like you, once you are properly dressed—straight black hair with a touch of gray, clear blue eyes, good nose, strong chin, tall, slender, and," Pappas, paused in his inventory, "most important of all, an intellectual face with just enough of a look of suffering to make it interesting. Yes," he concluded as they left the terrace, "I would wager that she will like you."

Manto's residence faced on a quiet avenue. Its facade, like those of the adjoining buildings, was drab and unadorned. Only its doorpost, inlaid with intricate designs in amber and ivory, prepared Elisha for the magnificence of its interior.

In a vestibule, paved with mosaic, servants took their outer wraps. A steward led them into the reception hall where he left them. The room for all that it was small and almost devoid of furniture was one of the most luxurious that Elisha had ever seen. Vividly colored scenes painted onto the walls, a beamed ceiling and a tessellated floor endowed it with warm spaciousness. Small pieces of statuary, obviously of the best workmanship, stood in the corners, with bronze, many-wicked candelabra hanging over them.

Only one person was in the chamber when they entered it—a slight, white-haired man who, his back toward them, studied a picture.

"We are early," Pappas murmured.

At the sound the man turned. Pappas's face lighted up in a spontaneous smile.

"Antiphanes. What a pleasure! Let me present my countryman, Elisha."

The man came closer. His unlined face and bright gray eyes were surprisingly young. They greeted each other, and instinctively Elisha liked him.

Then other guests began to arrive. In the midst of a group of men, chatting intimately with one another, Elisha felt lost and alone. The depression from which he had been relieved by Pappas's indefatigable gaiety was just beginning to settle on him again when a servant appeared announcing, "The Lady Manto."

Elisha caught a quick glimpse of reddish-gold hair and of a flowing sea-green robe. Then his view was cut off by his fellow guests who hurried to extend their greetings. He hung back awkwardly until Pappas took him by the elbow and led him forward.

"Manto," he said, "I have taken the liberty of bringing a 'shadow' with me. May I present my countryman and lifelong friend, Elisha." She was startlingly beautiful with her very white face and gray-green sloe eyes. Her tawny hair, gleaming with metallic lights, was piled high on her head so as to make her appear taller than she actually was. A vivid robe, complementing her own coloring, swirled about her to her feet. But for all its looseness, it clung to her, revealing the lithe curves of her body. When she moved there was a suggestion of the feline in her grace.

She scrutinized Elisha briefly but with such directness that he was disconcerted. Then she raised her bare arm to welcome him and he scented her elusive, provocative perfume.

"You are doubly welcome," she said, her speech soft and slurred, "first for your own sake but also because you have taken the place of a guest who has disappointed me."

Ill at ease, he acknowledged her greeting stiffly.

She had already turned away. But the reserve in his manner brought her eyes back to him for a moment. Then she addressed the entire company: "Shall we go in to dinner?"

The large banquet chamber was decorated with soft-colored murals. The couches for the guests were already in place, arranged to form three triangles. At a huge cabinet, standing against one wall and heavily laden with massive plate and glassware, servants were filling wine cups from a silver bowl crowned with roses.

Each guest accepted a wreath and a goblet and, murmuring the name of some god, poured a libation onto the floor. Intent on conforming with their etiquette Elisha did likewise, only to realize that he had paid obeisance to a pagan deity. The discovery shocked him slightly.

The servants carried in circular tables already set and placed them among the couches. Manto took her place at the apex of one of the triangles.

"Will you sit here at my table," she said to Elisha, indicating the couch to her left, "with Lysander, Pappas and me?"

He would have preferred a less conspicuous position but, watching his fellow guests, he got himself onto the couch and reclined as they did. Those at his table were already helping themselves to the tidbits, some of which seemed to be meats, on the tray before them. For all his determination to be done with Jewish practices, it was too soon for him to rid himself of his aversion to forbidden foods. Carefully he selected some olives, a bit of cheese and what looked to him like an anchovy. Pappas watched and a malicious smile played on his lips.

"So," he mocked, "the habits of a lifetime are not easily broken, are they, Rabbi?"

Elisha lifted his eyes from his plate to discover that his table companions were staring at him.

"A rabbi?" Manto asked, surprise in her tone.

"I was," Elisha murmured.

"Oh, really? None of us has ever met a rabbi before. Please do tell us something about yourself."

But her request raised unwelcome recollections in him.

"I would rather not."

She frowned and her eyes were suddenly very green.

"I am sorry," Elisha apologized. "I did not mean to sound ungracious. But the memories of my service as a rabbi are not happy."

"As you choose," she said indifferently, and began to eat.

Cautiously Elisha bit into a morsel. Neither in taste nor texture was it what he had expected.

"I thought," he said half to himself, "that this was an anchovy."

"No," Manto smiled, "it is a strip of turnip dressed up to appear like one."

Pappas chuckled. "That is the way it is in Antioch. Everything is in some guise and nothing is quite what it seems."

"Still the incorrigible Cynic," Manto taunted.

"See, Elisha, what did I tell you?" Pappas cried. "From her very mouth she confirms my contention. I am the Cynic though I do not wear the robe of the school and Lyncaeus over there, dressed as one, is really a naive trusting soul."

"Oh, come." Manto chided. "Food should be eaten, not philosophized about."

In the momentary silence Elisha heard a fragment of conversation from another table.

"I tell you, it is arrant nonsense," Antiphanes was saying. "There is no more sense in our writing in the Attic style than there would have been for Plato to employ the Homeric manner. All that is important about prose is its clarity and naturalness. Everything else is affectation."

"Not so, not so," someone objected. "If men of unusual ability have created patterns as near perfect as man can attain, what other course have we except imitation?"

"Who are they all, Pappas?" Elisha whispered.

"Why don't you ask your hostess?"

"Very well then, don't tell me."

But Pappas put the question for him. Manto turned to Elisha.

"Haven't you met them, Rabbi?"

"I have been introduced to them, but that is all."

"Well, here at our table we have—aside from you, Pappas and myself—Lysander who is perhaps the greatest astronomer in Syria."

Lysander looked up and smiled deprecatingly.

"At the table to the right," Manto went on, "our literary lights are gathered: Antiphanes, a splendid rhetorician, and Nicander, his colleague."

"A parasite, you mean," Pappas interjected.

"And the third," Manto continued, disregarding him, "is Smerdis, the grammarian, the one who was just defending the classical style. At the other table the thin man in the blue robe is Pompeianus, the jurist. The big fellow in the philosopher's mantle is Hermonax, the Stoic. And the last is Lyncaeus, the Cynic. There now, you have them all."

"There is one thing," Pappas added, "which Manto did not tell you—out of modesty no doubt. And that is that everything here is the best— not only the best food, the best wines, Chian, Mareotic and Falernian, but also the best people. In this one room you have the best grammarian in Syria, the best Cynic, Stoic, jurist, astronomer and rhetorician. I mean, Antiphanes, of course, not that leech Nicander. You, Elisha, fit in here, even if some of your former associates disapprove of you. Only I am out of place. Except perhaps as a court jester."

Manto glanced toward Elisha at Pappas's casual allusion to him, curiosity flickering in her strange eyes. For an instant he was held by her gaze. Unaccountably he flushed and looked away. But he volunteered no information and after a pause she joined in the talk at another table where the men were contrasting human nature as it had been in ancient times with what it was in their own generation. Imperceptibly she drew all her guests into the discussion and kept them absorbed in it. No one seemed to notice the artfulness with which she converted sporadic conversation into a pointed debate. But Elisha, already alert to everything about him because of its novelty, marveled at her subtlety and the ingenuity with which she prevented the controversy from being diverted or monopolized. He noted too the lightness with which she kept it sprightly.

There was little agreement among the guests on the topic at issue. But they spoke uniformly well in a polished Greek that reflected careful training in rhetoric. Without exception they were learned, citing appositely to illustrate their points.

Meantime, the courses, served by unobtrusive servants, followed each other—platters of assorted meats, great trays with roasts of suckling pig, a dessert of frosted fruit, and with each dish an appropriate wine.

At intervals Manto silenced the gathering to present entertainers, one to sing the plaintive love lyrics of Anacreon, another to dance a Doric rhythm to the accompaniment of a hymn by Tyrtaeus, a third to recite a rolling passage from Homer. But after each interruption she picked up the threads of their argument again.

Several times she turned to Elisha to invite him to express

an opinion. In each instance he shook his head and smiled apologetically. His refusal puzzled and annoyed her but she did not comment on it.

When the meal was over and the tables cleared, the large silver wine bowl, crowned afresh with roses, was moved from the serving table to a stand amid the couches. Each guest handed his goblet to a steward for filling and, as he received it back, toasted Manto by name.

Eagerly the men resumed their discussion. It was then that, forgetting himself, Elisha spoke up for the first time.

"Is it not possible," he suggested in a Greek somewhat hesitant from unfamiliarity, "that there is an element of truth in both the positions maintained this evening? Granted that human nature never changes either for the better or the worse, nevertheless men may have exhibited at certain periods in the past greater nobility than is to be discerned in our own age. For though character is constant, the circumstances surrounding it are not. And it is these ultimately which determine whether personality shall be large or stunted. Consider, for example, the effect of the institution of slavery upon us. There was a time when almost every farmer tilled his own land. He had pride in his task. He was the master of his own destiny. Today the world's work is done by slaves. The rich grow soft with indolence, the slaves degraded by oppression. This may well be the resolution of our paradox. The individual at birth today possesses endowments akin to those of his ancestors. Not called into use, they degenerate like some muscle grown flabby which, exerted often enough, might have been hard and firm. Perhaps it is our times that rob us of our potentialities for the heroic."

As he spoke the other men who had virtually forgotten his presence looked at him with pleased curiosity. A murmur of approbation swept the room when he had finished and at once someone took up the point he had made. But Manto, though she flashed an appreciative smile at him, seemed to feel that a fitting climax had already been put to the discussion. Without her guidance the conversation disintegrated into small talk. A while later the guests rose, took leave of their hostess and departed.

It was quite late when Elisha and Pappas set out for home. The streets were dark except for lanterns burning in doorways and the glare of torches carried by slaves escorting their masters homeward.

"Well, what did you think of the evening?" Pappas asked after they had walked for some time in silence. "And for heaven's sake, stop stroking your chin."

Elisha pulled his hand self-consciously from his face.

"It was very interesting," he admitted. "A little bewildering and confusing, of course—new manners, new people, strange ideas, but definitely interesting."

"That's exactly what several people said to me about you. Interesting was the word they used."

Elisha was amused. "Why, I behaved like a clod. I could scarcely open my mouth."

"That may be, but what you did say attracted them. It was intelligent and altogether fresh in approach."

"Perhaps," Elisha suggested, "they approved of the fact that in the main I kept quiet. That was unusual enough in all that talk."

"Whatever it was, I am certain that you will be receiving invitations to dinner fairly soon. Nicander for one inquired whether you would visit him. How Manto ever came to have that schemer at her home is beyond me. Needless to say, I refused his hospitality bluntly and decisively."

"So it seems I was a success tonight. And for so little effort. It is really quite breath-taking."

"But there is more," Pappas added slowly. "Manto has asked me to bring you back soon."

"Why?"

"What do you mean 'why'?"

"What would she want with me?"

"Don't be naive, Elisha. You're a strange bird in these parts. You must have caught her fancy."

"Who is she, anyway, Pappas?"

"Well," Pappas drawled, "that's a long story. I hope it doesn't disturb you too seriously. The fact is that you dined tonight with a courtesan...."

"A courtesan?" Elisha repeated incredulously.

"Are you shocked, Elisha?" Pappas grinned. "Well, you'll have to get used to things like that in Antioch. This is not Palestine, you know. But I have not yet finished. The man who is keeping her is none other than Rufus."

"Not the governor of Judea?"

"The very same, Marcus Tineius Rufus, Pretorian Prefect of Palestine, commander of the Tenth Legion Fretensis, personal friend of Caius Publicius Marcellus, Proconsul to Syria, and, most relevant of all, one of the richest men in the Empire. He served with Hadrian while he was governor here, returned to Rome as a member of his personal staff and amassed a huge fortune—how, it is wiser not to inquire."

"But do you mean to say all those men were there, in the full knowledge...?"

"And why not? A beautiful and brilliant woman with high connections, the best food and talk in the whole province—why, her invitations are at a premium. And if she is not married to the man who supports her, if Rufus has a wife whom he discreetly has left behind him in Italy, what then? By the way, he is in Rome now and will not return to his post for some time. All of which is no concern of ours. Certainly, it ought not to prevent you from accepting her hospitality."

"I don't know..." came the hesitant reply.

"Don't be a fool, Elisha. No one is asking you to do anything wrong." Half-baiting, half-persuading, Pappas continued, "Are you going to be a rabbi here, or a freeman?"

CHAPTER II

A LOUD KNOCKING ROUSED ELISHA from a heavy sleep. Blinking to clear his eyes, he got to his feet and made his way to the door. It was early morning, and the night before, as on every night since his arrival in Antioch, he had retired late.

Two Roman officers stood in the entrance of Pappas's apartment.

"Elisha the son of Abuyah of Migdal in Palestine?" one inquired.

Suppressing a yawn, he nodded.

"A summons from the Basilica of Trajan," the man continued, drawing a scroll from his robe and thrusting it forward.

Too befuddled even for curiosity, Elisha accepted the document and unfurled it clumsily. But he came fully awake as soon as he read its terse message.

"Elisha the son of Abuyah late of Migdal, now residing in Antioch, will present himself immediately on the receipt of this order in the Basilica of Trajan before Sextus Erucius Clarus, Imperial Legate Juridicus of the Province of Syria."

"Have you any idea of the meaning of this?" Elisha asked.

The two men, their faces impassive, shook their heads.

Pappas looked through the curtain of his chamber.

"What's going on here?" he asked irritably.

"You had better come out," Elisha urged in thorough bewilderment.

Pappas shuffled forward.

"Read this," Elisha instructed, handing him the summons.

Pappas scanned the writing.

"By the gods," he cried, "from the Legate Juridicus himself."

"Wait for us," he addressed the officers. "We'll be ready in a moment."

"Come on, Elisha," he ordered and turned toward the bedroom. "That message is from the chief justice of the province, the direct representative of the Emperor, assigned to administer the courts. Only matters of prime importance come before him. It happens that I know him. But let's not presume on that fact. We had better go immediately."

"But what can he want with me?" Elisha asked as he followed his friend.

"I have no idea," Pappas responded, already busy with his clothes. "You have been in Antioch only a fortnight, too short a time even for you to get into serious difficulties. And as for Palestine..."

He broke off abruptly, startled by an idea that occurred to him.

"Hurry," he prodded testily. "Get yourself dressed. This business worries me...."

Following the officers, Elisha and Pappas mounted the broad marble steps of the Basilica of Trajan, crossed its high colonnaded porch and, avoiding the central portals of the great hall, entered a corridor that led by numerous courtrooms. Over the hum of conversation of the loiterers who crowded the passage, Elisha and Pappas overheard fragments of the high-flown speech of attorneys or glimpsed trials in progress through the open doors.

The chamber into which they were ushered was, in contrast with those they had passed, altogether quiet. On a throne set on a dais against one wall sat an imposing figure, clad formally in a toga. Two barristers argued before him in subdued tones that scarcely carried to the thirty or forty people who occupied the stone benches arrayed across the floor. On either side of the platform secretaries sorted documents or took shorthand notes.

Concerned though he was over the mysterious summons, Elisha had had too extensive an experience with Jewish law to be indifferent to the operations of Roman jurisprudence. Once seated, he observed the proceedings closely. It soon became apparent, as case after case was heard, that the court in which he found himself was devoted to preliminary hearings only.

For despite the presentation of evidence, the presiding justice engaged in no cross-examinations and issued no verdicts. He indicated merely whether a ground for action had been presented, instructed the secretaries in the drafting of a bill to be used for guidance at the trial, and assigned the litigation sometimes to a panel of subordinate justices, sometimes to a single individual for final determination. Elisha was impressed both with the appearance and the conduct of the Judicial Legate. A tall man with a shock of bristling black hair, deep-set dark eyes and heavily-lined face, he was obviously a master of the intricacies of the law. He moved with confidence and dispatch and Elisha was so absorbed in him, the issues on which he passed and the decisions at which he arrived, that he was startled to hear his own name called by one of the secretaries.

He rose, came forward and stood expectantly before the dais.

"You are Elisha?" Clarus asked, glancing up from a tablet which an attendant had handed him.

"I am."

"The son of Abuyah of Migdal?" the Legate continued.

"Yes."

"You left Palestine about a month ago?"

"More nearly three weeks," Elisha suggested.

"And what was your position in your homeland?"

"I was a rabbi and a member of the council of the elders."

"Then you are the man in question," the Roman concluded, raising his eyes from the document to which he had referred and fixing them on Elisha. "A communication has been received by the Proconsul from the authorities of your people demanding your forcible extradition to Palestine."

The room swayed before Elisha's vision. He had not dreamed that his colleagues would be so bitterly vindictive.

"But they have no right to make such a request," he exploded.

"Which," Clarus added dryly, "is the very point for me

to determine. Unless, to be sure, you are willing to return voluntarily."

"Certainly not."

"Then I shall have to go further with my investigation. Will you please answer the following questions. Is it true that you were thrice summoned to appear before the Sanhedrin of the Jewish nation to answer charges brought against you, that in each instance you failed to obey, and that in the end you fled the country to avoid the necessity of standing trial?"

"That is all true, except that there was nothing of flight in my departure."

"It does not matter," the Legate said slowly, thinking aloud. "What troubles me at this moment is the validity of the demand. Unlike most provinces, Palestine has no charter, either senatorial or imperial. The country has always been too disturbed for the issuance of one. As a result, the powers of its autonomous councils have never been defined. Still, it is the practice of Roman law, to uphold the authority of native legal systems unless they are explicitly superseded."

"But," Elisha interjected eagerly, "even if the Sanhedrin possesses the authority to ask for extraditions—and you yourself have indicated doubt on that score—it does not have that right in my case. I have violated no ordinance civil or criminal, either of Roman or Jewish law. The charges against me are entirely of a religious character as I am sure the letter from Palestine makes clear."

"As a matter of fact," Clarus admitted, "the document gives no indication of the nature of your offense. Yet, your insistence that it is against the Jewish cult does not improve the situation. Judaism is a legally recognized religion. Desecration of its sanctuaries, profanation of its rituals are no less punishable under the law than a violation of the shrines in Rome."

"But you misunderstand," Elisha pleaded. "I am innocent of any overt act against the Jewish religion. I have robbed no synagogue, I have despoiled no holy object. The indictment prepared against me in Palestine accused me of disbelief, of denial of the truth of certain doctrines taught by the Jewish religion."

"For all of which," Clarus commented, unimpressed, "I have only your unsupported statement, and you are scarcely a disinterested party."

"I can vouch for the truth of his assertion." Pappas had risen and was coming forward as he spoke.

"Ah, Pappas," the Legate smiled a cordial greeting. "I was wondering what you were doing in the dusty dullness of a court-room, a place so unlike your normal haunts. Now I understand. You are here on behalf of this man. You know him?"

"We played together as children."

"And you testify to the accuracy of his story?"

"Without reservation."

"But how can you do that? I was not aware that you visited Palestine in recent months."

"I do not have to be an eyewitness to the actions of my friends to give assurances concerning them."

Clarus smiled ruefully.

"Were we anywhere else, were this business other than an issue of law, I should take your word unhesitatingly. But the judge, in distinction from the man, can accept the testimony only of eyewitnesses. No, I am afraid that I shall have to draft a bill and order a trial. And, unless I am mistaken, the judge who presides over it will feel as I do, that this man must be returned to Palestine. If the decision there goes against him, he can always appeal to the pretorial courts or the Senate in Rome both on the facts and on issues of jurisdiction...."

"But I will not go back to Palestine," Elisha cried, his heart heavy with dread. "I will not stand like a criminal before them...."

"I am sorry, really," Clarus said earnestly. "But there is no alternative. I am even sorrier that I shall have to detain you until the trial."

"Detain him?" Pappas all but shouted his protest. "Why must he be put in jail because of the stupid animosities of a group of bigots? Would it not be enough if I stood surety for his appearance...?"

Clarus was obviously embarrassed.

"Under ordinary circumstances, yes," he demurred unhappily. "But this is an unusual situation. We are not dealing with a dispute between individuals. A whole people is involved. If anything went amiss here, the Jewish authorities would carry their complaint to Rome. It would be a bit awkward for me to explain to the Praetors there, to the Senate or even the Emperor, that out of personal regard for someone I had allowed the administration of justice in Syria and Palestine to be disjointed. In self-protection, as well as principle, I must guarantee the presence of this man."

The discussion between Pappas and Clarus continued for some time. But of his friend's pleadings and of the judge's reluctant yet resolute refusals Elisha heard little. A sense of his powerlessness, an aching disillusionment that men he had loved, men like Joshua, Akiba and Gamliel, should have been incapable of letting him go in peace, paralyzed his faculties. Mechanically he thanked Pappas for his promises of assistance. Then, dazed and unprotesting, he allowed guards to lead him out of the basilica into the open. Along the streets he walked, indifferent to his destination, unconscious of the gaping stares of passersby. Only after the massive doors had thundered shut upon him and he had sunk onto the mouldy straw that littered a dark cell, did his powers of thought reassert themselves. With deepening depression he surveyed his position.

Roman justice alone stood between him and the people that persecuted him. It was a mighty force, the law of the Emperor, and reasonably impartial. But it too could be swayed by influence and considerations of expediency. And worst of all, it was unfeeling. He could not expect it to protect him in his friendlessness, against an entire nation.

Inevitably, then, he would be returned to Palestine to stand trial, to be humiliated, to be coerced, if his former colleagues had their way, into submissiveness. That new life for which he had come to Syria, that lighthearted freedom of mind and body, of which he had tasted so briefly but with such refreshment of the spirit, would be denied to him. And the great quest to which he had set himself would never be begun, let alone brought either to triumphant conclusion or honorable defeat. It was when he arrived at this recognition that despair invaded him, dispelling reason and hope.

So through the interminable night he prowled the cell, his thoughts, like his movements, circling without surcease or egress. Not until the barred window showed green with the coming of dawn did he yield to exhaustion. Stretching himself out on the verminous straw, he sank into a troubled, drugged sleep.

The aperture in the wall glowed with bright daylight when he opened his eyes again. Someone was struggling with the bolt on the door. Metal rasped shrilly against metal, and the nail-studded surface swung open.

"Get up," a jailor growled. "You are free."

Elisha stared at him, uncomprehending.

"An order of the Legate Juridicus," the warder explained curtly, adding as Elisha rose, "A man called Pappas who brought the release is waiting for you."

In the warder room Elisha stopped to compose himself. With every fiber of his being he was grateful to Pappas. But all their lives they had veiled their feelings behind studied casualness.

"Behold, the freed convict," he called jauntily as he stepped toward the outer gate.

"Well," Pappas replied offhandedly, "that wasn't such a long confinement after all, though," he added as Elisha came into the full light, "it has done your appearance little good."

"Nothing," Elisha said happily, "that a bath and a fresh robe will not correct. But tell me, how did this good fortune befall me? I had begun to doubt the omnipotence of your influence...."

"Oh, don't thank me for your liberty. It was procured for you by Pompeianus who unknown to you has become your advocate."

"So he is responsible?"

"Not actually. He has taken your case. Incidentally, you are to call on him the day after tomorrow for a conference. But your liberator is really the Lady Manto."

"Manto? How did she become involved?"

"Simple enough. After I left the court yesterday I went to Pompeianus for advice, and it was he who suggested that we appeal to her. I must say, she needed no coaxing. Before nightfall she had spoken to the Questor and sent a message to the Governor. And when she appeared before Clarus this morning, he was quite prepared to release you in her parole."

"But why," Elisha cried, "why should she go to all that trouble and assume all that responsibility for a stray acquaintance?"

"It amazes me too. But there it is. And now you could use the cleansing to which you referred a moment ago, and then we'll go, you and I, to the home of our Lady Manto where you will express your gratitude appropriately."

"There is one other obligation which I must discharge before that." Elisha put his hand on Pappas's arm. "I owe you my thanks...."

"Please, Elisha," Pappas interrupted. "Certainly you ought to remember the saying in Scripture:

'A friend loveth at all times
And a brother is born for adversity.' "

As the two men emerged from the dim, silent apartments of the mansion into its central court, brilliant with the sunlight that poured through the rectangular orifice in the roof, Manto rose from amid the group of guests with whom she was seated. Her robe of shimmering yellow silk gleamed brightly as she threaded her way through the shrubs and flowering plants that grew in profusion about the pool and came forward to receive them.

"Welcome, Pappas. Welcome, Elisha," she greeted, extending a hand to each. "I am glad to see you again."

"I must tell you," Elisha began impulsively, "how grateful I am...."

"No, no," she interrupted, "please do not thank me."

"But it was so generous." he persisted, "to trouble yourself for a stranger."

"It was of no consequence. Fortunately you look none the worse for your unpleasant experience."

"The miracles of the bathhouse," Pappas deprecated. "Even a corpse would take on a semblance of vitality after the sweat room, the plunge, a massage and an ointment."

She smiled and turned away.

"Come, let me present you to my guests."

They followed her, Elisha relieved that a difficult moment had passed so easily, yet dissatisfied that he had given voice so inadequately to his sense of indebtedness.

The men and women reclining on the chairs and couches looked up expectantly as Manto and the two men approached.

"You all know Pappas," she said, "but I should like to introduce a stranger in Antioch, Elisha, who has come very recently from Palestine. This is Caius Julius Severus, commander of the Fourth Scythican Legion, and his daughter Lucretia. Next, we have Servius Atilius Quadratus, Questor of Syria, and his wife Pasiphae. Antiphanes, our only bachelor, you have already met."

"My apologies," Quadratus volunteered through the chorus of greetings, "for the inhospitable reception which our province accorded you. Manto told me about the whole incident yesterday. But also my felicitations on its successful conclusion."

"I wish I were in a position to be congratulated." Elisha smiled to conceal the quiver of nervousness occasioned by the Questor's reminder. "Unfortunately I am not yet done with the nasty business. Nor am I too certain of its final outcome."

"So," the Roman mused with a wry expression, "there is still litigation ahead of you. However, I would not be too concerned. With Manto as your ally, and with the assistance of her friends…"

"Enough," Manto chided. "Let us have no references to unhappy incidents. Gentlemen," she addressed the newcomers, gesturing toward vacant places, "put yourselves at ease."

Reclining on comfortable couches, Elisha and Pappas sipped frosted drinks served by slaves who appeared and vanished soundlessly. Weariness and anxiety ebbed from Elisha as he listened to the random talk of the others and idly observed the play of light and shadow about him.

In the center of the court all was bright as in the glaring street outside. The patch of sky, visible through the opening in the ceiling, burned with blueness. The slender columns that hung from it were lined with white fire. In the shallow pool directly below the aperture the sun was reflected blindingly. Even the marble Aphrodite, standing in the midst of the waters, glittered warmly, and that despite her nakedness and the thin sprays of the fountain streaming over her.

But in the corner of the arcade where they lounged, all was cool, scented with the fragrance of flowers and damp with mist. A caged bird trilled intermittently. And Manto in her brilliantly colored wrap seemed, when the branches of the shrubs stirred in the breeze and flashes of sunlight touched her hair and her dress, compounded of molten gold altogether.

Yet even as they relaxed, Manto was turning their conversation in imperceptible stages from trivialities toward literary discussion. And before long they were listening raptly to

Antiphanes who, from an apparently inexhaustible memory, quoted from poetry and prose the passages for which she called.

"One more recitation." she coaxed when the rhetorician gave signs of stopping. "My favorite, the oration of Dion of Prusa, *On Poverty.*"

The courtyard was silent except for his voice and the rustling footsteps of a servant who kept their cups full. Their sensibilities heightened by the brooding quiet and the exquisite artfulness of his speech, they lived rather than heard the story he unfolded. A man of learning and high position, shipwrecked off the coast of Greece, takes refuge at an isolated farmstead with a family of poverty-stricken peasants. At first, he pities his hosts for their meager fare. But, with time, he comes to discern in this hut the presence of all man needs for happiness: simple but nourishing food, protection from the elements, spontaneous piety toward the gods, and above all mutual love and harmony. In the end, he returns to the great cities of the world and their vain pleasures, aware that serenity resides eternally beyond their confines.

When Antiphanes was done the sun was no longer high. The sky had lost something of its brilliance. Manto sighed faintly, breaking the charm that held them fast.

"Ah," she said, "that is life as it should be lived. If only we had the courage."

"I wonder," Pappas reflected, "whether we would want to live as those farmers did. I mean, with leaking roofs, smelly animals, badly sewn blistering shoes, coarse clothes, an eternal succession of meals of half-baked bread and vegetables, varied on rare occasions with a piece of tough smoked meat. No baths, no theaters, and no servants. The answer, I suppose, can be discerned in the fact that we stay right where we are. It is all very attractive—at a distance."

Staring at the fountain and so absorbed in what he had heard that for a moment he forgot all else, Elisha broke his silence. "There is more to it than that. In another age, people found the realization of their dreams in the realities about them. We do not. Hence we construct, each of us, his own imaginary world to which he may escape. Out of our needs, we endow it with a glow...." He looked up to see how they were responding to what he was saying, and in a flash was aware of the smile on Manto's face. Abruptly he flushed and stopped talking.

"Go on," she urged, "that's a splendid point you were making."

But he was unable to continue.

She watched him closely, her eyes deepening in color.

"Just as well, perhaps. If we pursue this somewhat melancholy train of thought, we shall ruin the day for one another — like that Egyptian practice described by Herodotus by which the host at a banquet causes a skeleton to be exhibited to his guests for fear that they will enjoy themselves too completely."

Thereafter they talked inconsequentially and Elisha found no occasion to participate. But to his own surprise he had been inordinately pleased by Manto's commendation. He leaned back and savored it, looking at her in the meantime, at first vacantly, then seeing very clearly. How much like Beruriah she was, and still how different. Both women were vibrant, alert, sparkling. Yet the loveliness of one was delicate, uncalculated, almost astringent; the other's lush, voluptuous, frankly provocative. Missing Beruriah poignantly, he turned his eyes away from Manto and held them on the fountain until thought and feeling alike were lost in a half-hypnotic contemplation of the wavering of light upon water.

CHAPTER III

THE OFFICES OF POMPEIANUS OCCUPIED the entire first floor of what had once been a palatial private residence. The atrium, serving now as a reception hall, was thronged with clients, all like Elisha and Pappas awaiting interviews. In the chambers that opened from it slave secretaries copied documents and student apprentices pored over scrolls.

The water clock that marked the half-hours had been filled for the third time before a porter ushered Elisha and Pappas into the conference room of the distinguished advocate. Even then they found him still engaged, deep in discussion with two men. Without interrupting his conversation, he saluted them with a gesture, beckoned them in and waved them toward the chairs arrayed along the walls.

Pompeianus was a dry little man, somewhat past the prime of life. His thin graying hair disheveled, his robe disarranged, he was altogether unprepossessing in manner and appearance. But his eyes were alive with intelligence and his speech was direct and incisive.

After a time, he got to his feet in a gesture of dismissal of the men with whom he had been closeted. They rose reluctantly and trailed him to the door where they detained him for a final exchange before they bowed and departed.

"And now, Pappas, Elisha," Pompeianus addressed them briskly, turning toward them, "to our business. I have had a transcript made of the writ that came from Palestine. I should like you to see it before we settle on a line of defense."

He rummaged in a cylindrical book box that rested on the floor and drew from it a scroll which he handed to Elisha.

"The alternatives before us," he continued while Elisha perused the writing, "are these. We can argue that the Jewish authorities have no legal right to make a request for extradition. Frankly I am reluctant to adopt that course. Our courts as a matter of policy prefer to uphold local authorities. Or we can gather evidence that your offense was entirely a dissent from the doctrines of the Jewish religion rather than an overt act against it, as you contended before Clarus. I am not too hopeful of that approach either. . . ."

"Here," he broke off, "what is it?"

Elisha had leaped to his feet, his eyes shining with elation. His face was transfigured by a triumphant smile.

"Look, Pappas," he cried, giving his friend the document. "Read this. The whole thing is a fraud—I should have known that Joshua and Gamliel, yes and most of the others too, would never stoop . . ."

"Perhaps," Pompeianus interjected dryly, "you will be so kind as to take me into your confidence."

"The names!" Elisha wrested the scroll from Pappas and held it before the lawyer, pointing with trembling fingers to the seals reproduced on it. " 'Abba, President of the Academy of Caesarea,' 'Shraga the Levite, of the students of the Sanhedrin' and the rest. It is perfectly clear what happened. My enemies tried to get the Sanhedrin to demand my extradition. Failing in that, they trumped up a document that would look official, attached whatever signatures they could procure and dressed them up with descriptions that would impress Gentiles ignorant of Jewish affairs."

"Gently," the lawyer calmed. "I think I understand, but I would like to have a clearer statement. . . ."

"It's all quite simple," Elisha explained, forcing himself into coherence. "No publication of the Sanhedrin can be official without the hand and seals of its president, of the adjutant patriarch and of the vice-president. Well, Gamliel's name is not here. Nor is Tarfon's, nor Elazar's. The whole list includes no more than two or three sages and they are among the most obscure and unrepresentative."

"You mean," Pompeianus inquired excitedly, "that the responsible authorities of the Jewish people are not involved in this whole business."

"Exactly."

"But that's perfect," the lawyer exclaimed. "Now we are in an unexceptionable position. There is no case against you. And we have the men who concocted the document right where we want them. Tomorrow we go before Clarus and invoke against them the laws on false informers. They will be arrested, brought here for trial…"

"Oh, no," Elisha recoiled, "I will not have that."

"You will not have that?" Pompeianus echoed in dismay. "But the best defense is always attack."

"That may be," Elisha conceded stubbornly. "But I do not want revenge. I want to be let alone. When I left Palestine I swore I was done with my former associates. The very prospect of confronting them is abhorrent to me."

"But," the jurist pursued, "if you follow my advice, the tables will be turned. The burden of proof will be taken from you and put onto your accusers. Otherwise you will have to prepare and present testimony yourself."

"Then that is the way it will be."

"As you say," Pompeianus yielded. "It is not the method I prefer, but since you insist, there is only one course open to you. You must write to the President of the Sanhedrin and ask for a statement signed and sealed that that High Court has no interest in your extradition."

"But," Elisha stammered, "that is impossible. He will not respond to any communication from me."

"Then go to Palestine and see him in person."

"Equally impossible. I am under a ban of excommunication. No Jew may so much as speak to me."

Pompeianus threw up his hands in bewilderment.

"Then how will you get the evidence we require?"

"That will be my task," Pappas volunteered. "I am not exactly in favor with the rabbis so that a letter from me might be disregarded. But if I travel to Palestine, I am certain that they will not refuse the request."

"Would you?" Elisha murmured gratefully.

"Of course, though"—Pappas hesitated—"I should like, if possible, to put the trip off for a week or so. I am involved in a speculation in Arabian spices and perfumes, and I ought to be on the scene to protect my investment. Would it matter seriously if I delayed my departure...?"

"I think not," Pompeianus assured him. "I am quite certain that Clarus will consent to a postponement. The courts are rather lenient in that regard."

"And you will not mind?" Pappas inquired of his friend.

"Of course not," Elisha replied instantly, concealing his disappointment.

Recent developments had been favorable and Pompeianus seemed certain of the outcome. But the workings of the law were unpredictable. And Elisha foresaw that he would not be altogether at ease until the whole matter had been safely and irrevocably closed. The prospect that opened before him of a period, perhaps of months, overshadowed by apprehension was not inviting. Yet Pappas had been more generous than he had the right to expect.

"You must not leave Antioch," he insisted, "until it suits your convenience altogether."

"Unless," Pompeianus added, strolling toward the door, "unexpected difficulties should arise over deferring the trial. If you do not hear from me to the contrary by tomorrow evening you may proceed at your leisure."

With that he had brought them to the exit and was bowing them out.

Pappas's speculation in Arabian aromatics proved more involved than he had predicted. As chance would have it, a large supply of spices and herbs reached Seleucia, the port of Antioch, on the very next day, depressing the price of the commodity so sharply that he was compelled to withhold his stock from the market, to avoid taking a severe loss. Each morning he ventured forth, hopeful of unearthing some purchaser who would relieve him of his merchandise for a sum equal to his investment. From each expedition he returned contrite, abjectly apologetic and unsuccessful. So, day after day, his negotiations dragged on as though with calculated perversity. Recurrently he seemed on the point of winding up his affairs. Always they were protracted by unforeseen complications.

The passage of a fortnight found him still in Antioch, no freer to leave the city than at the very beginning. By that time, Elisha's nerves were frayed to breaking though he concealed his frenzied impatience as best he could. Pappas, fully cognizant of the strain under which his friend labored, cast about for devices to turn his attention from his anxieties.

When Elisha had first arrived in Syria, bruised and aching after his experiences in Palestine, Pappas had plunged him deliberately into a round of social activities. Even more eager to distract him now, he filled every moment with some amusement or other, with lectures and symposia, with visits to the baths, the gymnasia and the theaters. His program of diversion was made all the easier by the fact that on meeting Elisha people were attracted to him, taking an almost immediate liking to this thoughtful, reticent stranger, romantic both in appearance and background. In consequence, the two men did not want for invitations to banquets nor were they ever at a loss how to spend their evenings. Yet pleasant as he found the succession of dinners and receptions, Elisha was deeply relieved when, liberated at last from his unfortunate enterprise, Pappas set out for Palestine.

They had reckoned that twenty days ought to be sufficient for the trip. But when weeks went by without word from Pappas, let alone his reappearance in Antioch, Elisha grew apprehensive. Declining all engagements with those newly acquired acquaintances to whose care Pappas, before his departure, had commended him, he confined himself to his quarters. There he spent the worrisome hours in desultory reading, morbid imaginings as to what might have befallen his emissary, and unhappy speculations over the future. Nor was he altogether reassured by the brief cryptic note that reached him just after the month's end. Delivered by a merchant who had traveled at his leasure from Palestine, the communication indicated that Pappas had arrived safely at his destination and that at the time of the letter's dispatch he was in good health. It added that he was already engaged in the attempt to procure from the Sanhedrin the required document but that unexpected difficulties, whose nature he did not specify, had arisen. Relieved of anxiety for Pappas's welfare, Elisha now had additional reason for concern over himself.

Meantime, Pompeianus hounded him mercilessly. He urged upon him the necessity of haste, listened irritably to protestations of powerlessness and uttered dire warnings of the perils of further delay.

"It has come at last," he informed Elisha, whom he had summoned peremptorily to his chambers one afternoon after Pappas had been absent over two months. "This morning Clarus denied my petition for another postponement. On the day after tomorrow he will issue a formula and assign the case to a trial judge."

"But didn't you explain...?" Elisha cried.

"He is done with excuses. He told me point-blank that he has been too generous with us, that we have had abundant opportunity to procure any evidence we desire. In fact, he hinted rather broadly that, lacking a presentable case, we are resorting to tricks to avoid a decision as long as possible."

"Then all is lost," Elisha concluded in toneless resignation.

"No, there is still a way."

Elisha looked up in quick inquiry.

"Clarus may refuse my request," Pompeianus went on, "but it is most unlikely that he would not defer to Manto. If you can persuade her to intervene once more, our problem will be solved. Pappas should be back any day now. It is time that we must play for, and this is our only hope of winning it."

At noon the next day Elisha presented himself at Manto's house.

"Will you inquire of your mistress," he instructed the porter who accosted him in the vestibule, "whether she will receive Elisha."

Awaiting the attendant's return, he steeled himself for the interview. It had never been easy for him to ask for assistance from anyone, not even from his closest friends. It was particularly difficult in the case of this woman who, despite the fact that they were virtually strangers to each other, had already done him a signal unearned service. Had there been any alternative to this appeal, he would have chosen it unhesitatingly. But Pompeianus had made it unmistakably clear that Manto was his sole and last resort.

"Our lady will see you in the picture gallery," the porter informed him as he relieved him of his cape. "Please come this way."

In a little room, paved with gleaming mosaic and walled with vivid murals and panel paintings, Manto received him. She was sitting in a high-backed chair, a green woolen shawl about her shoulders, a great shaggy fur draped over her legs. The tang of early autumn was in the air and near her a charcoal brazier crackled and sparkled.

"What an unexpected pleasure," she greeted him gaily, putting aside the embroidery on which she had been working. "I had almost despaired of your ever calling on me again—at least without a formal invitation."

Acutely embarrassed by her salutation, he smiled uncertainly and took the chair to which she pointed. For a few minutes she talked brightly, trying to draw him out. But he who had been ill at ease with her at their previous meetings was now too burdened by the consciousness of the request he must make to be responsive. Nor could he endure that she continue longer under misapprehension as to the purpose of his visit. Regretfully he began: "I wish that it were true that I came only to converse with you."

"Yes," she encouraged when he paused in manifest disquiet.

"The fact is," he floundered, "that I am here to solicit your help...it was so good of you the first time...and now..."

Falteringly he described his involvement with the law and his need for her further assistance.

"And so," she anticipated his request and spared him the voicing of it, "Pompeianus would like me to intercede with Clarus."

"Except," he corrected, "that it is I, not Pompeianus, who asks for it."

"Then it is already done, and I am confident that he will not deny me."

"You can have no notion," he murmured unsteadily, his eyes averted, "how indebted I shall always be...."

She looked at him quizzically, a faint vertical crease of curiosity cutting her brow.

"Why are you so ill at ease with me?" she asked abruptly.

"But I am not," he protested.

"Ah, yes, but you are, and not only now, which I can understand, but on the other occasions as well."

Furious with himself for being so tongue-tied, he blurted, "You see, where I was raised, it is considered improper for men to be alone with strange women."

"So, that is it," she mused. "Then you find my company distressing."

"On the contrary," he ventured, "it is very pleasant."

She laughed softly.

"I am afraid that you have not had much practice in turning compliments. You lack the ease, the touch of insinuation that is a necessary ingredient in the flattery of a woman."

Elisha relaxed a little and smiled. "I suppose they forgot to teach me that, too."

She seized on his second reference to his early life.

"I have never asked you about your past or the causes of

your present difficulties, hoping always that you would volunteer the information. Won't you tell me?"

A look of distaste came over his face at the prospect of disinterring a past he was only too eager to bury.

"Sometimes," she suggested, "the pain of memories is relieved by dragging them into the open."

It did not seem likely to him. But feeling that he owed her an accounting, he began to narrate the tale of his life in Palestine and what had befallen him there. He spoke disconnectedly at first, referring to persons and events without interpreting their identities and meanings. So quietly that he did not feel himself interrupted, she extracted explanations from him and led him from the relatively recent events with which he had begun into what lay behind them. When he was describing the earliest memories of his childhood, she became silent and listened without moving. As he talked, the sense of constraint fell from him. He forgot everything except the experiences he was reliving. Out of his very intensity he re-created scenes and episodes and the moods of aspiration, defeat or bitterness that still colored them.

"And here I am," he concluded, "a heretic, an outcast from my people who may soon be returned to them against his will. Here I am, seeking in Syria what I could not find in Palestine."

The pictures he had just evoked faded from him. He was suddenly aware of his setting, of the fact that in his concentration he had been pacing the room, of her eyes, now deep green, fixed on him.

"I have bored you," he said.

"Bored?" she murmured. "Ah no, you possess one quality of which there is very little in Antioch. Earnestness. Besides, that was a fascinating story. One never knows in meeting a stranger what experiences he may have undergone. I suppose each of us is like Odysseus, 'a man of much wandering and many toils,' even the most prosaic and unpromising-looking. Not that I did not suspect adventure in you. And I should scarcely feel justified in characterizing you as unattractive. On the contrary... What I still do not understand," she said quickly to avert a return of his self-consciousness, "is this. What are you looking for? What do you hope to find here?"

"Certainty," he answered simply.

"But certainty about what?"

"About the universe, in the first place. Is there a God directing it, or is it just brute accident? And if there is a God, what is His character? Certainty about how man ought to behave. Is there a right and wrong, and what are they? You see, I am one of those unfortunates who cannot be content with conjecture."

"I must be stupid," she apologized, "but I still do not see it."

"Then let me put it this way. Do you know Euclid's *Elements of Geometry?*"

She nodded.

"And you remember how every proposition in it is proved by rigid logic?"

"Yes, of course."

"Well, that is what I want to do, to proceed as Euclid does, only not with points, lines and triangles, but in the large domain of man's ultimate beliefs and principles. If Euclid's method can be successfully applied to the things with which religion, philosophy and morality are concerned, see what results. Instead of doctrines accepted on blind faith or conjecture, mankind will possess a system of demonstrations in which it can put fullest confidence. We shall know forever that such and such is the case about reality, that we must act in one fashion, not the other."

"But," she objected, "what if the last propositions in your geometry of thought and action—I suppose I can call it that— were to be disillusioning? Let us assume that by proving every step, you are driven to conclude that there are neither gods nor immortal souls, and that there is no such thing as right or virtue. What then?"

"Then," he asserted boldly, "the sooner we know, the better. At least, we would not deceive ourselves any longer.

Do you see what I mean?"

He watched her eagerly. It had somehow become important that she understand.

"Yes," she reflected. "And it is a magnificent thought. But why Euclid's method, and no other?"

"Because that is the only procedure in which one starts from assumptions so self-evident as to be unchallengeable and moves to conclusions that are equally indisputable. In an enterprise like this, the technique is all-important."

"But why did you have to leave Palestine for that? Could you not have built such a system there?"

In his enthusiasm he had resumed his pacing of the room. He stopped at her pertinent question and remained unmoving until it was answered.

"I had to leave Palestine. First, because my people there cherish a definite set of beliefs, which every Jew is expected to accept unquestioningly. For a long time their doctrines were mine too and, when I first began to doubt, I tried to find arguments to bolster them. But it cannot be done that way, first the conclusions and then the premises. It is like trying to build upper stories before laying a foundation. The whole structure collapsed. To my fellows, dissent was no trivial matter to be tolerated. Their resentment made it impossible for me to remain where I was. Besides, if I am going to make my attempt, I must learn philosophy. And aside from cities like Alexandria or Athens, this is the best place for that."

"And so," she concluded, "you have come here to study philosophy."

"Unfortunately," he said ruefully, "there is more to it even than that. I must first learn something of the sciences. And my knowledge of the Greek language and literature is faulty. I have been taught by bitter experience that an artisan must master his tools before he sets to work. Actually I must begin my re-education at the very beginning."

"But that would take you years!"

"What of it?" Elisha smiled wanly. "There is no occasion for hurry. My major concern right now is to extricate myself from this lawsuit. If that goes against me, if I am taken back to Palestine, everything is lost. That is why your co-operation is so important to me. Without it I could never avert the catastrophe. Even with it, I have my fears. What are the chances in any court of a lone individual, assisted though he may be by a powerful ally, against the demands of a whole people?"

"It does sound rather hopeless when you put it that way, especially since I know only too well that you are exaggerating my influence. But you are not stating the matter fairly. You have underestimated Roman law. I am less worried about political pressure than about the strength of your case. If I could be assured on that point, I would say that you are quite safe, regardless of who may be arrayed against you."

"I wish," Elisha commented, unconvinced, "I could share your trust in Roman judges."

"There are fools among them," Manto admitted, "and occasionally a rogue as well. Nor will I deny that at times they are swayed by considerations of expediency. But in the main they contrive to get justice done. And sometimes they show heartening stubbornness in defense of principles or persons. It is an amazing system of government which that city in Italy has invented and imposed on the world. I know it too intimately to be anything but respectful of it."

"Your admiration for the Empire bewilders me," Elisha said slowly. "It is so directly the contrary of my own and what I assumed to be the general opinion of thinking people. I have always regarded, or to express it more accurately, I have been trained to regard Rome as the great oppressor of mankind. It is difficult for me to conceive it otherwise."

"You will," she asserted confidently and with great earnestness, "when you have had an opportunity to observe it at work. Your own instance I am sure will prove my point." He smiled at the adroit obliqueness of her encouragement.

"Once upon a time," he jested, "I would have responded to a statement as welcome as this last of yours with the prayer: 'Amen, so may it be God's will.' "

She flashed an answering smile at him and then prompted, "But we are wandering. I am impatient to hear what you have accomplished since coming to Antioch."

"Not a thing," he sighed unhappily. "I have lacked the heart even to look for an apartment, let alone settle down to serious study. A kind of paralysis has taken hold of me and prevented me from thinking of anything except a particular document long since overdue from Palestine. If and when I hold that in my hands, I shall take the first step by engaging a competent instructor in grammar and rhetoric."

"But you must not delay," she urged in instant response. "You ought to begin at once—for your own peace of spirit in the first place. Unless you fill your time with work, you will go mad with waiting. Besides, you need not look far for a tutor. In all Antioch there is no one more capable than Antiphanes. I shall be delighted to speak to him on your behalf if you like."

He had been too distraught at first, too absorbed subsequently in their conversation and too grateful for her solicitude to notice her loveliness. But now as she sat, bent slightly forward in her eagerness, looking up at him appealingly, her eyes very bright, her cheeks flushed, her lips still open after her last word so that her firm white teeth showed, the awareness of her beauty broke through and shattered all else in his consciousness. In his delighted contemplation of her he forgot momentarily that she was awaiting his reply. When he did speak, it was hesitantly, with a trace of breathlessness in his voice.

"Would you do me that kindness, too?"

"Gladly, but subject to one condition."

He looked at her inquiringly.

"You must promise to visit me from time to time to report your progress."

Light of heart he laughed, "With pleasure."

CHAPTER IV

MANTO ACTED PROMPTLY ON HER twofold promise. From
Clarus she coaxed a postponement of legal action against Elisha.
She arranged an appointment for him with Antiphanes. On the
second day after Elisha's visit with her, he sat in the rhetorician's
quarters, watching him at work, with a student, and waiting
for him to be free. The pupil, a dull, gangling youngster, was
reciting a passage from a drama, reading its surging accented
lines in a monotonous, uninspired voice. From across the table,
his instructor interrupted from time to time with corrections
which the boy echoed mechanically, or explanations which for
all their simplicity he seemed not to understand at all.

When the lesson was over, and the signal of dismissal had
been given, the pupil rose instantly, slipped his scrolls into a
bag, and with a hurried farewell, left the room, neglecting to
shut the door in his eagerness to be off. With a sigh of mingled
relief and exasperation, Antiphanes got up.

"That's the life of a teacher for you."

"How can you stand it?"

From the doorway, Antiphanes looked over his shoulder
and smiled faintly. "It is ghastly sometimes, but one must live."

"But I cannot reconcile this with everything I have heard
about you. On all sides you are lauded as one of the most gifted
literary figures in Antioch. And yet I find you giving instruction to stupid boys. Certainly there must be other, less wearing
methods of earning a livelihood open to you."

"Not really," the rhetorician explained as he returned to his
seat. "There is little money in professional lecturing, and even
less in writing. How much can an author earn on an oration or
even on a full-length book when any slave-scribe can recopy it
for public sale? And as for the pensions of patrons, no thank
you. I prefer not to bow and scrape before some rich ignora-
mus for my keep. Besides, the good gods sometimes send me
alert, stimulating pupils whom it is a joy to teach. Which leads

me to what Manto told me about you."

"It means more grammar," Elisha warned. "At the beginning at least. Do you feel equal to it?"

"I should like a better notion of what you want before I answer."

For the second time within the span of a few days Elisha described the scheme of study he had projected for himself.

"And so," Antiphanes concluded when Elisha was through, "what you really want is a full course in every aspect of our culture, including a thorough grounding in Greek and Latin grammar and rhetoric, as preparation for philosophy. My dear man, have you thought of how long that will take you?"

"I am in no hurry," Elisha informed him as he had Manto, "except to get started. And what is more, I cannot be talked out of my obsession."

"Oh, no," Antiphanes protested, "I have no desire to dissuade you. In fact, I am excited at the prospect of having you as my student. Of course, I, too, have my limitations. The natural sciences and philosophy are out of my field. But grammar, rhetoric and literature, I will undertake gladly."

"Then it is all settled, all, that is, except the matter of compensation...."

"Let's not bother with that now," Antiphanes interrupted. "You can pay me whatever you choose."

"Indeed not," Elisha objected. "Teaching is your profession. You are certainly entitled to at least the normal fee."

"But that is just the point, there is no normal fee for instruction of this kind."

But Elisha was insistent and, after some coaxing, succeeded in persuading Antiphanes to stipulate a sum.

"Thank heavens, that is settled." the rhetorician sighed, pleased to be rid of an unpleasant issue. "Now, when shall we start?"

"Is there any reason why we cannot begin right now?"

"None at all," Antiphanes replied. He drew a wax tablet

across the table toward him and picked up a stylus. "Pull your chair closer and we can get busy outlining your course."

As they sat together, a painful yearning swept Elisha, a memory of Nicholaus sitting with a ten-year-old child, fretting over the same nouns and verbs. And with it went a sense of destiny, interrupted for years, now to be fulfilled.

For the next half-hour, the two of them were at work, compiling a list of subjects comprising Latin and Greek grammar; the poets, epic, lyric and dramatic; the orators, essayists, biographers and historians.

When they were through, Antiphanes looked at the two tablets he had covered with writing.

"I must say," he remarked, "this is an heroic program. And it is only the beginning."

"The heroism," Elisha smiled wryly, "is reserved for the future. We turn now to the first item of the series, humble grammar."

With a shrug of resignation, Antiphanes rummaged through a cabinet and drew forth several scrolls.

"Here," he said, placing them before Elisha, "these are texts that I have used with boys whom I have tutored at various times. They are a bit mutilated but still quite legible. Take the detestable things as a gift. You are quite welcome to them."

"Thank you," Elisha said. "Even the prospect of studying grammar is pleasant because of the instructor."

"I think you ought to know," Antiphanes cautioned, "that I do not share your interest in metaphysics and theology."

"So I suspected," Elisha nodded. "All through our conference I have been gathering my courage to ask about your philosophical opinions."

"I have given the matter so little thought." Antiphanes replied slowly, "that I scarcely know what to say. Of course, I do not believe in the gods of the myths. What is more, I do not know a single educated person who does, except the Stoics who interpret them as allegories for the forces of nature. I do attend worship at the temples occasionally. These are the rituals of the State. It is useful for society that they be maintained and so I regard it my duty to conform to them. As for the gods of the philosophers—Plato's Idea of Ideas, Aristotle's First and Final Cause, the Stoic's Cosmic Reason—it is hard for me to decide. Sometimes, depending on my mood or the last book I have read, I believe. Sometimes I do not. In the last analysis, it boils down to this: I do not know."

"But do you not feel that you must decide one way or the other? That you must be sure?"

"If I felt that way, I should be a philosopher, not a rhetorician."

"Then what do you live by?"

"The love of the beautiful. It is enough to hear inspiring music, read exalted prose, and respond to the color and grace of works of art. I have never quite understood why people like you are so concerned over certainty in abstract issues when you can, instead, watch a young man throw a discus or contemplate a statue carved by some great master. Which makes us even. I find your attitude as unintelligible as you find mine. You are enjoying Antioch," Antiphanes concluded abruptly, "are you not?"

"Immensely!"

"It is different from what you were accustomed to?"

"More than you can imagine."

"In what way?"

"In every respect," came the ready response. "In the joy in the body and its pleasures, in the theater, in that concern with beauty for its own sake to which you have alluded. But that is not all. You Greeks are at liberty to inquire, to challenge, even to deny anything. You can say that you do not know or much care whether God exists or does not. No rabbi would dare say that in Palestine, nor any Jew for that matter. My people has its doctrines and insists on the unquestioning acceptance of them, which is well so long as one has faith. Once one doubts and needs to discover for himself what to believe, freedom to think and inquire are indispensabilities. And that only your world allows."

"Then what is it," Antiphanes asked, "that attracts so many people to Judaism and the Christian sect of it?"

"The security of a truth revealed by a God, I suppose. The peace of mind, the clear direction for conduct which it offers."

Referring to the serenity that had once been his, a nostalgia came over Elisha. Fleetingly, he drew in the lingering aroma of dead flowers.

"But it was not good enough," he sighed. "It fell apart when I started to analyze it. Revelation must either be accepted or rejected. I had to choose between faith and reason. I have chosen the latter."

The two stood face to face, Elisha smiling affectionately now at the spare, silver-haired man. There was an answering smile on Antiphanes' face, but also a look in his eyes which escaped Elisha. It was wonder over the spirit of a man who, youth behind him, could renounce a world for a quest after truth. Something akin to awe and a sense of privilege flickered through him, as he said with gentle earnestness: "I hope that we shall be friends, as well as teacher and pupil."

"I am sure of it."

At the street door Elisha hesitated. Dusk had settled over Antioch. An early winter rain was falling in a gray torrent. A raw wind sighed between the houses. Slipping the scrolls under his cloak for protection, he plunged into the storm.

In the warmth and light of Pappas's apartment, he stripped off his sodden outer garments, and piled the books and tablets neatly on a corner of the table on which the attendant was laying out his evening repast. While he waited for the first course to be served, he wandered absent-mindedly about the room. From habit, he began to recite the old Hebrew prayers prescribed for the time of nightfall. Becoming aware of what he was doing, he chuckled with lighthearted amusement, shrugged his shoulders and sat down to his supper.

But he could never resist a new book. As he began his meal, he unfurled a scroll, propped it onto a dish and began to read, his food growing cold, so slowly in his absorption did he eat.

Lying abed but wide awake, Elisha paid no attention to the footsteps pounding across the courtyard. Pappas's apartment on the second floor of a five-story building gave upon a central inclosure shared by all the tenants so that the sound of people moving about, even late at night, was in no way unusual.

But when someone began to run up the private staircase which led to his quarters, Elisha rose quickly, sped through the intervening rooms to the door and, sliding back the bolt, swung it open. Instantly he was enveloped by powerful arms and billowing cloth.

"I have it," Pappas's voice cried in triumph. "Here, you may see for yourself."

Pappas stepped back to kick the door shut behind him, undoing at the same time the catch of a leather wallet that hung from his waist. Incapable of speech, Elisha extended a trembling hand for the wooden-backed, hinged tablets.

"Let's have more light first." Pappas whirled away, picked up the one lamp that burned in the chamber and touched wick after wick with its flame.

"Now," he said, pushing his friend onto a stool and tossing the document into his lap, "read it."

"The Sanhedrin," a firm hand had written in Greek on one waxed leaf, "the only court of the Jewish people authorized to treat with matters of state, has no interest in the return to Palestine of one Elisha the son of Abuyah, late of Migdal, now resident in Antioch. Nor has it ever petitioned the government of the province of Syria for his extradition."

On the other page, set in grooves, were the seals of Gamliel, of Tarfon and of Elazar ben Azariah, their signatures and official titles inscribed beside them.

Scanning the lines, Elisha felt relief surge through him and, unexpectedly in its wake, a numbing weariness. He had been living in such high tension that the relaxation of strain left him empty of energy.

"You have been very kind," he said with difficulty. "But why did it take you so long?"

Pappas dropped onto a chair and waved an arm in a gesture of disgust.

"Not by choice, I assure you. But I wasted a week in Jamnia waiting for Gamliel to return home and another five days trying to get an audience with him. Rebuffed there, I dashed off to the home of Elazar ben Azariah who as adjutant patriarch was my next resort, only to discover that he was away in Galilee. From there I went to Tarfon. He simply refused to trouble himself on your behalf. He admitted that he had no desire to penalize you, but neither would he go out of his way to be helpful. As he put it, since you cut yourself loose from the Jewish people you had no right to appeal to it for assistance. By that time I was almost frantic. I knew that speed was all-important, that the longer the delay the greater your danger and yet I had no idea where to turn."

"But Joshua," Elisha interjected, "did you not know that he too is an official of the Sanhedrin?"

"Please, Elisha," Pappas evaded. "Let me tell my story in my own way. Just when I was beginning to despair, Akiba sought me out. He had heard of my purpose and unsolicited joined forces with me. Together we retraced the entire circuit. I was present when he convinced Tarfon to affix his signature. 'It is forbidden,' he reminded him, 'to cast a stone after one who has fallen.' In brief, if anyone is to be thanked, it is Akiba, not I. Had it not been for him, I should still be in Palestine, and you..." He shrugged.

"It was to be expected of him." Elisha murmured. "He was always kind and a devoted friend. As you are, Pappas. But you still have not explained why you did not go to Joshua."

"Joshua..." Pappas paused and then continued with a rush, "Joshua is dead."

"Dead," Elisha breathed, staring so blankly that Pappas averted his eyes.

"He died just before I reached Palestine. That is why Gamliel was away from Jamnia."

"But what happened to him?" Elisha cried in anguish. "He was an old man, but strong, and in perfect health when I saw him last—only a few months ago."

Pappas was strangely silent.

"Don't you know?" Elisha pressed. "You must have inquired. Or is it something you are reluctant to tell me?"

Pappas nodded.

"Then let me hear it now, at once."

"People said," the other replied miserably, "that it was for grieving over you. At the session of the Sanhedrin at which you were excommunicated, he did not utter a word and, like Akiba, he refused to vote. He sat there, tears streaming down his face. But when it was done, he got to his feet and reversing the position of a lifetime, introduced a resolution putting an interdict on Greek studies. Needless to say, it was adopted. Then he went home and died. Everyone in Palestine believes..." Pappas hesitated.

Elisha's hands mounted jerkily to his breast. In accordance with the rituals of a religion which he had renounced, supposedly for all time and to its last and least injunctions, he ripped the cloth with a long ragged rending. So this hour which should have been elation over escape from a grave peril was converted into guilty sorrow, regret, remorse.

Claras's chamber in the Basilica of Trajan was already crowded with spectators when Elisha arrived in the company of Pompeianus and Pappas. As they made their way to the first bench reserved for litigants, Elisha noticed Manto and her distinguished escort, Antiphanes, Quadratus the Questor and the philosopher, Hermonax. Nicander the rhetorician was seated by himself in a corner. Others of his acquaintances were scattered about the room. The assurance engendered in Elisha by the presence of friends was strengthened by the manner with which the Judicial Legate greeted him. For, looking up from the lawyers arguing before him, Claras smiled a cordial welcome.

But his confidence ebbed when he heard Pappas whisper in his ear, "There are Jews here—in a body to the rear."

"Who are they?" he asked perturbed. "And why have they come?"

"Antiochene sympathizers with Shraga's war party, doubtless," Pappas conjectured. "But do not concern yourself over them. Claras is not the sort either to yield to intimidation or to tolerate disturbances."

At that point their subdued colloquy came to an abrupt close. For, having disposed of the matter in which he had been engaged, the Legate called Pompeianus and Elisha forward.

"Gentlemen," he began, "I owe you apology and thanks— apology for the skepticism with which, I am frank to admit, I regarded your contention of the spuriousness of the demand for extradition, and gratitude for your assistance in sparing me the commission of a judicial blunder. I have studied the document you procured in Palestine. It is indisputably genuine and official. Needless to say, there is no longer a case against the defendant and I have already ordered his name stricken from the docket."

Through his own exhilaration, Elisha was conscious of the congratulatory pressure of Pompeianus's hand on his, and the murmur of approval among the spectators behind them. He smiled and moved to express his appreciation both to Claras and his advocate. But the Legate was speaking again, this time in a voice raised so that everyone in the chambers might hear.

"Despite the fact that the action has been dismissed, I cannot refrain from utilizing this occasion to make clear the position of Roman law on the issues involved. The courts will protect any legally recognized religion. They will not, however, prosecute mere opinion. One may with impunity think of his fellows as he chooses, so long as he does not by physical act or malicious slander inflict harm on their persons, property or rights. Similarly, freedom of intellectual attitude toward any cult within the Empire is the privilege of every freeman, assuming always that he does no violence to its sacred objects nor speaks in wanton derision of its doctrines. In support of these principles, let me cite the Digests of the successive Imperial Governors Proconsular of this province as well as relevant decisions rendered at Rome...."

As the Legate proceeded to quote legal precedents, Elisha recalled Manto's prediction of the workings of Roman justice and her endorsement of the Empire on which it was based. Too confused at the moment by his own elation and the necessity of attending to Clarus' speech to think clearly, he nevertheless foresaw that, like so many of his opinions, his political judgments were destined to drastic revision.

In the corridor outside the judicial chambers, his acquaintances milled about Elisha, expressing their enthusiastic felicitations.

"Let us celebrate," Manto called excitedly over the hubbub. "You are all invited to my home for the festivities."

Touched though he was by the suggestion, Elisha shook his head.

"But aren't you pleased?" she queried.

"Of course."

"Then why will you not allow us to share the happiness of your good fortune?" His fingers touched the little, almost inconspicuous tear with which he had marked all his garments.

"I am in mourning," he explained, "over the death of a very dear friend."

"You can have no notion," he confessed to Antiphanes

some days later, "how decisive a reversal in attitude I have undergone. And you must not imagine that I am generalizing merely from my own isolated experience. It is simply that my eyes have been opened."

They were lounging on a couch in the rhetorician's apartment, the scrolls and tablets with which they had been occupied strewn over the spread between them.

"But how were you accustomed to think of the Empire?" Antiphanes wondered.

"To me it was the brutal power that conquered peoples, stripped them of their liberties, despoiled their shrines and drained them of their wealth by rapacious taxation. You will have some idea of the nature of my sentiments from the fact that less than a month ago I could not understand that Manto should speak sympathetically of Rome."

"But you can't possibly have conceived it as altogether evil?"

"No," Elisha reflected, "I suppose not. I recognized that it had its virtues. But it never occurred to me to include among them those I have recently discovered, the most significant which any government can exhibit, the impartial administration of a system of law designed to protect each man in his rights. I see now that there is a sense in which no human being is altogether friendless in any struggle for self-preservation as, at one time not so long ago, I conceived myself to be. In all the world from Britain to India an invisible guard stands watch over every person...."

"Hold on," Antiphanes cautioned. "Aren't you slipping into the opposite error—that of idealization?"

"I think not," Elisha replied. "I have not forgotten that there are ugly spots in the picture. The point is this, that whatever the deficiencies—and they are many and real—they are far overbalanced by the benefits."

"On that," Antiphanes agreed, "there can be no dispute. As you may have guessed, I, like so many others, take for granted the political structure which shelters me. Normally I concern myself with public affairs even less than with metaphysics. But I am never completely unaware of the fact that at no time in history and nowhere else in the world have men enjoyed peace, security, latitude in action and thought, such as is conferred on us by the imperial system."

CHAPTER V

EVER SINCE HIS ARRIVAL IN Antioch Elisha had planned to rent an apartment for himself. At first he had been deterred by the protestations of Pappas who dismissed the idea indignantly whenever Elisha referred to it. Later, distracted by his difficulties with the law and uncertain of his future, he had been incapable of acting on his intention. But once the charges against him had been annulled and he attempted sustained study, he discovered that he required more privacy than was possible in shared quarters. By chance, a desirable suite in a superior building was available for immediate occupancy. The tenant, a merchant who had fallen on evil days, was eager to be relieved not only of his residence and its furnishings but of the services of his attendant as well.

The four-room dwelling was exactly to Elisha's taste. Over the servant, a decrepit and unsightly freedman named Libanius, he hesitated. But there was such unspoken appeal in the old retainer's eyes that Elisha, taking over the establishment and purchasing its equipment, did not have the courage to turn the fellow out.

The discipline of study he had acquired in years gone by now stood Elisha in good stead. Quickly he recovered the habit of rising early each morning and working indefatigably not only through the day but often deep into the night. The texts he read were different from those which had concerned him in Palestine, and he recited no prayers before and after them. But once again his life centered on books.

At regular intervals he returned to Antiphanes to report on the ground he had covered and to discuss obscure and recondite points. The rhetorician, who had sensed intellectual maturity in Elisha on first meeting him, was amazed by his diligence, thoroughness and comprehension.

"I do not know," he commented on one occasion, "what

they taught you before you came here, but they certainly did teach you to learn."

Even Pappas was impressed. To be sure he scoffed, but he too had had a reverence for scholarship implanted in him in his childhood, and deep within him he admired Elisha for the very practices he pretended to scorn.

So the weeks worked themselves into months. Elementary treatises on Greek and Latin grammar yielded place to more advanced studies and these in turn to Homer and Hesiod, with the notes of the Alexandrian scholiasts on them. By midwinter, texts of the dramatists appeared on Elisha's table.

Yet even when he was working most intently Elisha was by no means a recluse. He visited often with his acquaintances or entertained them in his own home at dinners prepared and served none too skilfully by Libanius. With increasing frequency he called on Manto.

"How goes the great enterprise?" was the invariable greeting with which she welcomed him. But although she spoke half in banter, she was genuinely attentive to his answer, an interest that both flattered and stimulated him.

Nor was Antiphanes content to be merely a mentor. He insisted on presenting Elisha to the distinguished literary and scientific personalities of Antioch. He introduced him to the great public library as well as to smaller collections privately owned and housed but open to students properly recommended. He escorted him to theaters and concerts and symposia. And when Elisha protested that much of this gadding about was a waste of time, the rhetorician countered by pointing out that there was more to Greek culture than books, that its spirit could be acquired only by participation.

As a result, there was scarcely a public function of significance from which the two men were absent. The lectures they attended together were generally illuminating, or at the least informative if not always exciting. But one of them, confusing and disappointing in itself, turned out to be the first in a series of experiences which revealed to Elisha the less attractive side of the Greek world about him.

At Antiphanes' invitation, Elisha accompanied him to hear an address by Saturninus, leader of the Gnostics of Antioch. The meeting was held in a temple of Mithra, a building which by its fantastic architecture and decorations, made its contribution to the air of strangeness that invested the entire evening.

The vestibule was dominated by a weird statue in human shape, with the head of a lion and a snake coiled about it in a six-fold spiral. Its arms were clutched to its bosom, the right hand holding two keys, the left grasping a thunderbolt and a jagged flash of lightning. About its feet stood a cock, an anvil and hammer, a trident and a miscellany of other objects. The figure in its gigantic proportions suggested the fabled horrors of Greek legends.

As they came in from the street, Elisha gasped, "In heaven's name, what's that?"

"That," Antiphanes replied, "is the great god of the mysteries of Mithra. Sometimes they call it Kronos, sometimes Aeon, but most often Zenda-Akarana. In the doctrine of the cult it represents eternity from which all things have emerged. It is all elaborately symbolic. The lion's head is Time the Devourer, the snake the signs of the Zodiac, the keys the Last Judgment and the Resurrection. And these things at the bottom stand for various gods; the anvil and hammer for Hephaestus, the cock for Aesculapius, and so on. And this fellow here," he pointed to an attendant standing near by, "collects the admission fees."

They paid for the privilege of entrance and descended to an underground auditorium, the door of which was guarded by two statues of young men holding torches, one upright, the other inverted.

"The two Mithras, the rising and setting sun," Antiphanes explained as they walked between them.

The subterranean hall, heavy with the musty smell of a cellar, was brilliantly lighted by a multitude of little lamps. On both sides benches rose in tiers toward the walls where votive tablets shone with warm colors. At the far end, before a raised platform, stood a rostrum, two altars and another strange sculpture, the figure of a man emerging from a rock. The entire wall beyond it was covered by a great curtain, concealing, Elisha guessed, the most sacred symbol of the cult.

There were only some thirty or forty people scattered about the auditorium, and Elisha and Antiphanes had no difficulty finding seats near the pulpit.

Two men were standing before the rostrum, talking to each other in undertones: one large, loose-jointed, with a dissolute face and puffy eyes; the other an inconspicuous little person obviously deferential to his companion.

"It is a small crowd," the tall man was saying.

"Yes," the other replied, "but good. From their dress, they are people who count."

"I guess we may as well begin," the first man continued. "I doubt that anyone else will come."

Slowly and without enthusiasm, he mounted the platform.

"That's Saturninus," Antiphanes said.

"Men and women of Antioch," the lecturer began, lounging against the lectern, "or as I should put it, fragments of God that have descended the seven spheres to be imprisoned in the flesh."

He paused to allow his hearers to comprehend his unusual salutation and a solemn silence gripped the room. Somewhere through the stillness a woman whispered, "Fascinating, don't you think?" A faint smile of pleasure passed over Saturninus' dissipated face. His position at the rostrum became more indolent.

"It is my purpose to save you from the blindness of those who fail to distinguish the gods from one another. There is only one true God who was before Time came into being. He so far transcends human comprehension that in effect, so far as man's mind is concerned, He does not exist at all. From Him and from Sophia, who in His wisdom, was born the demiurge, creator of things physical, whom most people mistake for the true God, and whom they worship. It is this lesser being who gave the Law to Moses and the Jewish prophets, their doctrines to the Greek, Babylonian and Egyptian sages."

Elisha made every effort to follow the lecture as it moved into an involved account of minor gods, planetary spirits and the descent of the soul from Heaven. Occasionally, he heard quotations from Plato or Philo which he recognized or references to Greek philosophers whom he could identify. But for the rest it was a conglomeration of fantastic unrelated ideas.

Yet, strangely enough, his interest did not waver. The soothing, contemptuous voice of the speaker lapped about him like the waters of a warm bath. The lights and swimming colors engulfed his sight. A pleasurable sense of unreality pervaded him. He sat, wallowing in a half-hypnosis, listening to words that made no sense, but which he was for the time convinced were infinitely meaningful.

Saturninus himself freed him from the trance, first by a subtle change in tone and then by the unmistakable purport of his concluding remarks.

"I have presented to you this evening only the barest outline of our doctrine, the faintest indications of how man and the world must attain salvation. The heart of our truth I have not touched. That is a mystery into which only a few of special aptitudes can be initiated. Those of you who are interested in further study should apply to me privately for instruction, which, if you possess the necessary qualifications, I shall undertake in person. It is a long and difficult course. But the rewards are great. By putting aside the vile corruptible cloak of the senses and donning the luminous garment of Heaven, one enters into communion with the ineffable God."

"Well, what did you think of him?" Antiphanes asked.

They had left the auditorium and had come into the cool fresh air of night.

"It was nonsense. At least, so it seemed to me."

"Of course it was."

"And yet it fascinated me."

"Naturally. That rascal is one of the cleverest charlatans in Syria. And I may as well tell you that I had a reason for taking you to hear him. I feared that you were too enthusiastic about Antioch, that you saw only its virtues. As your friend I wanted you to see that the shield has another, less attractive, side—painted in greed, charlatanry and deceit."

"Thank you," Elisha replied, "for preparing me. But so long as it has freedom of inquiry and the facilities for investigation, it will give me what I came to find."

Of that "other side of the shield" to which Antiphanes had referred Elisha remained for some time blissfully unaware. It was only months later, and then quite by accident, that he caught his first glimpses of it. He was present at a dinner which he did not wish to attend, and he accompanied Manto on a shopping tour. In these chance experiences, the glittering shell of Greek life was cracked open, and the ugliness beneath it exposed for a moment. Thereafter he understood what his tutor had meant.

Elisha met Nicander on the open street where he could not avoid him. The rhetorician was all smiles and ingratiating cordiality.

"I would so much like to have you dine with me and meet my friends. I can appreciate the fact that you have been busy. But you must be settled by now. And I have asked you at least a half-dozen times."

"I have so little time," Elisha explained. He had not forgotten Pappas's comments about the fellow.

"I know," Nicander went on, determined not to take offense, "that Antiphanes absorbs you quite completely. Yet surely he can spare you tomorrow night."

Elisha shook his head.

"Or the night after?"

Shamelessly Elisha protested an imaginary engagement.

"Name your own evening."

It was becoming difficult. Elisha was running out of excuses. It might be just as well, he thought, to get the matter over with, and as quickly as possible.

"Perhaps," Nicander went on, his smile fixed, "you are, by some good fortune, free tonight."

"Yes," Elisha responded suddenly, "I am and I shall dine with you."

Then he was startled to discover a look of consternation in Nicander's face. "It just happens," he explained, "that this will be my only opportunity in weeks. Of course, if it is inconvenient..."

"Indeed not," Nicander hastened to reassure him. "As a matter of fact, I am receiving guests tonight. Only I am not certain that you will like them. Now, on these other occasions..."

Elisha, his curiosity roused, insisted.

There was about Nicander the air of one who, through his own precipitousness, has committed some irretrievable blunder. He smiled waveringly and rushed off as though there were matters that urgently required his attention.

The building in which Nicander occupied an apartment was situated in one of the most fashionable neighborhoods of Antioch, but just on its fringe. A succession of mansions and palaces flanked it on one side, markets and tenements huddled against it on the other. Seen from afar it was an imposing structure, large and ornate. On closer view it appeared run-down and shabby. The frayed and ill-fitting livery of the porter who tended the gate was presumably an heirloom from stouter predecessors in his post. The fountain in the courtyard was not playing, the flower beds about it were overgrown with weeds. And the rhetorician's quarters to the rear of the top story were the least accessible in the entire establishment. As he mounted the seemingly endless steps, Libanius panting after him, Elisha could not help thinking that his host's home, like his reputation, was a little shabby.

They had just begun to climb the last flight of stairs when through the open door above them they heard the dull thuds of a rod beating on a bare back. The rhythmic sound was accompanied by a mounting lament and a voice which bellowed, "I will teach you to steal wine."

"But I did not steal your wine," someone wailed. "You drank it yourself this morning."

"Do not argue with me," came the reply in words blurred with fury.

On the landing Elisha shuffled his feet hastily, noisily. At once the house was still. A moment later a servant appeared in the doorway, and on his heels Nicander, his breath irregular, his face flushed and his hands smoothing his disordered clothes.

"These slaves," he complained in the manner of one man of the world with another, "one treats them kindly, and the result—insolence. The whip is the only argument they understand. But come in."

Chatting gaily, Nicander led Elisha through a vestibule, where Libanius relieved him of his cloak, into a reception hall. The chamber was furnished with a not too harmonious collection of massive pieces, all elaborate. Here Nicander drew Elisha onto a couch, seated himself by his side and set about questioning him as to his plans. Devious as he was, there could be no doubt as to his purpose. Elisha was running out of evasions when to his relief a loud knocking at the door and a babble of voices, male and female, proclaimed the arrival of other guests. Several women, modishly dressed, a half-dozen men and a number of attendants burst into the room. Nicander, obviously displeased with the interruption, rose to welcome them.

"I have somebody here whom I am eager to present," he said after the first exchange of greetings.

The group quieted and looked at Elisha with curiosity.

"This," Nicander went on, "is Elisha who has come from Palestine to take up residence in Antioch."

Among the guests was a teacher of gymnastics, a huge hulk of a man with a loose and, as it became apparent, obscene mouth. On meeting Elisha he immediately blurted, "You must be the prospective pupil—"

Nicander cut him off.

Then there was an Epicurean philosopher who, at first glance, seemed thoroughly normal but who on scrutiny appeared warped and twisted, as though he were seen in an untrue mirror. Last of all, there was a Stoic philosopher, a thin little mummy with piping voice and trembling hands.

Aside from these three, of unfavorable distinction, the others were so obscure and unimpressive as to be forgotten as soon as they were met.

"And now, dinner," Nicander called over the boisterous conversation.

"It is really a group of learned and important people," Nicander whispered impressively as, arm in arm with Elisha, he led him toward the dining room. Just inside stood a flustered, harassed woman who had obviously seen better days. "And this is my wife."

Elisha paid the lady his respects to which she responded nervously, glancing apprehensively toward her husband as she spoke. Then in a body the guests drifted toward the wine bowl to receive their wreaths and drink their toasts.

As he sipped from his cup, Elisha looked about.

Like the reception hall, the dining room was ostentatious. The murals on the walls were done in the most striking colors. The draperies on the couches were heavily embroidered. And the tables which the attendants were moving into place were crowded with trays and plates of silver and bronze.

Meantime, Nicander was constantly at Elisha's side, talking incessantly and interposing himself, as it seemed, between him and the other guests.

"Come sit with me," the rhetorician suggested when it was time for the dinner to begin.

Elisha followed reluctantly to the head table at which the old Stoic had already taken his place.

For the first course, the waiters brought in steaming platters of boiled cabbage.

"You had better take some," Nicander urged Elisha. "There is going to be plenty to drink—good, expensive wines, I assure you—and nothing is more effective in keeping one sober."

Elisha managed to consume his share of the dish. But of those which followed he ate, despite the coaxing to which he was subjected, almost nothing. Ever since his first glimpse of his host in his own home and of his fellow guests, he had had but little appetite. And what was left of it was ruined by the sight of the old man opposite him who wolfed his food, stuffing it into his mouth so eagerly that the gravies slopped down onto his beard and philosopher's mantle.

The dinner was half-over when a large-boned man loomed in the doorway.

"Hail, Eucritus!" someone cried. "Were you invited?"

"Invited? Of course not. I do not wait for an invitation. As Homer puts it, 'Menelaus came of his own accord.'"

Unsteady on his feet, the man called Eucritus came into the room.

"Come now, Nicander, am I welcome or not?"

"Of course you are," Nicander replied helplessly. "Sit down."

"Nonsense," Eucritus warned. "I am no weakling to recline on a couch when I eat. I am a philosopher, a Cynic, I eat on my feet. And when I get tired, there is always the floor to lie on."

"A rascal," Nicander explained desperately, "who despises everything conventional as a member of his school should. But a brilliant mind and a noble soul."

Skeptically, Elisha studied Eucritus for some indication of nobility. The Cynic, a wine cup in one hand, walked up and down among the tables, picking up portions that caught his fancy. He stopped and lifted an expensive silver bowl, heavy and of expert workmanship.

"Where did you ever get a piece as good as this?" he called to Nicander across the room. "Have you acquired a wealthy pupil, or have you just borrowed it to impress us? And all these servants too, where did you get the money to hire them? I tell you, Nicander, you need the philosophy of Cynics. You would know not to lay such importance on finery especially when it is so obviously not yours."

Nicander flushed and said nothing. In the end Eucritus drained his goblet, wiped his lips on the back of his hand, stretched himself out on the floor deliberately, and with a massive forearm resting under his head sank into a heavy sleep.

By now everyone was drinking continuously. Elisha too had taken to the wine. As time went on, the outlines of the room blurred before his eyes. Once his goblet slipped from his fingers and rolled beneath his couch. Libanius, who stood behind him, stooped to pick it up. As Elisha turned to receive the cup he caught a glimpse of the teacher of gymnastics surreptitiously stroking the leg of a handsome slave boy. Too drunk to be shocked, Elisha shrugged and asked a passing servant for more wine.

The room became progressively noisier. One guest declaimed lines from Pindar, Hesiod and Anacreon combined so as to make an amusing and obscene continuity. The Stoic, who had eaten his fill, was ostentatiously reading a book which he had taken from his wallet. Late in the evening, the drink and the food having finally run out, someone suggested a visit to Daphne. The women protested but the men milled about excitedly and paid them no attention. In his befuddlement, Elisha agreed to join the others nor did he think to inquire as to the nature of their expedition. And when several men, his host among them, approached him to borrow money, each offering some excuse—a mislaid purse, a captious banker—he proceeded straightway to hand out coins indiscriminately, to whom or in what amounts he could not recall afterward.

Elisha looked about for Libanius. The old man had seated himself on a bench in the corner where he dozed.

"My wrap," Elisha called, weaving toward him.

"My wrap," he repeated, shaking him gently.

Libanius opened his eyes with a start and got painfully to his feet.

"Go home," Elisha instructed with kindly impatience. "You have had more than enough for one night."

The streets were quiet, emptier than Elisha had ever seen them before. Of the route they followed he had only the foggist notion, but everywhere along it irate householders thrust their heads out of windows to protest angrily against the noise they made, and once a police patrol held them up in a brief altercation.

It was only when they arrived at the vale of Daphne and passed gaily illuminated houses before which half-dressed women lounged soliciting trade that Elisha realized the purpose of the trip. Sodden as he was, he turned in his tracks and disregarding the calls of the others retraced his steps.

When he awoke next morning in his bed his tongue was thick and fuzzy, and nausea twisted his stomach. It was only with an effort that he contrived to sit up. Discovering that he was fully dressed and that his clothes reeked of wine, he got to his feet, stripped to the skin, bathed and dressed himself afresh.

Later that day, Pappas dropped in to see him and Elisha, describing his adventure of the night before, expressed his disgust over it.

Pappas listened, unimpressed. "Simpleton, what did you expect? It serves you right for going."

"But it was revolting," Elisha insisted.

"Of course it was—from your point of view. You know, Elisha," he ventured shrewdly, "you may have become an infidel but you are still a rabbi."

CHAPTER VI

AMONG ELISHA'S ACQUAINTANCES LIBANIUS' incompe-
tence became a theme for jests. The poor old man was willing
enough to discharge his duties. But he was somewhat feeble
with age, altogether incapable of executing more than one
simple instruction at a time, and invariably too drowsy by
evening to be even passably efficient.

It was because Pappas twitted Elisha over his servant in
Manto's presence that the two men happened to accompany
her on a visit to the slave market.

"Why don't you get yourself someone who can attend
you properly?" Manto inquired after the laughter over one of
Pappas's witticisms had subsided.

"I want to, desperately," Elisha admitted helplessly. "But if
I discharge that fellow he will certainly starve."

She studied him, a cryptic smile on her lips, a brooding
light in her eyes.

"Very well, retain him, but get a boy too. I am going to the
exchange tomorrow to buy a girl for the kitchen. If you will
come with me, you will provide me with an appropriate escort,
and we may find someone suitable to your purposes...."

When Elisha and Pappas called for Manto the next afternoon, they were shown not into one of the several reception
halls but into the business office of the household. The little
chamber off the vestibule was quite bare of ornament. Its only
furnishings were several chairs, a massive ironbound chest
against one wall and a table strewn with tablets and scrolls at
which Manto, dressed for the street in the long linen robe of
a matron, was seated.

"I am sorry," she apologized, "to receive you here. But I
have just finished going over the accounts with my steward,
and there are still a number of matters—tradespeople and
things like that—which I cannot postpone. Would you mind
waiting? If you will take chairs in this room where I cannot

help seeing you, I shall probably be through with my business all the sooner."

The Manto whom Elisha watched for the next hour was a different woman from the gracious hostess he knew. With firm dispatch she consulted an overseer concerning her country estate, instructed the porter whom he was to admit that evening, placed orders with the agents of wine merchants, butchers and greengrocers, and together with the meat and pastry cooks arranged menus for a formal dinner. Elisha was amazed that the administration of a household could be so complicated and staggered to hear Manto casually refer to sums larger than a year's income from his own estate. In the end, she tore herself free by refusing to see anyone else. With a smile of contrition, she indicated her readiness to leave.

They were a party of five when they emerged, for trailing behind came Manto's steward and Doris, her maid, carrying her mistress' vanity case. Their progress, once they reached the main thoroughfares, was slow. The streets were choked with wagons, litters, horses, camels and occasionally some lumbering dray. The sidewalks were narrow and, especially before busier shops, almost impassable. As a result, the men were forced to follow Manto in single file.

But if their passage was difficult through the streets, they scarcely moved at all on the Forum. As soon as she was recognized, Manto was surrounded by a crowd of men. Some were personal friends and acquaintances; others total strangers who felt it advantageous to be seen talking to important people such as the mistress of the governor of a province. In Antioch, as in Rome, whom one knew determined in great measure one's social acceptability, advancement in career and credit with the bankers.

At long last, Manto extricated herself, and flushed with excitement, led her companions into the comparative quiet of a side street. Protesting weariness, she nevertheless seemed quite pleased with the adulation she had received.

En route to the slave exchange, they stopped at several shops, at one to examine a table which had been offered to her for sale, at another to buy an antique marble statuette, at still others to make various purchases for her household. So by slow stages they reached their destination.

The market consisted of a series of cells opening onto a central court. On platforms men stood stark naked while groups of prospective purchasers examined them. Dealers, slaves and idlers lounged on benches about the side walls.

A blustering trader came up to them.

"What can I do for milady?"

"I am interested in buying a girl for my kitchen, a young girl, healthy and, above all, obedient. My steward got one for me at this very market not so long ago. She turned out to be a quarrelsome nuisance. You'll have her back tomorrow."

The merchant shrugged his shoulders.

"We never guarantee a slave's character. Will you come this way?"

He led them to a vacant platform.

"And now, what would you like—an Egyptian, German, Britain, Gaul, Negro, or someone home bred?"

"It does not matter so long as she is obedient and speaks Greek."

Summoning an attendant, the trader whispered instructions into his ear. The assistant crossed the courtyard, opened a cell door and led forth a corpulent Negress.

Manto waved her hand at once and the woman was returned to her pen. Next the assistant brought out a flaxen-haired girl dressed in a scanty shift that descended to just below her loins. Her body was robust and magnificently developed.

"She is a Saxon," said the trader, "and speaks with an accent but understands Greek thoroughly. Shall I put her on the block and have her stripped?"

Idlers waiting for such a moment rose from their seats

and sauntered forward to get a better view of the woman. But Manto shook her head.

"No. Too good-looking. She will merely make trouble among the men slaves."

The third girl exhibited was a Cilician, dark, slender and timid.

"This," Manto said with approval, "is a little nearer to what I want."

She engaged the girl in conversation to test her knowledge of Greek, asked after her training and inquired as to why she had been sold. Then she questioned the trader as to her pedigree. Satisfied on all scores, she ordered the girl to ascend the block and strip. Mounting the platform to examine her, Manto's steward pulled back her eyelids and stared into her eyes, looked into her mouth, scrutinized her teeth, kneaded her arms, ran his hands over her abdomen, flexed her legs, and then nodded approvingly to Manto.

"I will take her," Manto decided, "if the price is right. I suppose it would be futile to try to get the truth about her health and disposition."

"By the gods, I swear," the trader exclaimed, "that so far as I know she is even-tempered and healthy."

"Never mind, you would swear so if she had the disposition of an Xanthippe and were at death's door. What is her price?"

The girl slipped on her tunic quickly and looked down anxiously while the two came, after some bargaining, to an agreement.

"Good then," Manto concluded. "Deliver her to my house tomorrow. My steward will pay you. And now, Elisha, we will attend to your purchase."

"I have changed my mind," Elisha informed her abruptly. "I'll engage a freeman in addition to Libanius."

The whole incident had distressed him. He had been shocked at the callousness with which women's bodies were exposed, even more by the prurient curiosity of the bystanders, but, most of all, by the realization that human beings were bartered for so unfeelingly. There was slavery among the Jews in Palestine, but it was nothing like this. There both Scriptural and Rabbinic law gave at least partial protection to the bondsman. He saw all at once that for all its limitations there were in the old Judaism elements of moral dignity of which Antioch had not the slightest notions.

It was on the way home that Manto looked about for Elisha.

"Why so aloof?" she called back to him. "Come, talk to me."

When he had made his way forward to her side, she remarked casually, "That girl is a good purchase."

"I can't see," he broke out, "how you can do it."

"Do what?"

"You bought a statue and a human being today—and both in the same offhanded manner."

"It's the way of the world," she responded noncommittally.

"Then there is no equity in it."

"Maybe not, but it has been ordered so—by the gods, Fate or Fortune. No one knows."

"But you might just as well have been the slave and she the buyer."

Manto did not answer. Her eyes were suddenly veiled.

"Don't mind him," Pappas interjected. "He has the soul of a reformer. It is not Elisha who is talking but the rabbi in him."

"Don't you ever get bored with that comment?" Elisha retorted. Turning to Manto, he explained, "Every time I become concerned about moral issues, he insists it's the rabbi in me."

Manto smiled.

"Perhaps that is what I like in you."

She slipped her hand through his arm. At the warmth of her touch and the scent of her perfume, a tremor passed through him.

CHAPTER VII

SELEUCIA, PORT OF ANTIOCH, CLUNG to the precipitous seaward flank of Mt. Pieria some four miles to the north of the mouth of the Orontes. The upper town high on the hill was a place of simple residences, the homes of merchants, naval officers, captains and customs collectors. A broad road cutting through solid rock gave upon the lower city, crammed onto a narrow beach between the base of the cliffs and the Mediterranean. All winter long, when boats dared not venture beyond the breakwaters, the ocean front was almost uninhabited. But during the remainder of the year, its alleyways and taverns swarmed with sailors and stevedores, its quays were laden with bales of merchandise, its warehouses and banks throbbed with activity. The wharves and the bay, protected by moles, presented an ever changing spectacle of lumbering freighters from distant lands, fishing smacks and, on the roadways of the naval station, giant triremes and low, ominous Liburnian galleys.

One day in early June, an imposing procession of officials, civil and military, surrounding a luxuriously appointed four-wheeled carriage drawn by a double team of horses, descended the inclined road from upper to lower Seleucia.

Idlers in the central plaza onto which the highway debouched stared upward curiously.

"Somebody who is somebody," Pappas commented to Elisha, "is due either to sail or to arrive."

Elisha squinted through the glare and shrugged indifferently.

"All I want to see," he muttered disconsolately, "is some trace of that boat of yours."

The presence of the two men in the harbor town was the result, unfortunate in Elisha's eyes, of one of Pappas's commercial speculations. Summoned from Antioch to receive a shipment of furs, Pappas had invited his friend to accompany him to the port to await it. He had pleaded and coaxed, he had argued the advantages of a change of scene to one who spent so much of his time indoors. And Elisha in a moment of weakness had yielded. In the five days that had passed since their arrival he had had abundant occasion to regret his decision. The heat on the waterfront was oppressive. The constant bustle in the streets nerve-racking, there was no sleeping in the tavern where they lodged, for the noise. Worst of all, he was wasting precious hours which might have been better employed.

"Come on, Pappas," he urged, resuming the aimless stroll on which they had set forth.

"No, let's wait and watch. We have no place to go."

As the cavalcade drew closer, Pappas seized Elisha by the arm.

"Look, the driver of the carriage, isn't that Manto's livery?"

"It looks like it."

"And that first fellow on horseback is Quadratus, and there is Lysis, a legate of Rufus' staff. It must be she."

"But what can she be doing here?"

"We'll find out soon enough."

As the vehicle came by them Pappas peered through its half-drawn curtains.

"Manto," he hailed.

She looked out.

"Hold the horses," she ordered her groom.

"Elisha, and Pappas too!" she cried in unconcealed delight. "How very nice to see you. But what in the world brings you here?"

Elisha felt his heart stop its beating and then race at the unexpected encounter.

"Just what we are wondering about you," Pappas spoke up. "We've been here for days, waiting for a freighter that must have foundered."

"I've come down to meet a boat also." Her words halted with a sudden unaccountable reserve.

"I know," Pappas exclaimed; "Rufus must be coming back."

"Yes. A fast galley that sailed from Rhodes the day his ship put in there brought us the news that he ought to arrive today, or tomorrow at the latest."

She glanced toward Elisha.

He had averted his eyes.

"Well, I must go on," she added quickly. "I am holding everybody up. Come and visit me. We are going to stop at the house of the port overseer."

At her word the cortege swept on. The two men continued their stroll and came at last to one of the wharves. Picking their way past sheds and between bags and boxes, they seated themselves at the end of a jetty. Pappas chatted animatedly but Elisha remained abstracted and taciturn. On a ledge at their feet several boys fished. To either side of them at adjoining docks the sky was strung with a tangle of masts, sails and ropes. Far off, toward the open sea a low breakwater stretched, the breaking waves glistening about it. Between two towers that guarded its mouth, the horizon was visible. The air with its salt tang and vague smell of fishiness was pleasantly cool and refreshing.

"What's more," Pappas gaily ended his babbling, "I don't care now whether my boat gets in or not. We're in for real entertainment with these Roman soldiers as hosts. You have never seen a banquet until you've dined with them."

"I can dispense with all that," Elisha commented dryly. "All I want is to get back to Antioch."

"What's come over you?"

"Nothing," Elisha replied irritably and rose to his feet. "Let's return to our rooms."

But just as they reached the plaza, a brass horn sounded deeply from out at sea. Echoing calls answered from the breakwaters in the harbor. At once the square resounded with cries: "A ship! A ship!"

Shading their eyes, the men stared into the westering sun. Beyond the quays, the snare of ropes and masts that hung over them, and the waters of the bay, a white sail rose at the open gates of the moles. From one of the watch towers, a trumpet blared in a series of complicated flourishes. The plaza was silent while those who understood the code of signals listened.

"Government vessel from Ostia!" they interpreted when the horn was still.

"Manto's luck," Pappas commented disconsolately. "We wait days and her boat gets in within an hour after her arrival."

Merchants who, like him, had been expecting vessels of their own returned disappointed to their counting rooms and warehouses. The public buildings seethed with heightened excitement. Figures appeared at the windows to look out. Crowds streamed from the doors toward the wharves.

"Let's go down and watch the landing," Pappas suggested.

"I'd rather not."

"But you'll have a chance to meet Rufus."

"No, thank you."

"Oh, come on," Pappas urged, already on his way. "It's a spectacle and there's no sense in missing it."

Hesitating momentarily, Elisha followed him as far as the base of the wharf. There they halted.

The ship was now well into the harbor, its great bronze prow nodding before it. Its mainsail, painted with the crimson eagle of Rome, was being lowered slowly. Of its three tiers of oars two were suspended, motionless and glistening in the sunlight. Only the bottom-most still beat the water in half-strokes, propelling the vessel forward parallel to the shore line. Majestically the boat slid on until it came abreast of the wharf-head. A whistle sounded on board. Concertedly, all oars on the landward side dropped quickly into the water, swinging the great vessel alongside the pier.

In a tumult of calls, whistles and trumpet blasts, the dripping oars were pulled back into the ports. Ropes flew through the air, to grow taut and groan with strain as the shore crews checked the forward motion of the boat. The next minutes were mad confusion. Hatches were opened, rope ladders swung downward. Men poured onto land.

From where they stood, Elisha and Pappas could not see through the dense crowd that milled on the pier. But it thinned rapidly as people made their way singly or in little knots toward the town. Within a few minutes, the dock had cleared sufficiently for persons to be distinguished.

"That's Rufus there." Pappas pointed toward a band of officers standing in a circle.

"Which one?" Elisha started to inquire only to break off at the sight of Manto, waiting to one side.

As he stared, a man detached himself from the group and moved rapidly toward her. The two figures embraced. When they separated Elisha saw Rufus for the first time. Bald and short and potbellied, he seemed as though he would be moistly warm and pudgy to the touch.

All this time Pappas had been edging forward, Elisha trailing him by several steps.

"Well, Pappas," Rufus drawled. "What an unexpected honor for you to trouble to meet me."

"Sheer accident," Pappas bantered. "I'm here on business, waiting for a freighter, and you arrive instead. In any case, I bid you welcome."

"At least, I get honest answers from you," the Roman laughed.

"Rufus," Manto said hesitantly, with an awkwardness quite unlike her, "I should like to present someone else, someone who has come from Palestine during your absence.... This is Elisha, a friend of Pappas... and mine."

Rufus looked sharply at Manto and turned his gaze to Elisha, who had come close to acknowledge the introduction.

Elisha's first impression of the Roman was revised at once. He was not bald. A fine yellow fuzz invisible at a distance covered his head. His hand, when he extended it, was hard and firm. If his face was all curves, his lips were a thin line. And his voice when he drawled, "I am always glad to meet another of

Manto's intellectuals," pleasantly soft though it was, had in it undertones of amused contempt.

His eyes shocked Elisha. They were of a blue so pale that the irises were scarcely demarked and the pupils were black points that shone out of watery whitenesses. They suggested sightlessness. Repelled, Elisha withdrew his hand.

"Come on, my girl," Rufus said, slipping his arm possessively around Manto's waist. "It's a long time since I've been with you."

As the two made their way down the now empty wharf Elisha looked after them, an unreasonable fury raging within him.

From where he sat alongside Pappas far back in the imperial box Elisha could scarcely see the arena at all. The scene to the left and right was cut off by high marble ramparts and the huge statues that rested on them. A solid array of backs and heads obstructed the view in front. When they moved, he caught a glimpse of Manto in the first row and of Rufus, dressed in the full regalia of a pro-praetor. Antiphanes, too, was about somewhere, like himself ostensibly a guest of the Legate, but actually present at Manto's invitation. The other occupants of the box were governmental officials. They were gathered to witness games presented by the returned Governor in honor of the Emperor's birthday.

This was Elisha's initiation into an amphitheater. When he first entered he had gaped with amazement at the great stone bowl. It had been almost empty then. Now it was packed with people whose talk and movement seemed almost to shake the structure. A sudden silence, followed by the sound of a chant, moved Elisha to stand upon his seat for a better view. Before an altar against a far wall a group of men surrounded a bull. Its horns were gilded and garlands trailed down its flanks. Intermittently a trumpet blared. Between calls, a voice intoning a liturgical formula came faintly across the expanse. Rising and falling, it prayed for the genius of the Emperor. Then metal flashed, the animal reared and lowed in pain, and the little knot of priests wrestled with it to keep it still. A red spurt stained the yellow sand. The beast sank slowly to its knees, knives working upon it. Meantime, the murmur of prayer continued. The top of the altar smoked with burning meat and incense until the offering on behalf of the Emperor had been completed.

When fresh sand had been strewn, a troop of dancers came upon the scene, their voices chanting in chorus an old Greek hymn, their bare arms weaving in intricate patterns, their feet working rhythmic designs. They were followed successively by acrobats, clowns and comedians. Through it all the sound of voices and rustling garments persisted steadily. For the audience was indifferent, waiting impatiently for the climactic numbers of the program.

Abruptly the hum mounted a pitch with excitement.

A sleek Numidian lion trotted out of an underground cage and stood in the arena, blinded by the unwonted light, bewildered by noise. At the same time but from the opposite side of the amphitheater a lithe young gladiator appeared, naked except for a loincloth and armed only with a thin sliver of steel. Calmly he sauntered across the floor and disregarding the beast raised his sword in salute to Rufus and the citizenry of Antioch. Then, facing the animal, he strolled toward it. The lion, frightened and confused, watched him warily but seemed disinclined to fight. The gladiator, only several feet from his antagonist, stood waiting. When it did not move, he stooped quickly and threw a handful of sand into its face. It snarled with rage and tossed its head. Then, while the spectators gasped with horror, the man deliberately turned his back to the beast, and looked up at them, shrugging his shoulders in the manner of one who has come to the end of his devices. But it was only a pretense for, veering, he edged toward the animal's side. It circled with him, its long tufted tail beginning to swing. Everyone understood the sign. The animal was being successfully baited. But on the gladiator's face the fixed smile did not waver though his jaw muscles stood out taut and a shiny sweat covered his forehead and shoulders. He took a careful stance and lunged forward. As the shaft of steel touched the animal's flank and came away, its tip red, the lion snapped, flew into the air, and descended in a scurry of dust.

There was no need for further prodding. The tail swept with slow ferocity over the sand, a continuous snarling sounded through the enclosure. The great head, held low to the ground, hung motionless before a body crouched to spring. Then, when the tenseness became intolerable, a brown streak hurtled through space. Claws flashed. But the man dodged and thrust at the same time. The sand cloud subsided; the smile was still frozen onto the man's face, while the sword, wet halfway to its hilt, dripped blood. Again the lion charged, again the sword darted forward. Another red trickle stained a yellow flank.

But this time the gladiator had not come through unscathed. An angry streak ran down the side of one calf where the claws had torn the tight white skin. So the game went on, in a succession of roaring leaps and quick blows until, in the timelessness of concentration, it seemed as though it might continue forever. But they were tiring. The foot-beaten sand was widely spotted with brown drops. The grimace on the gladiator's face no longer concealed his mortal terror. Desperate with awareness of his failing strength, he lunged as the animal rose toward him. They went down together, the beast on top, but the sword had found a mortal spot, and though the claws ripped once, they were powerless to move again. Slowly the man squirmed from under the quivering yellow mass. He was, when he got to his feet, drenched with blood. His cheek had been ripped open, leaving his teeth and jawbone exposed. His left hand rose jerkily to press against it. Limping on his bruised leg, he wove toward the imperial box and brandished his sword jauntily before it. Hysterical applause thundered about him and a purse heavy with coins plummeted to his feet. When he bent to pick it up, he straightened so slowly that it seemed he would never come erect. He pulled his head up and a forced mirthless smile contorted the uninjured half of his face. Then he staggered across the arena to the exit, leaving a trail of blood behind him.

As the great bronze grille closed, Elisha awoke to the fact that he was standing on the bench. The palms of his tightly clenched hands were moist. From head to foot he was atremble. Shakily he dismounted and sank onto his seat. A quick wave of nausea swept away the last traces of the excitement that had held him hypnotized. His mind began to function again and with a rush he despised that vast assemblage for the amusements with which it beguiled itself, and himself for responding to them.

While he sat unseeing, he remembered Rabbi Joshua identifying the theater and circus with the seat of the scornful of which the Psalms speak. He recalled his teacher's condemnation of the amphitheater as the basest of all idolatries, the sacrifice of human beings. He thought of a prayer which some rabbi—he could not remember who—had once recited:

"Happy are we for we sit in houses of prayer and study while they sit in theaters and circuses. We labor and they labor, we in God's eternal law and they in vanity and emptiness."

Half-rising he looked out at the crowd again. Seated though it was, it danced before his eyes in blurred tides of tossing arms and bobbing heads. Voices deepened by blood-lust stormed and subsided. His eyes turned to the arena for relief. Fresh sand had been strewn over the bloodstains, slaves were raking the surface smooth for the next spectacle.

Trumpets blared and, from subterranean rooms, two men emerged, armed with shields and broadswords, and clad, one in a red loincloth, the other in a green.

Elisha's bowels twisted into a knot at the prospect of another fight. He saw again a flap of cheek held in place by a drenched hand. This time there might be a vote for the life, or the death, of the vanquished—an incredible decision of thumbs up or down, while glazing eyes awaited the agony of steel plunging through shrinking flesh to an overlabored heart. He could not stand it. Rising in panic, he stumbled blindly across Pappas's sprawling legs and disregarding astonished questions fought his way out of the box into a corridor. He was halfway down it when he heard Antiphanes call to him.

"Wait for me, I am coming, too."

At the end of the passageway his tutor came abreast of him. They stood for a moment in the shadows—the streaming white sunlight awaiting them like some bath of liquid fire. The roar of the crowd reached them hoarsely like the growl of a distant animal.

"By all the gods," Antiphanes broke out, "by Isis our Mother, it was horrible. I have not gone in years. I shall never go again. Such naked, twisted ugliness."

" 'Whosoever preserves one life, it is as though he had preserved a world; whosoever destroys one life, it is as though he had destroyed a world.' " The quotation, an echo of his past, slipped from Elisha.

What they had witnessed was not ugliness. It was sin. For a fleeting instant Elisha was about to explain how he felt. Then he caught himself. What matter whether one hated such things because they were unlovely or because they were wrong? The great sadness was that humanity was so friendless.

"It is hard," Antiphanes murmured, "to reconcile that spectacle with the Musaeum and libraries, with the law courts and their justice. Yet, at times like this, we must force ourselves to remember that these too exist, and are part of our world, the larger, saving part."

Elisha smiled wanly at his tutor.

"Always the balanced judgment. 'The Empire must be respected but not idealized.' 'There is another side to the shield.' And now, 'Against the arena stands the Musaeum.' It is good that I have you to remind me. Otherwise, I might despise the good because of the evil intermingled with it."

With that they stepped out into the sea of painful light.

CHAPTER VIII

From a little room adjoining the vestibule, the porter called to Elisha, "There is nobody at home. Everyone has gone to the games."

"I know." Elisha, still tense with excitement, continued on his way through the door. "I have just left them, but your mistress asked me to wait for her party here."

He walked slowly through the atrium into the court where a shaft of sunlight, like Jacob's ladder, golden and firm, stretched from the opening in the roof above to the waters of the pool. For a few minutes he wandered restlessly from room to room, coming at last into Manto's private garden, an open space, half-roofed over, between the mansion and a vine-covered wall. Under the shelter of the eaves, chairs and couches had been placed. Beneath the open sky, shrubs and flowering plants grew luxuriantly. Where the light and shadows met, a fountain threw a thin spray upward. Elisha slipped onto a divan and idly watched the wavering movement of water flowing over many-colored tiles. From afar he heard, dulled by distance, the murmur of the city. Near by a bee hummed from flower to flower. The air was warm and heavy with fragrance. His eyes closed....

Manto's voice woke him. He did not know how long he had dozed, but the sky overhead was still brilliantly bright. She stood over him, dressed in a street cloak. He started to rise.

"Please," she protested, "do not disturb yourself."

"But where are the others?"

"They did not come home with me, after all."

"I had better go, too," he said, nervously sitting up.

"No, no, please stay. I am glad you came. Give me a moment to change to more comfortable clothes. Tensely he sank back onto the couch, rigid fingers intertwined under his head.

Manto turned away toward her chamber directly off the garden. "Talk to me. I can hear very well." she called from her room. "When did you leave? One moment you were there, and then, when I looked around, you were gone."

"After the fight with the lion."

"But why so early?"

"It was my first experience with that sort of thing. I must confess it was too much for me."

"The hero, the Agamemnon, glorying in battle," she taunted. "Of course it was cruel, but you missed something if that was all you felt. There was beauty in it, too. That duel of the swordsmen, lithe, shining bodies, poised to kill, circling each other in a deadly dance..." She described the spectacle vividly as though she were reliving every thrust and parry. Her voice took on a strange, throaty timbre. Its passion communicated itself to him. A sudden restlessness drove him to his feet to pace the courtyard.

"But even more exciting," she went on, her speech accelerating in tempo and growing deeper and huskier, "was the lion. It hypnotized me with its restrained ferocity, the rippling of its muscles under its gleaming hide, its slinking, crouching movements. I would love to have a pet like that—some great, murderous, graceful beast, dangerous and lovely at the same time. Haven't you ever experienced the frenzy of such a sight, the wild rapture...?"

While she spoke, the blood-lust he had experienced in the arena pervaded him again. Then she appeared in the doorway. A long flowing robe, pale green as the waters of the fountain, swirled about her and clung to her form. She walked toward him slowly. Fascinated he watched her approach, sinuous, feline, like the great cats of which she spoke. His breath came unsteadily, there was a throbbing in him that was pain and ecstasy at the same time.

She was close to him now, the scent of her body, her nearness enveloping him. Her eyes held him—brilliantly green with the intense fire of emeralds, unfathomably deep.

" 'Thou art beautiful, my love...and terrible as an army with banners' " he murmured.

"Elisha…"

At the sound of his name on her parted lips the desire he had so long denied and suppressed broke free.

His arms closed about her.

That night Tineius Rufus entertained several hundred guests at dinner in the gardens of his country estate. Over the level lawn before the villa, the tables and couches were arrayed in sweeping arcs. A multitude of torches, scented with aromatic oils, flared from the branches of the trees. Elevated on the marble portico of the house, the table of honor was set, with Rufus in the center. Manto was on his right, in a dazzling white gown, her golden hair piled high in a tower of curls after the formal mode. To either side of them were the chief civil and military administrators of Syria, and the princes of the allied and tributary states of the district. Somewhere, behind the house, where the light did not reach and the discordant voices of the diners could not penetrate, Mount Silpius loomed. The heroic mythological figures carved on its cliffs in ancient days brooded over the scene, their weather-beaten faces unmoved by its splendor.

All through the banquet Elisha exchanged scarcely a word with Antiphanes, Pappas or the other friends of Manto in whose company he was seated. The rare and exquisitely flavored dishes and drinks placed before him stuck in his throat whenever he attempted to partake of them. For he was present against his will and only because Pappas had been so fierce in his insistence.

"You accepted his invitation," his friend had argued angrily on arriving at his apartment and finding him not only undressed but determined not to attend the dinner. "You cannot afford to insult him by staying away."

"I refuse to go," Elisha had repeated obdurately. "I have had enough of his hospitality."

"What's come over you? You leave the games without so

much as a word. You disappear without trace for the rest of the afternoon, why or whither you will not say. And now you are mad altogether."

"He will never miss me in that crowd. And if he does, I am ill."

"He is not a person to be toyed with. His stewards will not fail to inform him of your absence. And he is no fool to be deceived by flimsy excuses. I have no idea of the nature of your obsession. But whatever it is, you are coming with me, and at once, or we shall be late."

Reluctantly he had allowed himself to be persuaded. Now, taciturn and withdrawn, he sat, his consciousness divided, each fragment pursuing its own existence, each struggling for predominance over the others. The memory of Manto's body and its love pulsated within him, sometimes vague and distant so that he could not believe that anything so incredibly breathtaking had actually befallen him, sometimes so convincingly vivid that he was afire with recollection as some hours earlier he had been with experience. Simultaneously, in different areas of his mind a tortured colloquy was in progress. She belonged to another man. Little wonder then that he, Elisha, was nauseated by the taste of Rufus's food and scarcely dared breathe the air of the garden in which he found himself. The marvel was that he was so brazen as to accept anything of the hospitality of one he had betrayed. Yet, she had wanted him—of that he was certain. In his life he had known dutifulness, remote yearnings, but never, until that afternoon, the full awakening of passion and a gratification which had left him fulfilled yet still avid. Meantime, fragments of epigram and doctrine, the splinters of the hard old morality of his youth pricked at his fevered conscience.

"Well, here comes our host." someone at the table announced.

The words shook Elisha into immediate awareness.

Rufus who had left the dais for a tour of the tables was

moving in their direction. His robe disarranged, his wreath at a rakish angle, he reeled from party to party, stopping long enough to exchange a few words with his guests.

"Greetings, gentlemen," he said thickly, swaying over Antiphanes's couch, one hand groping for support on the rhetorician's shoulder. "I trust everything is to your taste. My villa, my food, my entertainment. To all of which you are welcome.

"But one possession," he leered, "I will not share, my prize, my Manto. Is she not the most beautiful woman here tonight, yes, in all Antioch for that matter? I will go further," he continued in drunken seriousness: "I say she is the most beautiful woman in the Empire. But none of you will ever know how beautiful."

Elisha, his mouth in a tight line, his fists clenched, half rose. Instantly, Pappas's hand darted across the space between them to restrain him. Under its peremptory tugging Elisha sank back.

From the very beginning of Rufus's maunderings, the other men at the table had averted their faces in embarrassment so that they missed the by-play. But Elisha's movement had not escaped the Roman. Sodden though he was, his eyes narrowed into two slits.

The smile, warm and spontaneous, with which Manto greeted Elisha broke momentarily into apprehension when she observed his expression. Quickly it reformed and she began to talk at once.

"What a delightful surprise to have you call so early in the morning," she chatted nervously. "Please sit down. Did you enjoy the banquet last night? Wasn't it brilliant? I was so sorry that you were placed at such a distance from me. I wanted very much to talk to you. But you can understand how difficult it was."

He took hold of her wrist to silence her.

"Manto," he asked abruptly, "what are we going to do?"

"What do you mean?" she faltered.

He released her arm, walked to a chair and, seated rigidly on it, stared at her.

"What happened to me yesterday was the climax of my life. But there is one question you must answer before we go further. Was it as important to you as to me?"

A flush suffused her face but she met his scrutiny directly and nodded.

"Was it?" he persisted. "You must tell me explicitly."

"From the very first moment we met, I was drawn to you, as I felt you were attracted to me. And I knew then that sooner or later we would come together."

"That was what I hoped to hear. I have wanted you, I want you as I can remember desiring nothing else."

"You haven't been thinking that I was toying with you," she murmured.

"I could not be sure."

"I was never more genuine. Now do you feel easier?"

"Yes, but I repeat, what are we going to do?"

"I don't understand, Elisha."

"Don't you see that I can't go on this way—sharing you with Rufus, at the very time that I accept his hospitality as I do whenever I am under this roof. Nor am I made for concealment and deception. Besides, given my background, training and temperament I cannot be happy with...with doubtful relationships."

"Then what would you have us do?"

"Give up Rufus," he urged, "and marry me."

Her eyes filled with tears.

"You cannot know," she said unsteadily, "how great a compliment you have just paid me. But it's impossible."

"And why, pray?" he challenged, an edge in his voice. "Is all this so necessary to you?"

He got to his feet in a surge of hurt and anger, his arm waving in contempt of the room and what it represented.

"Or is it the position you enjoy? In any case, I cannot

continue this way. I thank you for everything you have done for me, your interest in my work, your favor of yesterday. But I shall not enter this house again."

Sadly she watched him as he stormed at her.

"Sit down, Elisha," she said gently, "there is something I must tell you."

Stalking the floor, he paid her no heed.

"Please, Elisha. A long time ago I listened to your story. Won't you do the same for me? It's fearfully important that you understand me. And though what I am about to tell you may drive you farther from me, I must take the risk. You must know. I could not bear it otherwise."

Shaken by the quiet, desperate urgency of her voice, he returned reluctantly to his chair.

For a time she sat abstracted, her eyes fixed on the folded hands on her lap. Then without looking up she started to speak, slowly, painfully.

"I am the illegitimate daughter of a Roman merchant and a slave woman whom he rented for a week from a friend. When I was ten years old, my mother's master sold me into a brothel in Sardis. Since then I have known men, white and black, young and old, drunken and sober, rarely kind, and never friendly. I might have spent my life so, but nature endowed me with some foresight, and I watched women of my class. I saw them when they got too old to earn their keep at their trade. I felt the terror with which they faced the future and the drudgery it held for them.

"Do you remember," she continued, "some months ago when you suggested that under different circumstances I might be a slave? You did not know how close to home you struck. At eighteen I saw all too clearly that, unless I took fate into my own hands, I would end in a kitchen. I planned and prayed, and the gods answered me. They sent me a patrician of Sardis, old and ugly, but rich and eager to be young again. All the skills I had acquired I used on him. He bought me free, set me up in a house of my own and showered me with jewels and money. His wife came to me pleading that he was beggaring his family for me. I was sorry for her, yet she had had everything and I had only a hope for the future. I was polite and sympathetic. I promised to let him go, but I held on. Meantime, I gave myself to men of letters so that they might teach me. Finally I had money enough for my plan. I sold the house and jewels quietly, and left Sardis for Antioch. Once here I could afford to be selective. I could choose as my lovers those who were not too demanding and who could pay me well. With Tineius I realized my ambition.

"For eight years he has kept me in luxury. And I have been faithful to him. I too have my honor. Always he has returned to me, from a visit with his wife in Rome, from long and frequent sojourns on official duty in Palestine. He has been kind to me—at least, as kind as he can be. Through him I have become a personage. He has given me ease, security, position. I thought that my course in life was set permanently.

"And then you appeared. You're a rare person, Elisha. I have never known anyone quite like you. At that first dinner here, your aloofness piqued me, but you interested me too. Later I tried to resist you—you represented unwittingly a threat to all I had attained. I did not have the will to do what I knew to be wise. And I am glad, despite all that has and may happen. For you permitted me to participate in your work, you paid me first the honor of sharing your dreams with me, and today of asking me to be your wife.

"I am indebted to you, Elisha. But I cannot do that which you demand and I desire. I owe Rufus something. And I am afraid—afraid to renounce everything for which I have struggled all my life...."

All through her story, Elisha watched her face grow tired and world-weary until its glamour was no more. Pity ached in him at the sight.

"But these are not the real reasons," she continued. "I must refuse to marry you—there is no alternative—for your own sake."

The compassion which had mounted steadily in him was gone at once.

"For my sake?" he echoed sharply, scornfully. "When you refer to your debt to Rufus, when you admit that you lack the courage to surrender what you have achieved, I am disappointed. But I understand and at the least I am compelled to respect your candor. But for you to pretend to be motivated by concern for me…"

She raised her eyes to meet his. They were bright with tears and so truthful that he broke off and waited for her to speak again.

"Naturally, you do not believe me. Yet I swear to you, Elisha, that I would forget Rufus in a moment and walk out of this house with you unhesitatingly, were I not convinced that I would be ruining your life."

"But how?" he cried, more in perplexity now than resentment.

"Rufus in the first place," she answered. "Do you suppose that he would leave us in peace? Whether from love for me, or from the desire for revenge against you—and he can be horribly vindictive—he would plague us every day."

"What could he do to us?" Elisha scoffed.

She smiled at him with sad wisdom.

"Remember, he is Governor of Palestine and a friend of the Emperor. He could summon you back to your estate time and again, on matters of taxation, for violations of this ordinance or that. He could trump up charges against you—treason, blasphemy, what not. He could decide that your services are needed for military purposes. Everything would be quite legal on the surface, trust him for that, and if you went into the courts in each instance, you could prevent him having his way with you. But we would be harassed and harried to the day we died."

"Then we can live elsewhere," Elisha argued desperately. "Out of the range of his power. Once before I was drawn to a woman only to be kept from her. That was only a pallid presage of what I feel now. It was idealization—not love. I will not be denied this time. We will go to Egypt, Asia Minor, Rhodes, anywhere...."

"And tear yourself loose from Antioch where you have just taken root? You have friends here, instructors. You are moving forward rapidly in your studies. Do you realize what a setback another dislodgment would be? Ultimately it is your work I am thinking of. You have made such heroic sacrifices for it, I cannot allow myself to interfere with it. That is the last reason why I will not become your wife—because I believe so in you and your future."

"But my happiness..." he began.

"Don't you see, Elisha," she interrupted, "you are a man apart, a man marked by fate for a purpose. Nothing, not personal happiness, not the love of wife, child or people must stand in the way of the fulfillment of your destiny. And there must be no entanglement to hold you back, such as I would be inevitably. That is why I say to you—you must not let me become too important to you."

Her head was bowed, her shoulders drooped as though she had been drained of all strength by some gigantic effort of will.

"After all," she pleaded, "we enjoyed our friendship and were helpful to each other. Perhaps we can go back to things as they were."

"I love you," he responded. "I shall always love you and be grateful for your companionship on any terms."

Shaken, he got to his feet, walked to her and with his fingers tilted her chin upward until their eyes met.

"I cannot believe," he whispered, "that I deserve such devotion. I hope only that I shall be worthy of it."

She smiled up at him.

He bent and kissed her lips.

CHAPTER IX

MANTO MANAGED ELISHA'S VISITS SKILLFULLY. She spaced them at such intervals that the friendship on which they had agreed might be encouraged. And whenever they were together, a third person was present to preserve appearances—someone who would not be a barrier in the way of free exchange of thought between them.

Their first meetings were strained and awkward. But as the memory of what had been receded, the tension eased. Elisha began to talk to her more easily than ever and in greater detail of his studies. He developed the habit of bringing to her choice passages from the books he was reading, the random ideas that occurred to him, and the difficulties that sometimes beset him. He found her invariably sympathetic and intelligent, even in matters too technical for her full comprehension. Always when he left her, it was with stimulation and heightened courage. And if, on occasion, she excited him, he quickly repressed his impulses recognizing that their relationship was becoming too precious to be jeopardized.

So he lived in the great city, seeing no one except Manto, Antiphanes and Pappas, concentrating more and more on his work. In this fashion, the months, long in passage, brief in retrospect, mounted into a year, then two, and three.

By this time, Elisha was thoroughly at home in literature, and, though he approached it as a means to an ulterior end, he could not but respond now to its passionate beauty as when he had sampled it idly in the anthologies which Pappas had sent to Palestine.

Especially was he devoted to lyric poetry with its songs of love, its laments over death and the parting of friends. And yet for all its blitheness, the verse of the Greeks saddened him too. There was in it, he came to feel, stark fear, artfully concealed. It had about it an aura of yearning and regret. Beneath its gaiety, melancholy stirred, the more desperate because unspoken. And with time he came to understand the great hopelessness that breathed through these polished cadences. The poet loved life so ardently because in the end he despised it for its meaninglessness and futility. Nothing then was left for him but to seize upon sensations, to savor them lustily, to abstract from them their last sweetness—always to find them flavored with ultimate bitterness. He laughed stoutly at each jest, otherwise he must weep. He loved his beloved feverishly, what else did empty hateful time permit?

Inevitably, contrasts suggested themselves between this literature and that Scripture to which so many years of Elisha's life had been dedicated. It was a sternly earnest book, that of the Jews, and yet animated for all its dour austerity by a confident serenity which the Greeks seemed never to experience. For, given its presuppositions, all things were good by virtue of the God who pervaded them. There was for men no burning urgency in the quest for the fugitive experience. Love and laughter were but transient manifestations of the joy-drenched essence of all things.

Wistfully Elisha admitted that, so regarded, the world he had elected was less happy and buoyant and, as he had guessed that day in the slave exchange and again in the arena, less merciful than that which he had rejected.

But whatever his disillusionments they were more than offset by the delight occasioned by his progress. And when, still under Antiphanes' guidance, he moved on to the study of history a compensating insight was afforded him. Month after month for over a year he pored over records of the nations, Berossus on the Babylonians, Manetho on the Egyptians, Herodotus, Thucydides and numberless chroniclers of Greece and Rome. And the more he read, the more he was confirmed in that judgment of the role of the Empire at which he had first arrived in the chambers of Clarus. For until Rome had conquered the world the entire career of civilized man had been apparently nothing but a harrowing succession of wars. Armies had marched incessantly across all lands, murdering, burning, looting. Thousands of lives had been extinguished in each generation, millions had been subjected to bereavement, pain and misery, treasures on which hosts might have lived in luxury had been consumed—all to no point or purpose.

The motives of the Romans in subduing the peoples were by no means altruistic, and their treatment of the lands under their dominion had not always been beyond reproach, but the effects of the spread of their power could not be denied. Wherever they had gone they had brought the Pax Romana. It was a precious boon which Italy had forced on civilization, that of peace. And with it had come security for the individual and the opportunity to live out his life without hindrance in pursuit of the dreams of his heart. Of what account compared to this was the coerced surrender of their political independence by the nations, whether Gauls, Spaniards, Egyptians or Jews?

Reliving the unhappy past of humanity, Elisha reflected often that a rabbi-priest had once put it well, saying:

"Pray ye for the welfare of the Empire, for, had it not been for the awe of it, men would long since have swallowed one another alive."

The invitation which came to Antiphanes to lecture in Athens and Rhodes, the two most honored and ancient seats of learning in the Eastern Empire, was both a tribute to his growing fame and an unusual opportunity for enhancing it further.

"Accept it, by all means," Elisha urged when the rhetorician consulted him. "It would be unpardonable to refuse."

"That is what everyone has been telling me. And yet I am loath to uproot myself from Antioch, and especially reluctant to leave you. I doubt that I shall find anywhere another friendship as intimate and satisfying as ours has become."

"I know," Elisha conceded. "Everyone will miss you keenly, and I, who owe you so much and love you so deeply, most of all. But you will make new associations, and you must not allow your affections to keep you from the triumphs you so richly deserve."

"If it had not been for the fact," the gray-haired man mused, "that my task with you is virtually over, I should never have given the matter a moment's thought. But in less than five years, I have exhausted my usefulness. You have learned as much as I can teach you of literature. And what you have not read as yet, you are capable of handling by yourself. The sciences are your next enterprise. And for these, as I warned you at the start, you would have had to go elsewhere in any event."

"Do you mean to say," Elisha marveled, "that had this honor been offered you at any time since we began to work together, you would have refused it on my account?"

The clear blue eyes of the instructor were fixed steadily on his disciple as he answered without the least hesitation: "I have never admitted this to you before. It is in such glaring contradiction with my whole philosophy of life. But I have long been possessed by an intuition, unreasonable perhaps, that your project will emerge in some heroic triumph of the intellect. After all, of what importance is my activity? At the best, I create felicitous phrases, graceful passages. But your dream—if you bring it to completion—will be of a piece with the achievements of the significant thinkers among men. Given your extraordinary abilities and the technique you propose to use, it is by no means unlikely. To be in a position to serve potential genius as has been my lot is no common privilege."

Elisha dismissed the compliment with a deprecatory phrase. But his heart was leaping wildly. They might not be in vain then, those tortured hours in Galilee when he had wavered between faith and denial, those days when by a supreme effort of will he had torn himself wounded and bleeding from the parent body that had nurtured him, the weeks, months, years when he had driven himself unsparingly to master the wisdom of a strange new world. For someone aside from himself, someone as keenly critical as Antiphanes had seen as attainable those visions which in discouragement he himself had at times declared phantasms.

"You can have no notion," he breathed, "how you have encouraged and strengthened me."

"Perhaps," the rhetorician went on, "I am speaking prematurely. One always does in venturing prophecy. But it is not only my opinion that I have voiced. You would be even more heartened if you knew how profound a respect you have won, or of the interest with which your work is followed among those who have learned of your program. Whatever ensues, do not be deterred from it. And someday when you may have put the world in your debt, I shall be able to say to myself, 'I too helped,' and in that find the justification for my career."

Humbled before his friend's confidence, awed by the role in which he had confirmed him, Elisha could not respond at all.

But the intellectual eagerness, the intentness of purpose that had always marked Elisha had been kindled into white heat by his conversation with Antiphanes. He spent the last days of the rhetorician's residence in Antioch constantly in his company and traveled with him to Seleucia to see him on board ship and to bid him final farewell. Then returning to Antioch, he threw himself with fierce enthusiasm into his exploration of the sciences.

Under the guidance of new instructors, all competent and estimable men, he ploughed through the great texts in the fields of mathematics, physics, astronomy, astrology and biology. Worlds of the existence of which he had been unaware opened before him. He penetrated the higher realms of mathematics in works such as *The Conic Sections* of Apollonius of Perge. He read astronomical treatises and attempted in vain to decide between the theory propounded by Aristarchus of Samos and others—that the earth like other planets moved about a sun perhaps three hundred times its mass—and the more conventional doctrine of Geocentrism which was stoutly defended by most scholars. The guidebooks of Theophrastus and Strato in hand, he studied plants and animals in the zoological and botanical gardens attached to the Musaeum.

Overcoming his aversion he made his way into dissection rooms where he witnessed surgical operations of great complexity and delicacy. He watched, cringing with horror, the vivisection of animals and autopsies performed on the human body, following meantime in the writings of the anatomists their speculations as to the function and nature of the parts of the living organism.

Elisha did not reason it out deliberately but he came to distinguish between the two Antiochs in which he lived. One was a vast city of temples, mansions, baths and theaters but also of slave markets and amphitheaters. It had appeared gracious and glittering when he first saw it. Much of its glamour was gone for him now. He knew it for what it was, brilliant but devoid of the decencies and pities to which he had been accustomed in Palestine. Had this been the whole of Antioch, he would unhesitatingly have returned to the world of his youth.

But there was another city peopled by a handful of men of letters, scientists and philosophers. On the surface it seemed a cold and inhospitable place. Each of its citizens was altogether preoccupied with his own interests. Friendships were rare among them, and such as existed, originating in common purposes rather than mutual liking, were terminated at the exit of the library or laboratory. And yet among these scholars there was a fellowship of sorts, aloof, impersonal yet somehow intense. For all alike shared a passionate love of truth unalloyed by expectations of reward. Living among them unnoticed except by those who had heard of his extraordinary objective, Elisha felt himself altogether at home. For these men who rarely paid him heed were no strangers to him. They were rather companions, adventuring along the road he traveled.

Then, in the forty-seventh year of his life, the eighth of his sojourn in Antioch, Elisha was projected unexpectedly from his position of humble obscurity in learned circles into considerable prominence. Having completed his survey of the sciences, he prepared for the next and final stage of his program, the study of philosophy. Before casting about for an instructor, he decided to put into writing the principles by which he felt philosophical doctrines ought to be evaluated.

One morning, in the room which he frequented in the great library, he wrote on a tablet the superscription:

Prerequisites for All Metaphysical Systems Derived from the Methods Suggested by Aristotle in his Organon, *and more particularly from those implied in Euclid's* Elements of Geometry.

The framing of the title was almost more difficult than the text itself. For his ideas had long since crystallized into clarity and he recorded them fluently, almost unhesitatingly. At nightfall some days later, as he was finishing the task, the chief librarian of the Musaeum, a crusty old scholar, grammarian by profession, drifted into the room.

"And what are you doing so busily?" he inquired in an awkward attempt at affability.

"Completing a monograph," Elisha replied, glancing up briefly and continuing his work.

A few minutes later Elisha tossed his stylus away. "It's done," he cried with relief.

"And brilliantly done too," a voice added at his side.

Startled, Elisha looked up to discover that the librarian, still with him, was reading his scrawl intently.

"What are you going to do with this?" the man inquired.

"Erase it," Elisha answered casually.

"Oh no, you're not. You are going to publish it."

"Publish it?" Elisha repeated amazed. "But I have not even begun my study of philosophy. All I know is what I have picked up incidentally...."

"Nonsense," the librarian snapped testily. "Do you suppose

we lack for the scribblings of pedants? This is different. It is bold, original, creative. All it requires is a bit of polishing in style. That should not take you long. Then I will arrange to have it copied and circulated. It is about time that something dynamic came out of this institution."

Protesting, filled with misgivings, Elisha yielded. When he transmitted a reworked draft to the librarian, the highest hopes that he entertained for it were that it might pass unnoticed. To his surprise, the reactions on all sides were enthusiastically favorable. Men about the Musaeum who had never spoken to him stopped to congratulate him. In time, he began to receive communications from scholars in distant cities, Athens, Rhodes, Pergamum. A letter alive with joy came to him from Antiphanes. Some of the messages were critical of details in his argumentation but all alike expressed admiration for the project he had outlined and urged him to carry it to completion.

Nor was Elisha's fame confined to men of learning. The larger Antioch lived ostensibly in blissful indifference of the Musaeum; it even pretended to a good-natured contempt for it. Actually, it stood in awe of its scholars. Again, as when he had first come to Antioch, Elisha was deluged with invitations to dinners, extended in some instances by men who had forgotten that they had entertained him years before.

Steadfastly he declined. His triumphs like his problems and defeats he shared only with Manto and Pappas.

The letter from the distinguished head of the Musaeum of Alexandria was one of the last which came to Elisha but by far the most significant. It had been penned by a world-renowned scholar, noted for his sparing praise. As he read the concluding words, Elisha was already on his feet, burning to show the document to Manto. He hastened to her home, fretted impatiently until the porter returned with instructions to admit him, and fairly swooped down on her in her private garden.

"Read this!" he cried and handed her the tablets, forgetting in his enthusiasm even to inquire after her health.

Somewhat startled and perplexed, she complied. But as she bent over the writing, a flush of pleasure mounted her cheeks, her eyes began to glow, and though she did not look up, words broke from time to time on her lips.

"The head of the Musaeum...! Such a tribute!"

"Elisha," she sang out as she tossed the letter aside and extended her hands to him, "it is too wonderful. Let me congratulate you."

But he had scarcely taken hold of her fingers when, in a burst of excitement, she withdrew them, got to her feet, and set about pacing the room, uttering phrases addressed as much to herself as to him.

"You're arriving...not in any vulgar sense...recognition and fame...that matters little enough.....But this proves you are on the right track...and the invitation to lecture, should you ever go to Egypt!"

He watched her intently and realized how thoroughly his enjoyment of his own achievement was dependent on her participation in it.

"You must work hard...press on," she had continued when the sound of quick, firm footsteps approaching through the vestibule into the atrium silenced her.

"Who can that be?" she wondered. "I was expecting no one. And why haven't the attendants announced him?"

In answer, Rufus appeared in the doorway.

"Marcus," she cried in amazement. "I thought you were still in Caesarea."

He looked scathingly from her to Elisha and back again.

"Rather surprised by my sudden return?" he sneered. "I expected to find the two of you together."

"What do you mean?" she asked with soft, ominous restraint.

"My only disappointment," he went on, his voice turning raucous, his eyes glowing with a pallid fire, "is that when I did come upon you, you were so innocently engaged."

"How dare you?" she breathed unsteadily. "No, Elisha"—she restrained him as he started toward the Roman. "This is my business. I will handle it myself. Now, Tineius, you will explain yourself."

"Don't put on airs of injured dignity with me," he shouted, moving closer to her with each word until they were face to face. "What do you two do in each other's company? Twiddle your thumbs? Or do you suppose that even when I am in Palestine I do not learn when he calls and how long he stays."

"So," she hurled her indignant reproaches directly into the raging countenance before her, "you have set spies on me. I should have foreseen that, knowing you as I do. Just as well. What do they tell you, the slaves you have bribed? Have they informed you that we are never, never alone, that either the servants or some third party has been present whenever Elisha visits?"

"A clever blind," Rufus rasped contemptuously.

"You wouldn't understand friendship between a man and a woman," Elisha spoke, unable despite Manto's instruction to contain himself.

"Stay out of this," Rufus turned on him. "This is the last time you will enter this house."

"Is it now?" Manto inquired evenly. "Not while I am mistress here."

"Then you are no longer that," Rufus shouted.

"As you say," Manto shrugged indifferently. "You see, Marcus, you have the right to insist that I fulfill my share of our arrangement. I will not permit you to select my friends. I presume that I may take some clothes with me?" she asked, turning away.

Elisha's heart leaped at the thought that she might be in earnest.

Rufus watched her, stonily at first, then his angry pride cracked.

"Please, Manto, I didn't think you would take me seriously. You know how I feel about you."

She hesitated.

"Please," he coaxed.

"After all these years," she yielded grudgingly, "you ought to have more faith in me."

"I know. But I have been insane with jealousy."

"I understand, and now let's forget the whole distasteful business. Elisha here has just received a really remarkable letter from the head of the Musaeum of Alexandria, commending him on his essay...."

But the elation of the afternoon was gone irretrievably for Elisha.

She broke off, her eyes swinging from Elisha's unhappy face to the malevolent stare with which Rufus regarded him.

"I think," she said abruptly, "that there is something else I ought to make clear to you, Tineius. If ever you try to use your power against Elisha here, I shall even the score if it costs me my life."

CHAPTER X

As the third largest city in the Empire, Antioch attracted to itself actors, musicians, scientists, authors and philosophers from all over the civilized world.

Scarcely a day went by without some visiting lecturer haranguing shifting crowds of idlers in the forums, speaking to fashionable audiences in luxurious salons and auditoriums, or addressing little groups of scholars in the privacy of libraries.

Inevitably there were charlatans among them: rhetoricians who had every equipment of the orator except sincerity, Stoics who were secretly voluptuaries, and Cynics, obscene in speech, rude in dress, vulgar in thought, whose mantles, wallets and staffs, symbols of voluntary poverty, were but a device for garnering pennies on street corners.

The earnest students of Antioch had learned from hard experience to be skeptical of the reputation of these newcomers. But even they were pleasurably excited over the arrival in their city of Demonax of Cyprus, moralist of the Cynic school, distinguished both for his own attainments and for the fact that during his long life he had numbered among his personal friends the great Stoic, Epictetus; the Pythagorean, Apollonius of Tyana; and the rhetorician, Herodes Atticus.

Elisha had made it a rule of late to avoid public lectures, having found them too disjointed to be meaningful, but he eagerly joined the throngs who assembled to hear a scholar of such glowing fame. The addresses to which he listened were altogether equal to his expectations. He came away from them inspired by the learning, wisdom and sweet gentleness of the sage. When it was announced subsequently that Demonax would remain in Antioch for some time and would accept a limited number of disciples, it occurred to Elisha that in him he might find the instructor he desired. Without delay, he sought him out to present himself.

As the house guest of one of the great families of Syria,

Demonax resided in a palatial mansion. And Elisha as he entered it was perturbed by the manifest discrepancy between the splendor of the philosopher's lodgings and his professed adherence to a life of poverty. But the first sight of the chamber into which he was finally ushered restored his faith. The room was tiny and bare, stripped of all furnishings except stools, a table and a straw pallet against one wall. The philosopher who was at his luncheon rose instantly to greet his visitor.

"Pray do not interrupt your meal," Elisha urged.

"I shall return to it as soon as we have introduced ourselves."

Elisha identified himself and explained his purpose briefly.

"So you are Elisha," Demonax mused. "I have heard about you. What is more, I have read your essay. May I tell you that I thought it brilliant."

"Thank you," Elisha replied, delighted.

"And now, if you will excuse me for a moment, I shall finish with my food. Then we shall be free to talk at length."

While Demonax ate calmly, unhurriedly of coarse bread and a salad of greens, and drank cold water tinged faintly pink by an admixture of wine, Elisha studied him. He was an impressive figure, tall, straight and vigorous despite his years. His white hair and beard were carefully combed. His features were large and strong, his eyes gentle.

"So," he said after he had finished his repast and drawn his stool closer to Elisha, "you would like to study philosophy with me."

"If you will have me," Elisha corrected deferentially. "Of course, I shall be ready to pay whatever fees you stipulate."

"We need not worry on that score," the old man answered. "I am a person of very simple needs. I carry my bed with me." He indicated the mattress on the floor. "A crust of bread and fresh, cold water are all that I need for food. There is always some friend ready to offer me lodging and, if not, the world is large enough to afford me shelter. The real issue before us is whether I can offer you what you expect. You see, I have done more than skim your dissertation. I have studied it. And while I found it stimulating, should your viewpoint still be that which you expressed in it, I cannot possibly be of service to you."

Elisha started.

"Let me explain," Demonax continued. "To you philosophy is science. To me it is an art. To you it is a method of discovering the truth. To me it is a guide to noble living. We are too far removed in essential attitudes to be capable of co-operation."

"I am afraid I do not understand."

"No, I suppose my point is quite obscure. And yet it marks a real difference. The great thinkers, from Heraclitus on, have approached philosophy as you do. Plato, Aristotle, Democritus, even Zeno and Epicurus, have all been builders of systems. But for all their prestige, they are not my teachers. If I were to list my favorite sages I would say I revere Socrates, admire Diogenes and love Aristippus. For I am the expositor not of a theory but of a skill. As a flute teacher imparts his art, first by personal example and then by simple, practical principles, without too much concern over the nature of sound, so I attempt to influence people to live beautifully by striving to live so myself, and by communicating those rules of conduct that have stood the test of time."

"But," Elisha demurred, "no art can be entirely divorced from theory."

"Perfectly true," Demonax replied. "That is why I have some interest in metaphysics, but only in the barest and most essential minimum of it. It is guidance in their behavior which men need, a vision of immediate, attainable objectives to which they can dedicate themselves, not high-flown schemes of reality. Of the latter a man has enough if he attains to a reasonable belief in God and a fairly consistent picture of the universe and man's role in it."

"But even that minimum," Elisha protested, "must be thought through. You would not say that men should accept belief in God unless first they have reasoned their way to it clearly, consistently and indisputably. Or that they ought to adopt a code of morality unless they have convinced themselves of its validity."

The sadness in Demonax's eyes became more perceptible. "It is almost," he sighed, "as though I am hearing myself speak as I was many, many years ago. I, too, once felt as you did. But I have grown older and, if you will pardon my saying so, wiser. I have studied all the major metaphysical systems with care and found not a single issue which they have demonstrated absolutely. To make matters worse, there is not one conclusion on which they agree. The schools remind me of nothing so much as the fable in Hebrew literature about a tower which would have been built to heaven were it not that all the artisans were afflicted by a confusion of tongues."

"But after all," Elisha objected, "there is just as little agreement in the realm of practical principle as in that of theory. Your own argument can be turned against you. One might well say: There is no unity of opinion as to ethics, no one has ever attained moral perfection, therefore the quest after the better life ought to be abandoned. If ever there was an instance of self-contradiction…"

He stopped, realizing that he was overstepping the bounds of good taste.

"You will pardon me, I hope, for my bluntness. I did not mean to offend you."

The sage was unperturbed except that the look of compassion on his face had deepened.

"You are right," he said. "I am not altogether logical. Here I tell you that the quest after metaphysical certainty is not worthwhile because after several centuries of effort it has not attained its objectives. And at the very same moment I say that one ought to devote his efforts to teaching people how to behave although there is no agreement as to the better life and, so far as we are aware, no one has ever lived it in its completeness. But the contradiction is not mine. It is nature's.

The human scene is not some philosopher's garden, but a confusing, dark struggle. Through its noise and obscurity men grope, all seeking for serenity, few finding it. And some of us, though we have not completely demonstrated our principles, believe that we know how they may make themselves both better and happier. Can we withdraw into books and their abstrusities when men need insight into their souls, balms for their wounds, and healing of their sorrows? Ah, yes, if you and I were the gods, as Epicurus describes them, we might devote our lives to debating the question whether or not Platonic ideas exist eternally in realms beyond space and time. But we are flesh and blood. We dare not, for an intellectual luxury, forget our aches or those of our brothers."

"But if so," Elisha cried out, "it will go on forever. If they possess no certainty and are never fully convinced of anything men will always take refuge in aphorisms and maxims. I am not insensitive to human suffering, but the slow cure is sometimes the surer. Suppose people are lost in some dark and threatening forest without food or shelter. Ought not someone climb a tree to discern the forest as a whole and the paths by which he and his fellows can escape from it? Or, to change the metaphor, if, as in Plato's dialogue, we are to sit forever looking at shadows, we shall never see the sun. Now consider Euclid's *Elements of Geometry*. A mathematician evolves a truth concerning space. Thereafter every builder, whether of a ship, a temple or a bridge, can proceed from it with confidence. So, only if there be first an indisputable interpretation of reality and a moral system drawn from it, will men be able to live, as engineers and architects work, with assurance."

"And the failure of the schools in the past," Demonax challenged softly, "their inability to agree, you are prepared to make the effort despite that?"

"I am." Elisha replied, "I hope to find conviction in some established system. Otherwise I shall create one for myself, borrowing from the older philosophies whatever is valid, but in any case proceeding like Euclid from unchallengeable axioms to unshakable conclusions, whatever they may be, however hard to accept. It is presumptuous, I know, for me to think that I will succeed where others have failed. But there were mathematicians before the author of the *Elements*. Someone has to try. Why not I? Someone will succeed. Perhaps I."

"Presumptuous?" Demonax breathed. "Aye, as Prometheus was presumptuous. If only I were not so old, so weighted by futility, so oppressed by the urge to give immediate assistance to those in need, and also of so little faith, I would work with you. As it is, I commit you to Athene, the goddess of inner light."

"But I must have an instructor," Elisha pleaded.

"An instructor?" Demonax echoed. "Not really. All you require is someone who knows philosophical literature thoroughly and who can supply you with a bibliography. And I can suggest the man for that purpose, a fellow Cypriote and a former schoolmate of mine, called Polemon. He has been in Antioch for years working on a commentary on the *Timaeus* of Plato. I shall send him to you. He can tell you the name of every book on philosophy ever written. Let him plan your reading. Under his guidance and with the libraries of Antioch at your disposal you should be able to proceed alone."

The sage rose to indicate that the interview was over.

"It surprised me, sir," Elisha said at the door, "to hear you quote the story of the Hebrews about the Tower of Confusion. Tell me, pray, how does it happen that you have read it?"

"Ah," Demonax smiled, "I am pleased that you too have discovered that book. It is a sublime creation, rich in the moral truths that mankind needs more than metaphysics. But then, let us not begin our controversy again."

And Elisha was startled and strangely confused to hear a commendation of the Tradition he had abandoned coming from the lips of the foremost exponent of Greek thought.

CHAPTER XI

POLEMON WAS THIN, HIS SKIN wrinkled and parched like
some crumbling piece of parchment, his voice dry like the rustling of papyrus. It was almost as though he had been left among
arid books so long that the moisture of his body had evaporated.

He was, however, as Demonax had promised, of amazing
erudition. It was apparent that he had read everything of which
Elisha had ever heard. But it became equally clear on closer
acquaintance that there was a vast pointlessness to his scholarship. His entire mind was a jumble of quotations. During their
first interview, Elisha thought wantonly of the homely saying
with which the peasants of Palestine were wont to characterize
a learned fool, "An ass laden with books." But for all his limitations Polemon satisfied Elisha's needs. He knew the bibliography of philosophy. And so they undertook to meet.

Each fortnight Polemon covered a wax tablet with a list
of books and collected his fee. They rarely engaged in discussion except for one occasion when Elisha refused for a time
to read the literature of the Middle Academy, that school of
philosophy which stemmed from Plato but which in contradiction of its founder argued that the human intellect,
incapable of certainty, must rest content with plausibilities.
The negativism of the doctrine, of which Elisha had already
learned something, and its denial of his purposes, alarmed
him. He preferred to avoid contact with it. But he yielded
in the end, less because of Polemon's shrill insistence than
because he knew that none of his conclusions would ever
be secure unless first he took cognizance of the challenge.
Hurriedly, he skimmed the works Polemon suggested, eager
to be done with them. When they were safely out of the way
he proceeded with relief to more sympathetic systems.

One summer day, well over a year later, the Emperor Hadrian
visited Antioch in the course of a tour of the Oriental

provinces. For weeks in advance signs on blank walls along the main thoroughfares announced the schedule of public games with which his presence was to be celebrated. The program included gladiatorial shows in the arena, as the gift of the city-senate; water sports on the Orontes under the auspices of the associated societies of artisans and merchants; chariot racing at the Hippodrome arranged by the governor of the province; and, finally, a day of public banquets for the freemen of the city and of the distribution of doles to slaves and libertines, the gift of the Caesar himself.

On the afternoon of the Emperor's arrival even the Musaeum was abandoned by most of its habitues. Events outside its walls rarely disturbed its routine. But the most unworldly pedant was interested in Hadrian, who had served as Governor of Syria before his elevation to the principate and who, as a man of culture, had won many friends among the scholars. He was not, those who remembered him admitted, quite the philosopher king of whom Plato had spoken, but he was genuinely interested in things of the mind and had himself written verse. One of his poems, a poignant bit addressed to his soul, was a fine piece and had been widely read. As a result, grammarian and scientist alike regarded him as a kindred spirit and put aside treatises, commentaries and texts to pay him honor.

Like everyone else Elisha was present in the Forum where, after elaborate parades, the Emperor appeared to accept the salutations of his subjects. Returning from the spectacle through streets impassable for the noisy jostling crowds, Elisha, in the hope of making his way homeward the more quickly, abandoned the main thoroughfares for side streets. In the maze of alleys and unfamiliar bypaths he lost his way. Night was falling when, in the course of his blunderings, he came upon a plaza. Deciphering Hebrew inscriptions on the walls about him, he knew that he had wandered into one of the Jewish districts of the city. An imposing structure, obviously a synagogue, stood ahead of him, a dim light shining through its windows. Vaguely disquieted, he walked on more rapidly.

As he passed before the building, a door opened and released a flood of light squarely on him. Several men, conversing in Aramaic, came forth. Stopping short to avoid colliding with them, Elisha caught his breath. He was face to face with Akiba. Amazed as he was by that, he was equally astounded to observe that the rabbi's earlocks had been worked back of his ears, that he was dressed like a Greek.

"Peace," Akiba said quietly while they continued to stare at each other.

"Peace," came the whispered reply.

Inside the synagogue someone closed the door. The band of light narrowed and disappeared. The two men became shadows in a ghostly darkness. For a frenzied moment, love, curiosity, gratitude struggled against one another within Elisha to translate themselves into speech. But before he could utter a word, the invisible wall of excommunication rose between them. Abruptly Akiba turned away to rejoin his companions. Long after he was gone Elisha remained motionless, reliving episodes from the past they shared, mourning that they whose mutual devotion was so strong might yearn for each other but on meeting must be denied even the privilege of simple, almost irrepressible inquiries after each other's welfare. Then, desolate in heart, hungry for a friend's voice he might not hear, he plodded homeward. When he threw open the door of his apartment, he found Pappas lounging on his bed. Instantly his face became a mask.

"I bring you tidings," Pappas reported. "Whether good, bad or indifferent I cannot say. Do you know who is at Antioch?"

"Akiba."

Pappas gaped. "How did you know? I intended to surprise you."

"I just met him."

"But where?"

"In some Forum in the Gamma quarter. I was cutting across the city to avoid the crowds. He came out of the synagogue just as I was passing."

Pappas whistled softly. "Did you talk to each other?"

Elisha smiled wryly. "We just managed to exchange greetings, when we both remembered that, by an official vote of the Sanhedrin, I am a perverse, rebellious sage and an excommunicate. And so we just passed on. It hurt, Pappas...." He turned away, ostensibly to put his cloak in a closet. "But what I don't understand," he continued, coming over to Pappas, "is why he's in Antioch."

"Some official business of the Sanhedrin, I imagine," Pappas evaded.

"Then why was he dressed like a Greek?"

"Really, was he? How strange." But he was too casual.

"Come now," Elisha insisted, "I can tell by your manner that you know. What is it?"

"There is actually no reason why I should not tell you," Pappas replied after a moment's hesitation. "The rumor has spread through Palestine that Hadrian is planning to rebuild Jerusalem as a pagan city. Akiba is here to raise money for war if the report proves true."

"Stories like that," Elisha snorted, "are always current."

"That may be, but they are taking no chances in Palestine. They have gone so far as to elect a commander-in-chief, a man from Koziba by the name of Simon. Did you know him?"

"Simon of Koziba?" Elisha shook his head. "I think not. But it is impossible—that tale about Jerusalem. The Romans know better."

"Yes? Then let me tell you something. A week ago our banker, Ariston of Rhodes, called me in to advise me to dispose of the Palestinian tax shares I own. The country is disturbed—close to insurrection." he said.

"What did you do?"

"I sold. But the point is this. Bankers usually have special sources of information. When they talk of rebellion, they must know."

"But to rebel against Rome, no matter what the provocation—why it would be insane! They will destroy themselves. And for what? For a mound of ruins which in their obstinacy they insist on regarding as possessed of some special sanctity. Suppose those stones are of great antiquity, what meaning has that for mankind today and tomorrow? Is that a justification either for suicide or for disturbing the world's tranquillity and bringing misery to millions who have never even heard of Jerusalem?"

"You know, Elisha," Pappas's eyes narrowed, "I do not like the way you say 'they.' "

"How would you have me express myself?" Elisha's voice was raised defensively. "After all, as an excommunicate I am scarcely one of them."

"You might use 'we' occasionally."

"Really, you surprise me," Elisha scoffed in astonishment. "I am not accustomed to thinking of you as a Jewish patriot."

"Granted that I am a bad Jew. At least I know I am not a Roman. But it is you we are talking about. Which side, I wonder, are you on?"

"Naturally," Elisha reflected, "I am sympathetic with my own people, misguided though they be. I should hate even in the privacy of my mind to be aligned against them. But there can be no comparison between the blind loyalties of one group to its past, and the peace of the Empire, nor between the superstitions of that group and the intellectual life of the rest of the world, so meaningful to me, so promising for all men. It is in this that my life finds its sole point and purpose. The few people who are left to me to love are all associated with it. Do I not owe loyalty to the society that makes all this possible?"

He paused and meditated a moment before concluding: "All I can say, if you insist on an answer, is that I hope I may never be compelled to choose."

Early the next morning a slave brought Elisha the request that he call at once, and without fail, at the offices of the House of Ariston of Rhodes. Disturbed by his conversation with Pappas, disquieted by the urgent tone of the message, Elisha put aside his plans for a day of uninterrupted study and proceeded forthwith to the building just off the Forum which housed the counting rooms of his bankers. He was shown directly into the presence of the chief clerk.

"I hope," the man began apologetically, when Elisha was seated, "that you will pardon the abruptness of our invitation. But matters of prime importance have arisen, decisions on which we require your authorization. We are in receipt of reports from Palestine—"

"I know," Elisha interrupted. "Pappas spoke to me yesterday."

"Then I will not have to explain. Let me tell you what we have done already. We have taken the liberty of transferring here whatever moneys you have had on deposit at Tiberias. You have no objection to the step?"

"No," Elisha replied. "I think that you have exaggerated the situation. But it makes no difference to me where my funds are kept."

"And now," the clerk went on, "I should like to submit to your consideration a recommendation that we are making to all our clients. We are suggesting to them the liquidation of their Palestinian investments."

"You mean, sell the estate?" Elisha asked incredulously.

"Exactly. If there should be war, all revenues from it will cease."

Elisha's reply was immediate and decisive. "That house and its grounds have been in our family for generations. In no circumstance will I dispose of them, in whole or in part."

"But what will you live on, in the event of an insurrection?"

"I doubt very seriously that there will be one."

"But if there should be?" the banker insisted.

"Then," Elisha answered, "I still have resources—whatever is on deposit with you."

The clerk picked up a tablet from the table.

"It's rather a large sum," he commented, studying it. "The property has been paying well and you have been spending much less than its income. Still, it would last no longer than three years at your present rate of withdrawals."

"A long time," Elisha countered. "And I can always live more simply." He rose to leave.

"One moment please. There is an alternative I should like to recommend. Would you agree to a mortgage? The money remains intact with us. In case of need, it is available. If not, it can always..."

"No," Elisha said resolutely. "I thank you genuinely for your concern, but I will not impair the security of my estate."

Thereafter it became a rule with Elisha to stop in the Forum every day to read the news bulletins. For ever since his conversation with Pappas an apprehension had settled on him, the dread that through force of circumstances he would be compelled to make a decision of loyalty. Fervently he hoped that the rumor concerning the Emperor's plans would prove baseless. Desperately he prayed that should it be confirmed, the Shragas among the Jewish people would not succeed in precipitating a senseless rebellion, to their own destruction and to the misery of innocent thousands. So the proclamation board on which there would appear ultimately either a message of reassurance or the notice he feared drew him irresistibly.

Then, one morning it was there, a boldly written placard posted alongside the other reports.

"The Emperor Hadrian, having seen the ruins of Jerusalem on a visit to Palestine, has determined to restore the ancient city. Colonists are required. To suitable candidates household sites and subsidies will be granted. Where the Hebrew Temple once stood a great shrine is to be erected, dedicated to Jupiter, in whose honor the reconstructed town is to be named Aelia Capitolina."

It was early in the day. The air was cool and moist with dew. Long shadows and bright bands of light alternated across the pavement. The Forum was quiet. None of the law courts, offices or banking houses had opened yet for business. But in Elisha as he stood, dwarfed by the towering columns that faced the inclosure, there was turmoil and despair.

He knew the Jews, in their schools, bazaars, workshops and farms. They might conceivably have permitted their sacred city to be made into a heathen town. But they would never tolerate the desecration of the Temple mountain. How could the Roman authorities be so blind as not to see that they were inviting rebellion? He must inform them of the perils of their course. Immediately he set out to enlist the assistance of Pappas.

But Pappas was not at his apartment. Normally a late riser, he had that morning gone off early to his favorite bathhouse. Wild with impatience, Elisha followed him there to find him lying on a marble slab, a masseur rubbing excess ointment from him with an ivory flesh-scraper.

Without introduction Elisha told him of the bulletin he had read. Pappas's face turned gray.

"The Romans want war," he muttered.

"Why should you draw that inference?" Elisha protested. "It is much more likely that they do not understand the gravity of the situation."

"Nonsense," Pappas snorted. "When has the Roman government acted without considering every relevant detail?"

"But it is altogether possible in this instance. Certainly, if we could, we ought to call it to their attention."

"Granted, but how?"

"Tineius Rufus. We must get an audience with him!"

"I am not sure that he is in the city," Pappas said dubiously. "And he would scarcely take anything we say very seriously."

But while expressing his skepticism, he was already waving to an attendant for his clothes.

"It is hopeless," he said as they set forth, "but it can do no harm. And we must try."

They learned upon inquiry that Rufus was at his country estate on the outskirts of Antioch and, though they hastened to the villa, the morning was far advanced by the time they arrived at their destination. The vestibule was already crowded with officials, some of high rank, and with personal clients of the Prefect of Palestine, interested less in seeing their patron than in receiving from his stewards either money or baskets of food. Requested by the attendants to await their turn, they sat fuming until everyone who had come ahead of them had been interviewed. At long last, after the reception room had been emptied, a secretary approached them.

"You may come in now."

They forgot their impatience in a surge of hope as they walked into Rufus' presence.

Neither his pink round face nor his fuzzy hair had changed with the years.

"Welcome, Pappas," he said, but his greeting was cold. "And Elisha," he added as though it were an afterthought.

For a moment he studied Elisha and through his sightlessness there flashed, Elisha was sure, a look of malevolence.

"And now, gentlemen," he addressed them, "to what do I owe this honor? It is not often that Manto's dearest friends seek me out here."

"We have read the bulletin about Jerusalem," Elisha began tentatively.

Rufus looked at him blankly, saying nothing.

"And about the new Temple."

There was no encouragement from the Roman.

Annoyed by his stolidity Elisha plunged into tactless protest.

"Are there no other ruined cities to be rebuilt? Is that the only hilltop in the world where a Temple of Jupiter can be erected?"

"Oh, I see," Rufus spoke at last, as though for the first time comprehending, "you object to the Emperor's plan. So for that matter do I. It strikes me as a sheer waste of time and money to rebuild that desolate spot."

"But does he not recognize that it will mean war? You must caution him against the project."

"War!" Rufus repeated blandly. "I doubt it. And as for warning him, I see that you do not know our Hadrian. He is a sentimentalist, filled with romantic nostalgias over everything ancient. It offends him that a place invested with such historic associations should lie vacant and uninhabited. And when he is obsessed by one of his restorations, no power on earth can move him."

"Then if he must resettle Jerusalem, let him use Jewish colonists."

"Now, Elisha," Rufus chided, irritably, "do you suppose that the peace of the Empire is maintained by rewarding intractability—and that is all we have ever had from your countrymen. Or that they will be more compliant if we restore to them the city which has always served as their center of resistance?"

"But there will be a war," Elisha cried. "I know the Jews..."

"Do you think I am deaf?" Rufus snapped. "I heard you say that before. And may I tell you that I have already been sufficiently indulgent. My time is too precious to be wasted on gadabouts and closet scholars who represent nobody but their unimportant selves."

"Then you will not address the Emperor?" Elisha persisted, controlling his temper.

"No," Rufus exploded, his color deepening. "Hadrian's order will be fulfilled to the last detail and without resistance. And to show we are not such fools as to need your counsel, I will tell you that as a precaution, and only as that, two cohorts have been ordered into Palestine and I am leaving for Caesarea tomorrow to be on the scene. But before we part, let me advise you to attend to your own affairs and leave matters of state to grown men."

Towering over the Roman, Elisha stared down on him contemptuously.

"Come on, Pappas," he addressed his companion. "It is one of the tragedies of even good governments that they must sometimes be administered by persons incapable of reason."

A bellow sounded from Rufus as they turned their backs on him. They should have stopped to hear him out. It was dangerous to goad his fury further. But as Pappas slowed to turn, Elisha seized his elbow and propelled him through the door so that Rufus was left speaking into empty space.

It was not until they reached the main highway without being overtaken by guards that they knew they had insulted him with impunity. What they saw there caused them to forget the peril through which they had just passed. The scene filled them with foreboding. For sweeping along the road from Antioch went a large body of regular Roman infantry in full marching equipment, accompanied by auxiliary detachments of cavalry and archers, and followed by a lumbering wagon train. Rank by rank, the soldiers reached the shoulder of Mount Silpius, where for a moment they were black against the sun, except that points of light flashed briefly on their armor and standards. Then they sank from view on their way southward and downward.

CHAPTER XII

THE EMPEROR HADRIAN HAD NO sooner left the Orient when exhausted couriers riding horses flecked with foam and sweat rode into Antioch from the south. The next day bulletins announced an insurrection in Palestine and the beleaguerment of the Roman garrison in Jerusalem. Fantastic rumors swept Antioch: Caesarea had fallen to the Jews, who were now preparing to march on Damascus; the Parthians had crossed the eastern frontier; the province of Arabia was in revolt and the land beyond Jordan in flames. All the reports were steadfastly, if unavailingly, denied by the authorities, except one: that of rebellion in Palestine. Within a few days, refugees began to arrive: officials of the civil administration of Palestine, slave-traders who had lost their wares, and later, long wagon trains carrying the wounded of the Tenth Legion Fretensis that had policed the country. It was they who brought the first trustworthy news. The Roman army of occupation had been cut to pieces; Jerusalem had been stormed by a Jewish general, Simon of Koziba, renamed by his followers bar Cochba, the son of the Star, an archdemon heading a host of devils.

At once the economic life of Syria deteriorated. Estates in Palestine and districts bordering on it and shares in the tax companies of the disturbed areas were offered for pittances and went begging for buyers. Trade with the provinces to the south and east of Syria came to an abrupt standstill. A paralysis took hold of commerce and finance.

In autumn the remnants of the Roman army encamped on the southern frontiers of Syria where it spent the succeeding months in awaiting reinforcements and in preparations for the resumption of the campaign. With the coming of spring it took the field only to be defeated once more, this time so decisively that gladiators were called from the arenas to military service and emancipation was offered to any slave who would take up arms. By fall, the Roman forces had again been expelled from Palestine.

The distress of the first winter was intensified during the second. Bankrupt merchants unloaded their last assets to their creditors. Bankers turned adamant in their refusal to issue new loans. The slave market was reduced to a chaos by forced sales. Slowly the paralysis of business activity spread downward into the lower classes. Demand ceased for anything except the barest necessities. Guilds of artisans met anxiously to arrange for mutual assistance by lending their corporate resources to members in need. But even these funds were not inexhaustible. Then craftsmen were forced to sell their tools and, in thousands of cases before winter was over, themselves. So the war cost many a freeborn man his liberty and many an emancipated slave all he had attained by years of self-denial. Only armor makers, commission merchants dealing with the army and speculators prospered, the last in anticipation of the time when deeds, mortgages and bonds would return to their normal values.

Inevitably, there were riots in Antioch. One day a mob looted the shops so that soldiers had to be summoned from their barracks to restore order. On another occasion a vast crowd of freemen and libertines assembled before the official residence of Marcellus, Governor of the Province, demanding a dole. By the time they had been dispersed the Forum was littered with corpses.

In the countryside virtual anarchy reigned. Villas were burned, their masters and mistresses tortured to death by bands of runaway bondsmen who had taken to brigandage in the hills. Frightened by the prospect of a slave rebellion, the authorities of Syria called superannuated legionaries from their retirement into active police service and set them to patrolling streets or sent them off on punitive expeditions. But the sight of them was anything but comforting, so feeble did they appear in their refurbished armor, so awkward with weapons, the use of which had long since ceased to be natural to them.

It was at this time that Elisha and Pappas were first affected by the general economic distress. Foresighted, the chief clerk of the House of Ariston of Rhodes pointed out to them that with the cessation of income their money on deposit had diminished appreciably. His suggestion that they reduce their expenditures was not pleasant to the two men who had always enjoyed revenues in excess of their needs. But caution demanded that they heed his advice. And, as Elisha pointed out, their lot was still infinitely better than that of thousands of others. At the beginning of the third year of the war they moved from their costly apartments to simpler quarters, disposed of the luxury of attendants, ceased to purchase clothes and adjusted themselves as best they could to a limited budget. So they hoped to insure themselves against the prolongation of the crisis.

Elisha was unaffected by the slight discomforts to which he was subjected. But he could not blot out the scenes of suffering which he had witnessed during these nightmarish years of the war. And as he watched the increasing wretchedness on all sides, the progressive disorganization of the pleasant, decent routines of living, his opposition to the Jewish cause was turned slowly into resentment against it.

"Did those war-mongers have to inflict all this horror, both on the innocent ones in their own midst and the countless others who never did them the least harm?" he railed at Pappas during one of their many arguments over the issue. "And having engaged in it, must they prolong it indefinitely, without reckoning the cost? Why don't they sue for peace and put a stop to the insanity? Don't they see that now is the time to quit, now while they still have successes with which to bargain for an honorable peace? What good can come out of the whole murderous business if they persist in it?"

"What good," Pappas challenged in answer, "came from the rebellion of the Maccabees?"

"Exactly," Elisha seized on the reference. "Answer your own question if you can. Besides," he went on derisively, "do you compare the rotten kingdom of Antiochus with the Empire?"

"Nonetheless, bar Cochba has held out for three years by his own strength. Suppose the Parthians join them or some other province rebels?"

"Suppose, suppose, all suppositions. Meantime, the Parthians have not stirred. And if they should or if the Jews unaided should be victorious in the end—what then?"

"Complete independence," Pappas replied softly but at once. "I know, I know, you are going to tell me once more that it is a grotesque impossibility. And I admit that even with the war going as it is, it seems unattainable. But it is not inconceivable. And if it should come to pass... Think of it, the Jewish people free again in a free Palestine. It's a desperate gamble, like a dice player wagering fortune and life on one throw. But if the fall is right..."

"Anarchy results," Elisha completed for him, "the maddest chaos mankind has known since the days of Alexander the Great. Don't you see that if Palestine becomes independent, so also will Syria and Egypt, Armenia, every province in the Orient. The Empire disintegrates piecemeal and each nation becomes the arbiter of its own destiny. Inevitably then every peoples' hand is raised against the other. I tell you, the earth will run with blood and perish in its own lawlessness."

"This intense adoration of yours for the Roman state baffles me," Pappas sneered, "especially in view of comments I remember hearing from you. Have you not on occasion condemned the heathen world for its lack of mercy, contrasting it unfavorably with the way of the Jews? Or have you become blind to the motives with which Rome imposes peace on the peoples? You lived in Palestine. Have you forgotten the taxation, the repressive ordinances? Do you suppose it is different anywhere else? Quiet, order, you claim. A corpse is quiet and orderly. And that is just what Palestine will become, and other provinces too in the end unless they emancipate themselves."

"Look here, Pappas," Elisha said dispassionately, "I have no illusions about the Roman Government. It is always rapacious, occasionally despotic and often brutal. But it is at its worst to be preferred to what preceded it and what will most certainly follow on its dissolution, a multitude of warring states, each misruled by its own petty tyrant. Was Palestine happier or more prosperous under its own kings, the Ahabs and Herods, than as a Roman province? But an even more important consideration seems to have escaped you altogether. For all its faults the Empire secures men in their rights. Men are free now, freer than at any time in history. True, the masses utilize their liberty only so that they may gratify their animal desires. But some, a handful I admit, employ it for the discovery of the truth, and the study of the good life. And it is this minority, this Rome within Rome as I have sometimes named it to myself, which is the sole hope of the human future. For if men and their governments are ever to be better, happier, wiser, it will be only because somebody has had the liberty to discover the way. Don't you see, Pappas, how, without intending it, the Roman state provides the instrument not only for remaking human nature into something sweeter and fairer but perhaps in the end for its own reconstruction?"

"But certainly," Pappas pleaded, "every people has the right to live its own life and determine its own destiny."

"Not against the best interests of mankind," came the confident denial.

But in the spring even Pappas lost hope when he saw the gigantic concentration of armed forces assembled about Antioch: cohorts from the Danube, the Rhine and Mauretania. The city swarmed with soldiery, negroid Moors, blond Germans, slender rosy-cheeked Britons. And still they continued to come: Arab cavalry from the desert, Cilician mountaineer archers wearing native caps and stiff goathair cloaks. A babble of tongues was heard jn the streets, the gods of all the peoples of the world were worshiped in the encampments. Meantime mountains of equipment arose on the plains outside the city: grain, cloth and ominous war machines. As further indication of his determination to bring the war to a speedy close, the Emperor, retaining Rufus as civil governor of Palestine, ordered Caius Julius Severus, commander of the Fourth Scythican Legion and a highly reputed strategist, to supersede him in the direction of the campaign.

The worried populace relaxed. With the struggle so near its end, a delegation from the city-senate requested Marcellus, Legate to Syria, to release impressed gladiators so that public shows might be resumed.

And then, just as the army was preparing to move, the plague struck. None could trace its source. Soldiers from different lands accused one another of responsibility for it. Some said it had been brought from Palestine; others that it had been induced by the Jews through magic and witchcraft. But it descended on Syria so wildly that its victims were countless, so virulently that the stricken died with incredible swiftness, and so horribly that even those who were spared scarcely dared breathe for fear of it.

Thus through the days of early spring when the air was fresh and soft and anemones and poppies blanketed the fields, Death made of the loveliness of nature an indecent, brutal jest. For the second time within one generation the Temples of Aesculapius, the God of Healing, sounded with unceasing incantations and smoked with clouds of incense. On the streets Egyptian witches sold spells to divert the evil spirits, and Babylonian soothsayers and astrologers traded in horoscopes, unfailingly favorable to those who purchased them. Over every door of hovel and palace alike protecting charms appeared, sprigs of hyssop, images of gods, and almost universally the inscriptions, "Mithra the Unconquered," and "Merciful Mother Isis, Have Mercy."

So each man took refuge with his own god, with some new

deity of whose special powers he had heard, or even in many instances in the synagogues of Antioch, for might not this horror be the vengeance of the affronted God of the Hebrews? As for those who had no gods to protect them, they went coweringly in their wonted ways or forgot their fears in the Gardens of Daphne.

The Musaeum and libraries were not spared. There, too, men fell ill, arranged their notes for the last time, entrusting them perhaps to some colleague for safekeeping, went home and did not return. But there was among the scholars less of hysteria than in the city at large. They tended to preserve their calm as befitted men who dealt with deathless things and knew full well that someday someone else would take up and complete their unfinished labors.

Except for his visits to Manto, who on his advice confined herself to her house, Elisha scarcely left the library at all. In his books he could forget the pain and anguish visible in the streets and the sword that ravaged his native land. He was, moreover, within sight of his goal, at work at last on that great enterprise to which all these years had been a preliminary. But each morning he was compelled to leave his home and in the evening to return to it, and horror waylaid his passage.

Late one afternoon he hurried to his apartment, trying not to see the pathetic charms on the doorways or hear the shrieks from bereaved households. On a main thoroughfare he met a funeral procession unattended except by a weeping woman and the slaves who shuddered away from their tainted burden. Instinctively he huddled against the wall of a building and covered his nose and mouth with his robe. His eyes stared after the bier until it was at a safe distance.

As he approached his own doorway, someone standing before it turned and ran toward him. It was Doris, Manto's maid.

"Master Elisha," she gasped, "I have been waiting here for you so long. Master Elisha, our Lady Manto is stricken."

A sharp stab of pain pierced him, contracting his heart.

"Have you had a physician?"

She leaned against a wall and began to weep.

"Oh, Master! Two slaves have died. The body of one is still inside the house."

He shook her gently.

"A physician...have you sent for a physician?"

"I went to fetch one yesterday. Two slaves were sick in the house then. Lycophron and—

"Never mind that. Did you get one?"

"No. He was dead when I got there, the physician I mean....I found another. He refused to come. It was late then....I went looking for still another. On Arrhidaeus Street some men got hold of me. It was dark. I screamed. A patrol came along. They let me go and I ran away."

"Who is with your lady now?"

"Nobody. The other servants have fled. She is alone."

"Alone!" he exclaimed. "Let's not waste any more time. Come along."

In the main court of Manto's house furniture had been overturned and clothes were strewn about. In one place ivory splinters were scattered, the fragments of a statuette from which the gold ornaments had been torn by some slave turned thief in the security of chaos.

Elisha hurried through the little garden to the door of Manto's room.

Doris clutched at his robe, drawing back.

"I am afraid to go in."

"Then stay here."

Alone he entered the bedchamber. Air, stale and fetid, assailed his nostrils. He moved quickly to a window and tore a shutter open. The last of the daylight poured into the room.

Steeling himself for what awaited him, he turned toward the bed.

Manto was lying asleep, one arm thrown back over her head. The night dress she wore was wrinkled and twisted about her. Its skirts had crept above her knees, revealing her long slender legs. There were stains on the crumpled spread and littered floor.

For a moment he was paralyzed by pain. Then he drew a deep tremulous breath. He must do something for her.

"I want a large basin of water," he called quickly to the maid at the door. "Fresh spreads, a robe, some towels, ointments and incense powder in a burner."

Within a few minutes Doris had collected the objects for which he asked. His arms laden, he re-entered the chamber and set to work in a frenzy. When he had done everything he could think of, he gathered the soiled clothes and threw them out of the window.

An idea occurred to him that sent him into the court again. "Doris," he asked, "have you informed Rufus?"

"Yes. But when I went to his villa they would not let me in. So I sent in the news. But he hasn't come or sent anybody else."

"Does Manto know?"

"I think so. I tried to lie. I did not want to hurt her. I said he had gone to Caesarea but she knew better."

"Very well, if Rufus will not risk his precious neck," Elisha muttered furiously, "he can at least furnish us with a physician. Go back to his palace. Do not leave until he promises. And now, hurry—you have been a brave girl."

"I love our lady," she said and was gone.

Elisha returned to the room, now darkened by dusk. Standing by the bed he watched Manto through the half-light. She stirred uneasily, her tongue flicking out to moisten her parched lips. With a start he picked up a basin of water, poured into it the contents of jars of scent and bathed her face and neck. He had just finished washing her slender fingers when he chanced to look up. She had awakened and was smiling at him. He forced a smile in response, put aside the bowl and sat down on a stool at her side.

"I thought at first you were a physician. But it is you, Elisha! I am so glad. I hoped you would get here."

"Are you comfortable?"

She looked down at the fresh spread and clean robe, and sniffed the fragrance of incense and ointments.

"Yes, thank you," she whispered. "You know Rufus would not come."

"Perhaps he could not."

"Roman duty," she said bitterly, "was never more expedient. But it is just as well. I didn't really want him." Then she was quiet so long that Elisha thought she had fallen asleep.

"Elisha," she spoke again, "I am afraid to die."

"But you are not going to," he promised, swallowing hard. "You'll get well again."

"That's what I've been telling myself. But it is no use." What was left of her courage crumbled. Tears rolled down her cheeks. She cried softly for a time while he pressed her hand to his lips. At last with a show of bravery, she murmured, "It is fortunate there is so little light in here. I must look dreadful."

"You are lovely."

She smiled.

"And you will stay with me to the end?"

"Of course."

A sigh of relief escaped her. During the next few minutes, while they were silent, the light from the window waned.

"Tell me, Elisha," she went on, her voice low and halting, "do you believe, really believe, what Plato says, that the soul is immortal?"

"I do not know," he confessed, wishing that he had a faith with which to comfort her.

"It would be pleasant, would it not," she murmured, "if it were true that the souls of the dead mount to the stars.... I have been a religious person in my way... initiated into the mysteries of Isis. I have a little image of her here...."

"I know," he said; "I saw it under your pillow. It is there now. Shall I get it for you?"

"No, do not move," she choked. "I shall know for myself soon enough."

After that she relaxed and fell asleep, but her forehead when he touched it seemed afire.

Some time later, how long he did not know, he heard steps resounding sharply on the stone floor outside. Fumbling his way through the darkness to the door he stood blinking in the sudden light of a lantern. Doris was there with a lean, little, worried old man beside her.

"You are a physician?"

"Yes, but—"

"Rufus sent him," Doris interrupted eagerly.

"Then come in."

"You should know," the physician protested querulously, entering with obvious reluctance, "that there is nothing we can do. Besides, I shall need more than this light. I am no cat to see in the dark."

For a moment Doris disappeared into the darkened house to return carrying in both hands a large three-wicked lamp. The old man came to the bedside, muttering protestations. With shrinking hands he touched Manto's forehead and felt her pulse.

She had changed since Elisha had last been able to see her. Her face was dry and waxen, except for two spots of high color over her cheekbones.

The man completed his cursory examination, rose and started out of the room. Elisha followed.

"Have you nothing to say?" he asked when they were in the court.

"It is the last stage of the plague."

"But is there nothing to be done?"

"Of course not. I told them," he broke out, "that they had

no right to endanger my life, especially when they knew it was to no purpose."

"How long will she live?" Elisha asked tonelessly.

The physician looked about the shadowy garden.

"Is that water fresh yonder?" he asked, indicating the pool which gleamed darkly through the marble pillars.

Neither Elisha nor Doris answered, but he caught the gentle splash of spraying waters.

"It is a fountain!" he muttered. "It must be clean." He hurried to it and commenced to wash his hands and face vigorously.

Elisha followed, overtaking him.

"I asked you a question," he reminded him.

"A question? Oh yes! I should say a day at most. Her pulse is weak and fast—a very bad sign. But she may recover consciousness." Then his voice became raucous with resentment. "Please get away from me. Here I am, washing away the humors and miasmas, and you stand so close."

Elisha stared at him contemptuously. Without further word, he returned to the room, drawing the curtain softly behind him.

"Someone was here," Manto whispered drowsily.

"Yes, a physician."

She was wide awake. "What did he say?"

"Your condition is good."

"You're not a very good liar, Elisha. But then you never were. Please put out the lamps. The light hurts my eyes."

One by one he extinguished the three flames. Darkness engulfed them.

"If I can find you in this game of blind-man's-buff, I am going to collect my forfeit," he said, with a pretense of gaiety. "And it will be a kiss," he continued as his hands touched her.

"Please don't," she warned weakly. "You've exposed yourself too much already."

"What does that matter?"

He slipped an arm beneath her but she averted her face so that his lips found her burning cheek.

"There are two things I must tell you before it is too late," she whispered with an effort, her mouth close to his ear. "You must finish your work. I denied my love of you for the sake of it.... It would be too terrible if anything prevented your going on.... You must promise me.... Maybe, if there is no other immortality, I shall live in the great book you will write.... Promise me," she repeated.

"I swear," he breathed.

"And you will let nothing, regardless of what it is, stand in your way?"

"Nothing in all the world."

"And now the other thing.... All these years I have wanted to say it outright... but I couldn't break our agreement... I love you, Elisha.... Don't be too angry with me for breaking my promise."

"Oh, my dear," he said unevenly, "angry with you?

"Haven't you felt," he cried, his arms tightening about her frail body, "how difficult it was for me, too?"

"I know that. But it is sweet to hear you say it."

Again and again he told her of his love, mourning for the lost years.

"Don't feel badly," she gasped after a while. "Perhaps it's better so.... But talk to me... I can't stand the stillness. Tell me something to give me courage."

Her voice was so feeble that he could scarcely hear her. Anxiously he searched the wisdom of philosophy for lines which might sweeten the bitter taste of death. But among all the books he had studied there was none invested with such potency. Then in the fierceness of his need, there came to him from the vanished yesterdays of his youth verses instinct with an understanding softer than the sharp-lined wisdom of the Greeks. And never had he wanted so desperately to believe as in this hour when she leaned upon a faith he did not possess.

Holding her to himself he spoke of the gentle Shepherd Who leads men beside still waters causing them to walk unhurt through the valley of the shadow, Who cannot be fled, not in the grave, not even if one were to take the wings of the morning and dwell in the uttermost parts of the sea.

She listened and like a child, insatiable of some marvelous tale and reluctant of slumber, asked for more.

" 'My heart is not haughty,' " he quoted, " 'nor mine eyes lofty. Neither do I exercise myself in things too great, too wonderful for me. Surely I have stilled and quieted my soul, like a child with his mother, like a child is my soul within me.' "

With that Manto's body sagged in his arms and, after a moment, muffled sobs escaped him.

CHAPTER XIII

NOT EVEN THE OLDEST MEN in Antioch could remember a winter as hard as that of the fourth year of the war. From early in September, rains fell continuously until mountain streams ran in torrents and the Orontes overflowed its banks. Wild gales blew and traffic by sea, always perilous during this season, ceased altogether even along the coast. And in December at the time of the solstice when Romans celebrated their Saturnalia and devotees of Mithra the rebirth of the Sun-god, when Phrygians burned the pine log of Attis, and Jews kindled the eight lights of Dedication, a great blizzard swept down from Armenia, covering Syria and Palestine with deep snow. In its wake came an intense cold that persisted unbroken week after week as though it would endure forever.

Wretched with discomfort, men wrapped themselves in woolens, huddled close to braziers and remained confined to their houses. The roads even where passable were deserted except for military couriers traveling between Antioch and Palestine. The Roman legions had at last fought their way into Jerusalem where they were encamped for the winter. There they lay waiting for the spring so that they might resume their campaign against the Jewish army, broken at last and withdrawn to a fortress deep in the wilderness of Judea.

Elisha suffered acutely from the inclement weather. The preceding autumn, with his funds almost exhausted, he had mortgaged his estate and so had succeeded in raising a sum sufficient to keep him for several years. The prospect of a speedy Roman victory had had its effect on the money market. But shortly thereafter a letter came to him from Nicholaus. Conditions in Caesarea, on the fringe of military operations, were worse than in Antioch, and the book dealer, his business at a standstill, was on the verge of starvation. Immediately, Elisha went to his bankers, only to discover they would make no additional commitments. Nevertheless he authorized them to divide his monthly withdrawals so that a regular remittance might be sent his friend.

As a result, he was compelled to change quarters again, moving to a humble lodging house that was nerve-rackingly noisy. By day, ragged dirty children played over the slimy flagstones of the courtyard, and women gossiped through open doors in high-pitched voices, interrupting their conversations to shriek at their offspring below. At dusk, men lounged on the rickety staircases throwing knucklebones. And scarcely an evening passed without a brawl in some apartment. Worst of all, the tenement was insubstantially built. The wind penetrated through the casements of windows, the crumbling walls were always cold and damp. But a charcoal brazier was a luxury in which Elisha could no longer indulge. And his unreplenished wardrobe was stocked now with cloaks, some ragged, some frayed, all worn. In his efforts at economy he resorted to skimping on his food, until, between hunger and fatigue, his slender form became painfully thin, his face pale and haggard.

It was not absorption in his work that accounted altogether for the many hours he spent in the library. An ever-present consideration was the quiet that prevailed there and the fact that its public reading halls were partially heated, a happy circumstance whenever he could no longer abide the enervating cold.

Yet, despite his discomfort, despite his continuing grief over Manto, he was content. He was fulfilling his pledge to her, proceeding rapidly in the formulation of that great system for which he had been preparing so long. The wax tablets containing the outline and accumulated notes of his book were piled high on his desk. He had rewritten his published essay to serve as an introduction. And of the main body the first chapters containing the basic philosophical definitions and axioms were already finished. It was hard for him to be patient, so eager was he to get on. Nevertheless he proceeded painstakingly with each phrase, testing cautiously every step in the argumentation. Restless, sometimes frenzied but always intent, he worked without surcease.

During the second week after the great storm a courier entered his room in the Musaeum. The soldier handed him a sealed tablet and waited impassively for the reply. Elisha turned the packet over curiously, undid the binding thread, and read:

"To Elisha, formerly of Migdal in Palestine, now resident in Antioch:

"An order to travel with all possible speed to the city of Jerusalem in Palestine. He shall there report to M. Tineius Rufus.

"For a horse and funds for the journey, he may apply to the treasurer of the Fourth Scythican Legion, who upon presentation of this letter will provide him with a good mount and money sufficient for his trip.

"A similar order has been issued to Pappas, formerly of Migdal, now resident in Antioch.

"Seven days will be allowed from the time of delivery of this order to the appearance of both men at their destination in Jerusalem.

"By order of

M. Tineius Rufus, Imperial Legate, and C. Julius Severus, Commander-in-Chief of the Roman Armies in Palestine."

Astonished, Elisha looked up at the messenger.

"What do they want of me? Do you know?"

"No."

"Have you delivered the second order?"

"If you mean to the man called Pappas, yes. He said he would come to you here as soon as he had dressed. My orders call for an answer from both of you. The other man said he would undertake the trip. Will you?"

"I do not see that I have any choice." Elisha grimaced.

"Yes, you have," the courier smiled bleakly. "Prison."

"You mean that you have been ordered to arrest us if we refuse."

The messenger nodded and went on, "You will find the treasurer of the Fourth Scythican Legion in the Temple of Fortune, just beyond the Forum, on Seleucia Street. Show him this letter. As for travel, I suggest the highway to Damascus, then the fords of the Jordan and so to Tiberias. That far the road is safe. But when you go farther you may have to have a military escort. There are still some enemy in the hills. Now, is there anything else?"

Elisha shook his head.

"You had better take warm clothes," the soldier stopped at the door to add. "And remember," he concluded significantly, "the highway to Palestine goes south, not east. It is the only road on which you will not be arrested."

He had hardly gone when Pappas hurried into the room.

"By the sanctuary," he swore, dropping into a chair, "a fine time to order men to undertake a journey." He shivered and pulled his hastily donned robe closer about him. "And by my life, it is no warmer here. I have new respect for scholars. I never realized that learning involved such hardship."

"Pappas, what do they want?"

Pappas's facetiousness disappeared instantly.

"How should I know?" he grumbled. "Roman generals rarely take me into their confidence. It is an order and we shall have to obey."

"But have you no notion?"

"While coming here I tried to puzzle it out. The only interpretation that occurred to me is not a very happy one." He brooded in silence.

"And that?"

"With the war in its last stages, Severus and Rufus order two Jews to come to them. What do they want? The pleasure of their company? Scarcely. Expert advice most likely. Counsel from the inside, from those who know the character and the spirit of the conquered people. It is a highly plausible guess."

The cold of the room was only in part the cause of the chill Elisha experienced.

"But it may be something else," he fended, "something to do with matters in Antioch. Pappas," he asked accusingly, "have you been doing anything here—I mean, raising money or sending information to Palestine?"

"Of course not," Pappas replied with an impatience that convinced Elisha at once. "I have behaved myself beautifully. No, it has nothing to do with Antioch. If it had, it would have been handled on the scene. I am convinced my first suspicion is correct."

"What are we to do?"

"These are the courses we can adopt," Pappas held up three fingers. "One, disregard the order and stay here, be arrested and taken to Palestine by force. Two, attempt to get over the eastern frontier...."

"No use," Elisha interrupted. "I was warned by the messenger against that. The roads are closed to us. In all likelihood, we are being watched as well."

"And that is not all," Pappas went on. "I should not be surprised if any disobedience on our part were rewarded by scourging, if not crucifixion. This is war, you know—normal civil rights are suspended. And if you are thinking of Rufus' friendship..."

"I know better than that," Elisha commented dryly.

"The third course is to obey the order and hope for the best when we get there."

"But what will we do if your guess is correct?"

"What will *you* do?" Pappas hurled back.

"Everything that matters to me is in this library," Elisha said thoughtfully. Then his entire body shook, his face turned haggard with the pain of recollection.

"I have given a promise. I have sworn that I would allow

nothing in all the world to stand in the way of my work."

"You have sworn," Pappas challenged. "To whom? To yourself no doubt. And you will put a petty, private resolution above —"

"What matter to whom?" Elisha interrupted quickly. "I have made a vow..."

"You still have not given me an answer," said Pappas, staring into his eyes. "Pledge or no pledge, what are you going to do if my surmise proves true?"

"How can I answer that question," Elisha whispered in anguish, "when my instincts pull me in one direction, my reason, my ideals, my most sacred commitments, in the other?"

Moved by an intuition of his struggle, Pappas soothed him.

"Let us not quarrel over that again. There is still time in which to decide. But if you must know"—his voice took on a tone of mock secrecy—"what I am going to do right now..."

Elisha studied him anxiously.

"I am going to the best bath in Antioch and get myself properly thawed out in the steam room. Then I am going to soak in warm water for hours. I have been cold for years, it seems. I am cold now, and tomorrow on the road shall be cold again. But today, for a change, I shall be warm. And what is more, you are going to be warm with me. You shall be my guest."

Seizing the half-willing Elisha by the arm, he dragged him toward the door. But before he consented to depart, Elisha arranged his notes and manuscript, tied his papyri and wax tablets into orderly piles, and turned them over for safekeeping to the curator of the library against the time of his return.

Four days later they forded the Jordan at the Springs of Panias and entered Palestine. It was so cold that their limbs were stiff under their clothes and jets of mist shot forth from the nostrils of the horses and from their own mouths whenever they spoke. It was here in upper Galilee that they saw the first devastation of warfare—houses and barns gutted by flame, villages deserted. The road was untraveled except for an occasional mounted patrol which halted them long enough to examine their credentials and then passed on. Otherwise the country-side lay abandoned to fugitives hidden in the hills and to the wolves that howled by night.

But it was only when they entered lower Galilee, passing through territory they remembered well, that they were aware of the completeness of the ruin. They climbed rolling hills and looked in vain for the villages that once huddled in the valleys. Fire had swept the forest which had reached from the hills of Ephraim down to the sea of Galilee, leaving only blackened stumps protruding here and there from the rocky soil like ugly decayed teeth. And in Capernaum but one house remained, its door gaping, its shutters swinging in the frigid wind.

They were now a few miles from their homes. Sick with anxiety they rode on, skirting the ice-fringed, sullen gray waters of the lake, praying that by some miracle the torch and sword had spared the people and places they loved. At a fork in the highway, Pappas turned off to his own estate and left Elisha to ride on alone.

Rounding a bend in the road, Elisha looked up toward the house he had left fifteen years before. A fragment of a wall was all that remained of his villa. He had not dared hope for better. On the plateau the contours of the land were as they had been since time immemorial, but all else was gone. Where the house had stood, the store cellar yawned—a gaping hole. The rest was shattered brick, broken earthenware and splinters of glass gleaming dully through their coating of mud. Even the olive grove had been destroyed. Black patches on the ground testified to some encampment and marked the pyres on which the rich old trees had been consumed. Haunted by ghostly memories of his father, Deborah, Tobias, Uriel and those who for so many generations had lived in the place, Elisha wandered about inconsolably, to make his way in the end to the boundary stone where in years gone by he had been wont to find Pappas.

There the two friends met again, eyes averted to preserve the privacy of their grief, and rode away without a word.

The environs of Tiberias bustled with life. On the slopes and hills that ringed the city a large detachment of Roman soldiers was established in winter quarters. The late afternoon air, heavy with the acrid smoke of campfires, stirred with distant calls and laughter. The sounds seemed preternaturally loud to them, so thoroughly had they become accustomed only to the stumbling clatter of hoofs and an occasional muttered phrase. The city itself was half-deserted save for soldiers policing the streets and figures skulking wraithlike in the shadow of the houses. Even in the courtyard of a tavern, a place they had known well, all was silence. Only after they called again and again did the inn-keeper come forth cautiously. A little wisp of a man with shaggy hair and beard, he approached them hesitantly, and Elisha, who recognized him, noted the timidity and emaciation in his face.

"What can I do for you?" he asked in Greek.

"We should like lodging for the night," Pappas replied in Aramaic, the folk tongue of Palestinian Jews.

At the sound of his own dialect the tavern-keeper looked up with relief.

Reading his feeling aright, Elisha added, also in Aramaic, "You need not be afraid of us. We, too, are Jews."

A faint smile curved the lips within the beard. "Then welcome. Blessed be ye who come. Dismount, if you please."

As he held the bridles of their horses, he judged them critically, taking in their clean-shaven faces and their robes made after the manner of the pagans. His cordiality disappeared. Watching them suspiciously, he showed them into the large room of the tavern and through its emptiness into a chamber beyond.

"If you will excuse me," he said through the curtain he had pulled aside, "I shall stable your horses."

"Will you please prepare supper for us, also?" Pappas requested. "We have been on the road for several days, and we are hungry."

The tavern-keeper nodded and disappeared.

"Not very talkative, is he?" Elisha commented with a wan smile.

"He does not recognize us," Pappas explained as he wrestled with a strap of his saddlebag.

"Just as well in my case," Elisha went on bitterly. "If he knew me, he would not talk at all."

"But he may have information for us. He may be able to tell us.... By the way, what is his name? It will help if we know it."

"Ezekiel, I think," Elisha replied.

As though evoked by his name, the tavern-keeper returned with a tray which he placed on a little table and then turned to leave.

"Do not go," Pappas detained him. "Your name is Ezekiel, is it not?"

A shifty look came into the innkeeper's eyes. Wordlessly he nodded his head.

"Do you not remember me?"

He scrutinized Pappas's face, and answered, "No."

"I suppose I should be offended. Many a good coin has passed from my pocket into your hand. I am Pappas; my villa is—was on the hill just over Migdal."

The man nodded, muttered an apology, and then indicated Elisha craftily.

"And this gentleman?"

"A friend of mine," Pappas replied after a barely perceptible hesitation, "a Jewish merchant from Antioch. But perhaps you can give us certain information we want. Do you know what has become of the people of my estate?"

"No."

"Or on that of Elisha the son of Abuyah?"

"No."

"Can you tell us," Elisha pleaded, unable to restrain himself, "about Deborah...Tobias...Uriel?..."

"The slave-traders got Tobias and Uriel," the tavern-keeper

replied, his fear of spies yielding for a moment. "They are gone, God knows where. And as for the Lady Deborah they say that when the Romans began to plunder the house she turned into a raging maniac. In the end they set fire to the place and held her so that she would have to see. Then they drove her away. I have heard that she is at Gerasa beyond the Jordan now."

"Has she any money?" Elisha asked anxiously.

"How would I know?..." He broke off abruptly, his face twisting with suspicion.

"The gentleman from Antioch," he insinuated slyly, "knows people in this neighborhood, so far away from his own home?"

"Never mind that," Elisha urged, "please tell me..."

"But I know nothing more," Ezekiel protested and not all their coaxing could get him to admit that he possessed any further information.

They turned to the food on the table, a quarter-loaf of bread, some pickled olives and a flagon of wine.

"Oh, come now," Pappas pointed. "We are no beggars. We have funds for better than this. Let us have a full dinner."

"You can pay for food, but where is one to get it?" asked Ezekiel, forgetting his caution. "The country has been eaten naked as by the locust plague of Joel. Most of the people in this city are living on roots, the garbage of the army. For these times, this is a banquet. Those accursed..." He stopped, frightened by his self-betrayal.

"It is all right," Elisha reassured him, "we know how you feel."

As they ate the tavern-keeper watched them sullenly from the doorway.

"Where do the courts and schools meet? Have you heard anything about Akiba or a disciple called Meir?" Elisha queried.

Ezekiel shrugged his shoulders in answer. But Elisha's last question and the one about Deborah had set him peering thoughtfully through the half-light at his interrogator. He started.

"Are you not Rabbi Elisha the son of Abuyah?" he whispered.

"You have found me out," Elisha smiled in an attempt to be disarming. "But you need have no fear. I am not..." His words died away as Ezekiel edged from the door.

They saw no more of their host either that night or the next morning. When, at dawn, they went into the courtyard, their horses were already saddled and hitched to the post. To their insistent calling there was no response. They left a little pile of coins on a table in the public room, mounted and rode away.

The next afternoon brought them into the vicinity of Jerusalem. So exhausted in spirit were they that they saw without feeling the ugliness that made foul the environs of the ancient city. For it was ringed with heaps of refuse, the accumulated waste and debris of thousands of men. Abandoned scraps of clothes, armor and military machines rotted on the oozing ground. Still farther on along the road was a colony of tents of sodden tapestry before which women sat, dressed despite the cold in thin shabby finery, their faces painted, their palms hennaed, their eyes dark with kohl.

And just outside the camp itself, stood the huts erected by pagan slave-traders about which a swarm of men, women and children shivered, half-naked and exposed to the elements. Some of those nearer the highway looked up at Elisha and Pappas. One or two, their faces pinched with cold and white with despair, rose to beg hoarsely for alms. Before a well-constructed hut, apparently the residence of some important slave-trader, a Jewess was being beaten. Her figure was naked to the waist, her hands lashed high to a crossbar above her head. Her hair tumbling down over her back tossed each time the overseer swung his long rod. The air resounded with her screams and the regular cracking of wood against flesh. But the other captives sunken in their own miseries did not so much as raise their eyes to look their sympathy.

Only because they recognized their powerlessness did

Elisha and Pappas resist the fierce urge to interfere. With this tragic picture as the last recollection of their harrowing journey they reached the crest of a hill and came upon the Roman army sprawling over the mountains and valleys that had once been the city of Jerusalem.

The encampment was a vast orderly arrangement grouped around central plazas in which legionary standards had been erected. At the northernmost point where the road led into the camp a group of sentries challenged them. They produced their letters. Escorts were provided and they were conducted down long avenues.

The configurations of the landscape were so concealed that it was only through the fact that they were climbing steadily that they knew they were ascending the Temple Mount. Pieties long dormant stirred in both of them. They considered the inaccessibility of the place and the calculated contempt that had impelled Rufus to pitch his pavilion there.

In a barely audible tone, Pappas cursed the Romans from the Emperor on the throne to the lowliest sutler in the army.

CHAPTER XIV

A SENTRY LED ELISHA AND Pappas into the tent of Rufus, a great enclosure of weather-stained canvas that billowed and thundered with each movement of the wind. Despite the drafts that blew across the rock floor, the air within was smoky with the fumes of charcoal fires and foul with stale breath and the smell of unbathed bodies. Directly before the center pole stood a table, illuminated by feeble lamps and littered with parchment maps, swords, belts and wax tablets. Behind it sat Severus and Rufus flanked on either side by their staff, all officers of the High Command, though they wore no insignia on their shabby campaign cloaks. Dimly visible in the gloomy recesses of the pavilion, orderlies and attendants loitered.

The Romans looked up as they entered and watched them approach. Severus nodded in greeting, as did Quadratus, the Questor of Syria. But Rufus, his face no longer round and pink, his fuzzy hair streaked with white, neither rose nor asked them to be seated. Without preliminaries he opened the conversation.

"It is good that you came at once. The business for which we wanted you is urgent. The war is virtually over. That does not mean that there will be no more fighting, and hard fighting, too. But most of the country is in our hands now. Another year, and order will be restored. Now last month we got special orders from Rome. The Emperor is determined that what has just happened here must not occur again. This province has rebelled three times in less than seventy years. We have been instructed to adopt such policies as will make another insurrection impossible. We are going to cut out the root of the trouble." Rufus' blunt thumb descended toward the table and rose again as though gouging something from the wood. "You know this people. We have summoned you here to advise us." He watched them closely, watery eyes gleaming.

Elisha's thin face was pale and rigid, his body motionless.

"It has come," Pappas whispered to him in Hebrew.

"What did you say?" asked Rufus sharply, suspiciously.

"Nothing of sufficient consequence," Pappas replied blandly, "to justify interrupting our conversation."

Now that the dread moment was upon him, Elisha knew how he would decide. But there was still one hope, wild and fantastic, of averting the harrowing choice.

"I have a suggestion," he began cunningly, controlling the sensation of sickness in himself, "which might solve your problem."

Pappas looked at him in horror. Elisha reached out and silenced him with a touch.

"You yourselves," he went on, "have indicated how stubborn the Jewish people is. Every repressive measure has failed. But there is one policy which has never been tried, conciliation. You now hold the country completely in your hands. This is your opportunity to prevent another war. Instead of attempting to crush the Jews, why not cut out the root of their bitterness? Reduce the special taxes. Recall the expulsions. Release the prisoners."

"And I suppose," added Rufus sarcastically, "allow the Jews to rebuild their Temple, and perhaps grant them some measure of local independence."

"Why not?" Elisha argued. "This one hill means nothing at all to the Empire. It would be a slight price to pay for a permanent solution to an old problem."

"And the Emperor's edict?" Quadratus broke in. "We are simply to disregard it? I should like to see the fellow who would dare offer that advice to Rome."

"Gentlemen, I would ask you not to treat us like children," said Rufus, his eyes blanker than ever. "No skillful artifices, if you please. We are not interested in throwing away our victory. We want to make it permanent."

Neither Elisha nor Pappas spoke.

"Well, what do you say? Speak up...! We cannot spend all day with you."

"You are asking us," said Pappas desperately, "to assist you against our own people."

"Your loyalties are your own affair," Rufus snapped. "Though both of you, you, Elisha in particular, were ready to accept the protection of the Empire when you needed it. In any case, your information belongs to us and we are going to have it."

"Then you must give us time to decide," Pappas persisted doggedly. "It is a hard choice."

"We want the advice immediately. And may I remind you that there are ways of compelling you to speak. I have not referred to them because you have, on occasion, been my guests and because I remember that you, Elisha, were not only a friend of Manto but tended her in her last illness." Rufus' face twisted into a grimace and his voice choked in his throat. "But I swear by the gods that I will crucify the two of you before sunset if you do not—"

He stopped abruptly as a man burst into the tent, announcing excitedly, "My scouts have spotted their main forces."

"Good—well done—where?" the officers cried in unison, rising from their seats.

"Look here, Polyander," Rufus roared at the intruder, "we are busy…"

"Nonsense," Serverus interrupted, "this is more important. Tell us, Polyander!"

"Go ahead," another added.

"The gods have intervened on your behalf," Rufus said unsteadily to Elisha and Pappas. "They have granted you time to deliberate. But when you are summoned again, you had better have your answer ready. Meanwhile, you are under arrest. Marcus," he bellowed, and a young attendant rose from a rug on which he was squatting, "these two men are not to leave this mountain. See to it that they are here when I want them."

Trailed by the orderly assigned to guard them, Pappas and Elisha walked aimlessly across the plateau until they came to its rim.

"Elisha," Pappas pleaded, "have you made up your mind?"

Elisha stared into the distance. Below twisted the Valley of Jehoshaphat where for uncounted, unremembered centuries, his forefathers had been laid to their eternal rest. Beyond, on one of the hills, was the slave encampment where that very day he had witnessed the suffering of his brothers. And under his feet was ground sanctified by the tread of prophets and sages, made holy by the blood of martyrs. Here, he had stood once before in his life, an ugly old man by his side. At the thought of Joshua, his heart contracted so that he could not breathe. Scalding tears filmed his tortured eyes and, overflowing, ran down his cheeks.

"I am going to obey them," he whispered in a voice so low that for an instant Pappas was not certain he had spoken.

"You can't mean it," came the fierce, incredulous protest.

"I have known it for a long time. I have no alternative."

"In God's name," Pappas groaned, "don't talk to me about the peace of the Empire or personal freedom or Rome as the hope of mankind. I will not be able to endure it. Merciful heaven, do you realize that this is no academic question to be determined by pretty words and syllogisms? It is against your own people, your own flesh and blood that Rufus asks you to act."

"But these are real considerations." Elisha's words, still choked by anguish, were at the same time firm with finality. "Do you think I was toying when I discussed them with you? But they are not all. There is still another reason."

"You mean," Pappas, blind with frenzy, struck at him, "that you are afraid to die?"

"In a sense, yes. Not because of pain, or the pleasures I might miss in a future that would never be. But for another reason altogether. My own fate would be of little consequence were it not that long ago I assigned myself a task. I have no illusions about my powers or importance. But if I can finish what I have started, I may have taken the first steps toward something of great significance to all men. Besides, I must complete my work. I gave my oath...."

Through the torment of that moment of decision, the dull ache that had never left him since Manto's death was unbearably acute.

"If I do not discharge my commitment," he whispered unsteadily, "a great sacrifice made by me, and, what is more important, by someone else, shall have been for naught."

"What are all these dark sayings?" Pappas assailed him angrily. "Can you not answer me intelligibly, reasonably? All I want to know is this: Is there in you nothing of the simple loyalty of a human being to his own kind?"

Elisha's face twisted like that of a man whose open wound has been struck. Then it was composed and when he replied, his speech was soft, deliberate.

"You are right. We are going at this stupidly, employing passion rather than thought. Let us, as you suggest, try to be objective, impersonal, to allow our reason to function. Very well then. Among the Stoics, there is an old riddle—"

"In heaven's name," Pappas exploded, "more puzzles, philosophical puzzles this time. This is no occasion for piddling in metaphysics."

"On the contrary," came the perturbed answer, "this is just the time. It is at moments like this, when men are confronted by terrible decisions, that they must deliberately suppress blind emotions, as I am now doing, and think their way through.

"As I was saying, among the Stoics, there is an old riddle that runs as follows: A man is traveling in the desert. In his gourd he has enough water for one drink. He comes upon two men dying of thirst—one, his own father, the other, a philosopher. Now the problem is, to whom should the water be given? Who ought be saved? Among the wise there is some doubt whether most men would be strong enough to act on more than instinct. But there is no hesitation as to what is both reasonable and right."

"We have so short a time," Pappas's voice rose hysterically, "and you spin parables."

"But don't you see, Pappas, that is my dilemma? It is a terrible choice that is forced on me. But, given it, there can logically be only one answer."

"And for such wisps of your imagination," Pappas cried hoarsely, "you will set your hand against your fellow Jews?"

"The people is doomed in any case. Years ago I realized that. Do you suppose it can outlive this war? A generation, two generations at most, and the very name Jew will have been forgotten."

"Never," Pappas exclaimed confidently. "This isn't the first time that men like you have made that prophecy. Were there not some in Babylonia long ago who said, 'Our hope is perished'? And we outlived the Babylonians and the Greeks as we will outlive the Romans."

Elisha shook his head sadly.

"Inconsistent as it may seem, I wish I could believe that. It hurts me to hear the final accents of the sad story of which I was once a part. But it is impossible. In Egypt, Cyrenaica and Cyprus the Jews were ruined forever by their rebellion twenty years ago. Elsewhere, in Asia Minor, Italy, Greece, they are falling away by the hundreds, either into heathenism or into Christianity. And Palestine, the heart and brain of the whole organism, is dead. No, the fact that other prophecies have been mistaken proves nothing. This time the drama has reached the last act. But even had the Jews won the war and conquered Rome itself, I could not have decided otherwise."

"And the normal, decent devotion of a man to his own?" Pappas repeated passionately.

"A powerful instinct that tortures me now," Elisha completed, his voice choking once more. "Yet like all irrational feelings, something to distrust always, to renounce resolutely whenever it collides with reason."

"So," Pappas concluded in despair, "you have convinced yourself of the wisdom of treason."

"Treason," Elisha burst out, the more fiercely because of his anguish. "Yes, it is that, I suppose, a betrayal of every impulse of my being. But it is loyalty to something stronger. This much at least I have learned from philosophy, that, having caught a glimpse of the ideal, man must follow it no matter where it leads him. Mine has taken me out of my people into a strange world. Now, my vision compels me to become an enemy to my own blood. I tell you I am sick to death at the prospect of what I am about to do. But I know that ultimately it is right, the water must go to the philosopher, the work I have begun must be completed. And knowing that, I have no choice."

Pappas read the determination on Elisha's face and, over-whelmed by defeat, lacked the heart to speak again.

Someone called from Rufus's tent. The orderly tapped their shoulders. "He is ready now." But when they returned to the pavilion, they were kept waiting. Four prisoners under guard, who had just been brought up for questioning, stood in a group near them. Their clothes were rags, their wrists manacled, but defiance was written large in their carriage.

"Peace unto you!" Pappas greeted them in Hebrew.

Their eyes came to life with sullen suspicion.

"You need not be afraid of us," Pappas reassured them. "We are Jews, too."

They did not answer.

"But really we are."

"How do we know who you are?" one muttered back.

"What do we care?" another added.

"One of us," the first voice grumbled, "and yet at liberty here." Sardonic laughter swept through the group.

"Do not say anything." another counseled. "They are informers."

Suddenly one of the men leaped forward pointing a finger into Elisha's face.

"I know him," he screamed in Aramaic: "he is Elisha the son of Abuyah; the heretic. God pardon me, I was once one of his pupils in Usha and thought well of him." He spat toward Elisha. "Leper!"

One of the guards raised the staff of his spear and struck the prisoner across the face.

"Talk with respect," he ordered in broken Aramaic.

"Respect?" The captive ran the back of his hand over his bleeding nose. "Respect for that core of all uncleanliness, that offal of our people? May his bones waste!"

The soldier looked to Elisha for instruction. Elisha shook his head and turned away.

"Elisha," Pappas pleaded, "you must not allow this to influence you...."

"It does not matter. My mind was made up in any case. This merely proves that I have no people to renounce."

Then they were admitted into the pavilion and led before Rufus.

"What is your answer?"

Pappas spoke first. "My answer is no, and you can do your damnedest."

"Arrest him for treason," Rufus ordered instantly. Two soldiers stood at Pappas's side, pinning his arms.

"And you?"

Elisha drew a deep breath.

"I agree."

Rufus' face fell in disappointment.

"But on one condition..."

"We are not bargaining with you." replied Rufus coldly.

"Ah yes, but you are."

"One more word and I will arrest you, too."

"Very well," said Elisha, throwing up his hands in resignation, "call on your soldiers."

Eagerly Rufus signaled, but Quadratus checked him.

"Oh, come now, Rufus, let us hear him out. We will get

nothing out of him this way. It is quite obvious that you do not like these fellows but that is not a reason for throwing away their help."

"Very well, state your condition," Rufus yielded.

"Pappas here must be set free."

"Why not?" Severus responded. "He means nothing to us."

"Besides," another chimed in, "we don't need them both. And of the two, the fellow who is willing is the better informed. He is the one who was a rabbi."

The other commanders rumbled their assent.

"Release him," Rufus ordered reluctantly, and the soldiers stood away from Pappas.

"Elisha," Pappas pleaded in Aramaic, "no man can betray his own blood and face himself afterward. You were ready to risk your life for me; certainly you ought to do the same for a whole people."

"No," Elisha said quietly, "I am giving the water to the stranger, even though he is not so wise and so virtuous as in the Stoic riddle."

The resentment in Pappas's eyes turned slowly into a blaze of incredulity. He turned to the officers crying out in amazement:

"To this moment I did not believe him. Merciful heaven, the poor fool really means it."

The acrid smoke of the lantern burned in Elisha's nostrils and got into his eyes, so that they alternately teared and smarted. His body was clammy with perspiration. And still they tortured him with requests for further information.

For the first hour it had been easy. They had put questions which anyone might have answered. There was nothing secret about religious ceremonials, synagogue services and the authority of the rabbis. But as the evening wore on, they probed deeper, groping toward the hidden vital organs of the Jewish people whence flowed its loyalty and its capacity for courage. Like gardeners surveying the far-reaching roots of some hardy but undesirable plant, tracing the lines where incisions must be made to cut off its sources of life, the Romans proceeded deliberately to formulate a series of decrees. They planned to forbid, first of all, the observance of the Sabbath and the performance of the rite of circumcision. They decided, after some debate, not to ban worship altogether, lest thereby they encourage secret conventicles. They preferred to lay an interdict upon the recitation of certain favored or essential prayers—a device well-calculated to rob religious assemblies of their appeal. The Sanhedrin would be dispersed, its sessions declared illegal. All schools were to be closed. The ordination of new rabbis was to be prohibited. So item by item their program of repression emerged.

Dismay filled Elisha in the presence of their unpitying thoroughness. He had long known that Roman soldiers could be cruel, but it had never occurred to him that they were capable of such enormous ruthlessness, so cold-bloodedly undertaken. His heart chilled, his face twisted with revulsion. It was a foul business, fouler than he had conceived, in which he had involved himself. But if he had been in the right in engaging in it in the first place, then he had no choice except to persevere until it was done.

"Do you have it all?" Rufus asked at last of the secretary who had recorded each decision carefully.

"Every detail."

"Then rewrite it tomorrow so that we can send it on to Rome for approval. And as for you, Elisha, you will remain here, as a technical consultant to supply us with the names of leaders, interpret the reports of our informers, and suggest further measures as the situation shall require. We shall register you as a member of our staff with the status of Centurion. As a precaution, you will be put under detention. You are to have the freedom of the camp but may not leave it except by my explicit consent. And now the meeting is adjourned."

Elisha stood at the door of the tent in which he had been quartered. The weather was moderating and the air was orange-red from many campfires and sharply scented with the smell of burning wood. It was still cold but so damp that clothes clung to the body, and hands and faces were sticky as though dipped into some syrupy fluid. Elisha had felt like this once when, as a boy, he had bathed in the Dead Sea and had come out of the strong blue water coated with a film of slimy oils. He had been so uncomfortable then that Nicholaus had bathed him clean again at the springs of Jericho.

He was keeping his word to Manto. Not even his people had he allowed to stand between him and his work. There was comfort in the thought. But the philosophers in whom he had put his trust had been mistaken in one regard. They had insisted that serenity went with the performance of moral duty. Now his conscience might be clear, but there was no peace in it.

A fine rain began to fall. By instinct he lifted his face to its touch for cleansing.

The next morning Elisha dispatched a letter to the chief librarian of the Musaeum in Antioch.

"From time to time," it read, "you will receive from me scrolls or tablets which you will be so good as to deposit with the documents I left in your care. Also I may send you requests for books I shall need. Ariston of Rhodes is my banker and while my funds on deposit are slight they should be more than sufficient to purchase the volumes for which I may ask. I am loath to trouble you but it is most imperative that I continue my work. In view of your sympathy for it, I am emboldened to ask your assistance."

Elisha discharged his duties as adviser to the intelligence service of the Roman army like an automaton. On a specific hour each day he resorted to Rufus' pavilion, scrutinized without the least sign of emotion the reports of spies, evaluated events, identified persons. Then he returned to his hut, not to leave it again until his next visit to headquarters.

"What does he do with his time?" Rufus asked suspiciously of the soldiers assigned to guard him.

"He sits in that shack and writes like a madman all day."

"Writes, eh? What does he write? And does he receive or send letters? We shall have to look into that."

"Well?" he inquired of Marcus, his orderly, on the following afternoon.

"I went to his place while he was here with you, as you ordered. He is working on some sort of philosophical volume."

"And his letters?"

"He left one uncompleted. It was addressed to a librarian in Antioch. Those he has received and preserved come either from the same man or from a bookdealer in Caesarea named Nicholaus."

"Did you examine them for cryptograms?"

"I had little enough chance for careful study. But there does not seem to be the least trace of code."

"So he scribbles philosophy," Rufus mused, shrugging in contemptuous dismissal.

With the coming of spring, the Roman army left Jerusalem to take the field, and Rufus and other members of the civil administration of Palestine set forth for Caesarea. Traveling in the Governor's entourage, Elisha was like a wraith among men, so emaciated, haggard and taciturn had he become. Not once on the entire trip did he address anyone, nor did anyone speak to him. But behind the blank eyes through which he looked unseeing onto the world, frenzy seethed, an unbearable impatience that three days should be taken from his work for the journey.

And in Caesarea, he immured himself once more, this time in a little chamber in the Governor's mansion, writing from dawn to midnight without surcease.

CHAPTER XV

THE WILDERNESS OF JUDEA, A desert of barren stone, burned with midsummer heat. By day, the sky was a sheet of flame so intense that the hills beneath it glowed with white incandescence and writhed as if unable to bear the torment. By night, the stars were pinpricks of fire dancing through a darkness that swarmed with waves of warmth.

In the heart of this expanse of desolation, the fortress of Bethar on the crest of a great jagged rock rose sheer above the plain. From behind its massive ramparts the remnants of the Jewish army still defied the Empire.

Like a serpent basking in a triple coil, the Roman camp surrounded the beleaguered stronghold. A line of trenches, mounds and military machines hugged the foot of the cliff. Next came a broad belt of tents, and on the outer rim, a fringe of baggage wagons and the huts of camp-followers and slave-traders.

For three months they had lain so, the besieged on their inaccessible plateau, the besiegers ringing them in below. The Romans had been confident on first taking up their positions against the broken host to which all was lost except this one refuge. But the Jews had proved stubborn. They had repelled assault after assault with storms of spears, arrows, stones and scalding oil. Finally the investing army had settled down to bury its dead, nurse its wounds and starve its enemies out.

But the Romans had not reckoned with the sun. Each morning it rose brighter and hotter than the day before. Men began to go blind from the glare. Soldiers from the Danube and Rhine told of similar occurrences in cold lands when a snowfall was followed by a brilliant sun. Occasionally, some- one who had exposed himself too long grew dizzy and lay in the shade of a tent moaning with sunstroke. But most of all, the army suffered from the fact that its water, transported by ox-cart and camel-train from springs miles away, was tepid, brackish, sickening to the taste and insufficient. In their fretful sleep men dreamed of cold, fresh springs and lakes in which one might bathe and drink to satiety.

Nerves grew frayed, tempers sharp. Men who had been friends snapped at one another and developed murderous hatreds. Weary with sleeplessness and sick with blinding headaches, officers issued senseless orders to which grumbling soldiers squinted back insubordination. Inevitably, feverish minds exploded into insanity. One soldier tramped a scavenger dog to death and pounded its body into a crimson pulp with his great boots. Again, a Cilician archer, gone stark mad, ran through the camp with drawn sword and slashed at everyone in his path. A lieutenant in the Danube Legion cut the throat of a fellow officer in his sleep. Most shocking of all, someone stole a jug of sacred water from the shrine of Mithra, favorite god of the army. When the news of this sacrilege was known, men shook their heads in awe and noted with foreboding that the sun, angered by the affront, gained steadily in fierceness.

All this time the enemy bowmen lurked on the heights, their infantry crouched to spring at the first sign of relaxed vigilance. They did not come out of their gates often, but their sorties, unpredictable and savage, kept the Romans tense with alarm.

Into this monotone of discomfort, exasperation and ever-present danger, the elements introduced a lone note of variety. One day early in July a breeze began to blow, scorching hot to the touch. The sky turned yellow and a dull haze obscured the hills. The Roman soldiers taking the change in weather as an augury of rain went wild with joy. Eagerly they felt the mounting strength of the ever-whispering wind and watched the looming clouds creep closer. Only the Arab auxiliaries and the Mauretians were not pleased. They knew the desert and its ominous signs. The others refused to heed their prophecies. Nor were they concerned lest a rainfall replenish the cisterns which served as reservoirs for the besieged fortress. Nothing mattered except the prospect of cold, fresh water in abundance.

The storm which broke was such as they had never experienced before—a tempest devoid of moisture. The air came alive with swirling dust that filtered through clothes, gritted between teeth, insinuated itself into food and drink, and coated the perspiring skin with a rasping paste. Eyes, already half-blinded by excessive light, now burned with sand. For three days the wind blew until the whole camp was on the verge of hysteria.

Then more quickly than it had come, it was gone. The desert burned once more in clear whiteness.

Discipline in the ranks deteriorated steadily. The threat of mutiny grew apace. Alarmed officers assembled in staff meetings to consider their peril and to devise some means of averting it. Too fatigued and irritable to be clear-headed, they quarreled angrily but to no purpose, and dispersed.

It was then, when the morale of the Romans was at its lowest ebb, that the incident of the jug occurred.

The Jews had seen wagon trains carrying water into camp. Interpreting the mood of their foes aright, they made a game of taunting them. Occasionally some daredevil climbed to a conspicuous position on one of the battlements to drink water from a vase, bathe his hands and face in it, splash it about tormentingly, and then pour it out, to be wasted before thousands racked with thirst. It was dangerous sport and more than one foolhardy Jew paid for it with his life.

Once in mid-August, the spectacle was re-enacted. A soldier stood silhouetted against the sky drinking in long draughts. He enjoyed his role so thoroughly that he did not observe a Balearic bowman dart from rock to rock and work into range. In the shadow of a boulder at the very foot of the cliff, the archer unslung his bow, aimed carefully and released the string. The arrow, flying straight and sure through the breathless air, pierced the Jew's throat. He threw the jug from him. It dropped like a plummet and crashed on the rocks. For a moment the man swayed at the very edge of the rampart, clawing at the empty air for a hold. Then he, too, fell.

The Romans behind their earthworks cheered, but feebly and without enthusiasm. They had witnessed such episodes before. But the archer, driven by an impulse which later he was unable to explain, went after the jug.

From the wall the defenders released arrows and rocks in the hope of revenge. Awakened to new interest, Roman bowmen sent up protecting volleys under which their comrade succeeded in getting hold of some bits of baked clay and retreating with them to safety. Secure again in a trench, he was too short of breath to be able to speak at once. But he waved a jagged piece of pottery before the soldiers who had collected about him, pointing wildly to it. At last he managed to gasp, "Dry...dry!"

For a moment his fellows did not understand. Then, as though it were some great jest, they began to laugh in gusty gales, pounding one another on the back. For they knew there had been no water in the jug, which could mean only that the cisterns on the hill were running out, that the siege was almost over, and that in a few weeks they would be quartered in cool places where they could drink to satiety, eat to surfeit and consort with women.

A few nights later, sentries stirred uneasily at their posts, and soldiers sleeping fitfully in their tents awoke with a start.

From the fortress came the sound of many voices chanting. The words could not be distinguished but the melody was solemn and exalted, like the litany of a mystic sacrifice. In the light of the full moon the ramparts on high shimmered uncertainly. The Roman soldiers stared upward and marveled at the eerie sound. They wondered whether it might not be the intoning of some spell that breathed black magic. Uneasily, they noticed that the choir diminished in volume as though the voices were being silenced one by one. By the time the morning star arose, Bethar was quiet with a weird preternatural stillness.

On the next day the Romans, occupying a fortress they had not taken, gazed horrified and awe-stricken upon the bodies of men who had died on their own swords rather than surrender.

CHAPTER XVI

THAT AUTUMN FOR THE FIRST time since the outbreak of the war, merchants assembled on the outskirts of Lydda for the annual fair, set up their booths and put their wares on exhibition. But the country was still unsettled. Poverty after four years of turmoil was widespread and, to make matters worse, the rains began early, keeping prospective buyers at home. As a result almost no purchasers appeared. The traders who had gathered so hopefully brooded disconsolately from their huts over the deserted grounds, recalling unhappily the crowds, profits and excitement of pre-war times.

On the last night of the fair there was a stirring in the bazaars. Under the cover of darkness merchants, fully dressed, rose from bales of merchandise on which they had lain unsleeping and slipped out into the rain. In a caravan station nearby three Arab camel drivers peered cautiously from the opening of a goatskin tent before leaving it stealthily. Two Syrian slave dealers, who had remained in town long after their traffic had ceased, stole from their huts. And in the city itself, householders wakened guests and sent them forth like dark shadows along the wet streets.

There were Roman sentries about, stationed to prevent unlawful assemblies and breaches of the peace. Lulled by a deceptive stillness, they dozed at their posts or nodded in the shelter of arches and doorways. Undetected, the furtive figures converged on an obscure house, climbed an outer staircase to a garret into which they gained admittance after subdued whispering through a barred door. By midnight, some thirty rabbis—disguised variously as merchants, peasants, Bedouin and Syrian slavers—were seated on the attic floor, talking quietly to one another. A dimmed lamp wrestled with the shadows in the room. Heavy curtains hung over the windows to keep its light from shining out. Nitza, in whose house they had gathered, watched at the foot of the steps for Roman police.

A man arose, Simeon the son of Gamliel, who had succeeded his father in the hereditary post of the President of the Sanhedrin. Softly he summoned the court into session, briefly he invoked God's blessing and, in the absence of a secretary, called the roll. Those present responded to their names. For those who were dead, under arrest, in exile, or whose fate was unknown, no one spoke, but memories of them haunted the room, making it seem empty for want of them.

Simeon the Patriarch was a frail man, timid in manner, hesitant in speech, indecisive in action. Dominated in his youth by his strong-willed father, Gamliel, he was now, in his middle years, already overshadowed by a brilliantly gifted son, Judah by name. In his shy manner, he had once described himself as a fox, born of one lion, and by a strange miracle, the sire of another.

"My colleagues and brethren!" he began. "The purpose of this meeting must be known to all. The decrees of Rufus issued three months ago have thrown our entire people into despair and confusion. For that reason, it has been necessary to summon our assembly, even at the risk of our lives. I had not realized," he broke off irrelevantly, "until we came together the magnitude of the losses we have sustained. It is one thing to learn of the death of one man, the exile and imprisonment of others. It is another to see our ranks depleted as they are tonight. There are about thirty of us here, less than half our number. Well may we bewail the conflagration which the Lord kindled." His thin voice became a penetrating trickle of wordless lament. Eyes filled with tears, hearts grew heavier. All would have begun to weep had not someone spoken in a sharp whisper.

"Simeon, this is a dangerous situation for all of us, but particularly for Nitza and his family. Out of consideration for them, we ought to proceed directly to the business at hand."

"You are right," agreed Simeon hastily, like a chided child. "But what are we to do?"

Someone spoke from against one wall.

"There are a number of questions to which we must find answers. It would be better to take one at a time, and quickly, too, or the Romans will answer for us."

Simeon peered into the shadows.

"Akiba," he guessed.

"Aye," the speaker responded, his voice strong despite his great years and the hardships he had undergone during the war.

"Very well," the Patriarch suggested, "state the issues for us."

"There are two of supreme importance," Akiba said at once: "The first concerns us alone. Shall we continue teaching or not? The second affects every Jew in Palestine. The edicts of Rufus have forbidden the observance of the commandments under the threat of a death penalty. The people come to us for guidance. What shall we tell them? Shall they obey the will of God or the law of Rome?"

"And there is a third," said Hanina, Beruriah's father. "What shall we do about new ordinations? There are thirty of us left here. Some are already suspected by the Romans, others of us are undoubtedly being spied upon. In all probability, some of us will be under arrest, if not dead, in the course of a few months. If we adopt a policy of resistance, everyone of us may lose his life. We must provide for the appointment of new rabbis. Otherwise, our people may be left leaderless."

A rumble of assent went around the room.

"You are right," Simeon agreed. "That is an important matter. If there are no objections, we shall proceed—"

"But there are," Ishmael interrupted from the half-darkness. "Certainly we ought to be informed as to what has been done and can still be done to get the edicts modified or withdrawn."

"Let us not waste time in discussing that," Judah ben Baba called out in a full voice which sank at once in obedience to the fierce hisses demanding a quieter tone. "It is perfectly apparent the Romans will not be moved. We have only five hours till dawn. Let us use them to advantage."

"Nonetheless," Tarfon seconded Ishmael's request, "we are entitled to know what steps the Patriarch has taken to get the edicts recalled. It may be heroic to talk of defiance, but better a live dog than a dead lion."

Torn between opposing sentiments, Simeon hesitated.

"If we continue to argue about procedure," Akiba finally said, "we shall never get anything done. I, for one, agree that the Patriarch tell us what has happened, provided we do not take too long with it."

"I did what I could," Simeon said apologetically. "As soon as the edicts were issued I went to Rufus. I had to go by myself. To appear with an embassy would look as though we had already met in violation of the law. He would not see me."

"Did you try influence?" someone asked.

"Friends, acquaintances, rich men?" others added.

"I tried everybody and everything," said Simeon with a gesture of helplessness. "He simply refused to grant me an interview."

"And what about Rome?"

"I attempted that, too. I have just received a communication from the President of its Jewish community. The Emperor is determined. It is worth a man's position, if not his life, to suggest a change of policy. That, in brief, is how matters stand."

"But who told them what to do?" someone burst out. "No Roman could have known so exactly where to strike. A Jew, and a well-informed one, must have drawn up those regulations."

"I know who it was," Tarfon muttered.

"Hush," Akiba silenced him.

"I will not be quiet. It's time that everyone knew who suggested this policy. Your friend Elisha..."

A gasp of horror swept the room.

"They say," Tarfon went on, "that he has become a regular member of Rufus' staff. He occupies an office in the palace at Caesarea."

"So," someone brooded, "this is his revenge."

"Not revenge, I'm sure," Akiba defended, "just misguided idealism."

"Protecting him again," Tarfon retorted.

"I am neither defending nor accusing him," Akiba insisted wearily. "And may I suggest right now that we would do better to fix our attention on important matters."

"Right," Hanina agreed. "Let us resolve to resist the edicts and proceed to work out the exact details."

"Easy, easy," Ishmael cautioned. "There is another course. How long does the Roman Government persist in a policy or the Emperor in a mood? A week, a month, a year, ten years? What of it? We can afford to be patient. Tomorrow we order the people to conform. Eventually if we hold out long enough, the edicts are recalled. Remember that Scripture itself says concerning its own commandments, 'Thou shalt live by them'—*live by them,* not die because of them."

"But what becomes of the study of the Torah?" Hanina challenged. "Will you dismiss your pupils? Will you refuse to teach them?"

The argument might have continued indefinitely had not the door been thrown open. With a gust of wind that shook the lone flame, Nitza rushed into the room.

"A patrol," he panted, "on the street."

Instantly the lamp was extinguished and the room was a blank of dark silence through which the tramp of approaching steps sounded and then, after a period of painful suspense, died away. By unspoken consent the light was not kindled again.

Thereafter their deliberations moved with dispatch. It was agreed to adopt the principle of resistance to the edicts and to continue to give religious instruction in defiance of them. Next they formulated a policy for the people. No Jew, they decided, ought deliberately to invite death. He must, if the Romans so ordered, transgress any of the precepts of Scripture, except for three—the injunctions against idolatry, murder and sexual immorality. These commandments he must not violate in any circumstances, even if he die for his adherence to them. To this provision they appended a restriction. A Jew must give up his life for the slightest tittle of the Law should the Romans attempt to exploit his departure from it as a public example.

In the last hour of the night they came to the final issue. Quickly they reviewed the list of disciples still surviving upon whom ordination might with propriety be conferred. They settled on five, Meir included among them, and authorized Judah ben Baba to elevate them to the ranks of the sages, at his own discretion as to time and place. The ordinations, they ruled, must be held in the open country so that no city might be penalized for breach of a Roman ordinance within its confines.

With that their business was at an end. It was still dark outside but they were loath to part. For Death seemed very near, chilling them with the threat that they might never see one another again.

At the first signs of dawn they rose, slipped on their robes, shook hands while peering through the half-light of the new day to discern, once more and perhaps for the last time, the lines of well-loved faces. Then, burdened by sadness, they stole forth, one by one.

Shortly thereafter, a Roman officer, passing through the street, glanced up at the attic of Nitza's house. The door was wide open, proclaiming innocent emptiness.

Within the year Palestine was converted from a Jewish province into a half-pagan land and its natives into aliens within it. For in the spring, colonists broke the soil of confiscated farms to find it rich with blood and moldering bodies. Villages depopulated by sword, torch and the slave trader, were resettled by immigrants from all over the Empire.

Meantime the country swarmed with spies and informers whose reports, passing from hand to hand, were transmitted finally to Elisha in the palace at Caesarea. The Romans did not always require his suggestions. They had, independently of him, marked the entire membership of the Sanhedrin for extermination.

On the eve of the Feast of Weeks the blow fell. There had been arrests and imprisonments heretofore, but always of the obscure and the undistinguished: a peasant detained for circumcising his son, a village teacher crucified for conducting a class secretly, a merchant lashed for observing the Sabbath. But now the great leaders were seized. Bands of soldiers moved through the land. At Bnai Brak they arrested Akiba; in Tiberias, Ishmael. At Jamnia, Simeon the Patriarch was taken from his marble mansion. Within two days almost all the sages were imprisoned.

At once delegations of Jewish merchants and landowners appeared in Caesarea, cajoling, pleading and hinting at succulent bribes.

The Roman authorities laughed scornfully in their faces.

It was then that Rabbi Judah ben Baba, still at large, dispatched letters to the disciples selected for ordination. His message was cryptically phrased but its purport was clear to the five men to whom it was addressed.

On the appointed day, they met in a narrow ravine on the outskirts of the wilderness of Judea. All had come by indirect routes to make certain of throwing spies off their track. Rabbi Judah had traveled most deviously of all. His course was like the meandering scrawl of a child first learning to write. The trip had exhausted him, his silver beard was dulled with dust, his great head bowed with fatigue. Even his spirit was weary for he felt intuitively that despite his caution he had been trailed.

The place of their meeting was a narrow gully that twisted between two cliffs. Its entrance was difficult to find and so narrow that but one person could pass through at a time. There was an opening at its other end to serve as an alternative exit. And it was in the desert. No community could be penalized should they be detected.

Troubled by the suspicion that he had been followed, Judah set about conferring ordinations without delay.

"Come, my son," he called to Meir and raised his feeble hands over his head.

Breathless, trembling, he intoned: "Moses received the Law at Sinai from the Holy One Blessed be He. He transmitted it to Joshua…"

On he went in quick spurts of speech. The formula was completed only to begin again. It was just when the fourth ordination had been concluded that the clatter of hoofs penetrated into their retreat. With one gesture the old man signaled Meir to the entrance and summoned the fifth of the disciples to him.

By the time Meir had returned from the mouth of the defile Judah was halfway through the prescribed rubric. Without the least pause in his recital he questioned Meir with a look.

"Roman cavalry," Meir replied. "They may find the entrance at any moment."

The Rabbi nodded, and his words poured forth softly, but with greater speed and urgency, to their completion.

"Now go," he ordered not stopping for breath and pointed to the other opening.

They did not move.

"Quick," he whispered, "there is no time to lose."

Still they waited.

"I will not be able to keep up with you," he explained.

"But, Master…"

"No, no," he waved, "get away at once. I command it. Leave the country, too. If you do not go, everything is lost."

"But what will become of you?"

"When they come upon me, if they do, I shall tell them (God pardon the falsehood) that I have withdrawn here for meditation."

"They will not believe you.…"

"In heaven's name, flee before they find the exit. Do you not see that the longer I hold them in conversation the better will be your chances? For the sake of the Law," he urged.

Hastily the five men embraced and kissed him in turn, and slipped quietly down the ravine.

They were no sooner out of sight, than with surprising agility Judah stole to the entrance and looked out. A Roman soldier stood so close that he could almost touch him. Noiselessly the Rabbi slipped back to the narrowest point of the defile. Here he planted himself, his feet astraddle, his hands fixed against the rock walls on either side. In this position he waited.

"This looks like an entrance... by Jove, that is just what it is!"

A succession of calls sounded along the mountain. Another voice, apparently that of an officer, rang out.

"Go ahead, go in. What are you waiting for?"

The soldier shuffled cautiously inside.

"There is someone in here. I can see a piece of cloth."

"Speak to him," came an order from farther back. "Ask him to come out."

"Ho, there. Come out!"

At the command, the old Rabbi fixed his feet more firmly.

"Come out, I say, or I will come in and get you...."

"Who is it?" the officer called.

"He doesn't answer," the soldier reported in bewilderment.

"Doesn't he see you?"

"He has his back to me."

"Get around him."

"I can't. The pass is too narrow."

"What do you carry a spear for?"

Now it was time for Judah to speak. Still unmoving, he addressed the unseen Roman over his shoulder.

"Please, sir," he called in Greek, "do not be impatient."

"Get out of my way!"

"But I cannot," said Judah.

"Move, and quickly, too!"

"It is impossible."

"Impossible—why?"

"Ask what he is doing," the officer commanded.

"What are you doing there?" the soldier communicated "Why can't you move?"

"I am meditating on sacred matters. It would be a sacrilege to change my position."

"He is meditating...."

"Meditating!" the commander roared. "Why, you idiot, he is deliberately holding us up. Force him out of the way."

Something sharp pressed against Judah.

"Come out, I say."

The pressure was insistent. Judah's back ached terribly. In an undertone he recited his death confessional, listening anxiously all the time for some sound from the other end of the ravine. The silence was reassuring. A little longer and the disciples would be safe.

"He refuses to move," said the soldier.

"Let him have it!"

Judah felt the spear sink in, ripping his flesh. Waves of pain radiated from it. Weariness swept up, dimming his brain. Yet he stood firm.

"My spear is stuck," the soldier called with a violent tug that seemed to rip the old body apart. "Let me have another."

"You blundering fool! Push it through!"

An unbearable weight flashing brilliantly with agony moved forward through Judah. Looking downward he watched the cloak over his belly bulge as though some monstrous limb were being born out of his navel. His head drooped toward it, his knees sagged. Then he fell forward into seething darkness.

The soldier pulled his head up by the hair and looked into his contorted face.

"Why," he exclaimed, "it is only an old man."

CHAPTER XVII

THE NEWS OF WHAT HAD happened in the ravine spread to the entire Jewry of Palestine. At first there was great anxiety lest the disciples be apprehended and Judah's martyrdom be of no avail. But at last it was reported reliably that they were all safe in Babylonia, in the desert, and in Asia Minor. Thereafter the Jews held their heads higher, and their eyes were bolder whenever they passed officers in the streets.

The Romans, however, did not discover the significance of the event until later. An informer, lurking behind a partition in a tavern, picked up an account of it and embodied it in a memorandum. Although he gave a fairly accurate description of what had taken place, he failed to catch exactly the identities of the men concerned. In due course the document was referred to Elisha in his little chamber in the palace at Caesarea. In a moment and without difficulty he construed the garbled names aright and discerned the full meaning of the incident.

As, stylus in hand, he stared at the tablet, something seemed to snap inside him. For a year and more he had been unswervingly loyal to the decision which his reason had dictated at Jerusalem. All through that period he had lived as though it were a spell that held him hypnotized. Stubbornly he had refused to reconsider his course, resolutely he had suppressed his emotions and their protestations. But they continued to stir restlessly within him, biding their time, growing more insistent with the months, so that the effort to control them was progressively more difficult. There were moments when only by a supreme exertion of his will could he keep them in bounds. And he came to feel on such occasions that in his attempt to bury all his impulses he was endeavoring something unnatural, something impossible of permanence.

At the sight of Meir's name, at the recollections it evoked of Beruriah, the first breach in his defenses was effected. Like impounded waters penetrating a dyke through a tiny crevice, feeling oozed through him. A trickle to begin with, it grew, before he could shut it off, into a mad torrent—a wild, riotous exultation over the escape of the disciples—self-loathing, guilt, harrowing remorse over what he had done.

In a frenzied spurt he wrote at the foot of the document in Latin: "The men referred to in this report are unknown to me."

Only when he had dispatched the memorandum and his comment on it by the orderly who waited for it, did his reason reassert itself. He had thought the issue through, he had long since decided that he owed the Romans his assistance, that the water belonged by right to the philosopher. He strove to recapture the coolness of objective thought, to convince himself again against irrationality, against disturbing the close-woven consistency of logic and action. He was not altogether successful. An unusual confusion of mind persisted. The arguments that had persuaded him initially were still valid. Yet paradoxically, it did not matter that what he had just done was indefensible in the light of them. He was not in the least troubled in conscience. Indeed, not in a long time had he been so much at peace, so content with himself.

The orderly reappeared at the door.

"Rufus wants to see you at once," he announced in fright. "You had better go quickly. He is wild about something."

Rufus was seated on a formal high-backed chair at a table littered with papers. His pale eyes blazed with anger.

"What do you mean," he shouted, picking up a tablet and waving it at Elisha, "by lying to me? How dare you deceive me!"

A stream of vituperation poured from his mouth, filling the room and beating with high shrill echoes down the marble corridor outside. Then he paused for a moment to catch his breath.

"I have no notion of what you are talking about," Elisha replied, staring calmly at the raging man.

"No notion, eh? How about this?" He slammed the tablet

down so violently that its wooden back cracked.

Elisha picked it up and tossed it back onto the table.

"Well?"

Rufus' suffused face turned a deeper red.

"Do you see what you have written there?" He pointed with his finger to the words: "Unknown to me."

"You lied. I had the correct names of these fellows all along. They were formerly pupils of yours. You walked directly into a trap."

"That may be," Elisha said unperturbed, his face a mask.

"It is a dangerous game you are playing," said Rufus in cold hatred, "standing on both sides of the fence. I never did trust you and we have always checked your reports. But this is the first time you have been caught red-handed. You are relieved of all duties at once."

"Just as well," Elisha shrugged. "I am not too certain I would have continued in any case."

Rufus half-rose from his chair only to sink back, his face coming alive with cunning.

"So," he drawled, "that is the way it is. May I add then, that you are also under arrest? You may not leave this building without my permission."

"As you say."

"Now get out," Rufus roared, "before I throw you into prison."

The next day Elisha learned of Pappas's arrest. A memorandum, delivered to his room, bore only the inscription:

"Pappas the son of Joseph of Migdal and Antioch detained for treason by order of M.Tin.Ruf."

He jumped to his feet and stormed down the corridor to Rufus' office. The sentries stationed at the door crossed their spears before him.

"Whither in such haste?" one jested.

"Out of my way. I want to see Rufus."

"You do, do you? Well, he isn't here."

"Where is he?"

"He forgot to take us into his confidence."

Elisha started to turn away when he heard, through the great carved door, the tinkling of a lute, the rhythmic clapping of hands, and intermittent chuckles of masculine laughter.

"Not here, is he?" he cried furiously and with one hand threw the crossed spears out of the way, with the other forced the door.

Rufus half-reclined on a great comfortable chair. Other officers lolled on stone benches. A musician sat cross-legged on the floor and plucked at a stringed instrument. About the room a lithe naked girl danced, twisting her body in vividly provocative postures. She whirled at the sound of creaking hinges, caught a quick glimpse of furious eyes, squealed with sudden fright and faltered.

"Get out," Rufus called to Elisha, waving his arm impatiently. "Get out," he repeated, his tone rising.

"I want to talk to you."

"By all the gods," Rufus stormed, sitting upright, "get out, I tell you!"

The officers on the benches stirred tensely. Sentries crowded him from behind. But Elisha walked straight up to the Roman's chair.

"You have arrested Pappas," he accused, his eyes blazing and his whole body trembling with rage.

"Oh, so that's it!" Rufus sank back, faintly smiling. "What of it?"

"You promised to spare him."

"Did I now? When was that?"

"In Jerusalem—you know that. Do not toy with me," he threatened. "I will not tolerate it."

"Gently, gently," Rufus taunted gleefully. "I am sure I did not intend to arrest him."

Elisha relaxed but, still suspicious of Rufus' affability, asked cautiously, "When will you order his release?"

"Order his release?" Rufus mused. "I wonder. Unless my memory fails me he was free only as the result of a bargain made with you."

"You vile dog!" Elisha broke out.

"Come, come," Rufus chided, "there is no need to become abusive. It is not my fault if you do not keep your word and so compel me to detain him, and perhaps in the end to crucify him."

The room grew hazy before Elisha. He raised a clenched fist to strike the round, grinning face, but his arms were immediately pinned. The mask of pretense dropped away from Rufus.

"I call all present to witness," he cried out, "that this man has attempted violence against me. Hold him, hold him fast, until I have done with him!"

Rufus planted himself a foot or so from Elisha and talked directly into his face.

"I may as well tell you that I never liked your friend Pappas. I did not like him for his arrogance, but most of all because he was a bird in that flock of educated harpies that hovered over my Manto. They never fooled me. I saw through all their talk about philosophy and art. I knew what they wanted—her body. They wanted me to feed her and keep her in luxury so that they could enjoy her. I never said anything, but I despised them all, hated them...." Pinpoints of fury danced in his eyes. "And of the whole crew, I hated you most, because she thought most of you. It was Elisha this, and Elisha that, until I was sick of your name."

Elisha stared at Rufus with an aversion so manifest that the Roman's face turned purple.

"And now," he went on, infuriated beyond control, "I will tell you my plans. Your friend Pappas stays where he is in prison until I put him on a crucifix. As for you..." He floundered for some cruelty that would turn the expression of contempt on Elisha's face into fear. "I shall not have you crucified;

that would be too easy. You have a tender conscience, you are quite sensitive to the opinion of others. That is where I shall get you.

"I am going to let you live. Already every Roman despises you. Your own people hate you. But I am going to see to it that your name becomes a curse and a stink among all men. Your last act under my supervision will be to sit in my box to witness the executions of the rabbis we have condemned. You will be dressed in your gayest clothes with a harlot by your side making love to you. If, after that, there is a single person in the world, Jew or Roman, who will have anything to do with you, you are welcome to his companionship. Throw him out!"

The sentries seized Elisha.

"And I will put both of you on one crucifix to writhe against each other," Rufus vowed to them, "if you do not produce him on the day of the executions."

A spurt of globular saliva splotched the floor.

"Come on, dance," he called to the naked girl. "I am in the mood for further entertainment."

CHAPTER XVIII

THE WARDEN OF THE GREAT prison of Caesarea carefully scanned Elisha's parchment pass as though he were able to read. Between times, he glanced surreptitiously at his visitor's face. It was reassuring, but even more so was the Roman soldier accompanying the caller. Mistaking the guard for an escort, the warden smiled ingratiatingly and led Elisha into the general room where a group of jailers, off duty, squatted on the floor throwing knucklebones. There he picked up a fagot and dipped it in a charcoal stove. When it caught fire, he unlatched a massive iron-bound door and deferentially invited Elisha into the hallway beyond.

The corridor was dank and, except for the yellow light wavering from the tip of the torch, altogether dark. At regular intervals they passed heavy doors, into each of which square openings had been cut a foot or so above the floor. Through these little apertures came the sound of subdued stirrings. Occasionally a chain clattered. From one cell muttered profanity streamed, from another a sobbing whine. Elisha shuddered for the unseen bodies that rotted in foul darkness, for the figures crouched to the floor, eager to break the monotony of long years by the unwonted sight of passing feet. At one point they surprised a rat, cowering against a wall with eyes gleaming like those of the men whose confinement it shared.

The course they followed was tortuous. From time to time they halted to undo gates that led into other twisting corridors. Even the warden was not always sure of his way.

"It is confusing," he complained, as he handed Elisha his torch so that his fingers might be free to struggle with an unusually stubborn bolt. "Often we get lost ourselves. Sometimes we discover that we have forgotten to distribute food to a whole block of cells. How they curse us when we do bring it, as though it were our fault. I always tell them that if they didn't get themselves into trouble, they would not be where they are. That makes them wild...but never mind, this is the passageway we want. Now we must find your prisoner. Pappas!" he called so loudly that the name echoed and re-echoed down the stone tunnel. "There he is—that one, where a hand is sticking through."

Looking along the floor, Elisha caught sight of fingers waving through a vent. He passed a few coins into the jailer's hand.

"You won't mind if we talk in private?"

"No, no. Go right ahead," came the response.

Elisha slipped down onto the pavement and leaning on one elbow brought his face to the level of the square opening. It was much too dark to see. He clasped Pappas's hand with his.

"Pappas, it is I, Elisha. Hear me out, please," he said as he felt the hand being withdrawn. "There is something I must tell you."

Only silence was the answer from the wooden barrier. In a whisper Elisha hurriedly narrated the sequence of events which had led to Pappas's arrest. He felt the hand in his relax.

"And now you know the whole story. It is on my account you are here."

He braced himself for an outburst. Startlingly Pappas chuckled.

"The first decent thing you've done in months. Even though it's landed me where I am, there's hope for you yet."

Elisha winced and his voice was tight with pain.

"Don't jest, I beg of you."

"Why not? Besides, don't flatter yourself. I would have got here without your services. Rufus was merely looking for a pretext. If it hadn't been you, it would have been something else."

"It's good of you not to blame me," Elisha murmured.

"Well, I can think of a hundred places where I would rather be. But I do not hold you in the least responsible for this."

"How are you treated?"

"Not badly. What I need most is a bath. They are careless

about the slop pails too. Otherwise it wouldn't be intolerable...if only time didn't hang so heavily. We talk to each other, until that becomes a bore. It is a real pleasure when someone new arrives. If he is a Jew, we get our own news. If not, we get a life story anyway."

"And the food?"

"Wretched," Pappas said simply. "But then, peddlers come by. We give them our names and tell them what we want. They go around to the guardroom and the jailers bring us what we have ordered. Of course, that calls for a bribe...."

Without a word, Elisha untied his purse from his girdle and slipped it through the opening.

"Thanks," Pappas said, jingling the bag. "It should take care of me for some time."

They fell silent briefly and through the window Elisha heard a high-pitched voice intoning on the street outside.

"That must be one of those peddlers," he commented.

Abruptly Pappas began to describe, volubly and loudly, the grating in the cell wall, how high it was from the ground, how little fresh air came in, the attempts he had made to engage the jailers in talk.

Meanwhile the huckster's voice became clearer. Elisha caught occasional words.

"Needles, thread, thimbles...Needles, thread, thimbles..."

Something about the crying disturbed Elisha. It was the use of Hebrew. So far as he could remember there were no Jews in the vicinity of the prison, and even if there were, it was strange to hear someone hawking his wares in the tongue of the synagogue rather than in Aramaic, the speech of the street and marketplace.

"Why does he call in Hebrew?"

"Hebrew?" Pappas echoed. "You must be mistaken. It is so hard to hear correctly. Why I have climbed up to the grating to ask for food only to discover that they were selling cosmetics...." Pappas's voice, rising in volume, babbled on. Then suddenly he groaned, "It's no use. I have been trying to drown him out, but you have heard and will listen, no matter what."

"Needles, thread, thimbles...*Hakini has been arrested*... Needles, thread, thimbles...*A woman's husband has disappeared*...Needles, thread, thimbles...*Sold to a gladiatorial show*...Needles, thread, thimbles...*The case is before the court at Usha*...Needles, thread, thimbles...*Is the woman free to remarry on a presumption of her husband's death?*...Needles, thread, thimbles, all very cheap...*What is the Law on this point?*...Needles, thread, thimbles..."

A prisoner irritated by the singsong shouted in exasperation, "Go away, keep still!"

The voice of the peddler rose even louder.

"Needles, thread, thimbles...*The Book known as the Psalms of Solomon*...Needles, thread, thimbles...*What is its exact status?*...Needles, thread, thimbles...*That is all.*"

"How much are your needles?" a deep voice rang out down the corridor.... *"Alas for Hakini....* Are the colors fast in your thread?... *The woman is not free to remarry until someone testifies that her husband was seen entering the arena for the games....* Otherwise there is no presumption of death. What are your thimbles made of?... *The Psalms of Solomon are apocryphal, and not to be regarded as sacred writing....* Do you have my order?"

"I have," came the voice from the street below, "may God bless you for it...Needles, thread, thimbles..." The chant died away in the distance.

"Who is in that cell?" Elisha breathed.

"Akiba..."

Elisha started violently and the fingers through the opening tugged frantically at him.

"Not a word of this," Pappas begged fiercely. "Not for his sake—he is already condemned to death. But for those outside. Promise me!"

"I swear," Elisha assured him, and added haltingly, "besides, the Romans have dispensed with my services."

Pappas made no comment.

"So even from the dungeon," Elisha mused, "Akiba decides cases in Law. That must mean the courts are still functioning."

"Yes, and the schools, too…" Pappas paused and when he spoke again his voice was more reverential than Elisha had ever heard it. "I never realized how remarkable Akiba is. I met him near Sepphoris four months ago—walking down a lane with several disciples, lecturing to them. It was the only way they could meet safely. We stopped for greetings and I warned him that he had no right to risk his life, that the Romans suspected him already because of his participation in the rebellion, that they would gloat to catch him. In answer, he told me a fable."

"A fable?"

"Yes, the one about the fishes being agitated because of a marauding crane, and the fox suggesting that they come up on dry land where he could protect them. You know how it runs. The fishes see through the advice and say they prefer to take their chance on being picked off, one by one, rather than serve as a collective meal for the fox. He applied that story to the Jews aptly. As he put it, if Jews are not safe in their own element, they can be safe nowhere. Many individuals will die, he admitted, but the people can live only if it remains loyal to its tradition.

"It is magnificent," Pappas went on, "to believe so much in something that dying for it becomes easy. I have lived for nothing. In consequence, I have nothing to die for. And the supreme irony is this. Though it will go harder with him than with me at the end—when I am through, an insignificant atom of humanity shall have been obliterated, one pointless both in its existence and its extermination; whereas out of his death, greater life will be born."

Pappas's mood changed suddenly.

"Behold me," he mocked, "Pappas, the Epicurean wastrel, turned philosopher. Too late the skeptic looks for a faith."

"Do you talk to each other here?" Elisha asked quickly. "By the hour. Sometimes about things that happened years ago, sometimes about the war. We have refought the whole rebellion at least a dozen times."

"Does he ever refer to me?" Elisha ventured. It was desperately important that he know how Akiba felt about him. "Is he very bitter…?"

"Not at all," Pappas responded promptly. "He says that he has never doubted your integrity, that he has always been convinced that you have acted honestly in the light of your own conscience. I got the impression that he loves you, respects you but is sorry for you—much as one might pity a child who gets himself whipped because with the best intentions he misunderstands his father's instructions."

Pappas paused and waited, but Elisha, humbled with gratitude, dared not trust his voice.

"Most of all," Pappas broke the stillness, "we discuss religion, especially the differences between your attitudes and his. He doesn't agree with you at all about the future of the Jews."

"You don't mean," Elisha breathed in amazement, "that he still holds out hope…?"

"Not hope, certainty," Pappas corrected testily. "Why do you suppose he continues to teach from the dungeon?"

"One can remain loyal even to a cause admittedly lost."

"Which is exactly what he will not concede. As he sees it, the Jewish people possesses a unique religious truth, an unsurpassable morality of peace, mercy, justice and human equality—all indispensable to man's salvation—and, in addition, a Tradition or way of life in which they are embodied. It is for these and their communication to the nations of the world that we have been appointed. No sacrifice on our part can be too great for the fulfillment of so heroic a destiny. What is more, no power on earth can destroy us, provided always that we remain loyal to our purpose. Given that, we shall outlive the great empires to be present when God's Kingdom is inaugurated at the end of days."

"Years ago," Elisha brooded, "we argued that in a deserted

garden not far from here. We are no closer together now than we were then."

"And so far as the Empire is concerned," Pappas pursued eagerly, "he gave me the answer for that too. I did not admit it at the time, but once you almost convinced me of your point of view. Only an intuition kept me from accepting it and going your way. I tell you, Elisha, that man is incredible. It was he who put into words what I felt but could not formulate. You see, I told him pointblank about your contentions. He replied by pointing out what you seem never to have perceived. The Empire, he said, was conceived in the lust for power, is motivated now by the desire to protect a system of exploitation. Everything else in the sight of those who administer it is secondary. Therefore they will respect the beneficences that are the accidental byproducts of their purpose. But whenever the liberties of the individual or a group come into conflict with the interests they serve, they will destroy the former unhesitatingly for the sake of the latter."

"But it has not worked out that way," Elisha protested.

"He prophesies that it will. The Empire, according to him, must grow more rapacious until it shall have consumed the last vestiges of the tolerance it never seriously intended. All this he claims is inevitable since, with states as with individuals, the good which is born by chance out of the evil design is corrupt and rotten at the core. Only one type of government, he insists, can be permanent and morally justifiable: that which makes freedom for all men and all peoples not a pretty adornment to itself but the earnest goal of its being. And he is right, Elisha. That is the flaw in your argument on behalf of the Romans—you overlooked the character of their intentions."

"Perhaps," Elisha admitted uncertainly. "It was all so clear to me a year or so ago. Now it has become confused...."

"In any case," Pappas sighed, "it is my good fortune that he is near me. Even when we are not conversing I can hear him rehearsing Scripture, reciting his prayers or reviewing the Law." His voice sank so that it was almost inaudible. "I get to thinking, you know. One lies here so long that try as he will he cannot help imagining things. You would not believe it, Elisha, that I, the scoffer, sometimes wonder about what will happen after it is over. They may be right about the next world. In the dark here, anything seems possible. You can see how unnerved I get," he went on with a flash of his old sarcasm, "when thoughts like these trouble me. Whenever it gets too much for me, I ask Akiba to talk, and after a while I feel better."

The jailer at the end of the corridor stirred noisily.

"You will have to leave now," he called to Elisha. "The torch is low. If we stay longer, we will never find our way out."

"Elisha, before you go I have just one favor to ask." Again Pappas's hand reached for his friend's. "Please do everything you can to get it granted. I don't want to die, but there is no use in asking you to get my sentence commuted. That is impossible." His fingers clutched fiercely at Elisha's hand, pressing it until it seemed as though the bones would crack. "Try to arrange it so that it will be quick and as painless as possible."

"I will try," Elisha faltered; "I promise."

"Pappas," Elisha went on, his breath coming in spurts, "there is a favor which you must do for me, too. I want you to tell Akiba that I am going to be"—he groped for a word—"I am going to be present at the end in a box near Rufus. I want him to know, should he see me, that I shall not be there of my own choice. That is to be Rufus's revenge for my shielding the disciples."

"He would have understood anyway, but I shall tell him. Now, you must go."

They bade each other farewell softly. Their hands disengaged. Elisha rose slowly, his heart so insufferably heavy that he did not feel the ache in his cramped limbs. Halfway down the corridor he stopped for a moment, struggling with himself.

"Akiba," he whispered at last, "it is I, Elisha. May I bid you farewell...? Please forgive me...." He could not go on.

"Peace, Elisha," came the gentle response.

CHAPTER XIX

THE CHIEF EXECUTIONER, HIS POWERFUL body naked except for a scant loincloth, shivered in the autumnal cold, and began rubbing his huge hands over his hairy arms. His little eyes were intent on his plodding thoughts, his low forehead corrugated by them. He admitted that as a slave of the State he had no right to expect to be paid, but they almost always gave him something and the purse could not be less than fifty denarii for ten executions, especially since they were all rabbis. If he could make it exciting enough, the stands might throw money at him, as had happened before. Added to what he had saved...He brought his hands down from his shoulders and holding them before him tried to calculate the sum on his fingers. But he could not figure it out. It was so hard to translate Roman coins into their local equivalents. Besides, they might give him nothing. There was no point in counting his birds before they were snared. Through the haze of his mind, he felt depressed. It was taking so long to buy himself free. He shook his head and looked up.

A great crowd had gathered, the largest before which he had ever performed. The track was packed with people, jostling one another and bobbing up and down for a better view. The stands, full to overflowing, seemed like the inside of a honey pot left uncovered in summer. Boys hung precariously from the great pylons to either side. The whole countryside seemed to have turned out for the spectacle: peasants in broad-brimmed hats tilted back on their heads, carrying on their shoulders wallets with olives and bread, dates and figs; a band of Arab Bedouin, freedmen dressed in the colored uniforms of their societies; and even Jews, standing silent and long-faced in little groups.

A great roar went up. Into the imperial box which, jutting from the amphitheater, sloped toward the arena floor, a group of lictors made their way, their mounted fasces at their sides.

Behind them came the Governor of the Province in a gleaming white toga, his right arm raised in salute, his head bowing in acknowledgment of the cheers. His retinue followed, officers in armor and civil officials in formal garb. There was a woman among them in a startling red dress. Everyone in the crowd recognized her, the most expensive and notorious harlot in all Caesarea. The last person to appear wore a bright festive robe but walked with difficulty and acted as though he were reluctant to take the seat toward which Rufus pointed insistently. One of the lictors got hold of the man's arm, either to assist or push him, and led him into a place in the first row alongside the woman who straightway began to smile and chatter. His unusual entrance aroused general curiosity. A whisper went round, identifying him as the Jewish Rabbi who had sold out to the government. From all parts of the arena people stared at Elisha, fascinated by his brazenness and despising him for it.

The clouds slipped away from the sun. The gray day lightened as yellow warmth poured into the air and the headsman beamed with approval. Cold weather was bad for executions. The spectators were likely to be sullen and unresponsive. Besides, it was hard to work well with stiff fingers. Elated he walked over to his instruments in the center of the arena and awaited the signal to begin.

Two men mounted the starter's block. One, a trumpeter, sounded his horn to quiet the crowd; the other, a herald, began to read the indictments from a parchment scroll.

Then the trumpet was blown again.

At the far end of the inclosure the iron grates barring the stables were pushed open. Behind twelve soldiers, marching two by two, came ten rabbis in single file, clad only in loincloths and bound together at their wrists by a thin chain that dragged across the sand from one to the other. A great din rose throughout the amphitheater. In the stands, men climbed onto the stone benches. On the track, people stood on tiptoe or leaped for a moment into the air to see the victims more clearly. To the accompaniment of catcalls, hoots and jeers, the condemned men followed their guards to the center of the arena floor.

The crowd appraised the prisoners critically. Then it roared with laughter. Hands pointed, tongues wagged, mocking voices rose. The ten sages were a ludicrous sight in a place associated with youthful athletes. It was not only that they were old and that their flowing beards made their heads seem too large and heavy for their half-naked bodies, but some of them were quite grotesque. The Patriarch Simeon was all bones, spindly arms and thin, knobbed legs. Tarfon, behind him, rippled with rolls of fat. Still another, Hanina ben Teradion, held a scroll of the Law awkwardly against his body. The laughter dwindled. Some of the rabbis, despite their years, were not unprepossessing: Akiba, for example, and Ishmael, the former solid and firm, the latter lithe and handsome, his hair still untouched with gray.

Rufus rose to his feet. He was in a savage mood. Only the day before he had been informed that he was soon to be relieved of his office, and that Sextus Minicius Faustinus was to succeed him. The Emperor had decided that Palestine required more competent administration.

"These men," he called shrilly, "are all rabbis. It is they who, as Jewish leaders, are responsible for the war which took the lives of your kinsmen and robbed so many of you of your possessions. So perish all rebels who disturb the peace of the Empire."

He waved to the executioner.

From the starter's pedestal, the herald proclaimed, "Simeon the son of Gamliel, Patriarch of the Jews—by decapitation."

A guard released Simeon from the chain binding him to his fellows, seized him by the arm and pulled him toward the headsman's block. Simeon's face was white with long imprisonment and fear. His lips moved in prayer. Under the pressure of the executioner's hands, he bowed his head onto the block, timid and bewildered before death as before life. Ishmael started out of line, as far as the chain permitted, and spoke earnestly to the headsman, pleading with him. The executioner listened, shook his head in perplexity, and, with a gesture, ordered his two assistants to cease binding Simeon. Hesitantly he approached the foot of the imperial box. Rufus leaned over the parapet to catch his words.

"That one wants to die first," he said. "The other is their chief, or their head, some kind of very holy man. He does not want to see him killed."

"Take your orders from me," shouted Rufus, his neck instantly red with rage.

Frightened, the executioner returned to the block, picked up a great two-handed sword and brandished it to get its feel. Then, taking his stance, he regarded the kneeling figure and gauged the distance. The position did not suit him. He pulled Simeon's head by the hair forward an inch or so. His sword went up, flashed in a circle and came swiftly downward. A dull thud shook the amphitheater, followed by a tremendous shout from the spectators. The executioner grinned in approval. Sometimes he missed or did not get all the way through. This had been a good, clean blow. He turned about to acknowledge the applause and the coins spattering in the sand about him.

Ishmael strained toward the severed head. A shrill lament from his lips cut through the uproar, stilling it altogether.

"How is the tongue that taught the Law," he intoned, "brought low to lick the dust."

It was like a scene from the tragedies, like the fearful pictures that men of old had been wont to fix into eternal motionlessness on the sides of vases. Before its pathos, the excitement of the crowd became a sad, soundless brooding. Even the harlot at Elisha's side felt a stirring of compassion.

"Let that one go," she urged Rufus. "He is a handsome fellow even though," she added with professional appraisal, "he is old."

"Mind your business," he glared with rage. "I did not bring you here to give advice."

Furious with the crowd for its sullenness, Rufus rose before his seat.

"The one who wanted to die first," he shouted, "take him next. Flay him!"

The executioner paled. He did not like flaying. It was slow and bloody, and he did not do it well. One really ought to be a surgeon for that. He looked up at Rufus dumbly, moved to protest and then, recalling that he had already made one mistake, kept his tongue.

It turned out badly. Not a murmur came from his victim. Ishmael's eyes rolled with anguish, his breathing was labored, but he did not cry out. His silence made the spectators tense. As the minutes dragged by, the strain of waiting exhausted them. But when the skin parted from the center of the brow near the hairline, where for many years the headpiece of a phylactery had rested, a sound came at last like the rasp of metal on stone, and those who heard sucked in their breath. From some Jew in the crowd a blasphemy was wrested to go booming up the tiered seats toward heaven.

"God of Mercies, is this Thy Law and is this its reward?"

People shivered with horror and Rufus, reacting to their mood, commanded angrily, "Finish him—put him on the block!" Then he turned to the harlot and shoved her toward Elisha.

"Go on, laugh, caress him. What am I paying you for?"

Her face pale beneath its rouge, the crimson-clad woman threw herself on Elisha, her arms about him, her face close to his.

Eager for diversion, resentful that the spectacle was so depressing, the spectators vented their annoyance on Elisha.

"Look at him, enjoying the death of his own friends!" they hooted. "Traitor!" "Inhuman monster!" Gyges, eater of his own flesh!"

The thud of the sword sounded heavily and the head of Ishmael, its bloody face mercifully hidden, lay in the sand.

"Go on with it!" Rufus called fiercely. "Go on…the block, the block, take them in order."

Six times the sword flashed and struck, and with each the crowd grew more morose.

"One would think it was their own funeral," Rufus swore at last. "Something must be done or they will jeer me for this fiasco."

He rose, and no one cheered.

"Put the next one on the stake with a wool pack around his chest."

Preparing Hanina for burning, the headsman laid hold of the scroll of the Law that the old man held in his arms. The Rabbi resisted, and a struggle ensued.

"Let him keep it, you blundering fool," Rufus called.

"But I cannot tie his hands behind him this way," the executioner shouted back.

"Then tie them in front."

"But the fleeces…"

"Let him hold it, I say. And not another word out of you or, by the ghosts of my ancestors, I will put you where he is."

Muttering resentfully, the executioner led Hanina to the stake, bound him to it and piled fagots about him up to his knees. Great fleeces dripping with water were wrapped around him, enveloping his chest, arms and the book between them. Meantime an assistant held a torch in readiness. At a nod, he touched it to the pyre. The oil-soaked wood kindled about the Rabbi's legs. Within their fetters, his tortured feet twisted and writhed.

The air was suddenly sharp with the smell of burning flesh and broken by uncontrollable moans. A loincloth, moistened by the drippings of the fleeces, began to smoulder, a thin line of flame ascending it slowly. The water-soaked wool steamed and enclosed the old man in a pillar of vapor. Yet he could not die quickly for the fleeces protected his vital organs.

But when the scroll, more inflammable than flesh, began to burn, a strange portent took place. A piece of parchment, torn loose from the book, rose upward and hung wavering in the air, its edges defined in fire.

In the midst of continuous, inarticulate sobbing, Hanina screamed hoarsely, "I see, oh, I see!"

"What do you see, Master?" someone called.

"I see the scroll consumed, but its letters flying disembodied and free in the air."

The executioner was pouring water on the woolen cocoon when through the smoke and mist a voice called as from some other world.

"Man, man," it pleaded, "I cannot endure it. Man, man, help me to die."

"One kind act," the supplication continued, "may win God's eternal favor. Take off the fleece...Show your mercy and God will manifest His to you."

In the dark caverns of the executioner's soul strange impulses stirred, pity and a wild hope. He reached out, tore the steaming wool from Hanina's chest and neck, his hand scalding at the touch. The flame leaped up and kindled the Rabbi's beard. Crying out his last prayer, he lowered his face and drank in the soaring fire through his open mouth as though it were some cool refreshment.

Iron combs dug into Akiba's flesh, but he stood erect at the stake. His bald head shone in the sun above a circling wisp of gray hair. His beard, white with many years, swept downward onto his large-boned body. His belly and thighs were striated by deep bleeding lines, but on his lips there was a fixed smile, and in his eyes a look of ecstatic happiness. His face contorted from time to time but relaxed always into an expression of joy. The crowd, waiting intently for some sign of failing strength or waning courage, murmured in admiration. Still Akiba smiled. Through the expectant silence, a voice called out of the multitude: "Master, Master, is your endurance so great?"

Calmly, as though the question were addressed to him as a lecturer, Akiba answered in a voice steady except for an occasional wavering as the combs tore at him:

"It is written: 'Hear, O Israel, Thou shalt love the Lord thy God with all thy heart and with all thy soul'—even when thy soul is taken from thee."

Then his knees bent, his body leaned forward and his head was bowed. He died in this posture, as one making deep obeisance to a great king.

The vast multitude of spectators stirred uneasily and then, by unspoken consent, rose and moved slowly toward the exits.

Elisha alone remained, watching the executioner's assistants drag the sprawling corpses back to the barrier from which they had walked.

The arena attendants, coming into the amphitheater the next day, found him still sitting in the imperial box, a haunted ravaged look on his face, a vacant stare in his lusterless eyes.

With difficulty they extracted from him his own name and one other, that of a bookseller called Nicholaus.

All through that winter he lay abed in the Greek's house, broken in body, his mind tottering on the verge of insanity. But with spring something of his strength returned. Restlessness assailed him. He must return to Syria to his work.

Nicholaus sought to restrain him. Elisha was still too feeble, too uncertain in spirit to undertake so long a journey. But he was not to be dissuaded. Trembling with weakness, beclouded and harassed in heart, he made his way along the coast of Palestine, back to Antioch, to the library and his book.

CHAPTER XX

CHARICLES, THE PHILOSOPHER, SPOKE WITH mechanical fluency. He was in all truth more than a little weary of the particular lecture he was delivering, of the carefully polished phrases into which, years before, he had cast it for the first time, and of the studied gestures that went inevitably with certain passages.

He had been excited at the prospect of speaking in a metropolis like Antioch. A great city, he had hoped, might be a welcome change from the forums of small towns and their provincial intellectuals. But now, as he looked at the people seated on benches before him, he realized that the more it changed the more it was the same. This public garden in Antioch, bright with spring sunlight, might just as well be in Bilbis, Corinth, Tarsus or Utica.

In all the wearisome repetition of circumstance there was this time only one element of variety—a white-haired man seated in the last row, listening with an eagerness too fierce to be merely polite. But then, even this was no different. From experience Charicles knew that in every audience there was some overly earnest bore who, after the discourse, seized him by his tunic and talked at him interminably, trying to prove to him that he had been mistaken on this point or that. He must remember, he warned himself, to avoid that fellow.

"...Let us admit," he declaimed, his speech flowing on, his face a mask of assumed interest, "that the senses are not trustworthy since objects appear of different sizes and shapes to different people, and are perceived variously by the same person as he changes his position; since what is brown to one man is red another, and without hue to the color-blind; since the identical surface will feel coarse or smooth, warm or cold, depending on the sensitivity of the hand that comes into contact with it. Let us concede even that the whole of our experience is but a phantasm. A somewhat embarrassing assumption, to be sure, suggesting that neither you nor I may be really here, making you my pleasant dream and me, with my interminable talk, a nightmare to you, from which you cannot awaken too quickly."

Charicles took a deep breath and waited for the restrained laughter to subside. As was his practice, he began again before quiet was entirely restored. His sonorous voice rang out across the waning mirth as though he were too impatient to wait.

"But does that mean that there is no certainty, that accurate knowledge is and must forever remain unattainable?

"Not so. The skeptic lies, and here and now I throw his falsehood into his leering face. The truth can be won, provided one knows where to seek it and how to move toward it. For there is another method, independent of the senses —the technique of the founders of great philosophical systems of all times, the approach outlined in the *Organon* of Aristotle—the deductive process whereby one moves from lucid simple first premises through syllogisms to conclusions, more complicated but equally unequivocal and undeniable.

"See," he urged, "how generous nature has been with us, equipping our minds from birth with sure truths for which we need not labor and which no sane person ever challenges. Will the boldest skeptic deny that two and two equal four, no more, no less; that the whole is the sum of its parts; that equals, added to equals, yield equals; that every effect must have a cause; that A cannot be B and its opposite at the same time, that...? But why do I belabor so obvious a point. Each of you can list dozens, hundreds, perhaps thousands of principles of like character.

"Nature, I have said, has been kindly with us. A grotesque understatement. More than generous, she has been munificent. For, in addition to innate verities of the type I have just described, she has furnished us with the instruments of logic whereby we may through our own efforts derive from her original gift limitless treasures of larger richness.

"Can there be any conclusion but one to the sequence:

"All men are mortal;
Socrates is a man;
Therefore Socrates is mortal?

"Yet, deep within you, there is, I know, an unspoken question. If the truth may be attained, you ask how comes it that after generations it does not lie full-blown in our hands. Ah, my friends, let us not, in our disappointment, exaggerate. There are realms where certainty is ours already—areas of mathematics, physics, and even of metaphysics where old insistent riddles have been solved for all time. And as for the remaining areas of human interest, there, too, we are not without hope, provided always that we possess a triad of virtues—caution, probity and patience—caution in our selection of first premises, probity in the deductions from them, and, greatest of the three, patience. It is for lack of this last that the most colossal blunders have been made in the past. Too often have men, despising in their wishful impetuosity slow, safe plodding, overleaped all that intervened in a direct flight to their destination—only to find that they had arrived not at truth but illusion.

"It is, men of Antioch, of the part of wisdom to learn, but not to be discouraged, by experience. Let us then restrain our eager hearts, discipline our restless minds and we shall together penetrate ever further the frontiers of the doubtful and the unintelligible.

"Patience, my friends, and someday we, and if not we, our children or our children's children will yet be able to say in response to the choices, intellectual and moral, forced on mankind by an inscrutable destiny, 'At last, I know. After weary travail, I have come to understand.' "

The closing words were attended by a burst of applause. Charicles bowed gracefully and awaited questions. But no one raised a hand. After a moment he turned with relief to the bench before which he had spoken and picked up his robe and his long ivory-headed staff. At the signal, the audience rose, breaking into conversation.

In a few minutes, the garden emptied. One man only remained behind, the white-haired man with a ravaged face whom Charicles had observed in the last row. He worked his way forward, slowly as though lost in thought.

"My name is Elisha," he said abstractedly when he was face to face with the lecturer, "and may I congratulate you on your presentation, especially since I subscribe to it so completely? In a sense, you have stated my own case."

"Thank you." Charicles smiled his appreciation.

"But," Elisha went on, "I should like to ask you a question."

"By all means," Charicles murmured, feigning interest.

"As you spoke," Elisha continued, quite unaware of the interruption, "I detected a gap in your argument—you left unbridged the interval between innate ideas and the syllogism you quoted. After all it is a far cry from the assertion that if equals are added to equals the results are equals, and the major premise, 'All men are mortal.' The former is indeed a judgment of pure reason. The latter, on the other hand, involves the concepts 'men' and 'mortality' and an inference as to their association—all derived from sense and hence subject to all the uncertainties of physical experience.

"Now my question is this: how do you make the transition from innate ideas to such generalizations as the universal mortality of humanity? It is just that that has been holding me up in a piece of work of my own, a book....

"What's more," he pressed on as unexpectedly he envisaged a possibility that had never occurred to him before, "even if I concede that a chain of reasoning can be strung over the abyss, there are still unresolved difficulties that have just suggested themselves to me.

"You have posited the validity of the deductive process. But what happens when you form a syllogism. You take major premise A, minor premise B and deduce conclusion C. You say when you are through that C follows inevitably from A and B. But what do you mean by that? Only that you have a sentiment of congruity, an emotion of fittingness. Are sentiments the stuff of rational demonstration?

"Besides, I have been rereading the skeptical philosophers recently and have been impressed by one of their standard arguments. Every syllogism, they contend, rests on a first premise. Either you posit that premise as an act of faith, in which case it is patently impossible to speak of its absolute sureness, or else you derive it from another syllogism. But that demands still another premise, that another, so on to infinity. Somewhere you must stop and say, 'Here I shall believe without proof.' Then what becomes of the claim to certainty?"

"Not so fast," Charicles struck out. "You forget those premises which are sufficient to themselves without previous demonstration. In fact, you overlook the existence of an entire system built from such materials, namely geometry."

"Ah, yes," Elisha murmured, "an old friend, Euclid."

"But I don't understand you," Charicles queried, interested and perplexed. "You gave me the impression that you agree with me, that you believe in the power of reason...."

"I do," Elisha said confidently. "But to me Euclid is more than a book. It is, as it were, the visible proof of the possibility of proof. Under its inspiration I began a system of my own some years ago. On resuming it of late, after a long interruption, I found myself confronted by problems. What is more, I have stumbled on a work by the Epicurean, Zeno of Sidon, who has subjected Euclid to a critical analysis which, I confess, has left me somewhat shaken.

"Excuse me." Too intent to be altogether courteous he took the lecturer's staff from his unresisting hand and with its tip traced a figure on the ground.

Surprised, curious, Charicles sank back onto the bench behind him and watched.

"Let us imagine," Elisha went on, "that this is a straight line, and that a point beyond it. Together they form the diagram of the postulate that runs: 'From a point outside a line, only one line can be drawn parallel to the original.' Now, I ask you, what is the proof of that assertion?"

"Proof?" Charicles cried in astonishment. "It is a postulate and hence, by definition, needs none."

"But the point on which I have been unable to satisfy myself," Elisha insisted, distressed by his own words, yet unable to control them or the thoughts they voiced, "is why we should exempt Euclid who proves all things from assaying a proof of this?"

"Simply," Charicles answered at once, "because it is apparent that only one line can be drawn through that point parallel to the original. Any other line would coincide with the first."

"That's what I have always believed. But is it so? Is it self-evident to the same degree as the statement that the shortest distance between points is a straight line?"

"Of course."

"Not to me." Elisha shook his head stubbornly. "I have a much harder time visualizing and conceiving the parallel postulate."

"Very well then," Charicles conceded grudgingly, "it is self-evident, but not so immediately."

Elisha considered the reply, then, driven by the force of his own logic, asked gropingly, "But can there be immediacies more and less instantaneous? If so, must one not say that that which is less immediately evident must also be less certain? But in that case, geometry is based upon assertions, some of which are more certain than others."

"Nonsense," Charicles argued. "You might as well say that a complicated truth is less true than a simple one because it takes longer to comprehend."

At first glance the contention seemed quite valid and Elisha, apprehensive over the direction in which his reasoning tended, was momentarily reassured. But as he reflected, he saw that that too was no answer and he could not let the matter rest.

"A bad analogy," he said unhappily, "for demonstrated truth rests upon argumentation. The length and complexity of the proof have nothing to do with its validity. On the other hand, self-evidence, by its very nature, is a matter of immediacy."

Then because he was thinking relentlessly he perceived an argument that tightened his lips into a thin line of concern. Steadying his trembling hands, he traced a triangle in the sand.

"Look," he said unevenly, his eyes narrowed in concentration. "Euclid shows that the combined length of two sides of a triangle must be greater than the third side. You know the demonstration. But why does he bother with arguments to establish that proposition when it is easily as self-evident as the parallel postulate? Can we help suspecting that Euclid, able to prove one and not the other, took half a loaf because he could not get the whole?"

"Irrelevant and unjustified," the lecturer snapped angrily.

"Perhaps," Elisha said cautiously.

"And what's more," Charicles pursued eagerly, "even if the parallel postulate be not quite so certain as the others, it is still susceptible to an oblique demonstration. Its opposite is completely inconceivable. Can you think of more than one line being drawn parallel to another through one point?"

Panic-stricken though Elisha was, he was unable to restrain himself from a last assault on his ordered world.

"What do you mean by inconceivable?" he asked in anguish. "You mean you cannot picture it. But then can you imagine parallel lines at all, or for that matter, the infinity where they are supposed to meet?"

Incapable of further argument, Charicles retorted resentfully, "Very well then, have it your way. Let mathematics be reduced to myths, more or less plausible, since you are so insistent on it. But let me tell you that if man has not found truth in geometry, then he is incapable of discovering it anywhere."

Elisha's body shook, his pale face turned ashen as he realized the depths of the abyss which was opening beneath his feet. Watching him, Charicles was disquieted.

"By all the gods," he urged appeasingly, "don't take it so seriously. It's only an academic question. Why, you act as though your life could be ruined by it."

"It has been," Elisha replied.

But even as the edict of doom sounded on his stiff lips, his protesting heart rallied. Frantically he searched within himself for some principle which had not been dislodged, some unshaken axiom, some firm dictum to which he might cling and so save himself.

A tremulous breath escaped him and his shoulders sagged in defeat. For all at once this moment in a garden in Antioch was irretrievably one with what had befallen him in Galilee when another hope had been shattered by the sight of a boy falling from a tree.

Then the discipline of his senses and thoughts collapsed altogether. In his ears thundered the tumult as of a crashing edifice, before his eyes disjointed fragments of memory whirled giddily, and through the chaos of sound and vision he glimpsed figures whom the living knew no more and caught echoes of the long-silenced voices with which they had once spoken....

Again he was a child standing by a bedstead, receiving a father's last benediction...."I hope you will be wholehearted, not torn in two...." Fleetingly, he felt the warmth of Joshua's hand on his arm...."Only serve God and treasure His Law and I shall be repaid abundantly...." Then he saw himself rending his robe because he had brought down an old man's gray hairs in sorrow to the grave.... The two Simeons smiled up at him over a table in a tavern in Jamnia...."Elisha, my friend, my brother, turn back, and in time all things will be clear," Akiba pleaded, only to hang limp the next instant from a stake...."You must finish your work. Maybe, if there is no other immortality, I shall live in the great book you will write…." And now Manto was lost to all eternity….

One and all he had failed them—Akiba, the two Simeons, and Hanina, Beruriah's father, aye, the whole House of Israel which he had traduced….

He could not breathe, so intolerable was the torment in his heart. His forearms pressed against his breast to ease his pain. "Cain, Cain."

The uproar ebbed at last, leaving a quiet of infinite sadness in its wake. Charicles had gone, unnoticed, and the garden was empty. Unsteadily Elisha groped for a bench and sank upon it. With a breaking heart he considered the long, laborious quest for reasoned certainty that had ended in frustration, the travesty for which he had sold his birthright, betrayed his people and martyred those who had loved him. His face was now expressionless but tears flowed steadily down his cheeks as he confessed that his blasted years totalled into an abomination, that the tortuous course of his days must remain forever without the frailest hope of vindication.

CHAPTER XXI

ON A HOT SABBATH AFTERNOON when the hills of Galilee
were white in the sun and the olive trees and vines hung limp
in the motionless air, Elisha set forth from Tiberias on the
dusty highway that led toward Caesarea.

For the first time in three years, he looked again upon his
native land. The people he had just seen in the streets of the
city had once been his brothers. Now he had no portion in
their lives. And as for the soil, his last tie to it had been severed,
for that very day he had sold all that was left of his patrimony.

So rootless, unfriended he traveled by well-remembered
scenes, perceiving them vaguely but painfully through the
blinding light and the mists of recollection.

Down the empty roadway, a man trudged toward him, his
head bowed, his shoulders stooped. As they neared each other
something familiar in the form and gait of the stranger stirred
Elisha. His eyes opening wide with conjecture, his breath
coming fast with wonder, he continued to stare at the person
approaching him until, when they were upon each other, his
first incredulous surmise had become a certainty.

"Meir," he called, drawing in the reins.

Startled, the man glanced questioningly at the rider. Then
his body shook as though he had been dealt a violent blow.

"Master." he breathed, unsteadily. "Master, is it you?"

With a rush Elisha dismounted.

For an eternity that was but an instant they stood face
to face, constrained into immobility by their awareness of
the abyss between them. Then they drew together in a close
embrace.

They stepped apart but Elisha held Meir by the arms in a
grip so fierce that the younger man winced.

"Meir, Meir," he whispered brokenly, again and again. But
when he perceived that the golden hair was now dingy with
gray, that the face before him bespoke a deep familiarity with

the varieties of hardship, his voice tightened in a spasm of anguish. "Oh, my son, how you have changed!"

"Merciful God," Meir thought, "how he has changed!"

Elisha's hair, which was white, straggled down about his ears and over the nape of his neck. Beneath his untrimmed beard, his gaunt face was deeply furrowed, his mouth twisted by bitterness. And, most unbearable of all, disillusionment lurked in the eyes once so alight with eagerness.

"How have you been?...How are you getting along?...How is Beruriah?..." The questions poured forth, one crowding the other. "And what are you doing here?" Elisha's words quickened, his tone became strident with fear. "Isn't it dangerous for you?...The Romans..."

"They're relaxing," Meir reassured him. "I'm quite safe. I preached in Tiberias this morning. And we manage, Beruriah and I. A scribe can always make a living, even if he must ply his craft in a cellar or attic. But, Master," the momentary calm in Meir's voice became an urgency, "how are you? What has happened to you all these years?"

"Let's not talk about that. Tell me about Deborah. Do you know..."

Meir shook his head. "The last I heard, she was living beyond Jordan, quite comfortably. But that was some time ago.

"And our people?"

"It's been very hard. The land has passed into the hands of the pagans, its wealth with it. But we have raised a new generation of scholars. The Sanhedrin is meeting again. The roster is not full, but there are by now almost forty rabbis."

"Forty rabbis?" Elisha echoed, ruefully. "So the Romans have failed after all. Pappas always said it would be so."

"Master, what ever became of him?"

"They executed him," Elisha replied in a monotone, "the week after the ten sages...died....I had fallen ill and did not know at the time...."

"Rabbi," an agonized question was wrung from Meir, "did

you have to serve them so completely...? Forgive me, I didn't mean to ask that—but I never could understand...

"No more can I—now that it is too late. As Akiba once said to Pappas, I was too bedazzled by the external virtues of the Roman state to perceive the lust at its core." Abruptly he broke off, for at the mention of Akiba's name half-healed wounds opened, stabbing sharply. "It is hard, Meir," he brooded, "when one's dearest memories are too unhappy to be borne." Then, restless as ever of late, he reached for the reins of the horse.

"Master, shall we meet again?" Meir asked in quick distress.

"I am afraid not. I am going on a long journey." Impelled by his own words, he began to walk.

"Let me go with you a little way," Meir pleaded.

Elisha nodded, wordless. They went on together, the horse plodding behind.

But concern ached in Meir like some great hunger.

"Master, did you find what you sought?"

"Let us not talk about it."

"Please tell me. I love you. I must know. It will be easier if I can be assured that you found..."

"Aye, I found," the response came at last, soft-spoken and bitter, "I found vanity and a striving after wind."

"No more than that, Master, for all the struggle, all the sacrifice?"

"No more than that," Elisha repeated tonelessly.

He stopped and looked down into the eyes of his disciple, reading their unspoken questions. Slipping his hand under Meir's arm he started to walk again. Meantime, calmly, impersonally, as though he were narrating events altogether unrelated to him, he described his long pilgrimage to its last futility in a sunlit garden in Antioch.

"And now," he concluded wearily, "here I am with nothing—no God, no friends, no home."

"No home?" Meir cried out. "But, Master, that brilliant Greek world . . . "

"I can no longer abide it," Elisha completed heavily, "for its cruelty and violence, its brutality and contempt for man.

"Oh Meir," he pleaded, yearning all at once to make himself intelligible at least to one person he loved, "is it not clear why I blundered so horribly in arriving at my decision? In my eyes the pagan world was the seat of science and philosophy, hence as I supposed mankind's sole opportunity of ever attaining certainty in belief and action. What other course was open to me except to give it my absolute loyalty? I did not see then, what I perceive now with such fearful clarity, that no society, no matter how great the achievements of its scholars, can be an instrument of human redemption if it despises justice and mercy.

"Aye," he added after a moment's reflective silence, "that was my great error—this reverence for the intellect, this overweening reliance on it. It led me to condone the sins of Rome. It induced me to dismiss as blind emotion the impulses of loyalty and love for my people. Only when it was too late did I come to understand that the processes of life overflow the vessels of reason, that the most meaningful elements in human experience, sensitivity to beauty, devotion to one's kind, are not matters to be determined by syllogisms."

"But that method of Euclid in which you put such confidence..."

"It has failed me, like my faith before it."

"Perhaps, Master," Meir encouraged, seeking to discover some alleviating circumstance in all the ruin, "perhaps your defeat is only of the moment. Someday you, or if not you, another may yet succeed in winning a sure truth through reason."

"Never, not to all eternity." The words that denied hope dropped leaden and lifeless from Elisha's lips.

"But why?"

Elisha sighed wearily.

"In part, because as I have just suggested, neither reality

outside man, nor feeling within him, is altogether logical. There will then always be in the crucible of thought a residue of the irrational never to be resolved into lucidity. But even more because man's mind is too frail, too inadequate an instrument to achieve certainty.

"Do you remember, Meir, that epigram quoted in the name of Rabbi Johanan ben Zaccai: 'There is no truth unless there be a faith on which it may rest'? Ironically enough the only sure principle I have achieved is this which I have known almost all my life. And it is so. For all truth rests ultimately on some act of faith, geometry on axioms, the sciences on the assumptions of the objective existence and orderliness of the world of nature. In every realm one must lay down postulates or he shall have nothing at all. So with morality and religion. Faith and reason are not antagonists. On the contrary, salvation is through the commingling of the two, the former to establish first premises, the latter to purify them of confusion and to draw the fullness of their implications. It is not certainty which one acquires so, only plausibility, but that is the best we can hope for.

"Sometimes I have thought of myself as unique among men. As one who has been compelled to live apart because his only was a restlessness of spirit. But it is not so. In all men there is a relentless drive to know and understand. My destiny becomes then one episode in an eternal drama. In generations to come, others will desert the beliefs of their fathers and go seeking what I sought, others will put their trust in the intellect and strive to build philosophies and moralities after the fashion of the geometry book. If only I could discover some way of bequeathing to them my hard-won conclusion, that the light of man's logic is too frail, unaided, to prevail against the enveloping darkness, that to reason faith is a prerequisite— then my career should not have been unavailing....

The walls of Tiberias had dwindled behind them until they had become a low irregular strip of whiteness on the horizon. All unawares Elisha and Meir approached the roadside marker set up to indicate to the observant Jew the farthest boundary beyond which he might not walk on the Sabbath. Elisha stopped as they came abreast of it.

"Here is the Sabbath limit. You must not go farther. It is time for you to turn back."

Eagerly Meir seized on his words.

"Master, you, too. Even as it is written, 'Turn back, turn back, ye wayward children.' "

He laid hold of Elisha's arm as though to draw him toward Tiberias.

"No," Elisha said wearily, "it's too late. How could I live where I am so hated? I am shut off from returning as though a voice from heaven had proclaimed, 'All may repent, save only Elisha the son of Abuyah!' "

"But, Master," Meir pleaded, "back there is all that you have failed to find—a faith—a God...."

"Yes," Elisha said reflectively, "—and no. It is true that I seek, that I have always sought what they have in the city yonder. That is the fantastic intolerable paradox of my life, that I have gone questing for what I possessed initially—a belief to invest my days with dignity and meaning, a pattern of behavior through which man might most articulately express his devotion to his fellows. In a sense it has all been a long arduous journey in a circle, whereby I have returned to my point of departure.

"And yet I may not enter. For those who live there insist, at least in our generation, on the total acceptance without reservation of their revealed religion. And I cannot surrender the liberty of my mind to any authority. Free reason, my son, is a heady wine. It has failed to sustain my heart, but having drunk of it, I can never be content with a less fiery draught."

"Then what awaits you, Master?"

Elisha raised his eyes to the distant hills. "Older, sadder, wiser, I go seeking now, through faith and reason compounded, the answer to this baffling pageant which is the world, and this little by-play which has been my life."

Then he opened his arms to Meir. Again they embraced, clinging to each other in their reluctance to part. With an effort Elisha tore himself loose, threw the reins over the horse's neck and mounted the saddle.

"Farewell, my son," he spoke down at the upturned face. "The God of our Fathers remain with you."

Meir held to the stirrup, loath to let him go.

Elisha smiled affectionately and dug his heels into the horse's flanks. Meir's hand fell slowly away from the foot-piece as it slid from his grasp.

He remained standing where he was, looking along the dusty roadway, watching a figure travel down it toward the horizon and what lay beyond. Elisha's white robe gleamed in the sunlight, growing smaller with distance until it became an intermittent flash, now visible, now unseen in the larger whiteness of the world. Then it was gone finally and irretrievably, leaving earth and sky empty of him, as though he had never passed that way.

EPILOGUE

ON A NIGHT OF ANGRY winds and dripping rain, two peasants brought the news to Meir.

"Rabbi, Elisha's grave has been struck by lightning."

Shadows danced along the wall as the west wind blew in through the open door and shook the lamplight. The little room, chill with winter, was suddenly colder.

Meir turned to Beruriah, asking a silent question.

Fleetingly, her eyes came alive with pain. She nodded her head and looked away.

Meir picked up his cloak, threw it about his shoulders and left the house. Their bodies hunched against the gale, the three men made their way through the streets of the sleeping village, passing the darkened synagogue and the sprawling buildings of the Academy, where in one window a lone light burned, throwing a splash of yellow luminosity across the wet cobblestones. Like shadows they moved. Like wraiths, memories haunted Meir: the message from Elisha saying that he was mortally ill in Caesarea; the room where he lay dead, his body attended by a palsied old Greek called Nicholaus; the long slow journey back to Galilee; and the hours of coaxing before the authorities would allow him to be interred even outside the sacred confines of the town's cemetery.

Meantime, they left the city behind them and, reaching the crest of a bleak hill, stopped to peer through the gloom.

One of the men clutched Meir's arm.

"See, Rabbi," he whispered, pointing ahead, "there it is."

From a mound a column of smoke rose uncertainly into the darkness.

Overawed, the peasants would go no farther. Alone, Meir came to the side of the grave and looked down. A bolt of lightning had struck the place. A piece of wood, either the marker or a fragment of the coffin, hissed as it smoldered.

"Come back, Rabbi," one of the peasants called. "It is an omen from God, a judgment on the heretic."

Unhearing, unresponding, Meir contemplated his master's resting place. Long since the season's rains had gullied it. Now the lightning had broken it open altogether. He must return and tend it, he thought. But he could not bear to leave him, even until dawn, so exposed to the elements.

Slowly, as in a trance, he slipped his cloak from his shoulders and draped it like a blanket over the spot.

" 'Sleep through the night,' " he prayed, quoting the words of Boaz to another tired traveler.

Then he bethought himself of the poor shattered body before him, and of the weary search that had worn it into death. He recalled its beauty in youth, and set against it its likeness in old age, black hair turned white, eyes burned out like ashes, a face drawn with despair and lips too tired and too discouraged to speak. He wept silently, the tears streaming down his cheeks to mingle with the rain that beat upon them.

Thunder rolled in the misty vault of the heavens. From the cemetery down the hill, from the grave at his feet and from out dead yesterdays ghosts came stealing. And he wept not alone for his master, but for himself as well, for a woman who rarely smiled, for sweet children who slept near by, for a people crushed and persecuted, for all the sons of men, their aches of the body and soul, and their dreams that die.

THE END

447

AUTHOR'S NOTE

Elisha ben Abuyah is, as the reader may have inferred, a historical personality of whose life ancient rabbinic literature records a limited number of incidents, some distressingly obscure. These references, preserved mainly in the Palestinian and Babylonian Talmuds (those great depositories of information concerning Judaism during the Hellenistic and Roman age), have suggested the central motivation for *As a Driven Leaf.*

The student of the Jewish past will, for example, recognize Chapter I of Part I as a free interpretation of the anecdote found in the Palestinian Talmud, Tractate Hagigah, Chapter II. Similarly those conversant with classical literature will sense the influence of Lucian's *Lapiths* on the banquet scene in Chapter V of Part II.

Although source materials have been put to extensive use, *As a Driven Leaf* is intended as a novel, not a biography. Historical data have been widely reconstructed and amplified, the gaps between them unhesitatingly filled with imagined events. Thus, though the Talmud alludes to the Hellenistic interests of Elisha and to his activities as an informer in the service of the Romans, the entire first half of Part II is of the author's creation with no basis in recorded fact.

Again, the sequence treating with Elisha's relations with Akiba and the two Simeons, while deriving from a cryptic rabbinic passage is in form and interpretation fiction. Beyond all else, the conception of Elisha as a person in quest of intellectual certainty is without support in authoritative documents. Despite the liberties he has allowed himself, the author has attempted throughout to be true in spirit to the ancient world both Hellenistic and Jewish. That he cannot have been altogether successful, he recognizes. So much is unknown about both societies even to students of them, and so much more to him, that infidelities to the realities of the past are inevitable.

In a few instances, the author has departed deliberately from what is known definitely. He has disregarded the explicit statement in the Talmud which puts the year of Elisha's birth as before 70 C.E. He has passed over the fact that by tradition Elisha was survived by two daughters. He has contracted the execution of various rabbis by Rufus to form a single incident. The argumentation in Chapter XX of Part II, though not impossible to ancients who, as references in the text indicate, had developed their own skepticisms as to Euclid, does perhaps force the hand of history by making Elisha express himself in the idioms of a modern, drawing implications from non-Euclidian geometry. In fairness to an ancient personality, it should be indicated also that Pappas of the novel is not intended to represent the historical rabbi of that name. Last of all, some details of Jewish observance, including the rituals of the inauguration and conclusion of the Sabbath, have been presented in the definitive form they finally attained rather than exactly as they were practiced in Elisha's time.

On the other hand, it is suggested to the specialist that what may on occasion seem an inaccuracy will on closer study reveal itself, to be merely an alternative interpretation of events.

The description (Part I) of the abortive attempt to rebuild the Temple of Jerusalem will, to the reader of the monumental history of the Jews by Heinrich Graetz, appear to have been distorted, whereas it is in actuality another, more recent construction, advocated, among others, by Marx and Margolis in their *History of the Jewish People*. The existence of an antagonism between Elisha and Akiba, assumed widely by scholars, is at best no more than a dubiously plausible hypothesis. That Simeon ben Azzai and Simeon ben Zoma were not full members of the Sanhedrin is an inference of no greater validity.

In brief, *As a Driven Leaf* springs from historical data without any effort at rigid conformity or literal confinement to them.

PRAISE FOR
THE PROPHET'S WIFE

The long-lost novel by Milton Steinberg

"A sixty-year-old posthumous gift from
the author of *As a Driven Leaf,* which
was perhaps the most important Jewish
novel of the twentieth century. Milton
Steinberg's insights into the tormented,
sexually betrayed, and perennially
forgiving Hosea ring true and…present
a full-bodied portrait of a major figure
who until now was just a name."

—Rabbi Joseph Telushkin

FROM

THE PROPHET'S WIFE

by Milton Steinberg

WITH THE APPROACH OF EACH FESTIVAL,
Beeri's household went into a fever of uncertainty. How would
the master decide this time? Would he elect to disregard the
risks of an attempt at blood vengeance by Achimelech's kin by
traveling to Jezreel so that he might worship the Lord in the
high place at which his fathers had worshiped before him? Or
would his fears bind him to the safety of Samaria and the altars
sacred to the Lord in that city, even though they were not his
own? Or might he resolve to render the offerings of his lips
at some ancient, storied shrine, as he had in his earlier years,
when he was both more vigorous in body and less burdened by
a large and prospering household?

Among these possibilities, Beeri's household hesitated
during the sacred time of the first fruits, the harvest, and at
the great New Moon in the autumn. But not at Passover, the
one festival most properly celebrated in the family homestead.
For whence should the paschal lamb be taken except from
one's own flocks, and whence the grain for unleavened bread
save from one's own granaries? Besides, did not the stems of
new barley await their master that he might select a sheath,
mark it, cut it with his own scythe, thresh and winnow it, so
that an omer of it could be brought each day for forty-nine
days in thanksgiving to the Lord?

In all years then, even those of Gadiel's death and Iddo's
flight, the household traveled from Samaria down to the
valley of Jezreel, a procession of six ox-drawn carts groaning
under their bundles of goods, on top of which sat the women
and young children. On either side of the procession were

the bondsmen and sturdier maidservants who went afoot, as well as Beeri, Talmon, Hosea, and many of the more honored free laborers.

The journey was pleasurable or difficult, depending on family circumstances, the state of the weather, and the condition of the roads. The first spring after Iddo left, every heart brooded over the past and dreaded to look on familiar scenes from which two familiar faces and figures would be missing. As though out of fellow feeling, that winter had been unseasonably prolonged, so that the skies were grim, rain fell in solemn persistence, and a chill wind blew gustily. The roads were morasses in which the wagons mired time and again. The entire cavalcade seemed more a funeral than a festival procession.

But for the third Passover after Iddo's flight, when Hosea had passed his sixteenth birthday and was considered a man soon to be apprenticed to Noam the Naphtalite, every circumstance conspired for joyfulness, both on the road they traveled without obstacle and at the homestead at which they arrived in safety.

The sorrows of Beeri were by now old sorrows, somewhat mellowed. The spring was in him with a sweet potency that lifted the heart and brought song to the lips. The sky was so blue and breathtakingly high that it seemed not a heaven but in its exceeding loftiness a veritable heaven of heavens. The wind, blowing in long, even breaths was so strong in scent that all turned slightly giddy from the inhaling of it. And flowers were spread over the ground—crocuses, anemones, irises, and lilies—glowing and dancing in their many colors, looking like the jewels of some Canaanite trafficker, set against a cloth to show them off against the solid green of grass, solid green since there was no brown or barren spot anywhere.

At each dusk during that season, the world put away its daytime adornment of flowers, slowly and with reluctance, and put on, one by one, the spangles of hugely lavish, almost garish, displays of stars. The wind blew at twilight as strongly perfumed as before, save that it took on the coolness of a chilled wine and was moist as if with the vapor that condenses on a polished bowl. And night by night, the moon, which had been just newly born when the household came to Jezreel, grew prodigiously as the Passover approached and rose higher in the sky with each shining forth, until by the eve of the festival it was at the full, standing round and bright yellow overhead.

In its light, tables were spread in the courtyard of Beeri's homestead, as in every household in Israel and Judah in which men and women revered the Lord. A great fire was kindled for the roasting of the paschal lamb, which had been slaughtered at dusk, and a feast was made of its meat, together with unleavened bread and bitter herbs. Then, as they sat in the mingled light of the moon and the flames, still eating and drinking the wine, Been related to them the tale of Egyptian bondage and of the miraculous deliverance, after which they sang hymns of praise deep into the night.

On the next morning there began the annual "walking out" of the youths and virgins, of their going abroad in the fields and on the roads; addressing one another freely as was proper only two times a year, on the Passover and on the Festival of Booths; singing songs of love one to another and looking each to see who was fair and winsome.

Most of the young men went about in bands, as did the maidens also, compromising so between unconfessed eagerness and equally unconfessed timidity. Those whose hearts were already set on one person walked alone, as did those who were friendless, or so shy as to cringe at the company even of their own kind.

Such was Hosea. He knew no one whose company he might seek out freely and without embarrassment, his long absences from the valley having broken his acquaintance with other youths of like station. And such a flight of emotions had been awakened in him by the anticipation of walking forth—reluctance and ardor, desire, curiosity, and bashfulness—that he feared the presence of anyone by his side, lest he betray himself.

On the first morning, therefore, he went forth alone. Lacking boldness, he wandered side paths on the outskirts of the groves and fields rather than the main roads and other places where young people foregathered. He saw them from afar, heard their songs and laughter, and yearned, but did not dare, to approach them. Occasionally he encountered other youths as solitary as he, and once he encountered a maiden, a not uncomely maiden to whom he would have spoken. But she was hurrying toward the town and had brushed him by before he found words.

In his loneliness the day dragged for him, all the more painfully because he was aware of its passing and the slipping away of its promise. At its end he trudged home, heavy at heart.

Had he some pretext, he would not have gone forth at all the next morning. But a wine jug and a generous luncheon packed in a pouch had been set out for him at the doorway of his chamber. And he could not bring himself to face the mockery of the entire household which certainly would descend on him, and for a long time, were he to loiter at home. With studied nonchalance, therefore, he donned festive attire once more, raised the skirts of his mantle, pulling it up through the girdle so as to free his legs for walking, swung the pouch over his shoulder, and lifted the jug into the crook of his other arm. Calling casual farewells to all within hearing, he sauntered off. As he did so, a resolution which had been forming in him crystallized. He would not visit the places where youths and maidens congregated. Not again would he skulk about, looking and yearning from afar. Better to pass the day as best he might in solitude in some spot where no one would come upon him, amusing himself in whatever fashion he could until the dusk descended and it was safe to turn homeward. So at the least his pride would be spared and he would not be sickened at heart again with disappointment and self-reproach.

But though he struck off in the direction of the hills, he found himself drawn, despite himself, toward the town. He did not allow himself to venture inside, but neither did he go so far from it as to be beyond all hope of some happy chance encounter. He compromised by settling himself in an open space in a vineyard, as close to the midway point as he could determine between his home and the fields and paths where the other young people walked.

The hours did not go quickly. Having nothing else to do, he was compelled to invent matters, childish matters, with which to concern himself. He studied the vine leaves with painstaking and prolonged care, examining the network of veins, the mottled light and arc of the tissue. He watched a colony of ants at work. In the end, unable to think of an alternative, he took to staring up into the sky through half-closed lids, admiring the mysterious little luminous shapes that floated in and out of his vision. Hypnotized by the play of light and shadow, lulled by the whisper of the wind in the leaves, and somnolent with the mounting heat of day, he drifted into a half trance in which all thought and all awareness of time were blessedly swallowed up.

A shadow fell across his face, startling him into consciousness. He sat bolt upright, blinking up at a young woman's figure silhouetted against the sky.

He scrambled to his feet and set nervously to making himself presentable, brushing the dust from himself, pulling at the skirts of his mantle, all the time volunteering hastily invented and broken phrases for fear that the truth about his solitude be guessed. "I grew weary...all my friends..."

The girl's voice seemed strained, as from anger. "May I be your partner today?"

He wished, but could not bring himself, to say yes.

"Then you are not alone?" she continued after a moment, misconstruing his silence. "You have friends for whom you are waiting? I watched for a while and saw no one...forgive me...." She shrugged ruefully and turned to leave.

"Don't go," he interposed, hastening to stop her. "I am alone...."

"But your friends!"

He hesitated on the verge of lying again, but, being calmer now, he lacked the will.

"I have no friends," he confessed. "I did not tell the truth to you. I am alone."

She tossed her head defiantly. "As am I."

From his first startled glimpse of her, he had been aware that she was pretty. But now she suddenly appeared to him breathtakingly lovely.

Her hair was a swirl of very dark waves about her head, a cascade tumbling down her shoulders. The smooth olive of her skin was deep with sunburn and touched with the blush of her blood. Her eyes burned black under eyebrows that glared upward as though about to take flight. Her nose was not thin and her mouth was full, but there were hollows under her high cheekbones which lent delicacy and wistfulness to her face. She was tall for a girl, her eyes on a level with his. And there was in her an intensity which made her seem gloriously alive.

"You?" he wondered, "Why should you be alone?"

She struggled between shame and indignation.

"Because," she burst forth, "because the other girls will not walk with me, saying that I am a nobody. And the boys, when I go along with them, are over bold, mindful that with me they need fear neither a father nor brothers, since I am an orphan and alone. And because of this."

She swept the fingertips of both her hands down her sides, calling his attention to her robe, which he observed was threadbare, faded, and ragged at the fringes.

"And because of this," she went on in mounting passion, putting forth a bare, dust-stained foot. "It is not enough that I must appear in rags to be mocked at by all the world. I must also go without sandals so that I cannot even dance."

At this, he recognized her.

"Why, you are Gomer, Gomer the niece of Charun and the daughter of... "

"Diblaim," she supplied. "And you?"

"You do not know me?" he questioned, first touched by disappointment and then telling himself that he could not expect her to recognize him, as he had not recognized her. "We have met often before, but long ago. I am Hosea...."

She looked at him blankly.

"Hosea," he repeated, "Beeri's son."

"Of course," she cried, "Hosea, Iddo's brother. Where is Iddo? Is he still among the Philistines? Do you hear from him?"

"Not often, and then indirectly, as when some traveler comes from Ashkelon. That is where he is. He has become a captain of fifty of the palace guard of the city's seren."

For a long moment she said nothing, and while he waited, the misgiving beset Hosea that she would turn to leave.

"Will you eat with me? I have enough for two, for a whole company indeed," he stammered. "And it is not pleasant to be alone."

"Do I not know it," she replied solemnly.

"And you need not stay all day," he assured her, "though I would like it. You may go on whenever... "

She looked into his face. Whatever remained of sullenness in her face vanished in a swift, warm smile. "No, it will either be all day as I suggested when I first spoke to you or nothing. Which, I pray you, will you have?"

It was noon. His heart leaped with relief, with an onslaught of pleasure.

"To the very dusk," he said.

They turned at once to the pouch, undid its fastenings, and explored its contents—the cakes of unleavened bread, the meats wrapped in a cloth, the dried figs, dates, and nuts.

"This is a feast," she said. "One such as Solomon the king might have eaten."

They fell to zestfully, eating eagerly and steadily, and drinking from the jug as they ate, passing it back and forth whenever one or the other thirsted. The wine was, on Beeri's prudent instruction, well-diluted, but it was refreshing and had enough strength that, even if fleetingly, Hosea was partially liberated from his usual difficulty of speech. He talked with a spontaneity and articulateness which surprised and delighted Gomer, especially when he told her of Samaria, the multitudes who lived there, and the magnificence of its palaces and temples.

As he sobered from the wine, however, his speech faltered once more. She noticed that his courage began to fail him. He groped for things to say, lapsing into intervals of silence, from which he emerged into hesitant speech, only to slip back again with an ever heavier sense of anxiety and inadequacy.

Gomer was not without understanding. She suppressed any impatience she may have felt, and, whenever some period of quiet became intolerable or his inner anguish too painful, she tried to help him. As one supplies to a stammerer a word for which he struggles, she asked him leading questions.

But it was all slow and dull; she wished so very much that she were elsewhere that in the end her capacity for pretense was exhausted. She continued to sit, her face turned toward him as though she were all attention. But her fingers toyed with a twig, twisting and untwisting it interminably. Her eyes were either averted or, when she looked at him, vacant. Eventually, she stopped taking any part whatsoever in the conversation. Watching her furtively, anxiously, he came at last to the point at which he could no longer conceal from himself that she was bored. Despair overcame him. He gave up and fell as silent as she.

How long they sat wordless together he did not know, plunged as he was in a hopeless lethargy. But somehow, suddenly, he was aware of her again. And he was seeing her, all at once, not as someone who might leave him at any moment and whom he must strive to detain, nor as one with whom he must make conversation, no matter how difficult, but simply as one to be looked at and be marveled over for beauty. She was seated near him with her head somewhat bowed and her averted face visible only in profile. He had been lying on his side, his head propped up on an angled arm, his gaze fixed idly on the ground, his consciousness deep in the great, colorless tide of his loneliness. A moment later, nothing had changed except that his eyes had been raised.

He stared at her. His sight invaded and lost itself in the waves and curls of her hair. Recovering, it traced the clean line from her forehead to her chin; returned to her generous lips, where it paused for a trembling moment; wandered down her arms to her long, thin fingers, busy with the twig; retraced its way upward and forward as to round the swelling curve of her breast; then drew quickly away, returning to her face, where it found rest for a long interval on her lips, then on her long-lashed, lowered eyes.

A sweet tremulousness was born in him, a half-pleasurable, half-painful sensation in his chest.

She raised her eyes. He was too absorbed and lost to think of averting his own. Their glances locked.

"You are very beautiful," he murmured, speaking without forethought or self-consciousness.

She flushed at the compliment, a dark tide flowing upward in her face. Instantly he blushed too for the daring of his utterance, the openness of his self-disclosure.

AS A DRIVEN LEAF
DISCUSSION GUIDE

1. Elisha is depicted as both a philosopher/seeker and some-one who is unhappy in his personal life. What do you think is the major motivation that drives him away from the world of the Rabbis? Which aspect of his personality do you think was more dominant in influencing his choice to leave their world: the emotional or the intellectual?

2. Manto and Bruriah are two different models of women, yet both intrigue Elisha. What do you think of the way Steinberg portrays women? Is either character a compelling role model to you? What aspects of their personalities or situations can you identify with most?

3. Of the Rabbis who participate in the circle of the four, only Akiba emerges intact. What qualities in his character do you think distinguish him from the others? What strengths does one need to maintain faith in the face of challenge?

4. Elisha favors geometry because he believes Euclid, "started from the foundations," while the Rabbis, on the other hand, "have always tried to bolster a pre-established case." What do you think Steinberg is trying to say here about the relationship between religion and science? Do you agree or disagree?

5. Steinberg wrote a novel that serves as an allegory for challenges to faith in his own day. How do the concerns and challenges he raises resonate for us today? Do you think our challenges are the same or different from the ones faced by Steinberg in the 1940s? In what ways?

6. Rabbi Joshua's reversal of the decision to ban Greek learning is one of the turning points in the novel. Do you think limits on knowledge are *ever* appropriate? Do you think Rabbi Joshua's decision was ultimately in the interest of the Jewish people?

7. Steinberg seems to set up a sharp distinction between Roman and Rabbinic values—secular accomplishment versus sanctity and compassion. Do you think secular accomplishment and sanctity and compassion are mutually exclusive? Why or why not?

8. Why do you believe that Elisha is convinced there is no return for him? In the Talmud he hears a heavenly voice to that effect, but what psychological motivations can you imagine which would make him feel trapped, and without a path back to the Rabbinic world?

9. In the Talmud the incident of the child falling out of a tree while gathering eggs leads Elisha to claim that there is no judgment and no Judge. How central to the novel is this event and the question of evil in the world? How central is the quandary of why bad things happen to good people to your own understanding of religion?

10. What does this novel ultimately say to individuals who struggle with faith?

RABBI DAVID J. WOLPE IS the author of eight books, including *David: The Divided Heart* and *Floating Takes Faith: Ancient Wisdom for a Modern World*. Wolpe's column, "Musings," appears in *The Jewish Week*.